HIGH ON A CLIFF

COLIN SHINDLER

HEADLINE

First published in hardback in 1999 by
HEADLINE BOOK PUBLISHING

First published in paperback in 2000 by
HEADLINE BOOK PUBLISHING

10 9 8 7 6 5 4 3 2 1

ISBN 0 7472 6289 6

Typeset by Palimpsest Book Production Limited,
Polmont, Stirlingshire
Printed and bound by
Mackays of Chatham plc, Chatham, Kent

HEADLINE BOOK PUBLISHING
A division of Hodder Headline PLC
338 Euston Road
London NW1 3BH

www.headline.co.uk
www.hodderheadline.com

I've seen him crying. Not a lot but quite a few times. And I know it's about Mum. Has to be. There's something hollow inside Dad, something he can't shake. He's been telling me these stories since I was very small, about him and Mum and how happy they were. I used to like them a lot, particularly one we called 'High on a Cliff'.

It was a story about how he'd been really happy with her in one place, I think it was by a lighthouse or something, and so he scattered her ashes on the grass in front of the lighthouse where a family lived and watched him. I know I liked the last line of the story which was how Mummy's soul watches over both of us at all times. I was always happy when Dad said that, though I wondered why the family who lived in the lighthouse were so important. I couldn't work out how they fitted in.

All this, though, was when I a kid and I don't need to listen to 'High on a Cliff' before I can go to sleep any more. It's been twelve years since Mum died, almost the whole of my life. Surely he should have got over her by now. I don't mean forgotten her and I don't mean that he should stop treasuring her memory. I just mean I think he should move on with his life. There's a hole in Dad's heart. I want someone to fill it and I'm sure he must. Yet he constantly fights it because whenever there's a chance that someone might, he blows it.

Non-fiction by Colin Shindler

Manchester United Ruined My Life

This book is for my daughter

Amy

who is always kind to Captain Butler

ACKNOWLEDGEMENTS

Writing, as anybody who tries to do it for a living knows only too well, is a lonely and frequently bad tempered business. Writers are more than usually dependent on their families to keep them sane. My first debt of gratitude therefore is to my wife, Lynn, my own original California girl.

My agent, friend and mentor Luigi Bonomi was the key figure in the writing of this book. His judgement was impeccable, his honesty was vital and his enthusiasm was always inspiring. I owe him more than just his commission.

At Headline I have been treated with impressive professional efficiency and great personal consideration. My deepest thanks go to Amanda Ridout, Jane Morpeth, Ian Marshall, Heather Holden-Brown, Rebecca Purtell and Ros Ellis. They've become like family, but without the arguments in the bathroom.

Among the many people who helped me with research and advice I should like to record my particular thanks to Paul Wheeler, Conor Chamberlain, Tony Morris, Jim White and Rick Williams of the San Jose police department. However, in their defence, I have to confess that it's my fingerprints which are all over the following pages.

CHAPTER ONE

Danny

I CAN'T REMEMBER A TIME when I didn't know her and yet I can't remember a time when I did. She died, my mum, when I was eleven months, three weeks and two days old so there's no way I can remember much. Sometimes when I can't get to sleep at night I imagine her coming into my bedroom and kissing me goodnight. She bends over me and I can smell her perfume which is sweet and makes me want to bury myself in her. She is made up and dressed up ready for a night out at a big posh party. I tell her I can't sleep and she sits on the bed and I crawl out from underneath the sheets and sit on her lap while she tells me of all the things we're going to do together. Only she died when I was very small, so I suppose it never could have happened like that. Sometimes though, on nights like those, she seems so real.

I know what she looked like of course. Dad has lots of photos of her round the house and three big albums of them when they were students and after they were married. I've got the videos she made too but somehow that doesn't seem like my mum. They're not videos like homemade things. She was an actress and she made TV programmes — a few of them, anyway. It says 'Angela Frost' on the front of the video box and that was her name before she was married. Dad calls it her maiden name. He says all actresses keep their maiden names when they act because if they get divorced they won't have to change them all the time. But I can't imagine my dad and mum getting divorced. You've only got to look at the pictures to see how happy they were.

Sometimes the other mothers at school look at me with this strange look in their eye. And I know what they're thinking. They're thinking how sad it must be for me to be growing up without a mother. But I don't see it that way. Mothers spend a lot of time saying 'Don't do this' and 'Don't do that'. When there are mothers about there are always rules. Stupid rules most of the time. It's quite annoying really when you go to someone's house for tea and his mother says, 'Take your shoes off, wash your hands, turn the sound down, what about your homework?' over and over again. So why do they look at me as though there's something wrong with me just because I don't have a mother? When I see those mothers I'm glad I don't have one. In any case, I have Dad.

My dad is really cool. He's a freelance sports writer. He writes about lots of different sports and he goes to lots of games and he could do more but he says he likes to stay home with me so he mostly does columns and feature interviews. He brings me back souvenirs when he goes to games — like a Barcelona replica shirt when he flew to Spain to write about a big match with Real Madrid. It made quite a change in the playground from all the Arsenal, Chelsea and Man United shirts that the kids mostly have. I even wore it rather than my Spurs one for a while – but only till we signed Klinsmann.

So the other mothers might feel sorry for me because I have no mother but the other kids think I'm dead lucky and they really envy me my dad and his cool job. In many ways my dad is my mum and my dad all rolled up into one person. I mean, he used to dress me when I was small, he made my breakfast and he'd walk me to school when I was at primary school and he's nearly always there at the end of the day, waiting outside the school gates. Sometimes I go to my friend Jamie Kirk's house for tea and Dad picks me up about seven o'clock when he's been in London for the day. He always makes dinner for us. Dad talks about when he was a 'latchkey' kid when he was growing up. He says he doesn't want that to happen to me. But I've got my own key to the house so I suppose I am one anyway. I don't like to point that out to Dad. Somehow I feel he wouldn't like it.

My favourite picture of Mum is of her asleep in the garden. She is on a sun lounger. We've still got that sun lounger – it's in the garden shed but the sides of it are all rusty now. In the picture it looks brand new and Mum is wearing a red T-shirt and a pair of white tennis shorts. Dad says they played a lot of tennis that summer. I wasn't born yet and he says it was a golden time. I know he doesn't mean it – doesn't mean they didn't want me when I was a newborn infant – but he is trying to tell me why those

years he had with Mum and himself by themselves were
so special.

My dad is a good tennis player so when he says that
Mum was really good, he must mean it. She hit the ball
hard and timed it well but her backhand was weak. Dad
is very keen to make sure that my backhand is as strong as
my forehand. We spend hours on the tennis court during
the summer and he stands at the net and just volleys ball
after ball deep into my backhand court.

If I get back six in a row I get a Crunchie or an Aero
on the way home. One day I ran round my backhand
and got it back on my forehand but Dad said that was
cheating and I couldn't have the Crunchie. I was very
very very cross about that. I like Crunchies, particularly
the way the yellow bit in the middle is all hard and brittle
when you bite on it but if you let it stay on your tongue
it just sort of dissolves. Wicked.

I won the Under-12 school tennis tournament last year
so I guess Dad was right because Neil Wilson, the boy I was
playing in the final, his backhand was terrible and mine
was great and I won easily 6–2, 6–3. I got a £10 book token
presented to me by the headmaster (or headbastard as he
is usually called) on the last day of the school year. I wish
it had been a gift token for Eaden Lilley or Robert Sayle,
the big department stores in town. Then I could have
bought a computer game or a CD but it's just typical
of my old-fashioned school that they should give out a
book token. Who reads books these days unless you have
to for school or exams?

My mum was dead sexy. I know boys don't usually

think of their mothers as sexy and in the case of all my friends they're usually right — except Darren Foxton, whose mother wears low-cut dresses in the summer and everyone thinks she is really sexy but Darren says he's banned her from coming to school to pick him up any more.

Something must happen to women when they become mothers. You can't think of mothers as sexy and the ones who think they are — like Darren Foxton's mum — are just embarrassing to their children. I mean, I wouldn't even like to be best mates with Darren. Will Stevens is and he gets some fearful stick from the rest of us when he gets into the Foxton Range Rover after school.

But my mum was different from all the rest, just like my dad is different from all the rest. She was an actress, and not just an actress, as Dad keeps saying, but a star. So being sexy was, in a way, what she did for a living. And the reason I like that photo of Mum so much is that I think she looks supercool there. There's nothing made up about Mum lying half asleep on a sun lounger. She isn't trying to look sexy which is what those blonde bimbos in the tabloids are always doing. She looks so peaceful there, so contented, so happy. My friends see it and though they're sort of respectful because after all it's a photo of my dead mum, I can see they're thinking she's dead beautiful too.

I think of her as still around, kind of frozen in time. She died when she was only twenty-three and she met Dad when she was nineteen so there's only four years of pictures and videos and things. I suppose she might have started to age a bit if she'd lived, like Neville Thornton's mum who has great gobs of grey streaked through her hair — not that she gives a toss about how she looks. I like her for that. The point is, my mum will never grow old.

There's a bit in the Founder's Day service — something about 'they shall never grow old — at the going down of the sun we shall remember them'. Something like that. I get so bored with that Founder's Day service. But I like that bit. I always have. It reminds me of my mum. But I don't need a church service or the sun to set or one special day of the year. She's with me always. That's what I mean when I say I'll always remember her even though I can't actually remember her.

CHAPTER TWO

Ralph

WHEN I CAME BACK TO ENGLAND after the funeral, my first instinct was to bury Angela metaphorically all over again. I thought if the baby didn't know anything about his mother he wouldn't have a loss to adjust to. I'd probably marry again within a couple of years and to all intents and purposes that woman would become Danny's mother.

It didn't work out that way because of my own selfishness. Well, maybe not selfishness as such, that's being a touch harsh on myself. The point is I just didn't have the strength to cut Angela out of my life so I couldn't do it to Danny too. Maybe it would have been better for him as I had first planned it but whatever the baby's needs, I also had my own. I needed to grieve for Angela. If they had sackcloth and ashes at Sainsbury's I think I'd have loaded the car up with them twice a week. I went to see a psychiatrist and he was the one who recommended that I talk about her to Danny and show him pictures so it wasn't a shameful secret but a joyous celebration of her life.

That was the turning point really. As soon as I grasped the fact that not only was I allowed to hang on to Angela's memory but that I was positively encouraged to do so I started on the long slow road back to recovery. So I talked about his mummy a lot to Danny when he was growing up. I would tell him stories about how we met and the great times we had together and he would treat it as a kind of favourite story. Even her death became something glorious.

She was cremated close to where she was killed and I took the ashes to Big Sur on the coast of central California. It was a place where she and I had been particularly happy. I didn't want to cart her body back home in a coffin or stick the urn with her ashes in it into my carry-on luggage and then, inevitably, have it pulled out and examined going through that metal detector at the airport.

So I stopped the car just off the main highway and scrambled through the redwoods and the sequoias until I rediscovered that plateau of grassland stretching out towards the ocean. The plateau finished at a headland which fell precipitously to meet the pounding surf whose roar dimmed the constant noise emanating from the Route 1 traffic. Behind me was the forested wilderness of the Los Padres National Forest. In front of me the Pacific Ocean spread itself like a giant sapphire-blue tablecloth flecked with white.

I had no interest in the wishes of Angela's parents. They had never helped her, never liked me, never came to our wedding, never approved of our marriage. This was where she belonged. Here she would be free and wild, at one with the nature she adored. I unscrewed the lid and deposited the remains of the only woman I have ever loved where the sky meets the sea.

I know, in reality, that's not possible and I know, too, it's a reference to Bali Ha'i in *South Pacific* but Danny has always loved that description so, as far as I am concerned, that's the official version. 'High on a cliff,' I would always end the story, 'high on a cliff Mummy's soul sits, watching over us both always.'

In black and white that looks a bit ghoulish, not to say faintly New Ageish. I'm not like that at all. I support Tottenham Hotspur and the American baseball team the California Angels – now, disappointingly, known as the Anaheim Angels. I suppose it is possible for a man doomed to the reality of constantly dashed expectations to take refuge in a cult. However, I find that supporting the Angels who, unlike Spurs, don't even have a history of success to sustain them in their current mediocrity, it is necessary to keep both feet firmly planted on the ground. The story of Angela's end is one of the few poetic touches I allow myself.

Danny has always loved the story and I've always encouraged it as another means of getting him (and, if I'm honest, me too) to adjust to the reality of life without Angela. It was Danny who called the story 'High on a Cliff'. It had the same magic ingredient as 'Once upon a time' except that the familiar words came at the end so really it was closer to 'and they all lived happily ever after'.

I always thought it was comforting that he loved this story so much. To me it proved that he and I were living happily ever after. When he was three years old or so he had a number of favourite stories: one about an owl who was afraid of the dark, one about a hungry caterpillar who ate so much he turned into a butterfly, and one about a family who lived in a lighthouse. He loved them all and I had to read them to him every night for years and years. Maybe it was only two or three years but it certainly seemed like about five or six. But however much he loved the lighthouse story, I always had to finish with 'High on a Cliff' before I tucked him up in bed, kissed him goodnight and turned on the nightlight. It was part of a never-changing ritual but the most important part, I always felt, was saying to him 'high on a cliff Mummy's soul sits, watching over us both always'.

I moved back to Cambridge as part of the grieving process. It's ironic really. When we were here together as students, we couldn't wait to leave. We were desperate to go to London and start our careers, hers as an actress and mine as a sports journalist and/or comedy writer.

The move back to Cambridge meant that I was surrounded by memories of Angela for all time. Not just where we met and where we kissed for the first time, where we made love and where we fought and where we made up, but every year it seems to renew itself. Every year in October the town is overrun by the gown. Bicycles, now banned from the city centre in favour of buses (the spirit of Lewis Carroll appears to have shifted from Oxford to the Cambridge City Council), make a welcome reappearance in the pale autumnal sunshine and the median age of the town declines overnight by forty years.

Over the course of the academic year I can see relationships start to blossom. I know how it happens, I suppose, so I'm probably looking for it. Glances over lectures or during dinner in Hall, sizing up in the pub, long discussions with best friends over a late-night curry, the first date, the first kiss, the first fumble, the first sense of rapture. Then it all hibernates for the winter as the wind whips in across the flat Fenlands straight from the Urals and right into the vitals as you struggle your way round the great expanse of lawn in front of King's College Chapel, the coldest spot in the British Isles, North Sea oil rigs notwithstanding.

When the crocuses appear along the Backs, it all starts again. Cambridge isn't a campus, it's a town, so the evidence of young love is displayed not just to its contemporaries but to all the inhabitants of the town. In the fevered summer term the prospect of exams induces a general panic which only concludes after the last one has finished, with the day of general abandon known familiarly as Suicide Sunday.

I got over the envy long ago. If I had felt envious at the sight, I couldn't have stuck it and I would have raised Danny anywhere but here. Instead I welcome the sight of young couples holding hands or snogging on the banks of the river when they are supposed to be revising. I treasure the memories I have of Angela and me in the same position and it symbolises the triumph of life over death. I can deal with it all now because, despite the occasional bout of deep depression, I'm sorted.

All right, I'm not perfect, I have these black moods from time to time but I keep them well away from Danny. And much as I love him, there are times when I'm tired and frustrated and Danny's still a kid and I won't say he enjoys it but he knows how to get up my nose. I don't smack him but I do shout, perhaps quite a lot, but it's only under provocation. So, in general, I think it would be fair to say it's true, I *am* sorted.

CHAPTER THREE

Danny

MY DAD THINKS HE'S SORTED. I'm twelve and I know he's not. He thinks he hides it so well but he doesn't. I've seen it and if I've seen it, it makes me wonder who else might have. I can't tell him though. I don't think anyone can. There's no point to it anyway because he needs to think he is sorted. So I suppose if he thinks he's sorted and he behaves like he's sorted, he is sorted.

Only he's not. I don't mean the constant shouting when he's too embarrassed to admit he's made a mistake or when he tries to smack me when I'm in the back of the car and his hand snakes out just because I've asked him twice how long it will take before we get to wherever we're going. All grown-ups are pretty much like that, as far as I can see. So maybe I should just let him trundle along in the belief that he is sorted.

On the surface it certainly looks like he is. He's got this great job and we live in a nice house, nice enough for us, at least, though one of my friends' mothers said it was a stranger to Domestos. Peculiar word, 'domestos'.

I looked it up in the dictionary and it wasn't there. I thought it might be something to do with the Latin word *domus* meaning house but it's got a Greek ending. I asked my classics master but he gave me a weird look like I was making fun of him.

It's an old Victorian terraced house off the Chesterton Road, part of the inner ring road that runs round the city of Cambridge. It's got high ceilings which I like because we can play badminton in the living room with my friends or when Dad's in a good mood but apparently they are difficult to clean. I can't quite understand why this is such a problem since we aren't bats and don't spend much time clinging to the cobwebs, and anyway cleanliness seems overrated to me.

The general feeling among the adult population is that cobwebs are a bad thing. From a twelve-year-old perspective cobwebs are a) quite interesting things to look at briefly b) irrelevant if they nestle at the point where the wall meets the ceiling and c) only irritating if the shuttlecock gets caught in them when they become disgusting.

My room's up at the top. It's got all my favourite things in it – my posters, my stereo, my tapes and CDs, my games and my computer. Dad's got a computer too which he keeps downstairs in his study. I remember the day he got it. Dad was commissioned to write a sitcom pilot by Channel Four with a friend of his called Andy who lives in London. They wrote it by e-mail, transferring each scene as they finished it. Dad seemed to think this was some kind of major technological breakthrough but to me it just looked like common sense. I mean that's what e-mail is for.

I think Dad thought it was going to earn us a fortune. Andy was a comedy writer and Dad sort of tried to be one when he first started out after university but it never worked out for him so he concentrated on writing sports stuff for newspapers and magazines.

Anyway, Dad stayed in touch with Andy and they kept rewriting this idea about two girls and two blokes who live in a flat in Fulham. One day he came into my bedroom waving a piece of paper saying how Channel Four had bought their outline and we were all going to be rich and we could go and live in the West Indies. About six weeks later the move to the West Indies was off. Dad was in a really bad mood one day and it turned out that Channel Four had rejected his script because they'd bought a new American sitcom that was a bit like it instead.

It was called *Friends*. And Channel Four was right because I know my dad's cool and brilliant and everything but I don't see how he and Andy could ever have come up with anything as wicked as *Friends*. My favourite is Chandler because he's really funny. I don't think the writers have to write anything for Chandler. He just makes up those funny lines as he goes along. I also like Rachel, especially the way she's always having to push her hair away from her face. Wayne Singleton's a bit like that. The hair thing I mean. He's a boy in my class with long hair, not a TV star.

One of the big things about our house, though, is the garden. It's not that big, not like my friend Jamie's garden on Millington Road, but it's nearly all grass for a start, which is great for diving on, and it has very few flowers which are the bane of a boy's life. I go to my friends' houses and when we ask if we can play in the garden they have mothers who always say, 'Watch out for the flowers. I just planted . . .' and then it's some name I can't remember. I hate that.

You can't always judge where a ball is going to land. The Brazilian star Ronaldo, the best player in the world, can't do that so how can we at the age of twelve? And yet, and this is what really gets me, these mothers, who have never trapped, kicked or headed a ball in the whole of their pathetic lives, think we can control the ball so it doesn't touch their precious lupins or tulips or dehydrangas. See, that's what I mean about not missing a mother.

The reason I think Dad's not as sorted as he wants to believe is that he has this special sad look that comes over him on certain occasions. During the summer we wander through Cambridge and we see those disgusting students snogging on the banks of the river or lazing around punting when everyone knows they've got exams and they should be in their rooms working. I think Dad takes that route deliberately. Not that he's a dirty old man or anything 'cause he's not but he seems to need to remind himself of what it was like when he and Mum were young — well, Mum was always young, I guess — and they were in love.

He's always looking for her. Still. I can feel his eyes searching the back of a young woman with long blonde hair (like Mum had) and his pace of walking quickens just a bit and then we overtake and he shoots a sideways or backwards glance at her and of course it's not Mum, I mean how could it be? But Dad is always being disappointed like that and I can sense the expectancy escaping from him like the air from a punctured bicycle tyre. Believe me, I've had enough of those to know what that's like.

I want him to find someone. I do. Honest. He doesn't see it that way, of course. He thinks I'm dreading it and nobody can take the place of his precious Angela. Well, maybe he's right about that. No one can. But what really annoys me is that he thinks he's doing it for me and I know he's not. He's doing it for himself. That's another reason why he's not sorted.

I've seen him crying. Not a lot but quite a few times. And I know it's about Mum. Has to be. There's something hollow inside Dad, something he can't shake. He's been telling me these stories since I was very small, about him and Mum and how happy they were. I used to like them a lot, particularly one we called 'High on a Cliff'.

It was a story about how he'd been really happy with her in one place, I think it was by a lighthouse or something, and so he scattered her ashes on the grass in front of the lighthouse where a family lived and watched him. I know I liked the last line of the story which was how Mummy's soul watches over both of us at all times. I was always happy when Dad said that, though I wondered why the family who lived in the lighthouse were so important. I couldn't work out how they fitted in.

All this, though, was when I was a kid and I don't need to listen to 'High on a Cliff' before I can go to sleep any more. It's been twelve years since Mum died, almost the whole of my life. Surely he should have got over her by now. I don't mean forgotten her and I don't mean that he should stop treasuring her memory. I just mean I think he should move on with his life. There's a hole in Dad's heart. I want someone to fill it and I'm sure he must. Yet he constantly fights it because whenever there's a chance that someone might, he blows it.

Occasionally, and it's very occasional, there's a woman having breakfast with us on Sunday morning. It's embarrassing all right but usually more for them than for me. Dad always starts off by introducing us formally like we're in a play or something and then there's always a reason, like they're working together on an article or whatever and it got too late for her to take the train home. I mean quite pathetic stuff but it seems to be important to Dad that he should convince me that the woman only stayed in his bed because there was a reason other than they wanted to have sex together.

So I allow myself to be convinced and then Dad's like monitoring me for the slightest sign of emotional trauma. I think sometimes he's disappointed that he never gets what he's looking for. Why shouldn't he have sex? He's thirty-five years old and a widower. Jesus! I hope I'm a little more mature about all this when I get to his age. If I ever do. The school Under-15 team seems a long way off at the moment.

These encounters, you couldn't call them affairs, never

last and they've never stopped Dad from crying. He doesn't talk to me about them so I'm guessing here but I think he breaks them off and I think he uses me as an excuse. I can only tell that by the way these women look at me. Like they're thinking, 'So what's so special about you?'

I feel so sorry for Dad. He tries so hard not to show me when he's upset – unless it's Spurs losing at home to Arsenal and then he's not so much upset as angry and anyway I'm so upset myself I scarcely notice anyone else. There's something inside torturing him, something that makes him reject these women before anything can really start.

And though I know he's got a really cool job I think he came back to Cambridge not just to keep Mum's memory alive but to leave the competition behind. It's easier for him to do all his work by e-mail or fax. He doesn't go into an office; he says he hates something called 'office politics'. I'm not too sure what that means except it's not like the House of Commons.

But what I do know is that he is somehow hiding out here in Cambridge, in his study. There's something about the world that frightens him now. And it didn't when Mum was alive. When she died he closed up his feelings and ran away. In his work and in his heart Mum's death killed something there. He thinks I don't know about his troubles but I do. Now do you see what I mean when I say he's not sorted? Not sorted at all.

CHAPTER FOUR

Ralph

I USED TO HAVE SUCH grand dreams. I suppose they were not necessarily different to any other kid who has ambitions. I always remember that television programme which followed the lives of a bunch of real kids from the age of seven onwards — *7 Up* I think it was called. There was one boy who lived in the Yorkshire Dales. He was a farmer's son and he wanted to find out all about the moon. And he pronounced the word 'moon' like it was spelled 'moooon'. It was so utterly charming. It seemed to encapsulate the great breadth of his vision. I think he wound up teaching physics in an American university so maybe he did find out all about the 'moooon'.

As long as I can remember I've been desperately ambitious. Not for wealth, I was always terribly aware of those childhood morality tales in which the poor schnook who chooses the gold casket invariably winds up with the booby prize. I felt — oh God, this is going to sound so pompous, but it's true so I might as well admit it — I felt 'touched' by some kind of Destiny. I felt I would be famous, not in the television presenter sort of way and hopefully not in the serial killer sort of way either, but in a thoroughly laudable sort of way that would produce sycophantic interviews in the women's magazines and grudgingly respectful ones in the broadsheets.

I suppose it sounds even more big-headed if I were to describe the exact moment I felt the touch of Destiny on my shoulder. I was standing in the boys' playground – as opposed to the infants' playground – so I must have been about nine years old. A teacher blew a whistle or rang a bell and we started to line up. I looked at Nicholas Porter who was in the parallel line and I thought, 'Poor old Nicholas, he'll never amount to anything and I will.'

I'm not particularly proud of that thought; it's just that I seemed to know that it was true with an overwhelming sense of certainty. It wasn't that Nicholas Porter carried on him any distinguishing marks of failure. He was rather a colourless personality, never top, never bottom, never in trouble, never a goody-two-shoes, never particularly sporty but not the last to get picked to play either.

I suppose that was the startling realisation. Not that I would become Prime Minister and everyone else would go to prison. It was more the case that most of our class would live lives of total anonymity. Who, in future years, would start with sudden recognition when they heard the names of Lorraine Grempson or Philip Skinner? But Ralph Warren! Ah, now there was a name that would resonate. People would take photographs of this playground and say, 'This is where Ralph Warren went to school.'

I wasn't a boastful kid. I didn't tell anyone of my

epiphany. My father would have smacked it out of me if I had. So I continued to do what I had always done but I was buttressed now by an unshakable faith in myself. If I did badly in an exam or played poorly on the school team, it didn't upset me as would previously have been the case. I knew in my heart that I was going to succeed and, almost inevitably, that quiet but unwavering underlying self-confidence gave me the strength to battle and win.

It happened again at secondary school. I was always underrated, never one of the high fliers. I thought my English master would have a heart attack when I told him I wanted to try for Oxford or Cambridge. He could see no reason why any college of his knowledge would offer a place to me but the headmaster was putting up the fees that year by a scandalously large amount and he needed to justify it. A couple of extra kids into Oxbridge would do it so I was permitted to stay on after A level and have a go, along with half a dozen others who probably wouldn't get in but were more likely to do so than I was.

In the event they didn't and I did. Both the headmaster and the English master were astonished and put it down to the constantly unfathomable selection peccadillos of the admissions tutors, which bewildered them year after year. It turned out that I was the only entrant from my direct grant but would-be minor public school to get into either Oxford or Cambridge that year so the headmaster still had a parents' revolt on his hand when the new fee scale was announced. This exclusivity simply confirmed the feelings which had first surfaced in the playground nine years before when I had written off the prospects of poor Nicholas Porter.

Like all the rest of the intake in my freshman year I scrambled to find my place on the starting line in the fame race. I tried almost everything – journalism, acting, Footlights, speaking at the Union in that famous debating chamber, and it was all pretty successful. But already I was getting the sensation that there were over five thousand people in that town, all of whom had stood in their playgrounds aged nine and been overcome with an emotion identical to mine.

Arriving in Cambridge, I was eagerly anticipating a promised wonderland of sherry parties on the lawns in high summer punctuated by witty conversation, glamorous women and the offer of high-profile employment. I was astonished and disappointed when I found a hermetically sealed world in which the only chance of successful escape was offered by the magnetic charms of London. And then I met Angela and my world altered for ever.

It was the most unfortunate of opening acts. The only copy of the book I needed for my weekly essay was overdue at the faculty library. Despite repeated requests, the student concerned had failed to return it. With only twenty-four hours to go before I was supposed to hand in the as yet unwritten essay I smiled winningly at the faculty librarian (who was as affronted by the negative response to his severely worded admonishments as I was) and was handed a small piece of paper on which was written 'A. Frost, Jesus'.

I cycled slowly down Jesus Lane, rehearsing in my

mind the withering epithets I would shower on this selfish bastard Frost. The Porter's Lodge told me where Frost's room was located and I rapped smartly on the door before hearing a girl's melodious voice sing out, 'Come in!' I entered determined to find out from A. Frost's girlfriend where this selfish bastard A. Frost currently was because I was going to give him such a . . . when I was confronted by the sight of A. Frost in her underwear, smiling sweetly before pulling a rollneck sweater over her head.

It wasn't so much that I hadn't seen a real live girl in her underwear before, although I'm a little embarrassed to admit that I hadn't, but the fact that a) she was completely unfazed about appearing in a state of semi-undress in front of a strange man and b) she immediately got the sweater caught in a hair clip and was soon shouting for help. By the time I had untangled the sweater from the hair clip I had fallen hopelessly in love with her. By the time she had slipped into a pair of ripped jeans I would have walked barefoot to Palestine for one touch of her nether lip, and by the time she had put the kettle on I had entirely forgotten about strangling her and reclaiming the library book.

As it turned out I couldn't have timed my arrival better. Angela (rather than Alan or Andrew as I had imagined) was in the process of detaching herself from her old school boyfriend who was, I'm delighted to say, unfortunate enough to end up at university in Durham – a truly delightful city and an excellent university but far enough away from Cambridge to discourage the possibility of frequent meetings.

The following night we went to the cinema together for the first time — *Gandhi* which, despite its high-minded worthiness, was long enough for us both to become a little restless before the end. This necessitated a whispered apology which in itself necessitated the proximity of hot breath on ear hole. The erotic effect was precisely what each of the participants had planned so that when poor Ben Kingsley was ruthlessly assassinated, neither of us was looking at the screen.

I wanted to get married in the middle of our second term. We had already started sleeping together so in addition to wanting to erect warning signs to every other male, I felt I was morally obliged to make the offer which Angela laughingly dismissed as charmingly old-fashioned. She didn't see herself as getting married until she had won at least one Academy Award and the realistic forecast was that she wouldn't even gain a nomination until after graduation.

I took the decision with bad grace, I'm afraid. I was so utterly in love with Angela that every second she wasn't in my sight I feared some bounder, probably someone looking for an overdue book, would sweep her away from me. I don't think I ever felt completely sure that this wouldn't happen until after she was dead.

Clearing out her things after I came back to London, I found her diary which I knew she jotted in but had no idea it was quite so detailed. There were half a dozen large notebooks that allowed her to ramble on for as long as she wanted and to skip the days when she had nothing to say, which the tyranny of official diaries doesn't welcome.

I soon discovered that she knew all about my jealousy and possessiveness. Other women might have found all this emotional baggage distinctly off-putting but Angela was so laid back about everything that she found it endearing. I'm also short-tempered, impatient and lack quite a few of the social graces I've observed in others but failed to imitate. None of this fazed her.

She was quite used to the experience of men laying themselves at her feet. Had she lived in the Middle Ages, knights would have been charging at each other with lowered lances to seek her favour twenty-four hours a day, seven days a week — the evening jousts would obviously have had to take place under floodlights. They would have invented Kleenex seven hundred years early because of the number of her handkerchiefs that would have fluttered down to the jousting arena.

She had her own fantasy about me too. I was her writer, I was the man who was going to write a play or a film or something for her that was going to rocket her to stardom. We started with the Footlights. I had hoped to attract some attention myself in the Footlights and in the May Week revue I had written a passable slapstick sketch in which I played a demented Japanese visitor to Cambridge. It seemed to go down pretty well but there was no question but that Angela was the star turn. They had come to see her and they stayed to love her.

It took me a little while to come to terms with how much everyone loved her. There was a lot of jealousy involved, both personal and professional. Until Angela came along and blew everyone apart I was the one who seemed destined for Footlights stardom. Everyone was always looking for the new Jonathan Miller, Peter Cook, David Frost, John Cleese, and so on, those extraordinary Footlights graduates who went on to enduring fame. Then I helped get Angela in and after that there was no stopping her. I found myself writing more for her and appearing less and less myself. And when I did appear on stage I was acutely conscious that there was only one real star and it wasn't me.

I used to think it was pure sexism. They liked her because she had great boobs, in fact a great figure altogether, and she wasn't above exploiting her assets. She could sense how much she was desired and she used her sex appeal and that intensity of interest like a matador uses his cloak. Most men in my position would have enjoyed the salivating of other men but I was too possessive and too jealous. I wanted to lock her up in a tower like a storybook princess. I would have the only key. It wasn't particularly admirable, I admit, but I knew it was a hopeless fantasy. So I concentrated on becoming a writer, her writer.

I adapted *Antony and Cleopatra* as it might have been played by J.R. Ewing and Su Ellen from *Dallas*. I played J.R. with the traditional ten-gallon stetson and an accent as wide as an oil derrick. Angela looked quite stunning as Su Ellen, because she has, had rather, good cheek-bones, fairly plastic features, if you want to be rude, but they are, were, very useful because they attracted the stage lighting. She played it, of course, quite brilliantly, somehow portraying the essence of the Queen of Egypt crossed with a dipsomaniac Texan oil baron's wife. She was a genuine star.

The problem was that the sketch depended on the audience being literate enough to know the words of what we were sending up. That's not good comedy writing, I would later find out. I was OK, I guess, but Angela *was* both Su Ellen and Cleopatra of Egypt and even while she had the audience on the floor with laughter she was stretching beyond comedy for a touch of pathos, a touch of genuine tragedy. She was brilliant and at least I had the consolation of being the one to bring her talent to the notice of the public. On the first night we performed that sketch I effectively decided I would retire from appearing in public again. I couldn't stand the competition.

It was after that May Week revue that I knew what Destiny really wanted me to do — to tailor Angela's talents for the adoring masses. I was convinced that stardom would envelop my beloved Angela in her embrace as soon as she graduated from university. It was as inevitable as day followed night. Or so I thought. There was only one small problem. On graduation day Angela was eight months pregnant.

CHAPTER FIVE

Angela

(Extracts from Angela's diary)

31 October 1983

THE MEN IN THIS TOWN are so full of themselves. I'm glad I went to an all-girls school now. I know I bitched about it all the time when I was there because there were no boys but now that I'm living in a co-ed state I can suddenly see what I've lost.

Met another one of them today. His name's Ralph something. He came barging into the room really cross about an overdue library book, of all the unlikely things to get worked up about. Anyway, I pulled the oldest trick in the book, pretending to get my jumper caught in a hair clip, thereby giving him a jolly good eyeful for a moment or two. Totally disarmed him. Probably couldn't remember his own name at that instant. Honestly, men are so *simple*!!

Agreed to go to see *Gandhi* with him. Well, why not? I'm on this measly grant, my parents aren't contributing, I want to see the film and though I shall offer to pay my share he strikes me as the old-fashioned type who would regard a girl paying for herself at the cinema as a blot on his masculinity.

2 November 1983

Finished essay, gave Ralph library book back at cinema. He's cute. I really like him. He seems pretty keen on me too, which helps a bit but I wish he'd learn to disguise it. I mean, it's sometimes fun to make them run after you but if they come on strong right at the beginning it's just too easy.

Having said that I think this one might be different. He's not conventionally handsome which wouldn't interest me anyway but he has kind eyes and a lovely smile. He's also funny about the dons and he told me a very good joke about a girl who was stranded on a desert island with a one-legged jockey.

3 February 1984

Well! My first proposal of marriage! Technically I suppose it was my second but I tend to discount the one I got at kindergarten from Ian Bullivant.

It's been getting a bit hot with Ralph lately but even I never suspected this was what he was building up to.

He did it in style, I'll give him that. A corner table in the basement of La Traviata, a bottle of champagne which must have surprised the management as much as me — they probably went round to Oddbins for it. He'd put on a tie, too, so I thought it might be something to do with his parents coming down at half term and wanting to meet me.

But no, because we've been sleeping together he feels he's in love with me and wants to marry me. I told him we were both only nineteen and in our first year and weren't we a bit young? But he's been reading lots of romantic novels this term and I know for a fact he's written a good essay on nineteenth-century women novelists so perhaps he sees proposing to me as a kind of logical continuation.

I let him down gently. I told him there was nobody else because I think he's the jealous type. Then I told him that I loved him as much as he loved me though I think that might be a slight exaggeration. Then I said if we still felt this way about each other in our final term we should get married on graduation. Then I took him back to college and gave him a royal command performance.

Actually that was a mistake because in the morning when I woke up I found him looking at me with his big soulful eyes. When I asked what was the matter he told me he wanted to do this every day for the rest of his life. Wow! Fortunately he meant waking up next to me rather than me going through the royal command performance every night. I told him that could still happen whether we were married or not. At that he looked a bit brighter, thank God. A lot can happen between now and graduation. I wonder what.

15 June 1984

We opened the Footlights May Week revue last night after two weeks of frantic rehearsal. Actually it was less than two weeks because a lot of people didn't finish exams till last Monday so it's been a terrible panic.

The *Dallas* parody which Ralph wrote was a smash hit. I understood it as soon as I read it, felt a natural affinity for its comic rhythm. Ralph is a truly gifted writer although I think he still sees himself as a writer-performer in the tradition of Peter Cook and John Cleese. I don't feel I can tell him he's only average as a performer even though we're lovers. He's very sensitive and it would be too hurtful. I do tell him what a great writer he is though. One day he's going to write me a fabulous play and I'll star in it in the West End and it'll make both our names. We'll be like Diane Keaton and Woody Allen. I do wish he wouldn't be so damn jealous though. It's starting to grate on me.

31 October 1984

I've made a terrible mistake. I'd had enough of Ralph's jealousies and after that miserable summer inter-railing round Eastern Europe (neither of us would own up to who thought of the idea first) the prospect of two more years (and, arguably, sixty years after that) of Ralph seemed impossible to bear.

Anyway, I met this young director who's come up with a bit of a reputation from the National Youth Theatre. They gave him the main show to do — *Cabaret* — and I've always longed to play Sally Bowles. His name's Oliver and I loved his passion. Also he was a bloody good director, the best I've worked with though he was a real bastard when he couldn't get his own way — which wasn't often.

Oliver will be the head honcho at the RSC or the National Theatre in ten years' time I'm absolutely sure. And I suspect we'll end up working together when he gets there. Maybe we'll both be a little more mature by then.

The problem isn't the ten-day affair, it's what I've done to Ralph. He just crumbled. At first I lost my respect for him. If he wanted me so much why didn't he fight for me and to tell the truth I was fed up of him in a way. Put it this way, the brutal truth is that I didn't want to sleep with Ralph and nobody else for the rest of my life. There had to be something else out there.

There was. There was Oliver. And after ten days, when the first flush of sexual excitement wore off — quick, I know, even by my standards — I realised that I missed him dreadfully. I mean Ralph. For all his possessiveness and his peculiar ways and his obsession with tidiness and cleanliness that even my mother would find hard to live with, he did genuinely care for me, love me, and for all Oliver's flashing brilliance, he never would. Not just me, I doubt whether this man will ever love anyone but himself.

Last night was the first night of *Cabaret*. It went pretty

well but after I'd taken my make-up off and got dressed I went to the bar where I saw Oliver deep in discussion with one of the London critics he'd invited up. He looked up, saw me and quickly lowered his eyes, clearly anxious not to introduce me for fear that I should somehow spoil the wonderful impression he was creating. I stood there shocked for a moment. Had I been that bad?

It was like a film. A moment later I felt a tap on my shoulder. I turned round. It was Ralph. There were tears in his eyes. 'You were so bloody brilliant,' he said. And he meant it. In that split second I saw Ralph completely afresh. He just loved me. He loved me for what I was, not for what I might do for his career. He was so utterly reliable, dependable, trustworthy, lovable. I loved him so much. I suppose I always have. I just needed that shit Oliver to come along and make me realise it.

I wanted Ralph to come back with me but he wouldn't. I was hurt. Then I realised how selfish I was. What about him? He was still hurting from our break-up but he dragged himself in to see me in this new show, knowing that the guy I had dumped him for was directing me. If it was a triumph, it would merely cement me and Oliver together for ages.

And not only did Ralph come and see it, he stayed to tell me to my face how good he thought I was. No note stuffed in my pigeonhole. He waited for me in the bar knowing Oliver would be around and flaunting his triumph. How humiliating must that have been for Ralph who had so enjoyed that golden time around the May Week revue last summer? But he did it. What a guy!

Only now it's me who's running after him. He wouldn't come to my place, he didn't want me to go to his. Maybe he thought I was sort of teasing him. He's very sensitive.

I feel like Scarlet(t?) O'Hara at the end of *Gone with the Wind* when she says there must be some way I can get him back. I'll think about it tomorrow, for tomorrow is another day.

1 November 1984

I got him back.

Christmas Eve 1985

It's just the most ironic thing ever! Mummy won't let Ralph and me share a bedroom and yet we've come here to tell my parents that I'm pregnant. Ralph, of course, is the father. How's that for a definition of irony? My bedroom, with its prized collection of dolls (prized, I dare say, more by Mummy than by me) is not to be used as a venue for acts of illicit sexual relations. Though frankly, just at the moment, I feel like a tub of lard and have no interest in anything at night other than feeling my stomach and talking to whomsoever is in there.

We're planning to tell them after everyone's opened all the presents tomorrow but we haven't decided whether or not to do it before lunch. Will lunch be the saving grace or the last supper?

Will Mummy be shocked because a) I'm with child without benefit of wedlock, or shocked because b) my pregnancy means I'm no longer the virgin she still fondly believes me to be, or shocked because c) Ralph has literally screwed me out of a degree and/or career? My guess is she'll use c) as an excuse for b).

Dad just wants a quiet life so he'll settle for the easiest option available. Although I think Mummy was opposed to the Abortion Bill (oddly enough we haven't had much of a girly chat about the topic) I wonder whether she won't want it for me if it means a) getting rid of Ralph and b) restoring me to the bosom of the family.

I suppose there's always d) — Go and never darken my towels again, as Groucho said — but that's surely the least likely option.

27 December 1985

Well! Who would have believed it? It was option d)! That's why I'm writing this in the bedroom in Ralph's house. He's gone to play squash with an old school friend.

We told them, as planned, just before we sat down to Christmas dinner. My mother pretended she hadn't heard at first. She was pottering about the kitchen looking for the gravy boat as Ralph and I stood hand in hand by the sink.

'Mummy, we've got something to tell you. I'm going to have a baby.'

The amazing thing is I've heard those words on TV or wherever a million times and they always sound so corny, so clichéd. Yet, when it came to it and it was my turn for real, those were the only words that were somehow appropriate.

She did not take it well. She clutched the cupboard handle – a little melodramatically, I couldn't help feeling. (I was directing as well as appearing in this little playlet.) She cried out for Daddy who came running into the kitchen, instantly alarmed at the tone of Mummy's voice.

'Go on,' said Mummy, 'tell him. Tell him what you've just told me.'

You could see Daddy's face cloud over. Whatever it was, it wasn't going to be good news. And if it wasn't good news Mummy would be in a bad mood and that would last right through Christmas dinner and on into the fifty-fifth re-run of *It's a Wonderful Life* and *The Wizard of Oz*, which are Daddy's two favourite films of all time.

So I told him. Mummy then burst into tears and ran out of the room.

'Now look what you've done,' said Daddy and went after her.

Ralph and I set out the dinner in almost total silence – apart from the sound of James Bond destroying the underground cave of the megalomaniac who wants to blow up the rest of the world, which came from the television in the living room playing to a nonexistent audience.

I went upstairs to tell them everything was ready. Mummy was sitting on the bed dabbing at her nose with a Kleenex. Daddy was sitting next to her with his arm round her shoulder. He looked at me with such pain in his eyes. We left that night straight after supper and came here.

28 June 1986

Graduation Day. My parents didn't come. Mummy felt I would make an exhibition of myself. I was deeply if irrationally hurt when she told me but as it turned out she didn't know how right she was.

Well, I am eight months gone so I knew it would be impossible to hide. All the other mothers and fathers peering down on us from the gallery that runs round the Senate House must have been nudging each other and pointing at my enormous stomach – even under the wide maternity skirt and flapping undergraduate gown I wasn't going to disappear into the anonymity I (temporarily anyway) craved.

Fortunately, our long traipse up Trinity Street was conducted quite slowly although a gap occasionally opened up between my group and the one in front. Ralph offered to wheel me up there in a Sainsbury's trolley which he had liberated from the store in Sidney Street but I felt I was quite conspicuous enough. When we got to the Senate House we were organised into groups of four so that each of us could grasp a finger of the Praelector as he presented us to the Vice Chancellor.

He mumbled some words in Latin, some phrase which I was later assured meant something like, 'Here's a bunch of likely lads. Why don't you give them a degree?' We then had to kneel and place our hands inside those of the Vice Chancellor who would say something like, 'All right then. See if I care. Here's your BA.' Only in Latin of course. Then we'd rise to our feet and scuttle away through the side door for congratulations plus the inevitable strawberries and cream with a plastic spoon.

He was a nice old stick, the Vice Chancellor. If he wasn't shocked when he saw me, then he was certainly surprised. I found out later that he'd been a junior minister in the Macmillan government and a member of Ted Heath's cabinet ten years after that but as soon as Maggie Thatcher arrived he was out on his Old Etonian backside. So he wasn't too sprightly when he was doling out the degrees to us, maybe in his early seventies, but clearly a well-brought-up English gentleman.

The Praelector of our college had told us we didn't have to kneel in fealty if our religion forbade it. He obviously meant the Muslims etc. but he was looking directly at me when he said that. 'I'm C of E,' I pointed out. He coloured slightly but inclined his head towards my protuberant stomach. I pretended to suddenly click what he meant. Anyway, when it came to the crunch I wanted to go through the full kneeling down bit. I mean I am an actress, for God's sake. It was my little moment and Mummy and Daddy weren't there to be embarrassed.

'Angela Frost,' said the Praelector. I shuffled over to the throne and knelt slowly and ponderously in front of the old man. I put my hands together and placed them inside his. 'Here you are, mate. Have your degree. See if I care,' he intoned religiously in Latin. I inclined my head, deeply humbled by the honour bestowed on me. I tried to rise but I instantly realised I couldn't. So did the Vice Chancellor. He held out his arm for me to use as a lever to pull myself to my feet. I grasped it gratefully. He rose helpfully from his throne but the height/weight ratio was somehow imbalanced. I felt myself falling backwards. The Vice Chancellor tried desperately to steady me.

A look of fear flashed across the face of the Praelector. He saw it all unfold in slow motion but was powerless to intervene. As I went backwards, the Vice Chancellor inexorably came with me. As I fell flat on my bottom onto the marble floor of the Senate House in front of three hundred parents, one hundred and fifty graduands and the assembled dignitaries of the ancient University of Cambridge, the former Conservative Secretary of State for Employment toppled forwards and lay prostrate on top of me.

There was a collective gasp from the parents and an outbreak of barely stifled hysteria from the students close enough to observe the slapstick. The Praelector tried to lift the old boy from me but he seemed buried inside me — my first politician and certainly my first septuagenarian. I tried to help by lifting him from my shoulders but he sort of rocked back and forth over my swollen stomach which I dare say made the whole performance look positively obscene.

It took only a few seconds but it seemed like a lifetime

to everyone concerned. I was then hustled rapidly towards the exit door and out into Senate House Passage. The bloke with the funny hat and robes, whose precise function had been unclear, asked if I was all right but I suspect he was concerned in case I lost the baby and decided to sue the university.

The ancient ceremony resumed after I left with a rather chastened Vice Chancellor making no further gestures of gallantry. I assume I did get my degree. In the confusion I was worried that perhaps something was left undone and unsaid and I'm not really a BA at all. In retrospect I'm rather relieved Mummy and Daddy didn't make the journey.

23 July 1986

The happiest day of my life. Daniel Glenn Warren born today at 3.53 p.m., 3.8 kilos. Glenn, after Ralph's great hero Glenn Hoddle. Blue eyes (Ralph), bald (my dad), sweet disposition (modesty forbids). Baby doing fine, mother too wiped out to write more.

7 August 1986

While I remember (though I can't see how I could ever forget), I want to record my thoughts about the birth.

He was always going to be a big baby and at eight months he was still in the breech position. My mother, of course, told me that it would probably now be a Caesarian or a horrible forceps delivery in which they tugged the baby out and inserted fifty or more stitches into the mother afterwards. Fortunately the obstetrician turned him the right way up at the last moment but my mother had already put the wind up me and I knew it was going to be a very painful birth.

I didn't want to take any drugs, even an epidural, in case he came into the world hooked on something but when the pain started I'd have taken anything.

The fact is Danny came out like a rocket.

We'd gone out for a big Italian meal and I felt truly awful and bloated afterwards. I should never have had that tiramasu for dessert.

I felt the first contractions in the bath. Ralph timed them but they were more than five minutes apart. I rang the hospital but they said to wait till they were under four minutes. I decided to go to sleep. Nature would take its course. BIG MISTAKE!!

I had a dream I was drowning so I woke up about two hours later and I still felt really wet. It took me a good few seconds to realise that my waters had broken. I nudged Ralph who leapt to his feet stark naked and still ninety per cent asleep, I reckon, but mentally prepared. Actually I couldn't help noticing that he was also physically prepared but this wasn't the moment to do anything but giggle.

Thank God Ralph is so meticulous. He had had the suitcase packed and waiting by the front door for the previous week and within fifteen minutes of me realising my waters had broken we were on the way to the hospital. Four a.m is about the only good time to find a parking space in Hampstead and so even though the contractions were now coming at three-minute intervals we reckoned Ralph had plenty of time to park the car and see the birth of his firstborn.

By the time he got to the delivery room ten minutes later all hell had broken loose. There was one experienced midwife (thank God) and one junior doctor (probably still a bloody student a couple of years ago) and they were kicking bins across the room, racing to cope because, to everyone's astonishment, including my own, Danny was sprinting down the birth canal.

There was no time for the muscle relaxant, no time for the painkillers, Danny was on his way and nothing was going to stop him. His father strolled into the delivery room, tying on his mask and gown, to see half his baby son already through the trap door. I pushed without the need for the superfluous 'Push now, Mrs Warren' of the midwife. Danny wanted out and I sure as hell wanted him out.

I grabbed hold of Ralph's hand and squeezed. Ralph claimed later that I had inflicted more pain on him than Danny's birth had on me. I'd quite like it if we swapped roles next time. I'd happily impregnate him if he would like to be the one giving birth. Since it's not going to happen he, of course, said he'd be delighted. Bastard! That was the most terrifying pain I've ever been in. I suppose I've only got the time I fell off my bike and broke my arm when I was fourteen to compare it with but, honestly, childbirth is a lot worse though the end result of course is considerably better.

When the pain eventually stopped after about twenty-four hours (three, I was told later) I was too exhausted to care about anything, but Ralph was still in raptures that he had fathered a new England footballer. Then they washed off the blood and mucus and stuff and laid him, wrapped in a white sheet, in my arms.

I have never known a moment like it. I have never known anything as complete. Sometimes, during sex, I can feel like I'm a whole person but it's mostly a physical sensation. That evening when they laid Danny in my arms I felt whole in a way I have never felt before — as if there was a physical, spiritual, emotional hole at the centre of me which I never knew about until they slotted that missing piece into it. And it was a perfect fit.

CHAPTER SIX

Ralph

I LOVE CALIFORNIA. I GREW up in the sixties and seventies so my earliest television-induced images would have been of big American cars cruising down sun-drenched, palm-tree-lined boulevards with the Pacific Ocean rolling away into the distance and the sound of the Beach Boys' 'California Girls' on the soundtrack.

There's something enchanting about the prospect of California – to the non-American, that is. I believe that people who live on the East Coast think of California as some kind of lunatic asylum specialising in the collection of faddists and weirdos. But to me it is the very definition of life, liberty and the pursuit of happiness, particularly the latter.

I still believe in the promise of California even though I know it is no longer the new frontier. I know it is full of crime and pollution (Southern California, anyway), of people begging in the streets and physical labour done by exploited illegal immigrants fleeing from the poverty and killing fields of Central America.

But there is still the ocean and the beaches, the all-night diners and the bikini-clad girls. Oh God, this is all sounding so shallow but it would be disingenuous not to admit that the sybaritic lifestyle played some part in the attraction of that magical word 'California'.

I think that's why I took to the California Angels baseball team so readily. They seemed less interested in winning the pennant or the World Series than in being located two miles from Disneyland. At their evening home games, about the time of the fifth or sixth inning, Disneyland would let off its nightly firework display. The crowd would immediately leap to their feet and race to the back of the stadium, hanging over the walls to observe the whoosh and scream of cascading multicoloured rockets. The poor baseball players were left to conclude the inning almost unobserved. They didn't seem to care very much. They were owned by the old cowboy star Gene Autry and seemed to regard themselves as a branch of show business first and a bunch of serious professional ball players second. But they had the name 'California' attached and I was hooked.

I always wanted to go there because it seemed like Paradise on Earth. For Angela it was slightly different. I may be doing her memory a disservice here but she wanted something slightly more – fame. Not money, not glamour, not the Hollywood razzmatazz, but celebrity. Sure she was ambitious, I don't think people should think the less of her for that. Why shouldn't she be? She had talent and what she wanted was the chance to display it. She didn't want to give a series of magnificent performances of Ibsen above a pub in Stoke Newington – though she would happily have done so, I'm sure, when she had become a star.

It was following her star I suppose that killed her. At first we couldn't believe our luck when the call came. We used to joke about 'the' phone call – the one from Hollywood promising untold fame and riches. And then one day it came.

Perhaps it wasn't as entirely unexpected as I'm suggesting here. After all, she had left university as the golden girl – there's that California image again – despite not acting after January when she was three months pregnant. But already her previous efforts had created a small buzz amongst the London agents and they were there in force to see her play Nora in *A Doll's House*.

I thought, if I'm being honest, that it wasn't her greatest performance. There were good reasons. She was still upset by the way her parents had treated her at Christmas, she was suffering from morning sickness which seemed to afflict her most in the afternoons, and she didn't have a lot of time for her director who clearly thought it would make him look like a big shot if he treated the best actress in Cambridge as a juvenile incompetent.

Nevertheless, on opening night Dr Theatre worked his magic and she gave of her best. It was still, I felt, some way below her Amanda in *Private Lives* the previous year or even her Sally Bowles in *Cabaret* when she just blew me away but it was still mightily impressive. All the agents wanted to take her on immediately but she told them about the baby and they melted away – with one exception.

Martyn Frank didn't seem like an agent. That is, he wasn't boastful or pompous like so many of them seemed to be. He was quite shy, very soft spoken but he had vision. He looked way beyond the pregnancy and when he revealed that he, too, had seen *Cabaret* I knew he was the right one for Angela. He left his card listing an office in Soho, explained that he was really a one-man band with an invaluable assistant but that he had worked in one of the big agencies for three years and really knew the ropes. He had a number of young clients of whom we had both heard and it was obvious even before he left that Angela was going to join him.

She went up to London and had lunch with him before telling him the good news. She came back bubbling with words of praise for Martyn, energised by the prospect of the world he painted for her. I must admit something tugged at me, some antediluvian jealousy, no doubt because even though I liked Martyn, he was still, well, a man and all men wanted her — even when she was four months pregnant. I know I did so why wouldn't he?

By this time she was in the middle of her pregnancy and reluctantly hauling herself up the steps to the university library every day. I was quietly thankful that the pressure of exams might dull the enticing prospect of showbiz for a few brief months. I felt as if I was holding in my hands a rare and precious butterfly who was flapping its wings against my fingers, desperate for its freedom even though I feared that its freedom might also bring its death. How ironic! I only ever thought of that as an image, a metaphor, not a prognostication of tragic reality.

Just before we were due to go down for Easter, a scribbled message was taken at the Porter's Lodge and thrust into Angela's pigeon hole. Martyn wanted her to call – telling her to reverse the charges. An American movie was shooting in London. It was a so-called crazy comedy with Chevy Chase, one of those asinine pictures in which England is portrayed as a land of unchanging eternal values – Tower Bridge, red double-decker buses, Buckingham Palace. In one sequence Chevy's wife is taken to hospital after a supposedly hilarious accident and is mixed up with a pregnant woman.

Martyn thought Angela would be great as the pregnant woman and persuaded the casting director to meet her. Martyn was right. The casting director flipped, so did the director, and ten days later Angela was sitting in a corridor of Queen Charlotte's Maternity Hospital in west London. At least, we decided ruefully, if anything went wrong she was in the right place.

The scene was shot one day and forgotten about the following day as I hauled her up the steps into the university library again. When the cheque arrived about three weeks later we were very pleased she'd done the part. It bought all the baby things, with a bit left over for the scary prospect of the grown-up world we were hoping to enter when the baby was born.

The movie died as we thought it would but Angela's performance translated the Cambridge buzz into a London buzz. The casting director on the film mentioned Angela's name to the casting director at the Royal Shakespeare Company. Three weeks after Danny was born Angela was auditioning in Stratford. Two weeks later she was invited to join the company and six weeks after that she opened at the Barbican as Desdemona in *Othello*.

Yes, it was that fast. Her feet, our feet, barely touched the ground. She talked a mile a minute, she bubbled with life and I loved her for it. I had by no means lost my corrosive streak of jealousy but the sight of her with Danny eased my soul.

She loved that baby as much as I did. She left him with me for long periods while she rehearsed, of course, but she was always desperate to see him and since she was still feeding him she rarely went more than four or five hours without holding him to her. She conveyed an aura of such happiness and earth-mother contentment that not even the infamously randy male members of the world's second oldest profession dared to approach with anything on his mind other than Shakespeare or baby talk.

It was tough going in those early days after graduation. We were part of that Loadsamoney generation, the high water mark of the Thatcher-Lawson boom years between the blue collar recession of the early eighties and the white collar recession of the early nineties. We knew what money was, all right, and we liked it. We weren't like the sixties hippies with their contempt for material things. We were the children of the consumer age but Angela and I were as keen on fame as we were on fortune and we wanted to find them both in the West End rather than the City or Docklands. We had friends who were driving around in Porsches and Ferraris two years out of university. We were still waiting for the 9.30 a.m. watershed so we could qualify for the cheap day travel card on London Transport tubes and buses.

Angela's success in the theatre took little of the financial pressure off us because stage actresses get paid so badly but we just about managed to eat and feed and clothe Danny and still pay the rent on our overpriced, cramped, one-bedroom basement flat in Highgate. However, she fitted in a small but showy part in a successful sitcom and that paid relatively big money for work that was altogether less worthy, less challenging, just less in every way.

It was fortunate because I wasn't doing so well. I was getting bits and pieces — sports previews in *Time Out*, sketches on a late-night BBC Radio comedy programme called *Weekending* — but it was casual work. I felt like a labourer hanging around a bus stop at 6 a.m. waiting to be chosen for work that day — like Marlon Brando queueing up on the docks in *On the Waterfront*. My career seemed to be going nowhere fast. I had always felt sure of my talent but it was so competitive out there, so tough, and progress was nonexistent. I started to have real doubts about myself.

I couldn't even confide in Angela. She was surfing a gigantic wave of success that didn't seem to want to crash onto the shore. She kept encouraging me to write a play for her but I didn't have an idea in my head and the prospect of the blank piece of paper terrified me. The more she mentioned it, the more I froze. I started to feel like an incubus, the lead weight round her neck,

James Mason to her Judy Garland in *A Star Is Born*. When the phone rang, it was always for her. I could hear the disappointment in the voices on the other end when she was out and they had to deal with me. Especially if they were male.

This of course only helped to fuel my spiralling jealousy. Some days I couldn't work because all I could see, dancing in front of my eyes, was a vision of a naked Angela rolling around on a bed with a naked director, or a naked actor or a naked journalist or a naked PR guy. It was horrible and it was humiliating. I guess I wasn't the best husband in the world at that time. There were rows. Lots of them. I was a rotten husband, I know I was, but at least I was a good father. Thank God I had Danny. Without that little baby to look after I think I would have committed the *crime passionel* which would have kept me in prison for life. Ironic or what?

CHAPTER SEVEN

Angela

(Extracts from Angela's diary)

18 June 1987

WHEN MARTYN RANG THIS MORNING I thought it was a wind-up. He has always known how much I love *Gone with the Wind* so when he said a Hollywood studio wanted to see me because they were planning a re-make of *Gone with the Wind* I thought he was sending me up.

He had to reel off the director (Franco Zeffirelli) and the potential Rhett Butlers (Jack Nicholson, for God's sake, Redford, please no! Kevin Kline, please yes!) before I would begin to take him seriously. Ben Kingsley was going to play Ashley Wilkes (too old! Mind you, so was Leslie Howard) and they'd signed Michelle Pfeiffer to play Melanie.

Then what he said had a weird sort of logic. Meryl Streep wanted the part of Scarlett so much she sent Zeffirelli make-up and costume tests she'd had done at her own expense but he rejected her. Martyn heard that Zeffirelli wanted an English actress to play Scarlett because it had worked so well before with Vivien Leigh. So he'd sent a tape of that awful scene I did in the Chevy Chase movie to the casting director and a copy of my reviews from *Othello*. Apparently the tape got passed on to Zeffirelli who loved it. They want me to fly out there to meet the studio executives and the director and everyone. And they're paying me to go!

It actually fits perfectly because I don't start rehearsals for *Two Gentlemen of Verona* at Stratford until the first week in August and the RSC have been really great and said my understudy can fill in for the six performances I'll miss when I'm away. Then to make it even better Ralph got this great plan to write a series of articles on baseball for one of the magazines he's been wanting to get into for ages and today they said yes. Something's got to go wrong soon. This is just too good to last.

Actually, I know what it is. It's Danny. I wanted to take him with us but I know it's impractical. And besides, as Ralph keeps telling me, much as we love him we've had no time to ourselves in the year since he's been born. We're only going away for two weeks and I doubt he's going to be traumatised by our absence. He's been on solids for months and he's pretty much weaned off my breast.

Ralph wants us to leave him with his mother who has been going a bit potty recently. I would prefer to leave him with my parents even though they've not forgiven us for the Christmas eighteen months ago. The fact is they're still Mummy and Daddy and I know they still love me in their own repressed way and Mummy really wants to look after Danny, only her stupid pride gets in the way and she can't bring herself to ask. I know she has her faults but she's a good mother really.

Much as I love Ralph's mum I'd lie awake at night worrying that she's forgotten to feed him or she's left him in a trolley outside Tesco's. She is so scatty — which is probably why Ralph is exactly the opposite. It's funny that, the way children grow up directly opposite to their parents. I mean Mummy and Daddy are wonderful in their own way but they are products of the 1950s, a very repressive decade, and by the time the sixties came round they were married and mortgaged. Still, maybe it'll make them really great grandparents.

I wonder if Danny will grow up like that. They say that some character traits can skip a generation. He certainly doesn't behave like much of a rebel at the moment. He is such a sweet, angelic, placid child I am worried that there's something wrong with him. He's passed all his tests that the health visitor gives him. He's crawling now and trying to haul himself up on the leg of the sofa. He'll be walking very soon.

He smiled early and he's the easiest comic audience Ralph and I have ever known. He laughs at everything — well, gurgles more like. His face seems to crack open when he smiles, like Humpty Dumpty. Sometimes when he drifts into total silence I think he's become autistic or suddenly gone deaf so when he slips into one of those trances I ring a little bell in his ear. I know it startles him and he cries until I pick him up but I'm always so relieved to know that he's still normal.

At night it's even worse. It was the subject of one of our increasingly frequent rows. Last week I was really knackered. I came back from the performance about midnight. Ralph was waiting up, having cooked me a lovely piece of fish. He was being extra attentive, all right. After the fish (salmon steak, yummy) and the glass of white wine (Pouilly Fume, very fruity), we were relaxing together on the carpet. Ralph had obviously reached take-off stage, which I'm afraid I hadn't realised, when I was absolutely convinced that Danny was lying in his cot choking to death.

I pushed Ralph off me, which he took with unusually bad grace, and raced into the bedroom, buttoning my blouse as I went on the grounds that it was inappropriate for the grieving parent to find her dead child with both breasts exposed. Ralph came after me in an even worse mood, having scraped his willy on the zipper getting it back into his trousers.

'You see?' he whispered fiercely. 'Nothing wrong at all.'

I was not convinced. Seemed to me Danny's unmoving state indicated only that I was right all along. I prodded him in the stomach (Mummy says she always placed me on my tummy to stop me choking in the cot yet now we're given exactly the opposite advice – see what I mean about children being polar opposites of their parents?). I couldn't see Danny move or breathe. I jabbed him again much harder and this time to my indescribable relief he woke up and screamed the flat down.

It took him just thirty seconds or so to quiet down

again in my arms. I stayed in that room rocking him to sleep while I heard Ralph banging about in the bathroom, still cross with me obviously. It's going to be difficult, I dare say, when Danny gets older (and is joined perhaps by a sister and maybe a brother) but I really think it's possible to combine what I want to achieve as an actress with being a mother. I obviously can't be a full-time mother like mine was but then Ralph does so much with Danny and my father did almost no parenting at all except to take me to piano lessons on Saturday mornings. We are determined, no matter how successful we both get, that we will never hand the children over to a nanny. We don't want anyone else bringing up Danny. Why should they have all the fun?

21 June 1987

The tickets arrived this morning. First class! I've never travelled first class anywhere in my life. Neither has Ralph. He's playing it all really cool but I know that inside he's as excited as I am.

And we're going to be staying in the Beverly Wilshire Hotel. I asked Martyn if that was the same as the famous Beverly Hills Hotel with the Polo Lounge and everything, but apparently it isn't. It's very nice, I'm assured, and probably a cut above a damp basement flat in Highgate with the constant aroma of drying baby clothes. I cannot believe the clothes that baby goes through. Honestly, I wish I had a wardrobe his size. Well, no, I don't because

I wouldn't get my four dresses to hang up in a wardrobe designed to take infant's clothes.

The only snag is that Ralph's magazine cancelled last night. They've decided they haven't got the space for the baseball articles after all. Ralph asked why they didn't just hold them over till a month when they did have space but they got all shifty apparently and then claimed the articles might be out of date if they held on to them longer than a month.

Ralph said to me he expected that response and that it had never been a sure commission but I know he must be hurting inside. My career is going so well and his is slightly stalling. I mustn't be unfair. There's so much luck involved for both of us and he's not having much at the moment. I seem to be having it all for both of us. I'm sure it will even itself out but I've become aware in the last few weeks how fragile Ralph's ego is.

I remember when I was encouraging him to write more when we were in that Footlights revue, how he took it not as a compliment on his writing but as a criticism of his performance. He's got more touchy since we left university, though that's probably because things have gone so well for me. He's not resentful that I've done well, just anxious that he's being outstripped. I wish I could reassure him about his talent and about how much I love him but somehow I can never find the right moment. I have told him that he's got a great play inside him. He should get down to it and write it. He nods but, as far as I know, he's never even started.

It doesn't help that when the phone rings it's always for

me. He's rather thrown himself into full-time fatherhood as if to compensate for being unable to do the things he planned. I know this is what's behind all the rows we've been having lately but I'm so knackered most of the time I haven't got the strength to try to sort it out. I'm hoping that when we get away to America it'll all be different. We'll both be relaxed and we'll have had a couple of decent nights' uninterrupted sleep. That's going to help A LOT!

My big fear is that by devoting so much time to Danny, Ralph might be taking the easy way out – not that raising babies is easy, it's just that he's so sensitive. When I'm too tired to have sex he says he understands but I know he feels I'm rejecting him. So he gets an idea turned down by an editor and then I come home and I won't help put it right and he's been running round after Danny all day. Well, I guess that's a perfect recipe for the sort of rows we've been having. And then there's his stupid jealousy. It drives me crazy because I love him and I'd never be unfaithful to him but I know he thinks I'm shagging every dick in the RSC. I can see it in his eyes and hear it in his voice and it bugs me but I guess however unfounded, he sees this as yet another form of rejection. He hates rejection and he might just give up on me or his career because then he won't be rejected any longer. So thank God for Danny, the one person who will never reject him.

Of course, to be an actress you have to experience a lot of rejection. And when you're an actress people reject you personally. When Ralph gets a rejection it's because they don't like his ideas. But when an actress gets turned down it's because her face doesn't fit — literally. She's too tall or too short or too ugly or too beautiful or too confident or too mousy. And what they always forget is — WE'RE ACTRESSES. WE CAN DO IT BECAUSE WE CAN ACT IT!! They're all stupid, these producers and directors. They never want to give you a chance.

Except me of course. I've almost never known rejection. My career, although it's barely a year old, has been so easy and free of stress it's as if I've got a guardian angel riding on my shoulder. I sure hope he stays there when we get to Hollywood!

CHAPTER EIGHT

Danny

SOMETIMES, WHEN I GET LONELY or there's nothing on TV, I take out the scrapbook Dad made of Mum's short career and look through it. Other kids have family photograph albums or home video stuff but I have this scrapbook. I know it so well I feel like I was part of it even though I know I was just a baby at the time.

The bit I like best is when they went to America. That's when Dad started supporting the California Angels and he's bought me lots of their stuff which I've got in my room even though some of the players have retired now. I've got this big poster of Reggie Jackson who was a great hitter for the New York Yankees but not so great for us. He's in one of those *Naked Gun* movies. That's what I tell the other kids when they try to make fun of me for having a baseball poster on my wall. I've also got an amazing one of Michael Jordan from the Chicago Bulls like he's suspended in the air six feet off the ground just before he does a slam dunk. Jordan's famous, though, and anyway he advertises Air Jordans on the telly so everyone thinks he's cool.

They left me with my gran when they went to Hollywood. I don't see my gran much these days. She still sends me birthday cards with a cheque in the envelope for ten pounds but she and my dad don't like each other much. He doesn't say much about her. Just that she wasn't very nice to him after Mum died. My other gran, my dad's mum, is dead too so Gran is actually the only grandparent I have because both Grandpas died before I knew them. I don't care though. I've got my dad and he's all that counts.

In the scrapbook there's a picture of my mum that doesn't look anything like her – nothing like the other pictures I've got of her, I mean. Her blonde hair is very neat and she's got this weird smile on her face. I mean it's a nice smile and everything but it's sort of false. Like there's no reason for her to be smiling. It doesn't look like any of the other pictures we've got where she's smiling. I don't like it. Dad says that it was a studio photograph which means that the big studio that made them go out there wanted to have it even though Mum didn't want it taken like that.

She went because she was going to be in a re-make of an old film called *Gone with the Wind*. They didn't make it after she died. Dad says it was out of respect for her but I don't see how that can be. I mean she was my mum but she was very young and why would anybody not go and see a film because my mum had been killed a year before it was made? It makes no sense but I think Dad says that to me so that I'll be impressed with how famous Mum was. Actually, I think Dad says that for himself because he wants to remember Mum as being dead famous. I don't care how famous she was. I just care that she was my mum and she was special and I loved her.

Can you love someone you don't know? At times, at night, I screw my eyes up in the dark and think and think so hard and try to make the picture of my mum come back to me. I can sometimes do it but then I think I'm kidding myself. What I really know is that scrapbook and all the stories Dad has always told me about her.

They made tapes of Mum doing tests for the film and we've got them all. They show her in lots of different dresses and hats saying the same thing over and over again. It looks dead boring. Dad says they're only tests but if that's any guide it was going to be a really crappy film. Good job they never made it in the end, if you ask me.

The studio put them up in a big posh hotel which sounds wicked. They travelled around in limos, like a rock star, and they were only a year out of university. I mean a year before, they'd been pushing their bikes over Garrett Hostel Lane bridge. You can't get over that bridge without getting off your bike because it's a steep hill and you have to get a real run at it and you can't most of the time because it's full of tourists who are too thick to realise that bicycles travel faster than feet. I see all these students with bad haircuts and stupid clothes and I can't imagine any of them riding round Hollywood in a limo next year.

It must have been so cool when they found out that

Mum got the part. Dad smiles when he tells me about this bit and says they put the 'Do Not Disturb' sign on the door of the suite in the hotel. When I was little I used to think that was so people wouldn't come bursting into the room and change the channel on the television but now I know all about sex I guess that was another reference to sex. I mean, I know they were young and in love and all that but couldn't they have shown a little self-control? I get bored when all that kissy-kissy stuff comes on the telly or it happens in a film. It's OK when it's on video though – you can just fast forward through it. They look even more stupid with horizontal lines through them

After she died Dad asked the studio for copies of the tests or auditions or whatever they're called and they sent them back to England with a massive bunch of flowers. They were supposed to be put on her grave but they didn't know that Mum wasn't buried here. She was buried in California. Well, not buried. She was cremated and then her ashes were scattered on the cliff overlooking the Pacific Ocean with the lighthouse in the background.

That favourite bedtime story of mine, 'High on a Cliff', made me think that Mum watched over us from the lighthouse, that her soul was somehow trapped in the light that goes round and round. I suppose the lighthouse was my weird idea of Heaven when I was three or four years old.

The story wasn't as creepy as it sounds. It was more like a handsome prince and a beautiful princess sort of a story. There was this place, a magical kind of a place, where the sky meets the sea. Only my dad and my mum knew about it. Except I guess for the family who lived in the lighthouse on the other side of the cliff. But this piece of land was Mum and Dad's place and they used to lie there together.

Later, I realised Dad must have meant sex again but I don't like to think about it in that way. To me it's always meant that they lay down together looking at the clear blue sky like I do sometimes in the garden or looking at the stars at night when it's warm enough. Sometimes that makes me dizzy. I like to think of their private place as like the secret garden in the famous book I read when I was nine or ten — a magical, enchanted land full of colourful and exotic flowers.

She was badly hurt in that car crash and then the ambulance took her to a hospital where she died. The man who killed her, the car driver, he went to prison but not for a very long time. I don't know why he wasn't hanged. Dad said he had to go back to some kind of driving school after he got out and he couldn't drive on the roads for a long time. He had been drinking because his wife had left him. Well, big deal! At least he could still see his wife, and people get divorced all the time. Lots of kids in my class have been involved in a divorce and are living in a step-family or something like that. So what's the big deal? That doesn't give you the right to drink yourself stupid and kill my mum. I'd like to kill one of his kids then see how he feels. I hate that guy. Even more than Richard Brennan who stole my new trainers and pretended they were his because my dad hadn't written my name inside them.

Afterwards they asked my dad if he wanted to take her body back to England to bury her but he said no. They had been really happy in California. She had been given the part, you see, and that movie would have made her famous all over the world so Dad said he wanted her to be buried there. And anyway he's always had a thing about California. He must have had a really romantic image of the place because isn't California just full of gangs and shootings and drugs and everything? Dad seems to ignore all that kind of stuff. God, he even likes the Beach Boys! He plays their wrinkly music in the car sometimes but not often because I let him know I don't like it so he turns it off because he says I ruin it for him. If you ask me it's already ruined.

Anyway he wanted to take her body to lie in this magical place where they had been so happy but he couldn't bury her there so she had to be cremated. I think about it and I get so sad for my father. Fancy having to go through something as horrible as that by yourself. I wish I could have been there to hold his hand and give him a hug but I was just eleven months and three weeks and two days old when it happened.

But now I'm glad they had their private place next to the lighthouse, up on that cliff overlooking the ocean. I know my mum's happy there because my dad's happy for her. His happiness means everything to me but I know that really he's still sad inside and there's nothing I can do about it. I wish there was.

CHAPTER NINE

Angela

(Extracts from Angela's diary)

4 July 1987

I FEEL SO INCREDIBLY BLESSED. They told me last night I'd got the part. It wasn't quite as dramatic as Vivien Leigh. I think she was told when they were filming the burning of Atlanta. I was in the bath, or 'in the tub', as they say out here — a quaint saying making me think of a tub of ice cream — when the phone rang. Ralph called out from the bedroom but I was happily ensconced in the bath and asked him to take a message. He responded by telling me rather more urgently that it was Morgan, the agent from ICM Martyn had set me up with out here.

I got out of the bath, grabbed one of those luxurious towels that make life worth living and dripped my way into the bedroom — apparently many rooms now have phones in the bathroom to prevent exactly this calamity but we don't rate such indulgence — not yet anyway.

Morgan was incredibly excited — he could see the agency's commission and his own career advancement,

I'm sure — which in a funny way prevented me from joining in. If it had been Martyn and he had delivered the information in his typically deadpan dry way I would probably have been as hyper as Morgan. As it was I behaved like a perfect English convent-educated schoolgirl and thanked him courteously, replaced the receiver and sprang into Ralph's arms. The towel fell off and he got my wet body all over his nice new Armani T-shirt.

I know Ralph would never read these books. He sort of knows I write this semi-diary but he is a very honourable man and it's unlikely I'll ever come home unexpectedly early to find him in an armchair with a six-pack of beer to hand while he leafs through these pages. I can therefore commit anything about him to these notebooks in the sure and certain belief that nobody will ever read them except myself — and the rest of the world when I get ready to sell them because I haven't had a job in three years and I'm flat broke.

I think I've always been honest about Ralph and I'll continue to be so, otherwise what would be the point in this exercise? There was something wrong with our lovemaking last night. Well, not wrong, not technically wrong, although he came very quickly, more so than usual. No, what I'm writing about is a sense of something missing. He wasn't there emotionally. Given the news we'd just had I thought it might be one of the great fucks of all time but I accept that's probably romantic wishful thinking.

The great fuck of all time took place in my parents' double bed with Dominic Wharton when I was seventeen years old. They did not want me to see Dominic just because his name had been in the local paper for some court appearance — something to do with shoplifting — and anyway he got off.

We waited till my parents went to their weekly whist drive and I invited Dom round to the house. We could have done it I suppose in my single bed but the thought of defiling my parents' living space was overwhelmingly appealing. Dom was really good, though I don't know that my judgement was particularly acute since he was the only boy at that time I had permitted the ultimate reward. Sadly, he dropped me the next week, claiming that having to fuck me in my parents' bed had grossed him out. I cried for days.

I knew as Ralph and I rolled around on that American king-size bed, such luxury after the narrow confines of our regular double in the basement flat in Highgate, that something was wrong with him. Although he couldn't physically have been closer to me at that moment, he was also very distant. I think he must have been praying I didn't get the part. He must have felt I was on my way to a Hollywood career full of glitz and glamour with the now constant presence of other men. If the RSC had been difficult for him, what was the full glare of the studio spotlight going to be like?

I made it my task to reassure him. There never would be anyone else for me but him. I meant it. The sort of barflies you find in show business would never have an attraction for me. I loved Ralph and what we were facing was a test of my acting ability not a test of my marital fidelity. I could see he didn't believe me though.

So now we have to dress up for a big Fourth of July party in some mansion in Beverly Hills. Ralph has been swimming in the pool here, I can see him from the window slowly and methodically stroking his way up and down the (surprisingly small) pool. I think he's trying to put off the evil moment when we walk into that house and I'm surrounded by the traditional pack of hangers-on. I know it's going to happen but it isn't serious. Next week the same treatment will be accorded somebody else and she'll be queen for the day. It doesn't mean anything and it doesn't threaten our marriage. Why won't Ralph see that?

5 July 1987

The party was great. They really know how to put on a show, these Americans. There was so much food it almost caused me to become anorexic on the spot — I suspect some of those suspiciously slim women I met already were. There were lots of famous people there, none of whom I recognised — or rather I recognised them but I couldn't put a name to the face. Fortunately Ralph could, and I clung to his side all night so that he could make the introductions. He said he hated the whole thing but I think he rather liked it. None of the big stars, Dustin or Clint or Meryl or Redford, were there though, so maybe it wasn't quite as glitzy as I thought it was.

There were any number of beautiful women, many of whom took a shine to Ralph. I was glad. It must have been good for his self-esteem which is bothering me a bit these days and I felt supremely untroubled at the prospect of anything significant materialising.

In the evening there were fireworks which went on for ever. I remember my dad complaining every bonfire night that the cost of a small measly box of Roman candles and Catherine wheels was ruinously expensive. My childhood fireworks parties were like bad sex — always over in five minutes — unless the blue touch paper got damp in which case it would fizzle out before igniting the firework. So we would then have my father approaching nervously whilst my mother stood in the kitchen banging on the window shouting 'Don't touch it! Throw it away' etc. In that case the box could last anything up to fifteen minutes.

It was nothing like last night's display which was done with typical Hollywood professionalism. I mean that literally. There was a guy there whose profession it is to orchestrate firework displays, and pretty spectacular they must be too, judging by last night's show. It must have gone on for about an hour, that array of multicoloured showers of light. I wish my dad had seen it!

Now that I'm a big Hollywood star-in-the-making I got my agent, who slobbered all over me like a big grateful dog, to ring the RSC and pinch another few days' holiday. It's really important for my marriage that Ralph and I go away somewhere, away from this crazy town, and spend some time together. If we go straight back to London I'll be into work immediately and he'll be stewing about the prospect of moving out here and losing me permanently. He hasn't said anything but I can tell.

8 July 1987

Our last day in Hollywood. Morgan took us out to see some houses. They were ludicrous. I mean five bathrooms one of them had. Five! Admittedly they call the downstairs loo half a bathroom so the numbers aren't quite so mad but I kept explaining to Morgan that we lived in a damp basement flat in Highgate, the accommodation comprising, as the estate agent's spec sheet always says, one living room, one bedroom, kitchen and bathroom. Our bathroom has the loo jammed right up against the side of the bath — cosy but unhygienic.

The house we're going to take is in Westwood, near UCLA. We simply couldn't bring ourselves to live the other side of Sunset Boulevard in Bel Air or the foothills of Beverly Hills although the agency pointed out that the studio was paying anyway and it was important for my career (!) that we had a big house commensurate with my newly found status in 'this town', as they all call it.

Morgan was a bit miffed that neither Ralph nor I would accept his reasoning so he finally figured we were a bunch of Limey nincompoops and let us choose something we felt comfortable in — a three-bedroomed affair with a room for us, one for Danny and a spare bedroom for guests if we had people out from England.

Morgan wanted to know where the nanny would sleep.

We said 'What nanny?' He said didn't we have a kid? I said we had a beautiful baby boy named Danny who is nearly a year old but the sarcasm was lost on him – as was the idea that we had no intention of handing him over to the ministrations of some blonde airhead, in which 'this town' excels.

Ralph also bridled, making it quite clear that he had a major hand in Danny's upbringing and would be fully in charge of all elements of child-rearing while I was at the studio or on location. Morgan seemed quite relieved at that because it was one less thing that might go wrong for which he would get the blame. Ralph's house-husbanding was also good news as it would keep him away from the set where insecure, unoccupied, unemployed and unknown husbands of famous actresses have been known to wreak considerable havoc.

These extra few days have only one drawback – it postpones the time when I can hold Danny in my arms again. I just miss that little baby so much and I'm desperately anxious to be back to see him take his first unaided steps, which can't be too far away now.

I rang my mother this morning which was about 6 p.m. in England. She was just putting Danny to bed but I insisted that she bring him to the phone. She thought it was pointless but I know he recognises my voice and both Ralph and I thought it was important that he heard our voices as frequently as possible.

Sometimes I think my mother might well just be pretending to hold Danny next to the phone but this morning when we talked I heard that distinctive gurgle.

We were on the speaker phone so that Ralph and I could talk at the same time. My mother complained that we just sounded tinny but Danny didn't complain. That gurgle of his made us both smile for hours. We could really see it in front of us even though we're six thousand miles away.

I wonder so often how he will grow up. He's a sweet and lovely baby but so, probably, were the Moors Murderers. Hitler must at some point have sat in his pram or whatever they had then, making goo-goo noises at his mother. Did she point with pride to her child and say to the admiring neighbours, 'Little Adolf is going to be a brilliant doctor and save thousands of lives'?

How can we tell if we're doing the right thing as parents? Will Danny grow up kind and intelligent and sensitive and handsome? I really hope he's all of these things but maybe I'll be one of those mothers who just excuses everything in her children. 'I'm sorry Danny beat the shit out of your little daughter but I'm sure she must have done something to provoke him.' Ugh! It's uncanny but I can really hear myself saying that.

But maybe we're doing something wrong now. Maybe in our attempt to be the best parents ever we've already unwittingly done something to destroy Danny's life. Like Adolf's mum I've probably made the fatal error which has condemned my son to a lifetime of misery. Maybe just the fact of leaving him now for a couple of weeks will be enough to turn him into some anti-social Neanderthal devoid of brains or feelings.

All I know is I want to spend the years to come watching him (and his sister and/or brother) growing up, taking delight in each stage of their lives. I'll never let my career stop me from doing that. These actresses who leave their kids and their husbands behind while they're off on location for six months invariably end up in the papers for the wrong reasons. I can't wait for our family to be back together.

Ralph and I are talking about having another one soon. I actually think I might be pregnant now. I should have started two days ago and I'm incredibly regular. Only thing is, I've never been to California before and I think it may be that the long flight and the jet lag and the time difference and all the excitement and so on have confused my menstrual cycle. Maybe it thinks it's still back in England and when it was actually in the air over Greenland thought it was stuck in a tunnel on the Northern Line outside Camden Town tube station.

Next time we come, and there are bound to be make-up tests and costume tests and so on before we start shooting, I'm going to bring Danny with us. I don't want to be apart from him for so long ever again. I think Danny will do fine out here. Southern California is a pretty child-friendly place – if you can momentarily forget about the smog, the pollution, the drive-by shootings, etc. I don't think, in fact I'm sure I wouldn't like him to grow up and go to school here but living here for a few months when he's so small and we suddenly have money can't be a bad thing. Always assuming of course that Ralph sees it from the same positive point of view.

12 July 1987

We're in Carmel. Clint Eastwood used to be the mayor here, or maybe he still is. I'd vote for him. For anything. We've just been on this fantastic seventeen-mile drive round the Monterey peninsula and we kept looking for him but we didn't see him. At the southern end Ralph desperately wanted to get out of the car and play the famous golf course at Pebble Beach but when I said that was OK by me he told me it was a private club and that they'd never allow people like him to play there. I told him it wouldn't be long before clubs like that were ringing him up and begging him to play there. He just laughed and said I'd never met the sort of people who ran golf clubs.

It is absolutely gorgeous here in the central bit of California. So much nicer than Los Angeles which is best seen, I found out, through the tinted windows of a studio limo. Once we left LA, though, and drove up on the coastal route which they call 'Rowt One' we both started smiling again. Ralph had brought with him his Beach Boys cassette and we both started rocking in our seats to the sound of 'California Girls' and 'Surfin' USA'. It was truly glorious because all the worries that seemed to be wearing him down in LA just lifted from him like the heat which rose almost tangibly from the convertible when we took the top down.

I watched him as we drove north past Santa Barbara

and on to San Luis Obispo and my heart leaped to see him so happy. This afternoon we pulled the car over to a kind of picnic area. Shortly after you turn off the main road there are lots of parking and picnic tables laid out for travellers to use. It all seems very civilised, I must say, and a long way from those people in Vauxhall Cavaliers who spend the first sunny afternoon of the year in little canvas-backed folding chairs eating fish paste sandwiches in a layby on the A34.

We walked for quite some time parallel to the ocean until we glimpsed a gap in the trees. We had heard the sound of the crashing surf but been unable to see it because the forest ran directly to the top of the rocky cliffs. After we had been walking for more than a mile or so we saw a patch of green land, a plateau, reaching out of the dark and slightly dank forest, away from the constant noise of 'Rowt One' and isolated above the pounding waves as they gathered strength and dashed themselves unavailingly against the rocks.

We said nothing as we walked hand in hand but words weren't necessary. There was nobody on that grassy headland. Nobody could see us. Only the birds hovering overhead saw us as we stopped high on a cliff overlooking the ocean and looked into one another's eyes. It was a blissful, magical moment. Ralph's fingers slowly but with practised ease unbuttoned my blouse and gently cupped my breasts. A warm breeze (God's studio wind machine?) blew softly from the ocean and lifted my hair from my head. Eventually I stood there naked, glorying in Nature's privacy as Ralph quickly reduced himself to a similar state of playfulness.

There have been other erotic moments in my life but never anything as uplifting as this. Everything Ralph did was perfect. I have been thinking for some days that I might be pregnant but never said anything to Ralph because he seemed to have enough troubles as it is and I didn't want the prospect of another baby to be a problem rather than a joy.

Besides, there was the more relevant difficulty of how I could play Scarlett O'Hara while pregnant. You can shoot round it for only so long. The fact is, though, when I came for the third time, seconds after his climax, I knew I had definitely conceived. OK, I'm an actress, I'm probably dramatising this a little — but only a little. It was a perfect moment, the highest form of lovemaking, a sexual experience that transcended the physical and reached for something quite eternal.

Ralph is in the shower in our motel room. I have no need to show him what I've written. I know he experienced the identical emotion. If ever either of us doubted our love for each other, that magical hour high on that cliff must surely have banished our fears. I want to go back there tomorrow to prove that the place exists, that it wasn't some kind of absurd romantic fantasy.

But what if we went back and found it overrun with people, with picnic debris and cigarette ends, with empty Diet Coke cans and yesterday's copy of the *Los Angeles Times*? Worse, what if it doesn't exist? What if I've made it all up? What if I dreamed it because I wanted to believe it so badly? Does that matter?

It happened once and for all time. That place high on a cliff overlooking the Pacific Ocean is where I lived truly and fully for the first time in my life. I cannot believe that life has another experience of similar importance in store for me. I am complete.

CHAPTER TEN

Ralph

I WAS STILL IN A DAZE when I came back from California. There were two of me. First was the sports writer and father who had to earn a living, forge a career, look after a baby, raise a child. He was the practical one, the one who was for ever being complimented by people on how 'organised' he was.

He wasn't that organised. He never knew when the doppelganger would take over. The other me was like the zombie in bad horror movies. A blank face with dead eyes and a shuffling gait, he staggered through life in a trance. You expected him to fill his pockets with stones like Virginia Woolf and walk into the river with his hat still firmly on his head.

Had it not been for Danny I fear that is precisely what I would have done. I drove back from Heathrow to Angela's parents' house outside Coventry. I was possessed with the idea that I had to tell him what happened myself. I couldn't trust whatever it was Angela's parents might say. It was bound to be the wrong thing and I wanted so much to make the transition to single parenthood as easy as I could for Danny.

The fact that he was a baby, of course, and couldn't talk, never entered my calculation. Nor, I'm ashamed to admit, was the fact that Angela's parents were bound to have been devastated by the news of their daughter's death. My own pain and hurt and the terrifying prospect awaiting me filled my mind to the exclusion of all other thoughts.

I flew back on the return half of my first-class ticket. If I'd had my head screwed on I'd have cashed in the return half of Angela's unused ticket and lived off the sale for weeks but my mind wasn't working in that practical mode just yet. The cabin was full, apart from the seat next to me. The blonde stewardess made no mention of Mrs Warren, though whether that was because she knew what had happened and didn't want to mention it or had no idea what had happened and therefore couldn't mention it I didn't know.

I thought I was coping well, consuming enough free champagne to blot out the misery temporarily, eating too much with the hope that such indulgence would cause me to fall asleep. I welcomed the embrace of sleep so much in those early days. As far as the flight was concerned though, in this, as in most things at this time in my life, I was to be disappointed.

It was unfortunate but my mind, though numbed by the magnitude of the disaster which had overwhelmed it, was still functioning even if it had trouble processing the information and it refused to submit to post-prandial slumber. When the dinner tray was cleared away (real china plates, linen napkin and the tiniest but cutest salt cellar and pepper shaker I had ever seen), the movie started.

I'd already seen it, which was no help because it was *Terms of Endearment* in which Debra Winger dies slowly but romantically of cancer. I shut my eyes, I turned the switch on the headset viciously round the dial, seeking refuge, but I found none. Even while listening to selections from *HMS Pinafore* I heard the sound of Angela's voice. I opened my eyes to make sure it wasn't her, only to see Debra Winger expiring.

It wasn't Winger's death, I don't think, that set me off, or the deeply affecting nature of the film itself, it was the thought that Winger had won an Academy Award for the role. Angela had often said how it wasn't the performance that got you noticed or won the award, it was usually the role and in this movie Winger had the role of a lifetime. Angela was sure something similar would come her way and so was I.

It was puzzling. We were both so certain of what lay ahead I could have written Angela's biography for the next twenty years the day we got married. All right, maybe the stage career would take precedence over the movie life but neither of us doubted that golden future for a second. The offer of Scarlett O'Hara, the one role in the whole world which was guaranteed to make her famous from Alaska to Moscow to Rio, confirmed it. Who could doubt her destiny now? I cried silently from the time they brought round the over-priced duty free goods till we returned our seats to the upright position.

Danny was awake but lying peacefully in his cot when I rang the doorbell of his grandparents' house. I looked at Angela's mother and she looked back at me, a steady, unflinching gaze. I steeled myself to embrace her. Angela was dead, and whatever harsh words had passed between us and her, this was no time to recall them. But her body remained stiff and unresponsive. I felt a brief surge of anger. Now at this moment when we needed each other to get through our grief, couldn't she even now allow the emotion to take hold, allow herself to appear vulnerable for once in her tight-arsed life?

Then I thought, well, maybe this is what she needs — the stiff upper body. If she shows what she would call weakness she will have no place to go, emotionally speaking. She is of that generation for whom 'make do and mend' and 'muddling through' were admirable philosophies of life. 'Oh dear, the Nazis have bombed us out of the house. Never mind, let's put the kettle on and have a nice cup of tea.' 'You haven't got a bloody kettle,' I wanted to shout, 'let alone mains water or a teapot!'

I thought she should have been sitting there holding Danny on her lap. Angela and I both believed that you didn't stick a baby in the cot when he was awake just because it was more convenient for you. You kept him with you at all times so he could experience everything you did. That way he was constantly stimulated. Angela's mother believed the reverse. The best babies were the ones who knew how to behave, knew their place (in the cot) right from the start.

So we didn't hug; instead, we looked at each other with sadness in our eyes, knowing that Angela's death had probably broken the last link between us, unless I was going to go out of my way to ensure that Danny grew up knowing his maternal grandparents. I'm only human. I couldn't do it.

There was no declaration of war or anything, just a cessation of information. She was too proud to beg to see her grandson. I, selfishly I suppose, gratefully accepted her lack of communication as a lack of interest. I knew in my heart it wasn't so but it made my life easier and that, for a long time, was the only thing that interested me, apart from Danny's welfare of course. Easier emotionally, that is. There were times when, much as I loved Danny, I ached for time away to be myself, to rediscover who I was, apart from Danny's father. By rejecting the baby-sitting *quid pro quo* which stems from grandparent status, I had closed off a large conventional source of refuge.

So I poured into that baby all the love I would have had for my firstborn child anyway, as well as all the love I could no longer give his mother. And we, in the popular phrase, bonded. If anything positive came out of that terrible tragedy it was the hoops of steel that bound me and that boy. I knew when I sauntered back into the maternity hospital after parking the car to find Danny in a hurry to get out and join the party that he was special. Over the subsequent eleven years he has proved that original estimation to be correct.

We had only ever rented the flat in Highgate so I gave a month's notice and moved out. I decided I wanted to go back to live in Cambridge for practical rather than morbid reasons. It was a town I knew, a town where I still had friends who might be persuaded to look after Danny for a few hours if necessary. London was only an hour away by train and I invested in one of the first fax machines to hit the country because I could instantly see that by virtue of this dazzling new piece of technology I could communicate with most sources of potential work from my living room.

It wasn't by any means straightforward. Although I took so much joy in the developing Danny, I wouldn't wish to give the impression that it was unalloyed pleasure. Teething was a nightmare. Day after day, night after night of crying. I couldn't make him stop and I couldn't sleep myself so I couldn't work when he eventually cried himself into an exhausted nap.

Potty training wasn't much fun either. I was convinced I'd done it, all right we'd done it, so I left him with Linda Walling whose husband, my squash partner Ian, was then a research fellow at St John's College, because I had a commission to interview John McEnroe before the start of Wimbledon and he was one player you couldn't afford to upset. When I returned I found Danny in the garden up against the wall with Linda wiping him off with a kitchen towel and a bucket of soapy water. His pants and trousers lay in a revolting heap on top of a Sainsbury's plastic bag. Clearly he wasn't quite as potty trained as I had believed.

To all outward appearances Danny's life was completely normal. He went to playgroup at the age of two and a half, he started reception class at Grantchester Street Primary when he was rising five and he passed the exam for the local grammar school when he was ten and a half. He had a hot breakfast before he went to school and a conventional tea when he came home. Fortunately, his gastronomic tastes, which ran the gamut from fish fingers to baked beans and into the exotic foreign cuisine of cheese and tomato pizza, precisely complemented my culinary skills.

At school Danny did well, which I reckoned was a tribute to what we had achieved at home. He was reading and writing long before the rest of his classmates because he did so much at home. After I'd spent all day in front of the television watching England's bowlers disappear to all parts of various Test grounds, I was only too happy in the evenings to immerse myself in Christopher Robin and Winnie the Pooh.

Danny was my best friend as well as my son. We were sharing an adventure and that bound us as tightly as men roped together on a mountaineering expedition. It might have been his first few years of life but they were my first few years as a parent and, deprived of whatever input we would have had from Angela, we simply set off down the long road together hand in hand – like that illustration of Christopher Robin and Winnie the Pooh, I always thought.

He was a sporty kid, thank God. I don't know what would have happened had he turned into the class nerd.

I knew from my own experience the sort of status kids accord the best sports players in their group and though Danny was never the best he more than held his own.

One day I saw the Darwinian process at its rawest. All the kids line up against the wall and the two best players appoint themselves as captains of the respective sides. Each one then picks a player in turn so that it is hoped that the two competing sides will be of roughly comparable ability. In practice, what happens is that the best players get chosen first and as the remnant left standing against the wall diminishes in number you can see the fear in their eyes increasing.

The last poor sap to be chosen is almost paralysed by the humiliation and, invariably, he is the last one to be chosen every time until he finally gives up the game in despair. Even the penultimate duffer has the marginal satisfaction of looking down on him – until that terrible day when he himself is the last to be chosen. This process of natural selection, breathtaking in its raw simplicity, was going strong in my day and presumably will last as long as kids play competitive sports.

Watching the last boy to be chosen as he dragged his way reluctantly between the makeshift goalposts, I contented myself with the fantasy that in the capitalist world in which we live this shame might be sufficient to stir him to great acts of entrepreneurial success – at which point he could hire all the boys who were picked in front of him (except Danny, of course) at starvation wages and then fire them in the most public and humiliating of circumstances.

I fostered my love of Tottenham Hotspur on Danny from an impressionable age and took him to matches as soon as he was old enough to sit on my knee uncomplainingly for most of the game. For me Spurs were my local team and supporting them as my dad and my uncle did before me was as natural as complaining about the cost of living or the infrequency of buses. For Danny, growing up in Cambridge, it was a bit more of a leap of faith but then the changing culture brought about by the growing influence of money and television has completely destroyed the traditional philosophy that a boy supported his home town team as a matter of course.

Despite the changing times in which we live — I mean the rather more significant social changes like male unemployment, the increasing employment of women, the revolution in domestic arrangements — I was invariably the lone man outside the school railings at half past three. The women had their own support groups and I soon found out I wasn't a member of any of them. It was a big deal to be invited over for coffee when the kids were in playgroup or later at school but nobody ever invited me.

I can only assume that it was because the neighbours or the husbands would look askance at a single man coming round to the house in the middle of the day. The fact that we would inevitably be talking about the price of cornflakes or children's shoes rather than romping in the bedroom was irrelevant. They were perfectly friendly, those women, happy to have Danny over to play in their houses with their children after school or during the holidays, but for all their smiles of sympathy, the rules of behaviour dictated that I could never be admitted inside their circles.

I suppose I got used to the loneliness so that eventually it didn't seem like loneliness but normality. Something inside me started to shrivel up. Maybe that's why I clung to Angela's precious memory so tenaciously. It wasn't that I was frightened by the prospect of love, afraid in the modern parlance 'to commit'; it was more a case that the longer I went without a female relationship, the more difficult it became to believe that I would ever meet anyone.

I mean where would I do it, for a start? I began each day waking Danny, getting him dressed, cooking him breakfast, walking him to school. Then there was the shopping and the launderette and the seemingly minor matter of making a living. This consisted of reading, writing and telephoning which are largely solitary occupations.

I had a small select list (three) of people who could be relied upon to pick up Danny after school and keep him till after dinner. I didn't like to make a nuisance of myself and hated to ask anyone more than once during the term because the real bugger was how I got through the holidays as a single parent.

I realised that I needed to be higher profile in my work than I had been up till then. There was an explosion of sports magazines and radio and television programmes about sport which coincided with the start of Sky Sports, England's semi-final defeat in the World Cup in Italy in 1990 and the rapid growth of the Premier League in England which began in 1992. But this new trend was accompanied by the arrival of a whole new group of young and hungry journalists, eager to make their mark in the world too. And none of them were the sole support of a little boy. What did I have that made me more employable than they were?

American football had already taken off on Channel Four and I was one of the few British writers who knew his linebacker from his wide receiver, his Marcus Allen from his Mike Ditka. I had already made a bit of a mark with a series of articles on baseball for the *Independent* and I was the only British journalist to track down the late great Flo Jo after she won her gold medals in the Seoul Olympics. Turned out she was a big showbiz buff and had followed the casting twists and turns on *Gone with the Wind II* so she knew all about Angela. She was only too happy to co-operate after that. As an added bonus to that interview I learned more than I ever wanted to know about women's nail polish.

When sport on satellite and cable became big business the companies found they had to fill the airwaves with something. Television abhors a vacuum. They couldn't show a Steeple Bumpstead versus Chipping Sodbury tug-of-war contest without causing recent subscribers to unscrew their dishes or cancel their subscriptions so they decided to import vast quantities of cheap American sport.

The NBA, the NHL, the USPGA and Major League Baseball joined the National Football League as an important component of the satellite and cable television schedules.

Inevitably, in their wake came the ancillary marketing — the endorsed sports clothes and equipment and the magazines. My dream came true when *US Sport Today* started.

It was really a British version of *Sports Illustrated* but it was perfect for me. It was designed to fill what the American publishers, owned by a New York-based conglomerate, perceived as a gap in the European market. Jack McGinty, an old pal from my first days sniffing for work in the big world outside Cambridge, was appointed the editor and within days he had invited me to a slap-up lunch with too much red wine at Langan's bistro in Mayfair to offer me the coveted and probably slightly overpaid post of contributing editor.

On the strength of this new contract I moved Danny and me out of our cramped two-bedroom flat near the railway station and into the big terraced house off Chesterton Road we now occupy. Although there were only two of us, that flat was getting increasingly impossible to live in. Danny's bike had to be brought into the living room otherwise it would join the hundreds of stolen bikes in which Cambridge must lead the world and I was getting fed up with trips to the launderette so I invested in a washing machine and a spin dryer. We were drowning under the relentless tide of consumer acquisition.

The loneliness abated somewhat as the new work expanded to fill the emotional vacuum. I still didn't meet anyone — nobody special, that is. There was the occasional night when I wanted female company so badly I let my guard down. One was a student I met at the Arts

Theatre who expressed an interest in baby-sitting. I was always looking for someone who could be relied upon for a couple of hours so I could see a film or a play, and this girl, Melanie, seemed keen and reliable.

I got back after a showing of *The English Patient* which had won all those awards. I just loathed it; well, no, I didn't loathe it but I was bored after the first hour and a half and couldn't wait for it to finish. It turned out that Melanie had also hated it and was the only woman in her college to do so. A shared dislike of the film led to an offer of a glass of red wine which in turn led to other matters. I was so tired and so emptied by the experience that I fell into a deep sleep which wasn't broken until eight twenty the following morning when Danny woke us both up and wanted to know if I was going to make breakfast.

Both Melanie and I were covered in embarrassment although that was the only covering available to us. Ironically Danny, who I thought might have been traumatised by the discovery, appeared to be entirely unmoved. I told him quickly that I had been helping Melanie with an essay after I got back from the cinema and it had got so late that we had just fallen asleep on the bed.

He seemed to take the explanation in his stride, being much more interested in his breakfast and whether he would be late for school. It was probably cruel and unnecessary of me but I felt I couldn't see Melanie again so I kept on looking for a baby-sitter and a possible partner for sex or life but I abandoned the idea that they could be the same person. Years seemed to go by and though the baby-sitter position was filled competently and without further alarms, the partner bit remained permanently available.

CHAPTER ELEVEN

Helen

THE FIRST TIME I MET Ralph I was determined to fire him. Presuming, however, that the British do things in a more civilised manner than we do in the US, I had arranged for the bullet to be fired over a decent lunch. If I'd been a coward I could just as easily have told that old lush Jack McGinty to do it and not soiled my dainty hands. It wasn't that I enjoyed firing people (unfounded office gossip notwithstanding) but I maintained a naive view that people who were being let go were owed a rational explanation by the person who was firing them. I was always conscious of the human cost of unemployment but I figured if I did my job honestly and responsibly I had nothing to fear.

So how come I didn't can Ralph Warren when all my instincts told me his post was superfluous to requirements? Well, for a start there was the picture at the head of his column. Ralph had this regular column in *US Sports Today* in which he profiled a big US sports star of the month and for which he was being overpaid.

Next to his by-line was a colour photograph of himself which pleased me. These things are so small and usually so anonymous I rarely notice them but I noticed this one. I liked the slightly unkempt look as if he was concentrating so hard on the important things of life that he had no time to run a comb through his hair.

I suppose in a subconscious Freudian sort of way I rather envied that. I feel, rather like my role model Hillary Rodham Clinton, that if we all reduced the hours we spend in personal grooming we could lift humankind to the next level of evolution but, like Hillary, I've been forced to concede that people won't look at your ideas if you're a woman unless they want to look at your face and body, too. Men have not yet reached this evolved state and it's perfectly possible for them to show up to a meeting looking as though they'd been dragged through a hedge backwards and it is regarded as a harmless eccentricity. Let a woman do the same, however, and she's history.

I should also point out, however, that I liked his writing. Unlike some of his colleagues he had a certain sense of style and in other circumstances I would have been happy to have kept him on. Unfortunately it didn't really matter how great his pieces were, I'd been given the task of removing all the feature writers from their lucrative staff contracts and Ralph Warren had to go, no matter how good the quality of his prose was. I figured a writer as good as he was would have no trouble getting work if he had the necessary drive. I'd even see to it that *US Sports Today* commissioned a monthly piece but his gravy train staff job was being derailed.

The parent company, Waverley Bros. Inc., sent me over to the UK because they figured I was the one to get *US Sports Today* out of the hole its managerial team had dug it into. I had made my name in the States doing something similar in San Francisco when I turned around their business magazine *Profits* which had been losing millions of dollars.

I certainly rationalised the managerial structure, pink-slipped around fifty execs and middle managers, but the real dramatic growth in sales volume fostered by the Clinton economic resurgence was the most decisive factor. Still, there's nothing like being in the right place at the right time and I was happy to take all the corporate credit that was flying around. Like the old politician said, if you take the credit for the sunshine, you'd better be prepared to take the blame when it starts raining. Or something like that.

I figure I'd have made a brilliant general under Napoleon. He always used to ask about his generals not if they had ability but if they were lucky. I've been pretty lucky in life. I was born in London though I remember little about it. My mother is American though my dad was English. They split up when I was two years old and my mom took me and my older brother Michael back to the States to live.

I grew up in Boston, Mass., as an all-American kid. I don't recall ever travelling on a British passport so the fact of my birth in Britain was pretty much an irrelevance. My dad, the stuck-up British sonofabitch, never bothered to see us or helped my mom in any way, financially. He was having an affair, which is what caused Mom to throw him out, and he married the other woman and had a new family with her pretty fast. The three of us were a mistake he didn't want to be reminded of.

Mom wasn't the kind of woman to remind him of his responsibilities or to feel sorry for herself. She took the sonofabitch's studied insolence as a kick up her own rear end. She set herself to manage fine as a single parent and always taught us — well, I guess me more than Michael because I was the girl — the importance of being able to stand on your own two feet.

She knew it was vital for me to get to college but to get to the Columbia School of Journalism on which I had set my heart I needed a straight A, 3.5 or above grade point average, so I just put my head down, hit the books real hard and eventually got there. I thought it would have been easier if I'd been a guy because I could have gotten some kind of basketball scholarship or something because I knew it was going to be tough living in New York, paying the fees, putting myself through school.

Then I found out about this special scholarship, the Levenshulme Scholarship it was called. There was one awarded annually to the person who submitted the most original piece of journalism in a feature-length article. I went down to New York because I'd heard about these Russian, mostly Jewish, immigrants who had come pouring into the Brighton Beach section of Brooklyn in the early days of Gorbachev's *glasnost*. Later, everyone was after those guys but I spoke a little Russian and I got some really great and original interviews which I wrote up and submitted for the award.

On the panel were journalists and editors and publishers from the *New York Times*, *Washington Post*, *Chicago Tribune*, *Christian Science Monitor*, *Time*, *Newsweek* etc., a real impressive bunch of heavy hitters. Winning that scholarship was probably the most satisfying moment of my life so far. I realised that Mom was right. I needed no one to help me succeed; just self-discipline and determination. I have never forgotten the lesson.

While most of my fellow graduates went off to learn the business in Des Moines and Talahassie, I was offered a job on the *Wall Street Journal*. Initially I was surprised. All my ambitions and previous experience had led me to believe I was the new Woodward and Bernstein. I'd seen that movie with Robert Redford and Dustin Hoffman — *All the President's Men* — about how these two investigative journalists on the *Washington Post* had dug up the dirt on President Nixon's re-election campaign. Eventually Nixon was forced to resign rather than risk being impeached, so you could say that those two hacks had changed the course of American history. Wow! Yes, sir, I'll take a half pound of that!

My time on the *Wall Street Journal* changed that philosophy completely. I took the job because I had fallen in love with a man and didn't want to leave New York although, ironically, that fizzled out six months after I graduated from Columbia. I should have known, I suppose. He was a married man and much as I kept telling myself that it was doomed from the start I really cared for him. He cared for me too but he was older, quite a lot older, nearer fifty than forty.

Though that didn't matter to me because I loved him (I was always more partial to older men than men my own age anyway), it seemed to matter to him. He was convinced that someone twenty years younger would come along and sweep me off my feet. Eventually, after ignoring a million warning signs, it dawned on me that what he was really panicking about was not failing to get it up twice a night but starting over again in a one-bedroom apartment on the wrong side of the tracks and a beat-up Chevy in the garage after his wife kicked him out. In the end the pension fund and the house in Scarsdale meant more to him than I did. It was a sobering realisation. I cried buckets, feeling, as I have always felt in affairs of the heart, that I would never love another man again.

Ironically, this mess-up happened at exactly the same time that my work was trying to teach me that the only sign that mattered in life was the dollar sign. The other reason I had taken the job with the *Journal* was that I thought a year or two learning about the financial side of things was bound to be good experience – this was the eighties, remember, the time of Michael Millken and the junk bonds, Gordon Gekko, 'lunch is for wimps' and 'greed is good for you'.

In fact I became completely obsessed with this new kind of journalism. I was like an old political historian who discovers Marxism and suddenly realises that everything he thought about the way society operated is totally wrong. Money dominates society and has always done so. In learning to look at the world through gold-tinted glasses I found explanations where previously there had only been irrational behaviour.

Again, like one of Napoleon's generals, I was lucky enough to be in the right place at the right time. As the economy slipped into recession and the Millkens and Gekkos of the world crashed, I was in a perfect position to give them a helping hand on their way to Leavenworth. If I'd had my way it would have been Alcatraz — if Alcatraz had still been operating.

I did a good job for the *Journal* so I was given a bonus — a year in Stanford at the best business school in the country, Harvard included. That, too, was an eye-opener — a bunch of people as highly motivated as myself, and most of them far brighter. These were the future CEOs of the first years of the twenty-first century. I learned a lot from those guys and when I came out of California, the prospect of going back to New York and earning $43,750 a year when they were set to make hundreds of thousands suddenly became unappealing.

I don't think I did anything wrong. I changed in that new environment. Plus I liked California — a most unforeseen dividend. I didn't expect to. I was an East Coast gal, we prided ourselves on being cool and sophisticated — our firm belief was that California was peopled entirely by kooks and freaks. In Stanford you couldn't have found a kook or a freak if you'd put an ad in the paper. Plus the weather was great. Even in February I used to bike to the campus. I mean the winters in New York and Boston were just deadly. Literally. People died in the winter all over the US. Not in California though. At least not of the cold.

So when the offer came from Waverley Bros. Inc., it found me well prepared. The *Journal* pointed out, in a hurt sort of a way, that it had paid for me to go to Stanford so that I would return to the paper a better and more versatile journalist. Much as I wanted to stay in California earning a salary in six figures I steeled myself to return to New York to honour my contract. I think Waverley might have offered the *Journal* some kind of a financial inducement because they permitted Waverley a more direct approach.

The first inkling I had was when the doorbell to my apartment rang just after breakfast. FedEx were delivering a round-trip first-class air ticket to New York and a confirmed reservation at the Sherry Netherland. I was staggered. This was no way for the *Wall Street Journal* to behave! Then I took a look at the enclosed note. I was due to meet the CEO and COO of Waverley at nine o'clock the following morning. A limo would collect me in forty-five minutes. Good job I was in when the bell went. I took a look in my closet to see what would be suitable attire for the most important business meeting of my life. The answer was immediately clear. I had nothing to wear.

Thank God for the sisterhood. When I told Elaine and Rachel what I was up for they dropped their slightly reserved competitive edge which they'd held all semester and flung open the doors of their more expansive closets. I grabbed Rachel's electric-blue suit – though the skirt was an inch higher than my natural instinct thought was appropriate — and Elaine's little black cocktail dress which covered a multitude of possible social problems.

Waverley was a more diversified group of companies than Condé Nast but their core business was also print journalism. What they were offering me, however, was the chance to move from journalism into executive management while still retaining my contact with journalists. It was very hard to sit there for two hours knowing I'd have to say at the end of it, 'I don't know about this. It's a big decision. I'll have to sleep on it,' when all I wanted to do was to shout, 'Yes, please. Let me start now before you change your mind!'

At the same time I was genuinely impressed by Charles Schmidt, the CEO, who was dressed in an impeccable Savile Row suit and handmade Italian shoes. He seemed more British than the British but in fact he had been born in Germany and immigrated to the States as a teenager in the 1950s. His plans for expanding the company were exciting but practical, offering the potential for growth with limited exposure.

Over dinner, when Elaine's little black dress really earned its salary, I discovered that Charles was married to Gwen Larrenson, the former Broadway musical star who had retired at the height of her fame. I remembered going with Mom and Michael one New Year's to see Gwen in *Sweet Charity* in which she sang 'Big Spender' so brilliantly it made the hair on your neck stand on end.

So this perfect guy had a perfect wife and presumably two blonde perfect children as well. When it transpired that he had three children, one of them quite a difficult teenager, I was relieved but still aware that here was a man who was pressing all the right buttons with me. What is it with me and married men? I should have a scarlet 'M' for 'married' branded on my forehead like Hester Prynne.

He dropped me off at the Sherry Netherland with the chastest kiss on the cheek. I promised I would give him my answer first thing in the morning. He scribbled down the number of his mobile phone. Was this some sort of coded invitation or the action of a go-getting chief executive? I stood on the sidewalk outside the hotel watching the black limo speed away (never a white limo for Charles, this guy had taste!) wondering whether I should walk away from this chance of a lifetime.

In the tub I luxuriated in the bath salts, debating whether it would be stupid to walk away from the job that was made for me just because my hormones were raging. After all, he was based at head office in New York while it was suggested that, since I had professed an inclination to remain in California, I would probably enjoy turning around the leisure magazines which were currently losing money and were based in Los Angeles. It was therefore entirely possible that we wouldn't even run into each other at all apart from the three-monthly retreats all top managements went to. Maybe he had no sexual interest in me at all but he had simply spotted a genuine high flyer and wanted to give me a chance. Maybe I was dazzled by him and kidding myself that there was a romantic self-interest to be served.

Spreading my limbs in between the softest cotton sheets I have ever felt I decided that even if things did blossom on the personal front he could handle it and therefore so could I. It had probably happened before to him – it would be truly extraordinary had the opportunity never arisen. In any case he had enough excuses to be away from home and the office at any time and enough money to cover up whatever tracks his amorous advances towards me might make. He was either an expert adulterer or had never been one at all. I decided to take the job, zapped the TV onto standby with the remote and went to sleep.

Two hours of tossing and turning later I gave up the idea of sleep and flipped the TV back on. It was 3.30 a.m. but on Channel 57 Dick van Dyke and Mary Tyler Moore were puzzling how to tell Richie, their ten-year-old boy, how babies were made. I thought that somewhere in New York City at that moment some ten-year-old boy was probably making a girl pregnant. The papers had been full of such stories recently. I decided that this was somehow prophetic. It was a message that I should go back to the *Wall Street Journal* and get on with a career that was progressing quite satisfactorily. I didn't need the dangerous excitement that Charles Schmidt and his millions were offering. Secure in my decision, I fell asleep as Buddy made fun of Mel's bald head.

At seven thirty I was awake, already showered and wrapped in a voluminous Sherry Netherland bath towel. As I sipped a cold glass of freshly squeezed orange juice and observed the steam rising gently from the double espresso on the marble coffee table, I dialled Charles Schmidt's mobile phone number. He answered on the first ring, clearly in the back of the car reading the papers on the way to the office. His tone was civilised and warm. He said how much he had enjoyed the previous day and evening and how much he was looking forward to working with me.

The sound of his voice destroyed all my good intentions. The fact was that I liked this man, I liked his mind and I liked the job he was offering. I would be a fool to turn him down. Trying very hard to echo the deliberate speed of his speech I told him that after much careful thought I would be very happy to join his organisation. As far as I could tell from his obviously pleased reaction he was delighted to have another good person on his team. There wasn't the slightest hint that he saw me as a potential notch on his belt. Six weeks later we were lovers.

Charles decided that the California operation needed more of his time than ever before. He moved out to the Coast on a semi-permanent basis. Although he stayed at the exclusive Bel Air Hotel (not for him the obvious glamour of the Beverly Hills Hotel or the Beverly Wilshire) he encouraged me to buy a house outside of LA. A fellow big shot was selling his weekend place in Montecito, just south of Santa Barbara.

It was a wonderful, surprisingly modest place in the Spanish style with three bedrooms and four bathrooms, a neat living room with an inlaid fireplace and a patio overlooking a kidney-shaped pool. My first reaction was that I couldn't afford it but after Charles and the big shot talked some more, the price suddenly became affordable, particularly on the generous terms that Charles's bank was prepared to offer me a mortgage.

It was truly a blissful time. Mom came out to see me and was almost speechless with pleasure – for herself, I think, as much as for me. It was the realisation of all her dreams, a triumphant vindication that her decision to leave her husband, to struggle along with two kids as a single parent, had been the right one.

She was out there once, lying on the sun deck with her face covered in sun block and a wide-brimmed straw hat on her head, when Charles stopped by. She was hugely impressed that the boss should come out to see me on the weekend. Not for a moment did it cross her mind that the boss might have had other things on his mind beside the current fortunes and future prosperity of his company. Predictably Charles behaved with great charm towards my mother and no hint of condescension. She was besotted with him and flew back to Boston on the Sunday night almost purring with pleasure – as, by the time she landed at Logan Airport, were Charles and I.

In turn I behaved with the propriety expected of the mistress of an important man. I had already had a good grounding in the basic rules after my experience in New York. It was odd to realise that one reason for my coming to California in the first place was to rid myself of the difficulties imposed by having an affair with a married man. Now here I was in an identical position. It wasn't so much that I had no place to go on Thanksgiving or Christmas or New Year's but that I knew that I would not be spending it with him. I could give him a birthday gift or a Christmas present but it could never be anything intimate. It had to be precisely judged to the level expected of an employee, albeit an employee who was fast rising on the corporate ladder.

The affair lasted about two and a half years — almost as long as the traditional marriage these days. There were plenty of times when I wanted to call a halt, when I simply couldn't take the pretence a moment longer. What had started as an affair of convenience became an affair of the heart despite all my rationalisations.

I liked my job and I knew I was getting better at it day by day but I just loved being with him. He had such an air of command, an irresistible charisma, that being deprived of it was heart-breaking. It wasn't so much I resented his returning to Gwen or his waking up next to her. I found myself resenting the New York office when problems back East prevented his return to the Coast. I was somehow diminished as a person when I was deprived of his physical presence. Despite my own severe warnings which I had administered to myself on a hundred occasions since that first night at the Sherry Netherland, I had fallen in love with Charles Schmidt and the wise woman inside of me knew that the only way now was down.

We finished not because I finally heeded my own sensible advice but because Mr Schmidt found a new bright shiny object with a low-cut dress. I didn't mind. No, really, I didn't. I did not become hysterical when I found I was being replaced in his affections, because I think I was maturing too. We maintained a civilised courtesy towards each other in private and continued to work productively together without any of the tension that I had been dreading that night I lay

in the Sherry Netherland king-size bed tossing and turning.

I must confess, however, I was not terribly impressed
by the pinch hitter who came off the bench to replace
me. I am quite sure I never wore anything quite as low
cut as that simpering bitch flounced round the building
in. I was just slightly surprised that the man whose taste
in all things from mistresses to interior decoration I had
previously found impeccable should have been so easily
seduced by a pair of bouncing boobs. What puzzled me
even more was that I knew he was an ass man anyway
and she seemed to have been short changed in that
department. It was so small and tight you could have
struck a match on it. Maybe he did.

I'm not being catty. I was never even tempted to call
Gwen and spill the beans or, slightly more deviously, call
any one of a half-dozen friends on different (non-house)
gossip columns and let them have the story. I did, however, play my own game of brinkmanship by demanding
a raise. I suppose I was taking a risk in that Charles could
simply have fired me but I knew that even with his Calvin
Klein boxer shorts on he needed me. It would have been
an odd decision to have fired me having spent the previous
two years singing my praises at every opportunity.

He knew exactly the price he could extract from
me. I got everything I asked for in salary and pension
provisions. In return I signed a contract which exiled me
to Europe.

It was only when I got off the plane in London and
heard the strangulated sounds of English as spoken by the

British that I fully realised what had happened. Charles Schmidt was the big love of my life and I knew I would never see him again. Not the way I wanted to see him.

In immigration I broke down and wept. A kind Asian guy with a turban on his head helped me to the front where my passport was stamped. The rest of the line looked at me with undisguised hatred. They thought it was a transparent attempt to jump what the British quaintly call a queue. So it was with red eyes and a coat pocket full of wet Kleenex that Waverley Bros. Inc.'s ice-cold asset stripper arrived in London to fire Ralph Warren.

CHAPTER TWELVE

Ralph

BEFORE HELEN ARRIVED IN LONDON I had felt my life was as good as it was likely to get. Danny was growing up into such a great kid. I was always so proud of him. Although he 'only' went to a state primary school, he won a scholarship to the grammar school, beating off competition from kids whose parents had paid for them to have a head start in life by subjecting them to the torture of a prep school.

I had what I thought was a cast-iron three-year contract with *US Sports Today* which guaranteed me a decent income for almost the first time in my professional life. All right, there was no regular woman around but the memory of Angela was so strong, so all-pervasive, I didn't feel too badly about it. I didn't feel I was some kind of widower whose life was at an end, more like a husband whose actress-wife had been away on location for a long time – a very long time, eleven years. It was going to be a hell of a film.

I didn't like Helen Cooper at all when I met her,

though that's partially because I didn't meet her until some time after my telephone had started ringing with advance warnings. She had breezed into town and set about her with an axe, like some executive Lizzie Borden. OK, so the magazine hadn't exactly been *People* or *Hello!* but then it wasn't designed to be *People* or *Hello!*. It was targeted at a specialised audience and we all knew that it would take time to build.

Jack McGinty told me how sanguine the proprietors had been at the planning and dummy stages about the possibility of sustaining heavy losses for the first few years until people learned to appreciate the quality of the writing. Jack told me they had shown him a profit-loss account forecast in which the magazine wouldn't move into the black until its fourth year. Now, eighteen months after the launch, they were coming to town to close us down because we weren't making a profit. Jerks!

One Thursday morning I was sitting at home typing up my notes on the interview with Tiger Woods, whom I thought was a nervous breakdown waiting to happen, when the phone rang. It was one of those female voices which set you instantly on edge. Before she had finished saying, 'Is that Ralph Warren?' I knew there was a problem. She was the temporary secretary of Helen Cooper, yes, the very woman the mention of whose name caused grown journalists to tear their own heads off rather than upset her. The secretary herself sounded harassed to the point of distress.

She told me I was expected at the office in London at ten thirty the following morning. I told her that wasn't going to be possible. I had to take Danny to school so I couldn't leave until after nine which meant I wouldn't be able to get a train until after nine thirty which would take me to Liverpool Street rather than King's Cross so the best I could do was eleven o'clock. Even then Friday was inconvenient because the deadline on the Tiger Woods piece was close of play tomorrow and if I came up to town, that was effectively the whole day wiped out. Besides, Danny had cricket practice after school and I was one of the coaches. Monday would be far more convenient.

I might as well have asked for the moon. The girl on the other end of the phone made it quite clear that I was expected in the office tomorrow at ten thirty. I wasn't being asked for my opinion as to whether this was convenient for me, I was being told to be there or else. I dare say these tactics work in some places where all employees walk in fear of the chop every hour but I had never worked in any such place and I wasn't about to start. I was going to give this American bitch a piece of homespun English common sense.

I'm afraid I rather took it out on that poor secretary. Since her boss was too high and mighty to get on the phone herself she left me no alternative. In all fairness, as they say in all the best sports press conferences, I don't think the girl gave a damn. She didn't know who I was, she had been plucked out of obscurity to be the evil Helen Cooper's assistant for a day or two and the chances were good that by Monday morning there'd be another temp in her place.

I realise that this sounds like what Hollywood screen-writers call a 'meet cute' — a contrived situation in which the boy meets the girl who has her skirt caught in a suitcase or they are the only people on a bus that has broken down or they have each been booked into the other's hotel room by mistake. Of course they start by hating each other and then ninety minutes later they're living happily ever after. Maybe this sort of thing became a screen convention because it can and does happen in real life.

I mean, if people don't meet at a party or through an advert in the personal columns of the newspapers, they do meet through somewhat strange circumstances. One of my best friends met his wife only because she was too dense to understand perfectly comprehensible directions, got lost and was rescued by the man with whom she had three children and lived happily after. So it does happen.

I arrived at reception at the skyscraper in Marylebone Road at ten thirty-seven. I wasn't going to give the bitch the satisfaction of seeing me there bang on time, though usually I'm so anal that's invariably when I do show up. Just to make the point, to myself if nobody else, I actually arrived outside the building at ten twenty-seven. I purposely paced up and down outside the main entrance for ten minutes, much to the puzzlement of the receptionist whom I could see behind the glass door. In the end the gesture was entirely pointless because Helen was running late and I didn't get in to see her until after eleven. I could have got that Liverpool Street train after all and saved the money I spent on the taxi to catch the nine ten King's Cross express.

She was not exactly what I expected. A dark blue business suit of course, but no starched white blouse, shoulder pads or other standard issue female executive attire. For no good reason I had formed an impression of Helen Cooper which was dominated by a cropped haircut that would not have looked out of place in Cell Block H. Instead I found a thirtyish woman with good legs, thick curly black hair and minimal make-up and jewellery.

The overall effect was pleasingly feminine although her dress still proclaimed that she was one of those women whose main ambition is to be taken 'seriously' like a man. Too many women in business are so anxious to be seen as the equal of any man that they end up dressing like one. I don't mean the skirt and high heels of course (although I do know a couple of men who wear that stuff when they get back from the office after a hard day) but the unfeminine nature of their attire is their way of showing us that they have a uniform too: we are not soft dopey women whose only idea is to please a man; we wear these clothes to show that we have more important things on our minds than men or sex.

Angela used to spend considerable time fretting about what to wear because she liked to dress for a part she was auditioning for. Whatever she wore was always great and she never looked anything other than a gorgeous woman. She also had thick, lustrous blonde hair which she could do anything with. I personally always preferred it spilling down her back. It gave her a look of sexual abandon which I found constantly arousing.

Angela had instilled in me a sense that for a woman to look sexually attractive she had to dress in a particular way. It had been more than twelve years since I had found any other appearance to create that effect. The Laura Ashley look had become for me what the pneumatic blonde had been for fifties *Playboy*-purchasing man. I know Laura Ashley was now passé but so, I guess, was I. Until I laid eyes on Helen Cooper. This was a most unexpected turn of events. What other surprises did this morning hold in store?

I had to admit that Helen was pretty much on top of her brief. The meeting had been called so that she could meet all the contributing editors, not just me. Now it made a bit more sense as to why it was so important that I came at the same time as everyone else. Helen had all the tools of the trade – flip charts and all that presentation stuff that's so popular these days – and her performance was both eloquent and perceptive.

It was when she left her analysis of the business and the readership demographics and launched herself on the quality of the journalism that I felt the hackles rising. Now she was bound to put her foot in it. As far as I was aware she knew little about sports and less about Britain. She was going to fall flat on her cute little face. Oh yes, I forgot to mention, apart from the skirt and the hair and the legs, she had a soft round face with very kissable lips. I know I shouldn't really have been thinking this way, what with my job at stake (I

presumed) but when she talked so passionately she was
very cute indeed.

As it turned out she didn't know too much about
sports but she knew a hell of a lot about good writing.
I hadn't realised she'd been a journalist herself. I thought
she was a kind of management consultant figure who
simply fired people and increased profit margins, but she
really knew her stuff. OK, if you asked her which golfer
won the US Open two years ago she probably would have
had no idea but she had a built-in shit detector which told
her which articles were sloppy, poorly researched and
badly written. She got after two guys in the room in
particular – neither of them me, I was relieved to note by
this time. Mike Staunton had done a very ordinary piece
on the American players' performance at the French clay
court championships at Roland Garros and Jim Fullerton
had turned in a scissors and paste analysis on the decline
of Nick Faldo on the US PGA tour. She was right on
both counts.

The meeting broke up with all of us sweating. I believed
we were all going to lunch in Soho afterwards so I was
surprised when Jack McGinty shook my hand and wished
me good luck. Apparently we weren't all going on to the
restaurant together. It was going to be lunch à deux. A cold
shiver ran down my spine.

I had come up on the train only three hours ago
prepared to take some kind of bollocking and give it
straight back. The worst that could happen, surely, was
that we'd be made aware that we were on Easy Street and
the company had shown faith in us by giving us these

staff jobs and the least we could do in return was to write and fight for the good old parent company conglomerate and show we appreciated how lucky we were to be in this privileged position.

Instead, this woman had turned things round 180 degrees and I was completely wrong-footed. I now made the inevitable assumption based on Jack's soft apologetic handshake that I was about to be fired. Me! Fired! Well, I thought grimly, it will be fun finding out precisely what excuse she was going to dredge up for giving me the order of the boot. It was particularly devilish that it should be administered by a woman whom I was starting to find increasingly attractive.

She was civil in the taxi on the way to the restaurant, apologising for dragging me up from Cambridge at ten thirty when she knew I was a single parent. I was wrong-footed again. What was this woman up to? I said it was fine, I'd made alternative arrangements and I could see that if everyone else was coming in at ten thirty there was no point in my showing up half an hour late but the secretary hadn't told me that. She looked at me sharply.

'She didn't tell you there was a meeting?'

'Not a general meeting. I thought it was just the two of us.'

'I'm so sorry. That's inexcusable. You think I should fire her?'

'Good God, no. People don't lose their jobs in England over something as petty as that.'

'Maybe they should. Maybe that would keep people on their toes.'

'Is that a coded warning?'

'I thought you knew Americans have no sense of irony.'

I was flummoxed. I had no idea how to talk to this woman. Was I being softened up for the fatal bullet or was I being hung out to dry here? A clean shot with a pearl-handled revolver always seemed preferable to a life sentence without possibility of parole incarcerated in a dank prison infested with rats. I was probably guilty of letting my mind exaggerate but after that staccato burst of conversation we both fell silent and stared out of the window.

In the bright but noisy restaurant we were shown to a corner table for four. I wondered whether this might indicate some kind of social rescue was on the cards but as soon as the waiter had slipped the chair under Helen's bottom he gathered the other two place settings and removed them from the table. There was to be no rescue. Should I fall on my sword, I wondered, resign in high dudgeon so at least I could stage a magnificent exit with my head held high, possibly attracting a spontaneous round of applause from the other diners while she sank ever deeper in her seat with shame and embarrassment?

'I'm sorry about the noise. Is this place OK for you? We could go someplace else if you prefer.'

Another body swerve and she left my two-footed tackle sprawling on the ground as she headed for goal with the ball at her feet. Why this sudden humility?

'No. This is fine. Really.'

'I asked for the closest decent restaurant. Everyone I talked to recommended this place.'

'Seems great.'

'You haven't been here?'

I shook my head. Couldn't write, lived in the wrong place, didn't know which London restaurants to go to for lunch. I was dead meat, surely. Silence fell as we studied the menu.

'It always strikes me,' I declared ingratiatingly, 'that the national dish of America is menus.'

Halfway through the sentence I expected her to cut me dead with a blistering broadside on how backward Britain is and how advanced American cooking is, so it was another surprise when she laughed.

'That's great! Yours?'

I shook my head ruefully. 'Saw it on some travel programme on TV ages ago. It always stuck in my mind.'

'I like it.' Two games all, first set. Maybe I wasn't dead meat yet.

The appetisers arrived. Her salad was swimming in dressing. She sent it back.

'Surely you're not counting calories,' I smiled, implying, I hoped, that she was ever so slim but without needing to articulate the fact.

'When I grew up here, they doused every salad with something out of a bottle called salad cream. Now they think they're sophisticated they douse everything in salad dressing from a bottle. A salad needs dressing not drowning.'

'You grew up here?' I was astonished.

'I was born here. My dad's British.'

'He is? Where does he live?'

'If he's alive he's probably in this city.'

'You don't speak then.'

'How's your appetiser?' The subject was obviously closed.

'Good,' I said, 'good.'

'You're a good journo, Ralph.' Here it comes. I could sense the tone in her voice and what it meant. The pause at the end of the sentence was like that moment in cartoons when a character who is being chased sprints over the edge of the cliff but instead of falling to his immediate death appears to hover in mid-air for two seconds with his feet still kicking away before the law of gravity snaps into action.

'I sense a reservation.'

'I've got to make some changes.' For changes read firings, or 'redeployment'.

'Why? We're all having a great time.'

'The guys back home don't care if you're having a great time. They're just looking at the bottom line.'

'When Jack hired me he said you weren't looking for a profit for three years.'

'We invested heavily in the Asian economy. We got badly burned so we have to make cuts elsewhere to get back on track.'

'Cuts? What kind of cuts?'

'There are too many journos on high-paying staff contracts. They're going to have to go back on to freelance work.'

'You looking at me?' I wanted to say in my best Robert De Niro voice even while expecting her reply to be, 'Yeah. I'm looking at you, shithead!' I had been so relieved when I got that sense of financial security that came with the staff contract. Now this Yank was going to yank it away from under my nose. I couldn't get out of my mind that brilliant *Sun* headline which immortalised England's 2-0 defeat by the underrated United States soccer team: Yanks 2, Planks 0. Who was the Plank now?

'Does that mean me?' I affected an indifference to my fate I did not feel. She nodded, rather sadly. I liked that.

'I'm sorry.'

'You don't have to be.'

'I think you're an excellent writer. Truly I do. You'd be the last person I'd fire if it was a question of talent.'

'That's a comfort.'

'I can see you don't believe me but I assure you it's true. I really like the way you write and I think the magazine will be lucky to get you on a freelance basis. I'm sure you'll be swamped with offers of work.'

Another awkward pause. At this critical moment the waiter arrived to clear away the plates. Helen reached across and poured the sparkling water into both our glasses. Into my mind now came the image of a judge reaching for the black cap. What I heard was, 'Ralph Michael Warren, you have been found guilty of signing a lucrative staff contract. You shall be taken from hence to a place of execution where you shall be hanged by the laptop recharger extension cord until you are dead. And may the Inland Revenue have mercy on your soul.'

What she said was, 'Tell me about your son. I see you don't wear a wedding band.'

My mind crashed its gears as it changed down abruptly from top directly into second.

'I'm sorry?'

'No. I'm the one who's sorry. I shouldn't be sticking my big fat nose in. This is a business lunch. And it's none of my business.'

'I'm not divorced. My wife died.'

'Oh, that's so sad. When?'

'Eleven years ago. In California. She was killed in a car crash.'

And so I told her the story. *Gone with the Wind II* and all the rest of it. She didn't cluck with empty sympathy the way most women did nor turn monosyllabic with embarrassment as most men did. She asked searching questions but I felt they were genuine attempts to understand rather than prurient prying. The main course arrived and disappeared. Dessert was fashionably dispensed with and I smiled as she countered my decaffeinated cappuccino with a double espresso; one of us fighting off the perceived harmful effects of the coffee bean, the other welcoming the caffeine stimulus with gusto.

I looked at my watch instinctively.

'That's the twelfth time you've done that since we sat down.'

'You're keeping score?'

'I was wondering if you had some place more important to be.'

'I do.' I explained. I needed to get the two forty-five

train from King's Cross which got into Cambridge at three thirty-five so I could coach Danny's cricket team when school broke up at four o'clock. Besides, I was fed up of being dangled on the end of the rope like this. 'If you're going to make a change, why don't you make it? Put us both out of our misery.'

'I'm not feeling too miserable.'

'That makes one of us.'

She drank her double espresso like a cowboy downing a double shot of whisky. I slurped at the cappuccino, conscious of the danger of leaving traces of the milky foam on the tip of my nose. Would I be able to lick it off or would I have to use the napkin and make it look as if I was wiping my nose with it? How is it that a cup of coffee could be filled with such dangers?

'I want to talk to you some more.'

'Can we do it on the phone? Or on Monday? I do have that piece on Tiger Woods to e-mail in this afternoon.'

'How you gonna do that if you're out coaching batting practice?'

I gestured to the laptop. 'On the train.'

I could see her mind flicking through a number of possibilities. I knew she wasn't likely to rescind her decision to fire me but then again I'm a Spurs and Angels supporter and I believe that hope springs eternal.

'That train of yours full?'

'I'm sorry?'

'Do you have to book a ticket? I mean is it like a bus or an airplane?'

'More like a bus.'

'You want to get back to Cambridge right now?'

'If you don't mind.'

'OK. Let's go.'

I must have looked shocked at the impulsive decision. She smiled.

'I'm in therapy. He wants me to work on my spontaneity.'

'You're in therapy. Really?'

'I used to be. All Americans with incomes over a hundred thousand dollars have a therapist. You must know that.'

I could see that she regretted the sentence as soon as it was out of her mouth. She hadn't meant to rub my face in the spectacular difference between her guaranteed income and my own current situation.

'I've got no appointments this afternoon and I can talk to my assistant on the cell phone. I'm really interested in you as a writer. I'd like to be able to work something out and seeing you in your natural habitat might help us both. Make sense?'

What did I have to lose? 'Sure.'

She grabbed her bag and her mobile phone, marched over to the cash desk and insisted the bill be made up immediately. The maîtresse d' clearly did not believe that such intimate secrets should be disclosed to clientele and did so with an extreme reluctance. Helen waited, refusing to be intimidated, getting in a retaliatory blow by tapping rhythmically with her gold card on the edge of the desk until it was seized from her hand and swiped aggressively through the machine.

I watched as she took great pride in ignoring the space on the Visa bill for the gratuity but scribbled her signature illegibly, handed back the appropriate half, grabbed her card and thrust a five pound note into the hands of the surprised but grateful waiter. An imperious wave at a black taxi as we emerged from the restaurant and ten seconds later we were on our way to King's Cross station.

CHAPTER THIRTEEN

Danny

THE WHOLE THING WAS PROBABLY my fault. Right from
the first time I saw her. I was cross with her because I
was cross with my dad for showing up late. He'd told
my teacher Mrs Hargreaves that he could help with
coaching the school team and she put him on to Mr
Banks who ran the school first eleven. If you ask me
it was confusion on all sides because I think Mr Banks
knew Dad was a dead famous sports writer and he
probably thought Tim Henman would be coming down
to teach the school tennis and Ian Botham to umpire
the Under-14s cricket match.

At ten past four we were all on the playing field in our
cricket clothes except Rob Winston who thought we had
extra swimming after school not cricket and came with his
swimming trunks and towel. He was given a good teasing
but he just took his blazer and tie off, borrowed a pair
of trainers and rolled up his sleeves. By twenty past four
there was still no sign of Dad and it was my turn to get
the treatment. Mr Banks then came by and made some

barbed comment about Dad, and I cringed. He split us up into four groups and we'd just started catching practice when there was a loud blast from a car horn.

We all looked up to see Dad waving furiously from a taxi. If that wasn't embarrassing enough he was with some woman. The other lads didn't waste any time, calling her a tart and lots of other names which I didn't understand but which I knew were rude. I hated him for embarrassing me like this. How could he do it? He'd never done anything like this before, that was one of the reasons I loved him so much. And this woman! All right, I know I said before how I thought it was about time he found someone, but not here! I meant at home one Saturday night or something. Fancy coming to school with some bird in a short skirt. I saw Mr Banks coming over towards me and judging by the look on his face he wasn't going to give me the Man of the Match award. I just wanted the ground to open up and swallow me.

Turned out it wasn't Dad's fault. The train was half an hour late leaving King's Cross. He said there were leaves on the line but I didn't understand because it was nearly May and all the trees were in bloom. You only get leaves on the line in the autumn and only then if the trees are deciduous. If they are evergreens or conifers they don't shed their leaves at all.

But Mr Banks laughed when Dad mentioned leaves and said we must have started practising with the wrong kind of balls because we could none of us catch them. That wasn't true either but then Dad laughed and suddenly it looked like Dad and Mr Banks were best friends. Grown-ups are really peculiar sometimes.

Anyway it wasn't half as bad as I had feared. I knew Dad had spent two days with the England one-day cricket team at the start of the one-day international series, watching their pre-season training in the Canary Isles. That's why he was able to tell everyone the special exercises they do for strengthening what he called 'hand-eye co-ordination'. That phrase always makes me think of Nicholas Wallingford who is a bit of a spas and can't put a can of Coke to his mouth without spilling it all down his chin and onto his shirt but I guess Dad wasn't talking about that.

By the time we got to play a short game, not with the usual hard red ball but tennis balls in order to improve everyone's speed around the field, we had forgotten all about the bird. She was called 'Helen from work' and I thought at first, oh God, no, she really is one of his 'research assistants' or whatever he calls his short-term girlfriends. But she kicked off her shoes, sat on the grass beyond the boundary for a few minutes watching us, obviously got bored, lay back in the sunshine and went to sleep. She forgot about us and we forgot about her.

Afterwards Dad said we could go to Pizza Express but Helen said why didn't we buy something at Sainsbury's and she'd cook it? She never got the chance to usually, which I thought was weird. If she never cooked, how did she eat? Anyway, we went to Sainsbury's which I hated because you can't just go in and buy something and come out again like buying a sandwich or a bag of chips. You have to get a trolley and pay a pound and all that fuss and I was really thirsty.

I made Dad stop at a newsagent's and buy me a Coke first but he was in a funny old mood. He and Helen kept staring at each other and laughing a lot. They bought chicken drumsticks and baked potatoes which I like and salad stuff which I absolutely hate. I mean, if you're really hungry, and I was because once I wasn't dead thirsty any more after the Coke I discovered that I was starving because I'd had nothing to eat since lunch – if you can call that gruel we get lunch – then, well, the one thing you don't want is a salad. I know there are girls who eat salad because I see them in town on Saturday lunchtimes but they've all made themselves barmy with their dieting. Well, I'm not on a diet so I don't see why I should have to eat salad.

This Helen was American and apparently chicken and baked potato and salad is what people have for dinner in America – I thought they just ate hamburgers. When we got home I was sent upstairs to do my homework although I wanted to watch *The Simpsons* first. Usually Dad lets me while he's cooking dinner but this time he got all stern and said I had to start my homework because it would be too late after dinner blah blah blah. I think he was showing off in front of the American woman.

And she was American, this woman, American in her looks and in her way of behaving. Not like my mum. Mum was pretty, Mum was beautiful. She was tall and she had long golden hair like a fairy princess and she wore long flowing dresses. This Helen person is only average in height and her hair is dark and curly whereas I know for a fact that Dad likes women who have long fair hair. He's always going on and on about how beautiful Mum's hair was because he could run his fingers through it. I think it's a weird thing to do, run your fingers through someone else's hair. I mean, the only person I've ever seen do that is the school nurse and she's just looking for head lice. Is that what grown-ups do when they're making out? Like I said, weird.

In the end Dad did the cooking anyway because Helen's mobile kept ringing. She went into the study where Dad works and then she came back in saying she had to get online to talk to head office in America and she asked me if I could help because 'kids know so much more about the Internet than we wrinklies'. It made me want to puke right there.

I was starting to explain that Dad had told me I had to start my homework when Dad interrupted me and said he'd show her how to do it. When he came back he gave me this long lecture about how we always have to be polite to guests and he'd taught me all these manners and why didn't I use some of them occasionally — like now, for instance.

This made me mad because a) I hadn't been rude to Helen anyway, I'd only just met her; you had to give me time to be rude to the woman and b) how come this system of Dad's about being extra polite to guests only works the one way? Whenever we go to other people's houses Dad tells me how it's not only him who wants to be proud of me but Mum would as well. So when we go out I'm very careful to be polite and what Mum and Dad would call 'the perfect guest'. That means I can't do anything except what other people tell me to do. But when people come to our house I've got to be 'the perfect host' as well, which means I can't do anything and the guest can do whatever she pleases. Now is this unfair or what?

Anyway, Dad then decided that I could do my homework after dinner and that I now had to set the table with the best crockery, and I thought that was stupid too. We don't normally eat with the best plates and it wasn't like she was the Queen or the Prime Minister; she was just somebody from work. And she was getting a false impression of how we normally lived and ate. Particularly since there was live football on the telly.

It was only a testimonial match for some old Scottish player who had retired before the start of the season but it was Celtic v. Juventus and Juventus have been the best team in Europe now for years and normally we'd sit in the front room with the plate on our knees and watch the game on TV. Dad always said it was his work, it wasn't that he wanted to watch it but he had to. (That's a joke of course.) So now, when he had the chance to watch Alessandro Del Piero and that really good Frenchman with lots of Zs in his name, we were stuck in the dining room eating off the posh dinner plates.

I could see it wasn't worth having a go at Dad about it. I wasn't going to win so what was the point? I decided to be dead cool about everything, so when she came back into the room I was smiling and chirpy. Inside I was still sending her up but she didn't know that so that was my victory. I did suggest, just casually, that she might be interested in watching the Celtic v. Juventus game but Dad chipped in smartly, 'Oh, I think Helen would much prefer to talk to you rather than watch a meaningless friendly.' And his eyes were flashing warning signs, but of course she said, 'Oh yes, Danny, your dad's been telling me all about you on the train.' Which I hate because I hate him talking about me to other people.

Dad and me, we have a great relationship but it's ours. When he talks about us to other people I sometimes feel it's not special any more. The Red Indians, I think it was the Red Indians, they thought that if they had their photo taken their souls would be taken with it. It's stupid, I know, but I do sort of see their point. It's like you've got something dead private then it becomes public and everyone has a piece of it and suddenly it's not your private thing any more.

Which I suppose is why you never see a bunch of Red Indians in one of those passport photo booths pulling faces behind the curtain – like me and Darren Foxton and Will Stevens did last summer in the bus station till we got thrown out and the man said he was going to report us to our parents. So I told him both my parents were dead, which I know is a bit of an exaggeration but I reckoned it would make him feel sorry for me. It probably occurred to him that I might be lying but he couldn't take the chance. By this time

Darren and Will had run off anyway but the horrible man kept the pictures when they came sliding out of the developing tray. I hope he got all that slimy stuff over his fingers.

CHAPTER FOURTEEN

Helen

I'VE NEVER BEEN WHAT YOU might call a maternal person. I have never had that urge to procreate, never wanted to hold a baby in my arms, mine or anybody else's, never heard that mythical baby clock ticking anywhere near me. Sometimes I look at myself naked in the mirror and stare at my belly, wondering what it would be like if it was bloated by pregnancy. Confronted by my own body, normally I feel nothing but irritation.

I know, as a rational person, that I contribute professionally to the objectification of women. I know that something like fifty per cent of women are size sixteen and above. I know that the slimness of my waistline and the shape of my boobs and ass would not qualify me as a supermodel and that this should not matter. Not that any man has ever articulated these thoughts – I'd punch his lights out if he started down that road. I also know that I'm bright and sharp and resilient and loyal, which seem to me to be things that matter. So how is it that when I look in the mirror I figure my greatest quality is my flat stomach?

I was one of those who were not so much enchanted as grossed out by the sight of Demi Moore's notorious photo shoot in *Vanity Fair*. The sight of a pregnant woman does nothing for me other than to reinforce my desire to retain a figure unblemished by stretch marks. If the rest of womankind felt like I do, no doubt the human race would die out, but since there's no chance of that happening and the slight decline in the birth rate in the Western world in recent years has been more than compensated for by its rapid growth in the Third World, I would be more inclined to argue that my stand was the responsible one.

So when I met Danny for the first time I felt nothing special. In fact if anything I was kind of disappointed. On the train on the way down to Cambridge Ralph had talked endlessly about what a great kid he was, how if it hadn't been for Danny he couldn't have gone on after Angela's death and all that kind of crap, so that by the time the train rolled into the station half an hour late I was expecting to see a mixture of the juvenile Sigmund Freud and baby Jesus.

What I found, of course, was a normal kid, good-looking in a freckly pubescent way, in a British school uniform which made him look like all the other kids. On the way back to the house he set up this traditional whine about being thirsty and I could tell Ralph was getting increasingly impatient with him. I thought, 'Uh oh, I'm not getting involved in playing Happy Families with these two,' but as soon as we got to the house the cell phone went and I left the room to talk to the office.

When I got back, it was obvious that something had happened because the grumpy adolescent had turned into this really nice kid, so suddenly all was sweetness and light. Danny was cheerful and Ralph was relaxed and dinner went with a swing. I felt a bit guilty because we'd gone shopping for ingredients which I'd promised to cook but then the phone rang and I got online with California and then that turned into a conference call so by the time I'd finished Ralph had done all the cooking.

He's a good cook, better than me, I would think, if only because he's had more practice. For me, cooking is something I only do when there is no alternative. Because of my job I'm frequently being taken out to eat or else I'm so exhausted I'm crashed out in front of the TV and I wind up with a bowl of gourmet soup heated up in the microwave.

When Charles came for the weekend we had other things besides food on our minds. Even when I offered to cook during those rare times when we both had our clothes on he would invariably want to demonstrate his largesse and self-importance by sweeping me off to the best restaurant in town. Charles has never been a homebody.

Frequently when I go to people's houses for dinner I can't wait to escape. There is something about family life which gives me a royal pain in the ass. It's so damn smug, you know, so exclusive, so 'I bet you wish you could sit down every night with your own family like we do'. Well, those guys can just take a flying fuck because at the end of a hard working day I prefer to lie on the couch with a bowl of pasta and a bottle of wine and watch re-runs of *Seinfeld* than wash dishes for three untidy kids and one selfish lazy bastard of a husband.

I thought I might feel similarly about Ralph and Danny but my fears were soon calmed. For a start, I liked the way they talked to each other. It was gentle teasing on both sides and it was clear that Ralph was keen to allow Danny to develop his own ideas. So many kids of that age either parrot their parents' attitudes or are so set in their rebellious ways that they're just plain contrary. Danny was different. He had his own ideas and he wasn't afraid to express them because they were thought out and intelligent and well-articulated. Lots of kids get their original thoughts stifled at birth because their parents (usually the fathers) take great delight in ridiculing them. Not Ralph.

Over dinner it became clear to me that Danny and Ralph did have a special relationship, one I'd never seen before between a father and a son. Ralph welcomed what Danny was saying, took it seriously, asked Danny what he thought about everything from school to politics. And it was interesting — I mean interesting to me.

When he found out I lived in California, Danny's eyes lit up. He wanted to know if I'd been to Disneyland and when I said 'No' I felt like a freak. He knew everything about Disneyland — Tomorrowland, Space Mountain, all that kind of stuff — and he couldn't believe that someone who lived only a hundred miles away had never been there. I promised I would take him there. It seemed the least I could do. His eyes glowed with pleasure at the prospect. I was getting to like this kid.

Danny and Ralph washed the dishes. I offered to help but they wouldn't hear of it. This was a routine they did every day. Danny cleared the table, Ralph washed the dishes. I was surprised momentarily they didn't have a dishwasher but then I could see with the amount of dishes they had to wash, just the two of them, there probably wasn't the need. Besides, Ralph was tidy so it wasn't like there was going to be a stack of dirty dishes piled up at the end of the week.

One thing I couldn't help noticing of course were the photographs of his dead wife, Angela. They were all over the house. I wouldn't say it was creepy, like a shrine or anything. It's just that there were lots of them. None of them were posed studio shots or stills from her movies or TV shows. They were all Angela out in the garden, Angela with the baby (Danny, I figured it had to be), Angela on holiday, Angela with her folks, at least I guessed they were her folks, and so on. She was in all of them as if she was the only one that mattered. Now obviously Ralph did this so it wasn't like Angela herself was demonstrating some kind of superego. But I found it inhibiting, I have to say. It was like her presence hung over the house.

It was when Danny went to bed that the evening started. I had no real idea why I had gotten on that train other than I knew I wanted to be with Ralph a while longer. The girl in my office was too relieved to know that I wasn't going to be back till Monday morning to ask why I was suddenly re-routing myself to Cambridge. I didn't even call her at five twenty-five to check she was still there. Frankly, and most unusually, I hoped she was in the pub with her friends, which I gathered was traditionally where she spent her free time. I wondered why I was suddenly feeling like Ebenezer Scrooge at the end of *A Christmas Carol*.

The conclusion I reached was that running away from the office and getting on the train was the sort of spontaneous gesture my therapist would have approved of. I didn't get much in the way of positive affirmation in my new position, so this was a great start to a relationship. Was this going to *be* a relationship, I wondered. I had begun the day assuming that I would never see Ralph again, personally or professionally. Did I dare contemplate the prospect of something as meaningful as a 'relationship'? My last experience had been with a man so different from Ralph that it seemed incredible that the same species could have produced two such contrasting individuals.

But as the evening progressed I found myself becoming increasingly attracted to this new kind of male animal. I had always dismissed 'the sensitive lover' syndrome as a limp-wristed waste of time and space. I didn't want a man who would clean out the john; I could hire a cleaner for that or, at a pinch and with a certain amount of reluctance, do it myself. I always thought that what I wanted was a man who exuded power, who was fascinated by my mind and my body, who was strong enough to withstand my withering sarcasm and all-round cynicism.

It was certainly true enough that I liked men who were strong and hard in attitude as well as muscle, whose sexual manners were more suited to the bedroom than the drawing room. The men I went to bed with had to be as familiar with the way round my erogenous zones as they were with their own. I liked to be held, to be fondled, to be aroused as all women do and I didn't mind if he became a little aggressive with me just so long as he didn't mind when the tables were turned. I've always had sharp teeth and a firm hand and I was never afraid to use them in pursuit of my own pleasure. Such men, I soon realised, were rare. Charles Schmidt was just such a man. Ralph Warren assuredly was not. So how was it possible that Ralph Warren was now exercising this creeping fascination for me? Something deep and uncontrollable was happening to me and I felt powerless as well as unwilling to stop it.

Since the demise of the relationship with Charles I had also made a pact with myself to abandon any romantic entanglements with men who were in any way connected to me by our joint professions. I didn't want a re-run of my humiliating substitution in front of the rest of my colleagues and I never really anticipated the prospect of getting involved with a man who was in some measure my junior. I was so attracted to powerful men that the thought of a man who was less powerful than I was simply made me realise that I'd never want such a guy sexually.

It was the smell of Ralph which changed all these feelings which I had thought were such a certainty. It wasn't, modern television advertising notwithstanding, an artificial smell coming from his aftershave or his deodorant. It was his own body smell, a warm, enveloping smell that made me want to curl up inside of it. It seemed very safe and the more I smelled it as we sat on the couch after dinner, the more I wanted him. I made the first move because of it, unbuttoning his shirt and running my fingers up and down his chest, putting my face close to it. I suppose it was reasonable to interpret such a move as blatantly sexual but in my own defence I'd have to say it was, initially at least, more sensual than sexual.

He pulled my hands away but gently, whispering about Danny not being in bed yet upstairs, clearly anxious about where my hands were going next, understanding that I was expecting his hands to start delving too. But he did it beautifully. It wasn't a wimpish petulant act, it wasn't brutal or unfeeling. He managed to soothe my injured pride, if that's what he thought it was, and still retain a measure of masculine control.

In that very act of rejection, although as it turned out it was less rejection than delayed gratification, he showed me the true measure of the man. It was a tiny moment, capable of certainly more than one interpretation. If I'd been hyper-sensitive I would no doubt have risen grandly to my feet, gathered my things and called for a taxi. But I did no such thing. Instead, I just sat there and waited for him to return.

CHAPTER FIFTEEN

Ralph

I'M SURE THERE MUST BE some people who find sex the easiest and most natural act in the world and can't help wondering what the fuss is all about and why the rest of the Western world makes such an issue of it. I don't know where these people live, possibly on top of a mountain in one of the more remote parts of the Andes, but certainly I've never met any of these people myself and to judge by the contents of daytime television programmes and the shelves of every bookshop, there are absolutely none in the fifty-one states of America and Great Britain combined.

Angela was probably the nearest I've come to meeting someone of this nature but perhaps, I speculate on my darker days, that was because she was also an actress. Actresses get used to simulating making love and the ecstasy that is supposed to follow, so maybe they are just expert at letting go, being uninhibited and knowing how to make their partner feel good about the experience.

It was less than three years from the time we made

up (after that unfortunate interlude with that creep of a director whose name I've now blanked) until the moment of Angela's death but despite the domestic disputes which punctuated the relationship, I can honestly say I was never unfaithful to her. It wasn't that I wasn't tempted. It was a mixture of cowardice on my part, fear of rejection by other women whom I did find attractive, and a diminishing sense of self-worth compared to my starry wife. Plus I did love her and I think I might have found adultery a tricky concept to handle if it meant hurting Angela. Plus she was really good in bed.

Angela had the magical ability to keep the sex between us as fresh as the first time we made love. Because she was inventive and uninhibited, it encouraged me to be the same. If I was a good lover, and of course I never read any decent reviews of myself in the broadsheets, it was because of her.

It's not that it hasn't occurred to me that maybe it was all an act. Maybe she was setting me up, covering her tracks while she leaped from bed to bed. Maybe she was screwing her way round the Royal Shakespeare Company as I had imagined on occasion when she came back from rehearsals late or flushed with an exuberance which she always attributed to excelling in a difficult and demanding job.

I suppose there was no real threat to our happiness from any of those horny actors and directors she worked with. At my blackest I could just about build this fantasy nightmare of her running off with a big shot Hollywood director. In reality, though, it wouldn't have been an RSC actor; I knew her ambitions would have stretched further than Stratford-on-Avon and the Barbican. But I never, in my worst nightmares, thought I would lose her at the age of twenty-three to the drunken homicidal driver of an Oldsmobile.

I need to remember the rows and the jealousies that came between us because otherwise I would romanticise Angela into sainthood and she was never that ethereal. It's certainly true that she was my first and best and in many ways my only. The women who have come since have been unable to live up to Angela, I suppose because I never let them. It's not that I didn't want these other women — at the time anyway. There is a limit to the fevered imagination of even a sports writer's brain and it was certainly great to experience the feeling that I was still normal on those infrequent occasions when I spent the night with a woman. But there was always Danny.

I was stuck really. I loved Danny and I thought he was too young to deal with my remarrying. Then there would be all the problems that stem from step-families. Either the woman I married would bring her own children from a former marriage and I didn't think it would ever be possible to treat her children identically to the way in which I responded to Danny or, worse, she would be a bad mother to Danny even if she was a loving wife to me.

Then there was the problem of our having children together. I could not see how this could benefit Danny. It was bound to get in the way of the tight relationship that had developed between us. How could I possibly give myself to children from a new marriage knowing that

Danny would inevitably feel displaced in my affections no matter how hard I tried to reassure him? What sort of a father would I then be to the new children if I was always putting Danny's needs first?

If any of the women whom I dated had serious designs on me I was never aware of it because I was always too preoccupied with all these questions. After being married and revelling in the security of sex in such protected circumstances, it was a rude shock to discover that sex with women after Angela involved all these ancillary questions. No wonder the relationships rarely lasted beyond the first serious encounter. In my own defence it was rarely me who blew these women off, it was usually they who blew me — in both senses of the vernacular.

I'd make a rotten adulterer. I was for ever looking at my watch when I should have been concentrating on the person nearest to me. If I had to pick up Danny from school at three thirty, I'd be mentally calculating during the act of congress (is this what Metternich was really doing in Vienna in 1815? I wondered) how soon I could tease her into orgasm so I could make my departure without having the bedside lamp thrown at me.

The stories of women lying back, thinking of England and looking at the ceiling and wondering whether it needs repainting always induced in me a feeling of empathy. From my point of view, it was more a question of whether I'd make it through the traffic in time to get to school before Danny came out. Of course the irritating thing was, by letting my mind wander along these paths I had achieved what at the age of nineteen I had found impossible – namely to delay the moment of release almost indefinitely.

I have always been taken with the idea of Tantric sex which I understand calls for congress to be broken off frequently and then resumed at a later stage and at a higher point of intensity. I think the Kama Sutra advocates the idea of holding hands and staring at the moon, possibly wandering naked and unashamed through neatly tended ornamental gardens. I doubt whether it was to drive like a lunatic across Cambridge to pick up number one son outside primary school, go home, supervise homework, make dinner, feed child, wash up dishes, bath child, read to child, kiss child goodnight then drive like a lunatic across town to resume passionate sex acts with woman who has been waiting patiently for five hours for the yoni to return to the lingam – or vice versa. I can never remember which one is which.

So that first night with Helen threatened to follow the traditional lines of failure laid down over many years. She took the initiative, which was perhaps as well considering this was the woman who had been trying to fire me a few hours ago. I was acutely conscious that if the sexes had been reversed, she would have had every reason to have hauled me in front of an industrial tribunal claiming sexual harassment but, as she looked at me with most unprofessional eyes, I knew I was attracted to her and that this wasn't like the other abortive sexual encounters of recent years.

It was I who blinked first of course. It was instinctive,

accentuated by the knowledge that Danny was still awake upstairs. I excused myself on that basis, mentally calculating that by the time I returned she would either have recovered her professional poise and dignity or stripped down to bra and panties. Either way I would have drawn her into the first big declaration of intent.

Upstairs the conversation took a predictable turn.

'Is she staying the night?'

'That's none of your business. Have you brushed your teeth?'

'Yes. She's after you, Dad.'

'I don't think she is. She's just friendly. Americans usually are.'

'Why?'

'I don't know. They're less uptight.'

'Why?'

'I don't know. Maybe it's something to do with the American Constitution.'

'What's that?'

'Look, I'm just being hospitable. She's a guest in the house.'

'Can you record the highlights of the Celtic v. Juventus game?'

'They'll be on *Football Focus* at lunchtime.'

'Please.'

'All right. But only if you go straight to sleep.'

'Can you turn on the tape?' He had a tape recorder on which he played the audio cassettes we rented from the library. It was an excellent way to get him to go to sleep while hoping that he absorbed a little culture. By the time he was ten he had heard most of the great Dickens novels this way. We then experimented with Trollope but though *The Barchester Chronicles* sent him to sleep quite effectively, it made no impact otherwise and indeed it drove him back to rubbish authors who specialised in action adventure stories. We compromised on John Buchan so I switched on side six of *The Thirty-Nine Steps* and turned off the light.

I made a detour into the bathroom, unsure of quite what might be going on downstairs. A quick brush of the teeth, a swift floss of the chicken (nothing like kissing a woman with bits of poultry stuck between your front teeth) and a squirt of aftershave behind the ear made me feel better prepared for what might happen downstairs. Now that Danny was ninety-eight per cent secure, I was starting to get quite excited. Helen was a bright and attractive woman who had clearly taken a shine to me. The night was replete with possibilities.

I wanted her, there was no doubt. If she was all buttoned up when I got downstairs I was going to be disappointed – temporarily anyway, until the relief seeped through a little later. It did occur to me as I flicked off the bathroom light that the traditional manner of seduction – predatory male, reluctant yet interested female with child to worry about making a quick dash to the bathroom to effect emergency repairs before the big moment – had been completely reversed. It appeared that I was now the ditzy blonde, she was the suave hero. Did I care? Not by the time I was halfway down the stairs and I could see into the living room I didn't.

CHAPTER SIXTEEN

Danny

I KNEW SOMETHING WAS WRONG as soon as I woke up. Even the way he made breakfast was different. He had this soppy look on his face and he didn't listen to anything I said. And he'd forgotten to record the Celtic v. Juventus game. On the other hand I was going to be allowed to watch television all morning and usually I'm only allowed an hour on Saturday mornings.

'Is that woman still here?' I shook a large stream of Crunchy Nut Corn Flakes into my favourite cereal bowl.

'That woman's name is Helen. And yes, she's in the spare bedroom.'

I smirked but Dad didn't see it. Did he think I was five years old or something? Honestly! At least he didn't give me the old one about missing her train.

'We had a lot of work to do and by the time we'd finished, it was too late for the last train to get back to London.'

Oh God, here we go.

She came down a few minutes later, dressed in the same clothes as the night before. Well, obviously, I know she didn't bring a suitcase or anything but at least she hadn't nicked one of Dad's long T-shirts or his dressing gown or something that would have made it seem like she belonged in our house. One of the others had tried that once so I gave her marks for that. But not too many.

Dad made porridge for her, which she called 'oatmeal' which sounds like something horses eat. Anyway, it's good, even though he makes it with salt because I have it on cold days in winter when I have to get up for school and it's still dark outside. Only this was a warm day in late April and I was puzzled. I reckoned that all women were weird. She certainly was.

After breakfast they decided to go for a walk. Dad wanted to show her the sights of Cambridge. This wasn't unusual. He does this for all the people who come and stay with us. He shows them where he first met Mum and then takes them on a guided tour of their romance. Actually it's not quite as sick as it sounds because it's also a tour of the university. Now I live here all the time so I can't get very excited about looking at King's College Chapel or any building but lots of people seem to like it.

Summers in Cambridge are full of tourists and tour buses. I hate them. They don't come out where I live much but if you go into town you can hardly move. Plus they don't seem to understand that I can go dead quick on my bike and they casually saunter across your path even if you've rung your bell at them. That's one reason why I didn't much like Helen at first. She was just another American tourist. And I didn't like the way Dad was looking at her. It wasn't like the others. He seemed to ignore me entirely.

As soon as they left, though, it was OK. I had the house to myself so I lay on the couch and watched the cartoons on Junk TV and played with my Gameboy. I sometimes like to get my weekend homework out of the way on Saturday mornings and then I've got the rest of the weekend clear, but then sometimes I just don't want to do it and I leave it as late as possible. Sometimes I leave it as late as bathtime on Sunday nights and Dad screams at me but then he helps me with it so it's dead easy. I hate copying off other boys because I feel such a spas and anyway I know I'll get caught out if I haven't learned it. But when Dad helps me it's great because I know I'm going to get it right and he's a really good teacher so it's quicker and better.

This time, though, Dad forgot about it altogether because she stayed the whole weekend and we did things together as if we were a family which we weren't. When they came back from their walk I was watching a match on TV; I can't remember which one but Dad didn't seem to mind because he was chatting about sport and the magazine to Helen and she was smiling at him and they seemed to be having a jolly good time.

After lunch they decided we were going to play tennis. Dad still has an arrangement at his old college sports field which has a dozen quite good grass courts which are rarely used. The students were only due to come back up that weekend so he knew there'd be plenty of courts available.

Helen claimed she had no tennis clothes with her which wasn't surprising as she didn't have a toothbrush either. I hope she didn't use Dad's because that's really gross, using someone else's toothbrush. Matthew Lanchberry used mine once on a geography field trip just because we both had a blue one and I nearly killed him I was so grossed out.

Dad said that Helen could borrow a spare pair of his tennis shorts but since she was so slim she'd better come upstairs and try them on first. They took ages upstairs which I couldn't understand. I mean either a pair of shorts fits you or it doesn't. You look inside the waistband and if it's your size it fits and if it's two sizes too big it won't.

Anyway they were hours up there so I started throwing the tennis ball against the lounge wall and catching the rebound which I thought would bug Dad but he didn't come racing down the stairs to tell me off like I had expected. And when they did come down they didn't notice the marks on the wall.

What I wasn't too pleased about was that they'd borrowed a pair of my white shorts for her because all Dad's were too large and mine were just about the right size. 'Look, Dan,' said Helen, twirling round and showing them off, 'it's just like Goldilocks,' though Goldilocks didn't wear tennis shorts in any story I've ever read. And Helen had dark hair. It looked weird seeing her in my shorts.

Recently some of the boys had started talking about girls and how they bleed every month but it didn't hurt and they couldn't help it. I really didn't want her to start bleeding in my shorts but I knew I shouldn't say anything about it. I thought the safest thing to do was to examine them in the laundry basket and if they had bloodstains all over them I'd throw them in the dustbin. It seemed to me she was causing a lot of problems and she'd only been in the house a few hours.

She was an OK tennis player. She hit the ball hard enough but she couldn't run and she had a crap backhand but Dad was full of encouragement. Lots of 'well played's and 'great shot's but that's what he usually says to me and I'm miles better than she is. If the ball came straight at her and she happened to be in the right place she could hit it hard across the net but if you made her run about the court with the occasional drop shot she was easy peasy.

I won the set I played against her 6-3. I kept looking at Dad for approval because some of my backhand returns were really good, particularly off her serve because I was finally understanding what Dad had always told me about using the power of your opponent's shot to return the ball to him with interest — it's all in the timing — but he couldn't keep his eyes off Helen. He said afterwards that of course he was looking at me but I know he wasn't, not like he usually does.

They sent me off to buy three cans of Coke, a diet one for her, she said. I didn't think they sold that kind at the newsagent's so I said I'd ask but I wouldn't really. I'd give her the same Coke as Dad and I usually had and hope the sugar would make her explode or something.

When I got back he was teaching her to serve. Only not like he does it with me, which is to stand to one side and

let me copy his throw up and the way he moves his body
so that you hit the ball with your body falling forward so
that it takes you into the court. Instead he was standing
directly behind her and his body was leaning right into
hers. I don't think he was teaching her to serve at all. I
think he was trying to feel her up in public.

I decided I'd get his attention once and for all so I
shook up one of the cans of Coke and handed it to her.
She put it on the ground as Dad did with his until he
was finished with the exercise. When they picked up the
cans (I apologised really well because I couldn't be arsed
to buy her the diet one by saying that was all they had
left) I saw to my horror that Dad had picked up the
one I'd shaken to buggery. So of course, as soon as he
snaps it open it shoots all over his face.

Helen thought it was hilarious and burst out laughing and I would have done too only I could see that
Dad knew instantly what had happened. He might have
thought I was trying to get at him not her but he knew
I'd done it and that I'd done it with lots of spite and
malice and all those things. So I felt a bit guilty.

'When do you have to be back in London?' I asked
Helen, hoping for the answer 'In an hour'.

Instead she said, 'Oh, not till Monday morning. Tell
me, Dan, are there lots of fun things to do round
here?'

I wanted to scream at her that my name was Danny
not Dan but I didn't. Dad interrupted instead, grinning
all over his face.

'Sure. Cambridge is the funnest city on the globe, isn't

it, Dan?' Now he was starting it too. He'd never called me 'Dan' before. Ever.

'Yeah? Like what? I mean what's like a typical fun day for you?'

'Piano lessons, swimming lessons, tennis lessons, judo lessons, homework, TV and Pizza Express,' I said, running all the words together so she'd get the idea that there was no fun anywhere in Cambridge and she'd go home immediately.

Instead she seemed delighted. 'You know they never put anything like that in the tourist brochures. It's full of punting on the river and evensong in King's College Chapel. I never knew Cambridge had a Pizza Express.'

'Actually it's rather a good one. It's in a sort of mock classical building on Jesus Lane.'

'A Pizza Express on Jesus Lane? This I gotta see. Sounds like Disneyland in the Deep South. Would it be OK if I bought Danny a large pepperoni pizza with extra toppings and a giant Coke to go with it?'

I was salivating. Maybe this woman wasn't so bad after all. She wasn't trying to be Mum. She was just doing her best to be nice. She wasn't fawning over me. She was just acting naturally.

Dad looked dubious. 'Well, I don't know. I mean he's got an awfully busy schedule. He's got piano lessons, tennis lessons, swimming lessons, judo lessons, homework . . .'

I fell for it. I couldn't control myself. 'Please, Dad, we never go out to eat, please.'

'OK. You sure about this?' He looked at Helen as if awaiting confirmation.

'Never been surer of anything.'

We went to Pizza Express. We had to wait for ever for the food to arrive. But it was worth it.

I suppose I could see it that first day that Helen and Dad were falling for each other. I've never seen anyone fall in love so I didn't know that's how it would be. I've always loved my dad and my mum too but I never changed from not loving them to loving them, if you see what I mean. They were always there to be loved.

The boys at my school, sometimes they talk about their girlfriends but it doesn't really mean anything. Maybe they've seen someone in an arcade or the shopping centre on Saturdays and they've gone to the cinema that evening but nobody ever talks about falling in love.

A girlfriend is a kind of a status symbol but only kind of because most of us haven't got one and if one of us mentions that he has and he tells us her name, we always say, 'Oh, we know her. She's a slag,' even though we probably never heard of her till that moment. No one is too keen to get that sort of treatment so we don't do much boasting about girlfriends.

And if I'm being honest most of the twelve- or thirteen-year-old girls you see aren't like Claudia Schiffer or Kate Moss who really are beautiful. It would be worth boasting about a girlfriend if you had someone who looked like one of those but all the twelve-year-old girls I've ever seen are dead ugly or they've got braces on their teeth which make them look dead ugly. So you can't blame me for being sort of unprepared when Dad fell in love with Helen.

CHAPTER SEVENTEEN

Helen

IT WAS NEVER ON MY itinerary, never in my scheme of things. It wasn't that I didn't expect to fall in love ever again or that Ralph was not my type, it's just that the whole thing took me by surprise. I left the office that Friday lunchtime prepared to fire the bullet. I came back in on Monday morning bewitched, bothered and bewildered — by myself as much as by him.

In the intervening sixty-eight hours, most of my colleagues had slept, been to the pub, been to the supermarket, washed the car, talked to their parents on the phone, maybe been to a club, been out to dinner, gone to a soccer game. Substantially they returned on Monday morning very much the same people who had left on the Friday afternoon. But not me.

When I first 'did it' all those years ago I used to look in the mirror for days afterwards for some kind of telltale sign. I was changed inside, I was now officially a woman. So surely there had to be some kind of physical change that went along with it. Were my cheeks red, my cheekbones more pronounced, my graceless walk a little more poised? Or did I just have an enormous V with a line through it, like one of those no smoking signs or no dogs signs, to indicate that my cherry had been officially consumed in the conventional way? Sadly, none of the above appeared to apply and I was left to whisper of my new found celebrity status in the locker room at PS 158.

Irritatingly, very few girls seemed to want to believe me. The more I protested and added corroborative detail, the more I realised that I was digging a new grave for myself – one marked 'slag'. This infuriated me. For a start I really was moved by that first experience. It was a big deal for me, not just a quick fumble and grope in the back seat of a Chevy. I wanted to acquire status, that's why I did it, but the status I craved was tantalisingly withheld. It's bad enough that men should exploit all our vulnerabilities and insecurities in this area but I was horrified when I saw that my own sex was just as capable of inflicting the same cruelties with the added insult that they knew just how much these wounds really hurt.

I had a small re-run of those feelings when I walked back into the office on that Monday morning. I wanted so much to shout from the rooftops that I had fallen in love but I contented myself with sending a long e-mail to Los Angeles explaining why I thought the company should retain the services of Ralph Warren, guaranteeing his current salary while switching his status from staff to freelance.

I found it easy to justify the new arrangement to my employers. Ralph was by far the most talented of all the contributing editors and as part of our 'negotiations', conducted, I blush to admit, while curled up in his arms in a post-coital situation at 2 a.m. on the Sunday morning, I had persuaded him to increase his output for the magazine. He no longer had the staff benefits, but living in Cambridge most of them weren't relevant to his needs. I must remember how easy it is to negotiate in that position.

I couldn't, obviously, conduct negotiations with the other fall guys in similar fashion. Purely on a time basis it was cost ineffective. So I steeled myself to ten days of depressing lunches with the other contributing editors who couldn't write as well as Ralph. If they wanted to submit articles on a freelance basis we'd take a look at them, but judging by their previous efforts they weren't going to sell many. At least by the time I'd gotten around to the tenth guy I had the speech down pat. I wasn't looking forward to it but I just couldn't write those unfeeling letters of dismissal.

The process was nasty but successful. The company saved half a million pounds a year and I saved Ralph's ass — a cute deal however you looked at it.

I tried very hard to keep my business with Ralph separate from our relationship but it proved difficult. For a start that old lush Jack McGinty was clearly deeply sceptical when he discovered that I had kept Ralph's guaranteed income at its former level. Even the extra articles didn't fool him and I expect he made an immediate cause-and-effect link in his mind.

Also there was no real reason for me to have any contact with Ralph once the initial bloodletting on the magazine was through. We talked a lot on the cellular phone to stay away from the main office switchboard but every time his name came up in one discussion or another a little tremor went through me and my mind was filled with the memory of his touch and his smell, and a slow warmth permeated my body, which made my toes curl in pleasure.

In the end it emerged, like the election of the Pope, but without the white smoke – or smog as we call it in Los Angeles. One day I was having a wonderful secretive private affair with a lovely man and the next I was the clear target of smirks and whispered giggles. Two secretaries stopped gossiping and turned bright red when I came into the women's room. In the excruciating silence that followed, it was plainly obvious that I had been the subject of their conversation. Since that particular room is rarely anything other than the venue for gossip of a scandalous kind (the venue for office politics, I discovered, was the nearest pub) I knew the jig was up at that moment.

My new assistant then started smiling at me. She had never done it before in her miserable British way though I thought I'd been perfectly pleasant to her in my classic American way. Now, as the internal phone shrilled with the insistent manner of a fire alarm, she looked at me with new eyes – a mixture of sympathy and condescension. Now I wasn't just the American bitch with the manners of a man who had spread fear and loathing and P45s, as they call pink slips in the UK. I was a woman in love which made me human, hence the sympathy, but also vulnerable for the first time, hence the condescension.

I knew I was in love because I didn't care. I didn't care that these snooty secretaries looked down on me from their lofty perches behind the Tampax dispenser. I didn't care that Jack McGinty was now bringing his Jack Daniels or whatever it was into the office and hiding it in the filing cabinet as if I would never know or if I found out he had 'something' on me.

Previously I would have taken this as a flagrant disregard of my importance and have bawled him out in front of the whole office. Now I just asked him for a shot at the end of the working day and suggested that in future if he wanted one he came to my office after six thirty when most of the workers had left. I knew he'd never do it and he'd go back to the pub as he had always done in the past but I achieved what I wanted without the need for bad feelings or public executions. And it felt good.

Falling in love with Ralph Warren made me better at my job while making me care less deeply about it. I had been in love before, with Charles certainly, but it was a different kind of love – a hard, almost competitive kind of love and remorseless consumption of each other, it had an intensity which I had always supposed love to demand.

Not with Ralph, though. He was no less of a man than Charles, and in many ways, as a more rounded individual, you could argue that he was more of a man. His talents as I got to know them were just as impressive. He could write anything and he could lead the life of a domestic housewife without losing a jot of his mental sharpness. Plus he was an amazing father.

I knew how difficult life as a single parent could be because I had watched my mom struggle so hard for so long. I guess that's why I had never given much thought to motherhood. Charles would never leave his family and I didn't see myself as a single parent failing my kid and failing in my career. I had toyed with the idea of carrying his child, though not because I wanted children. As I explained before, I wasn't the maternal type. But I had wanted that power – to extract his seed and grow something inside me that would contain just enough of him that I could control. Somehow, in my mind, that might have redressed the imbalance of power between us.

But when it came down to the grim reality of single parenting I never even made it to first base, as Ralph would say – struck out, flied out, grounded out, I never showed the slightest inclination to set off along that ninety feet long line. (You can't work on magazines like *US Sports Today* for long without assimilating their language.)

There was just so much to *do*. Danny was twelve and in many ways I guess he was more responsible than many kids of his age simply because he had been used to helping his dad around the house. But still the sheer volume of stuff necessary to raise a kid and run a house blew my mind. It wasn't just getting him up in the morning because he was quite capable of sleeping through the sound of the alarm clock going off on the shelf over his bed and then making sure he had brushed his teeth before turning the bedroom light off at night. Spending time with Ralph and Danny made me realise that you could pass the whole day doing almost nothing but either thinking about his future welfare and planning for it or just keeping going now. It also made me realise my mom must have been some kind of a saint.

When he was at school I soon discovered that though this was the best time for Ralph to work, he still had things to do for Danny. By the time he got back from dropping him off, it was nearly nine thirty, and to pick him up at four he had to set off from the house just after three thirty. There was no yellow school bus which would have saved him an hour a day so the day, such as it was, didn't shape up remotely like any day I've ever worked. No wonder he kept looking at his watch during that first lunch.

Most weekends I went down to Cambridge. Danny (I thought) accepted me pretty quickly. I didn't think it was going to be that difficult. I just bought him stuff. There was that dinner at Pizza Express the first day and video games and CDs from new bands he hadn't heard of but had already made it big in LA and were on their way to Europe. Ralph said Danny couldn't be bought, that is, his affections couldn't be bought, but I soon found out different. They could be bought – it just depended how much you were prepared to spend.

He was a sweet kid, I soon saw that. I knew what Ralph was talking about that first time not so much because he was unlike every other twelve-year-old kid I've ever known (not many, I admit) but because he was like them but still retained this special bond with his dad. He had no problems hugging his dad, unlike I've noticed with a lot of kids — or rather I've noticed their fathers have a problem with that kind of physical intimacy, which makes the kids that much more self-conscious.

Ralph and Danny had no such problems. It wasn't that he came out of school and flung himself into his dad's arms but that they immediately slipped into a way of talking, a way of relating to each other, that was easy and familiar, not just parent and child, father and son, but also two old friends. It wasn't true all the time but I could see evidence of it often enough to be aware that it existed.

That summer was idyllic. Ralph and Danny liked to go to the Lake District region of north-west England. Since every time I look out the window it is either raining or just about to rain or just stopped raining I couldn't believe anyone would want to vacation in England voluntarily but apparently people do. I had to go back to the States on business after the World Cup finished in July but I arranged to take my last week of vacation with them in Keswick, a cute village in the Lake District.

Discreetly I booked a single room in the same hotel, some way away from them for appearances' sake so as not to embarrass Danny rather than to avoid whispers among the hotel staff. In my experience hotel staff see so much of the detritus of the human condition that nothing shocks them. Certainly not the prospect of two single people sharing a room. But this was Danny's special time with his dad and I wanted to make no waves. I wasn't sure they really wanted me to come but Ralph was insistent and Danny seemed to want me. At least I trusted that Ralph would be able to tell if there was a problem.

Considering the hours I work and my diet, I keep myself pretty fit. I belong to a gym but I don't go every morning from 6 a.m. to 7 a.m. and then into the office or anything stupid like that. Maybe on a Friday night after work I'll go and spend forty minutes or so on the Stairmaster, winding down and burning off some fat. My diet's maybe not the greatest but I'm not too crazy about red meat and I haven't got a sweet tooth so I manage to keep my shape.

So when Danny was telling me all about the mountains they climb in those parts I wasn't too worried. Of course when I called them mountains he was quick to correct me. Apparently the appropriate term is 'fells' which I'd never heard of. They decided because it was my first day on the fells they'd take me up something they called Bowfell which didn't sound too bad. It was less than three thousand feet to the summit and Danny had climbed it when he was nine years old so I was up for that.

Jesus! That was some climb. It was nothing like the fat-burning mode of the Stairmaster. It started off OK with a half-mile hike along a flat pebble-strewn path and through a farmyard. I kept looking a trifle nervously at the mountain, sorry fell, looming in front of us but I consoled myself with the prospect of little nine-year-old Danny leaping ahead and up to the top.

The two of them never stopped jabbering. The whole way up they talked about how magnificent the scenery was and how they could see all sorts of other mountains

with the weirdest names — Pike O'Blisco was one and
Coniston Old Man, which sounded like a song Paul
Robeson should have sung. Then the path gave out
completely.

'This is Esk Hause,' said Ralph. 'Over there's the Scafell
range and beyond is Pillar and Great Gable. They're my
two favourites.'

I said nothing, being incapable of speech. My calves
and the backs of my thighs were singing ('Climb ev'ry
mountain' it sure wasn't) and my lungs were bursting.
Sweat was pouring from my head down my face and
dropping off the end of my nose, splattering onto the
rocks. What made it worse was that Ralph and Danny
were carrying the backpacks. Ralph had the sandwiches
and drinks and the Ordnance Survey map, Danny's
contained my spare sweater. I couldn't imagine why I
should ever want a sweater. My whole body felt like it
had been heated up in a sauna. Except, oddly, my knees,
which were exposed because I was wearing shorts and felt
rather cold. I longed for the sauna, or more accurately a
swimming pool under the warm Californian sun and the
prospect of an iced drink on climbing out and lying on
a sun lounger. That was my idea of a holiday.

'It gets a bit harder till we get to the summit,' Ralph
said apologetically.

'You mean this isn't the goddamn summit?' I gasped.

'This is Esk Hause,' piped up the infuriating Danny.
'That's the summit up there.' He pointed towards Mount
Everest.

'I thought that was the next mountain.'

'Fell.'

'OK. Fell then.'

'Nope. That's the top of Bowfell.'

'Well, how many frigging mountains have we climbed today?'

'Fells.'

'How many fells?'

'We haven't climbed one yet. This is just Esk Hause.'

'If I hear that fucking name one more time—'

'You don't have to come to the top,' Ralph interjected quickly before the entire Lake District was submerged in blue. 'You can wait here if you like. We'll leave your sandwiches and drink and we'll pick you up on the descent.'

'Oh Dad, I thought we were going down the other side into Eskdale.'

'This is Helen's first time on the fells. We'll come back the same way and pick her up.'

'Oh no.' I breathed deeply. 'I'm coming up there with you. If you can do it so can I.' I set off in the lead, not looking back.

'Helen?'

'What?' I marched grimly on.

'I can help you.' Danny ran after me till he caught me up – a matter of some five or six yards. He looked at me earnestly although I had the faint niggling suspicion that he was making fun of me. 'I can put your earrings in my pocket.'

I stopped.

'They're long and dangly and they look heavy.'

Ralph was smiling broadly. I pretended to consider Danny's suggestion carefully then extracted the earrings and solemnly handed them over.

'What about your watch?'

My watch was a very expensive Rolex bought for me by my brother Michael when he was on United Nations business in Japan. I must have looked hesitant.

'I'll make sure he doesn't sell it before we get to the top,' said Ralph, still with that captivating smile on his face.

I unstrapped the watch and watched Danny put it carefully deep into his pocket.

'Feel lighter now?'

'Thanks! I feel like Flo Jo,' I shouted and sprinted ahead.

'Careful!' yelled Ralph. 'The next bit's the most difficult.'

Ralph was right. The climb to the summit was much tougher than anything we'd done so far. Soon I was faced with a huge rock buttress we had to scramble up. Frankly I was terrified.

'Shouldn't we have ropes or something?' I panted.

'No, no. That's for rock climbing.'

'Well, what the hell is all this?'

'This? This is just fell-walking.'

'I tell you one thing, Ralph Warren. I'm never going walking with you again. You don't know the meaning of the word.'

'I think you should just concentrate on where you're putting your feet.'

Even when we had climbed the sheer north face of

Mt McKinley, we still couldn't see the top. Or rather we could but the top we could see wasn't the top of Bowfell, as Danny took great delight in telling me. It was some kind of mirage because the real summit of Bowfell was two big climbs away. Now the cliff face was replaced by a series of large boulders on which even the tough climbing boots Ralph had hired for me from a store in Keswick didn't give me much of a grip.

I couldn't look around because it was too damn dangerous and because frankly I was angry. Not at them but at myself. I knew how much it meant to them and here I was acting like a Grade A grouch. In my defence all I could enter as evidence was the fact that I was exhausted and frightened and wished I'd never come. Somehow with Ralph occasionally guiding me over a particularly tricky series of loose rocks and even larger boulders and the sight of Danny steaming ahead towards the summit (I realised he had a lower centre of gravity and was a good twenty pounds lighter than I was even with my watch and earrings in his pocket), I managed to keep going.

'There it is. That's the top, over there by that pile of stones. Where those people are taking photos.'

I've heard some memorable phrases in my life. 'We'd like you to join the company at a starting salary of one hundred and twenty-five thousand dollars' was certainly one, as was, at an earlier date, 'I promise I'll take it out before I come', but no arrangement of words in the English language could possibly have been more gratifying at that moment. With a groan of release that would have done credit to the late John Holmes I flung myself onto the cool, welcoming grass, ignoring the jealous proximity of two aggressive sheep who, judging from my immediate surroundings, were having bowel problems.

St Paul experienced his enlightenment on the road to Damascus. I experienced mine on the top of Bowfell. For a full ten minutes I lay on my back gasping for breath, slowly feeling the agonising pain seep from my thighs and calves. My top, soaked with sweat, stuck to me as if it was Lycra. Then I felt the warmth of the afternoon sun caress my cheeks and a gentle breeze like the fan made by a giant palm frond being waved in front of my face dried my forehead. I sat up and looked around. Ralph and Danny were standing a few feet away looking at a map and pointing towards the horizon.

'Is that Scafell?' I asked.

'No, that's Mickledore. That's Scafell, the one behind.'

Danny slurped his drink carton through a straw and nodded in agreement.

I dragged myself across to join them, grasping Ralph's discreetly proferred hand. The squeeze that followed, I felt sure, meant more than a modest congratulation on my Herculean efforts. It seemed at that moment symbolic of an acknowledgement that this climb wasn't just to the summit of Bowfell but to a peak in our developing relationship. I returned the squeeze with interest then looked around me.

Only then did I fully comprehend the vista they were examining. Wherever you looked it was simply breathtaking. Mountains of different shapes and sizes but which all seemed to have special names and which

Ralph and Danny regarded as old friends surrounded us. The sunlight illuminated a valley with its myriad green fields enclosed by those ubiquitous dry-stone walls as if in a children's picture book. I felt as if we had climbed onto the roof of the world. It was like no other feeling I had ever known.

It wasn't just the range of mountain peaks which so overwhelmed me but the lakes which floated in the distance like huge white flags laid out on the ground for display. Windermere and Coniston Water were the two I could see but Ralph and Danny showed me the map and pointed to other lakes which were somewhere down there in the valleys, though I couldn't see them. I didn't want to know their names and I didn't want to talk to Ralph or Danny. I felt like I had been silently escorted to the most wonderful meal on earth, seated formally at a table for one, had a napkin unfolded onto my lap and a dish of great pictorial beauty and heavenly aroma placed in front of me. Before picking up my spoon I just wanted to absorb everything, inhaling before eagerly consuming.

For the first time I truly connected with both Ralph and Danny. Admittedly I had connected in a very basic way with Ralph some weeks before but there on the top of Bowfell I felt a genuine intimacy which no amount of sexual gymnastics could match. They had introduced me to a world I had never known, never thought about, had no wish ever to enter. I hugged Danny who, I thought, didn't object as many twelve-year-old kids might have done. Indeed he solemnly presented me with my own watch and earrings as if they were Olympic gold medals. I laughed and hugged him tighter. Then I did feel him tensing so I let him escape.

I turned to Ralph. I was a little hesitant because I didn't want to embarrass Danny. But I wanted Ralph to demonstrate more explicitly what the two of us meant to each other. I had entered his world as surely as he had entered my body that first night in Cambridge. My whole being cried out for him to recognise the fact and to deal with Danny's embarrassment (if that was what it would engender) later. He didn't fail me. The kiss he now imparted was not the kiss of a friend congratulating someone on a task successfully completed. It was not the kiss of a horny male who was turned on by the erotic possibilities of alfresco sex with the almost certain knowledge of public discovery. It was not even the kiss of a lover. It was the kiss of man who had found the woman who was to be his soul mate.

The kiss must have lasted all of three seconds but as Danny drifted away, drawn magnetically to the very edge of the summit from where he could look steeply down into what I later discovered was called the Langdale Valley, a party of noisy teenagers arrived, whooping with exultation at having made it to the top, and the spell was broken.

California has so many outstanding places of natural beauty that we kind of get tired of them or at least take them for granted. Instead Californians spend all their lives and all their money searching for inner peace and spiritual serenity. I don't know if any of them really do find it (as opposed to saying they do) but I know I found it for those few minutes on the top of a mountain called Bowfell in the north-west of England. But, I later asked myself, was it really the majestic beauty of the Lake District that made that moment so special or was it that for the first time in my life I was unutterably, indescribably, unbelievably, undoubtedly, incomparably head-over-heels in love?

CHAPTER EIGHTEEN

Ralph

I THOUGHT THERE WAS ONLY one way to be in love and that was the way it was between Angela and me. We met, we fell in love — correction, I fell in love with her — we made love, she dumped me for one brief millisecond of eternity, I hated her for the same amount of time, we found each other again, we definitely fell in love with each other, we got married and we had a baby. A deeply unoriginal scenario, I know, but one that dominated my whole life even twelve years after her death. I did not know whether it would ever be possible to fall in love again. On top of Bowfell I knew that it was.

I thought I remembered all those emotions — the joy that her presence could bring, the physical ecstasy that her touch could provoke — but I was wrong. It was all new again, nothing like what I had remembered. I was thirty-five years old, halfway through my allotted three score and ten, but I felt nineteen again. Not in the 'What the hell are all these spots doing here?' nineteen or the 'How am I going to get through the next week when all

I've got in the world is seventy-five pence?' nineteen but 'This world is a magical place' nineteen, and 'I have never been so happy in my life and this feeling will last for ever' nineteen.

I hadn't forgotten Angela and I could hardly have forgotten Danny but I was in love again and I wanted to shout it from the top of Bowfell. Instead, because I believe absolutely in the Right of Man to enjoy fell tops without having to stand in litter, I restricted myself to asking the kids politely to pick up their empty cans of Coke. They did so without the surliness that would surely have accompanied the request if it had been made at ground level. They, in their own way, were just as moved as we were by the splendour of the vista. Not even that prosaic conversation could puncture the euphoria that took possession of me.

On the descent Danny and I sang our way through our regular songbook (Beach Boys for me, Oasis for him) but the discovery that my darling beautiful new love had the worst voice on God's earth (as opposed to Angela, who, as you might suppose, sang divinely) perversely only increased my love for her. Even the sheep were put off and seemed to scatter, startled, baa-ing their dismay. I couldn't stop smiling. By the time we reached the car I felt that the man who had locked it up with great misgivings under a tree, attached to which was a notice proclaiming that car thieves operated in the area, had metamorphosed into an entirely new human being – a happy one.

Did I deserve such happiness? Was God playing a particularly cruel trick on me, I wondered, showing me the mirage of happiness only to snatch it away from under my nose? Was Helen real, real in the sense that she meant what she said? Were those signs which I interpreted as her having fallen in love with me also credible or was I just misreading the whole situation?

Such doubts consumed me as I lay in the bath surrounded by the pathetic bubbles stirred up by the complimentary shampoo and foam bath. The hot water, however, coaxed the ache from my weary limbs and the doubts were sucked down the drain with the dirty bath water. I towelled myself dry energetically and stood just for a moment naked in front of the three-quarter-length mirror, trying to look at my body through Helen's eyes. Was it OK? I wondered. Americans are sticklers for physical perfection and there were already signs of spider veins crawling up my thighs, a sensation of a fullness in the tummy area which almost certainly wasn't there last year.

Of course Danny chose this exact moment to race into the room to tell me that he had met a boy of his own age who had arrived from Manchester that afternoon. He discovered me examining my body with rare critical attention.

'What's up?' he asked anxiously.

'Groin strain,' I said offhandedly, making a grab for the towel which I had left annoyingly on a chair at the far side of the room. We hadn't seen each other naked for about three years. It was my way of giving him space to develop. I wanted him to feel comfortable about his own body changes. He'd let me know soon enough when he felt happy to resume our previous physical intimacy.

'I think I'll be fit for tomorrow,' I said as I draped the towel thankfully round my middle.

The food at dinner was excellent and to my great satisfaction Danny raced off after dessert with the boy who had just arrived from Manchester. They disappeared into the table tennis room, which left Helen and me the chance for a last walk under the stars as night closed in and the surrounding fells loomed even more menacingly in the gathering gloom.

Each night the hotel left on the doorknob of each room an order form for breakfast. You just had to fill in the blanks for fruit juice, cereal, cooked breakfast, etc. If Mother Nature had left something similar for me to request the evening climate of my dreams, I couldn't have arrived at a more perfect combination than the one provided that night.

All the anxieties which had attacked me in the bath seemed tiny and irrelevant beneath the stars and the sound of the lapwing and chaffinch. It was a still night in late summer, the first nip of autumn wouldn't be felt for a week or two yet and I doubted that a stroll on a Caribbean beach could produce a more congenial temperature. Helen's hand was clasped within mine, her perfume, fresh and delicate, intoxicated my senses and the warmth permeating from her body as I laid my arm across her shoulders and the way she turned her breast to press against me filled me with a confidence that simply banished those feeble-minded fears.

In the long grass beyond Keswick railway station we joined our bodies in warmth and security, to say nothing of pleasure. We had made love before of course, starting on that surprising first night in Cambridge, but nothing had prepared me for the amazing experience which now overwhelmed me.

I have always been a visual person and making love with the lights out always struck me as being almost entirely pointless. However politically incorrect it may be now to admit it, I have always loved women's bodies, constantly marvelled at the difference between the two sexes, devoured the look of the woman I was making love with as much as savouring her touch and feel. Now, in the almost total darkness and solitude of our love nest, I found something else to compensate for the inability to see Helen's body as I stripped it slowly of her clothes.

As I entered her I felt her spirit move towards me, an extraordinarily religious experience for a pronounced religious sceptic like myself. This wasn't just the physical union of two sexually aroused bodies but the emotional confluence of two beings in love. Now, I thought, now I will finally know the moment of coming together, but when I came it wasn't like that at all. Helen wasn't taking from me or giving herself to me, she was joining me.

The only way I can truly describe it is to conjure up those old movies at the moment when somebody dies and the spirit leaves the body and rises towards some kind of art director's vision of celestial paradise. Our bodies remained firmly interlocked on the ground but our spirits rose as one and wandered away together. It was such a perfect moment I doubted that it could ever be repeated.

I felt the hot pricking of tears forming in my eyes. By some miracle Helen must have felt the identical emotion for she held my face between her hands and slowly licked the salty tears from my eyes. Whatever she had previously done with her mouth and tongue, there could be no more intimate moment ever.

The weeks which followed that sublime experience confirmed that I was starting to live again. Not live as in earning a living and picking up the dry cleaning. I mean live as in opening up again to a range of emotions I had not known for twelve years.

It wasn't as if the pattern of my life underwent a major change. I still had my job, Helen still had her job. I still had Danny and the routine of my life was still built around him. But everything to do with that routine was changed by the way I felt. When I woke up in the morning I no longer had that awful, vague, unsatisfactory, empty feeling in the pit of my stomach. Instead the day was a field of unlimited possibilities. Would she call? Or rather, when would she call, because Helen seemed to have a telephone grafted onto one ear.

Every time the phone rang, a tremor of excitement passed through me. I tried hard to keep the note of disappointment out of my voice whenever it wasn't her, just as I tried to control it when I heard her soft musical tones. Occasionally, I would spring out of my chair when I was sitting at the computer keyboard because I heard the sound of a diesel engine and a car idling loudly. To me that always meant a taxi and a taxi might mean Helen had impulsively leaped onto the train again, grabbed a cab at the station and come to see me because she could stay away no longer. Constant frustrations never lessened the thrill of anticipation the next time round.

Even the certain knowledge that she was on a plane to Berlin or Paris or in a business meeting in central London failed to stem the romantic daydream that she would be able to stand it no longer and dash from her meeting muttering some lame excuse simply because she had found the need to lie naked in my arms too overwhelming to resist.

Is this not just the last word in revolting juvenile lovesickness, the sort of thing you tolerate at sixteen but you feel should be over by the age of eighteen? Possibly, but then who says teenagers don't feel their passions as deeply as their elders and not necessarily betters? We smile at them because their passions don't usually last but we shouldn't forget that they are no less deeply felt despite their short-lived nature.

When I turned Danny's light out at night I would think that the stage was now set for the next seduction and even if she hadn't arrived like a genie out of a bottle, I was certain that when the phone went at 11.15 p.m. it had to be her. In addition I had the freedom to call her last thing at night too so that if I couldn't have the comforting physical presence of her body in my bed I had the means of communicating my desire to her in words. I believe the operative phrase is 'talking dirty' and Helen had a first-class honours degree in the subject.

Just the thought of her and our future life together now made me happy. I was more patient with Danny, more resilient when interviews fell down or the car didn't start, more tolerant of all of life's many imperfections. It's a shame you can't bottle the sensation and sell it. Far more effective than cocaine or heroin or ecstasy, the buzz you get from falling in love lasts longer and gives you a bigger high than the conventional hard drugs.

It wasn't too difficult to convince myself that I had been blessed with the love of two amazingly talented, beautiful women and a truly wonderful son so I didn't have the right to expect any more out of life. Most people on this earth would willingly settle for less.

Such thoughts were idly running round my head as I sat at my desk one morning when the fax machine started to spew out the details of Mike Tyson's arrival in Britain. He was coming over to fight the latest of our home-grown heavyweight horizontals in yet another last desperate attempt to regain his former crown and glory. A press conference was being arranged for noon the following day at his training camp.

Noon is my favourite time for a press conference because I can usually get back home by four o'clock to meet Danny after school. And thank God it was tomorrow not today because today was Danny's big school game and I promised him faithfully I'd be there as always even though he was unlikely to do anything other than sit on the bench as usual. Just as I was looking up the train timetable, the doorbell rang. I wandered to the front door reading the fax as I went.

I had imagined the moment so many times in my daydreams yet I was completely flummoxed when it happened. There stood Helen, a smile creasing her face for a second before she threw herself into my arms. I kissed her and held her before I could bring myself to inquire the reason for her visit. She stood aside in the doorway and pointed to the shiny new BMW parked illegally in a Residents Only bay. I looked askance.

'One of our lifestyle magazines,' she explained. 'We get to test drive the car and stay overnight at a country house hotel built exclusively for honeymooners.'

I must have been very slow on the uptake.

'We're the honeymooners. Thought we could use an all-expenses-paid rehearsal.'

'I thought you were a high-flying executive not a journalist.'

'And I thought you were a journalist.'

'You mean I have to fuck you and then write about it?'

'What's wrong? Worried you can't do me justice?'

'Not worried about you. I'm just not a big fan of BMWs. Why couldn't you find a Mercedes?'

She laughed and nudged me inside, kicking the front door closed with her trailing leg, pushing me, not exactly unwillingly, into the lounge until I fell backwards onto the couch. She dropped her coat onto the floor like a stripper and proceeded to disrobe slowly in a mesmerising performance that convinced me she had missed her calling and that Soho was a lesser place for her absence.

'Well,' she said afterwards, 'I hope the BMW gives a ride of similar style and comfort.'

'I doubt,' I said, fondling her breasts, 'that the upholstery will provide such agreeable support.'

'My God, it goes from zero to sixty quicker than anything I've ever seen,' she marvelled, stroking my new erection with professional admiration.

'It's all down to what's under the bonnet,' I replied, gently easing her thighs apart.

'The bonnet?' she wondered. 'Oh, you mean the hood!' She ran her fingers delicately round the tip of the foreskin. I rolled on top of her, gently inserting myself.

'Luxury every time you ride,' I proclaimed as her muscles tightened around me.

'Cut the crap and fuck me,' she said, sucking my tongue into her mouth and grasping both buttocks, pulling me against her as hard as she could.

I must have been out of my mind. Well I was out of my mind. I knew I was. We were halfway to our country house hotel before I realised that I had forgotten about Danny and the school match. The school was playing one of its closest rivals and though Danny wasn't in the team he wanted me to come as usual and watch so we could work out how he could win his place back in the starting line-up.

I picked up the mobile phone and made a couple of calls. Elaine Kirk, who knew something was happening in my life and was deeply frustrated by my unwillingness to tell her precisely what, kindly agreed to pick Danny up after the match and bring him home to stay the night. I had never been away from Danny without telling him exactly where I was going to be but as Helen pointed out, he was twelve years old and he'd been staying with the Kirks on and off for most of that time.

I wasn't so sure. Danny and I both liked the security of our routine together. I had always tried so hard to keep things on an even keel for him. Just as I had when he was a baby and I came home without his mother, my first priority was always to create a happy and stable home environment for him. I played down Helen's significance, rarely mentioned her name, redoubled my efforts to help him distinguish between the French verbs which take 'être' and those which take 'avoir'. Either I was not very good at this dissembling game or Danny was even more perceptive than I gave him credit for but I knew in my heart that he knew I was in love.

Since we had returned from the Lake District I had made a point of spending one night a week if possible in London. I tried to settle on the same night each week so that again Danny would feel secure within a new routine but there was no point in staying away from the house if Helen was going to be in Rome or Paris so in the end the routine was never possible.

Elaine is the mother of Jamie, Danny's best friend, and usually he's quite keen to go there because the Kirks have a big house in Millington Road off Barton Road, a lovely part of town, and with a big garden the two boys can play football in. Jamie also has, I am reliably informed, an enviably cool collection of computer games which Danny tells me about in great detail and with the implicit understanding that it is about time I distinguished myself as a father by building up a rival collection.

When I first started to stay in town with Helen for my 'staff conferences', Danny seemed quiet and rather depressed when I returned. I asked Elaine if he'd been all right and she always seemed to think he had but after the fourth time I was surprised to discover that Danny wanted to stay at home by himself in the future. Of course I said he couldn't and sent him back to the Kirks the following week but it started to bug me. Why, I wondered, did he suddenly want to stop at home by himself when he had that big house and garden and game collection at the Kirks?

Answer came there none except a slight anxiety that either he knew what was going on and wanted somehow to punish me or he was up to something and wanted the house to himself to do it. Drink? Drugs? Sex? They went racing through my head like a corporation bus over the speed bumps but despite intense scrutiny I could find no evidence to support any one of those theories.

This time, though, I thought that maybe the whole thing was a product of my own too fevered imagination. Danny was twelve going on thirteen, the dreaded puberty. There was no point in worrying about him. He'd come out the other side OK and surely the best thing I could do was to show him the wonders of being in love. If I was sublimely happy myself, which I was, surely that happiness would transmit itself to him.

The journey to the south coast was wonderful. It was one of those bright autumn days when the English countryside can be at its most captivating. It wasn't as it could be in the full bloom of a hot midsummer's day but it was a last poetic reminder of the eternal promise it always held before the onset of winter frosts and rain.

As we neared our destination and the light faded rapidly, a soft mist rose from the fallow fields and bathed the rolling vista in a paler shade of grey. The Mozart clarinet concerto gave out its sublime slow movement from the CD player, the hot air from the floor-level vent of the temperature-controlled car interior gently massaged my toes, and Helen's left hand strayed from the steering wheel to find my own and squeezed it with such love and tenderness it sent a shiver of prickly heat up my spine. I didn't deserve such happiness. Something must surely go badly wrong soon.

'I love you, Helen.'

She turned the radio off. The silence that replaced the Mozart was deafening. She turned to look at me. 'I know. I love you, too.'

My heart was pounding. I meant it and she meant it. I wanted to say something, something that would seal the moment. My head pulsated as I sought in vain for the right words. I looked at Helen. She smiled. No words were necessary.

The hotel itself was almost an irrelevance. It was luxurious in both appointments and tariff but we decided not to eat in the Michelin one-star restaurant with half a dozen other couples who actually were on their honeymoon because we felt somewhat fraudulent. Instead we booked ourselves into the nearest restaurant with a good review in the guide book Helen had thoughtfully brought with her.

I called beforehand to make sure they didn't mind if I wasn't wearing a tie. In the haste of our departure from Cambridge that was one of the items I had forgotten to pack. The voice on the telephone was a little hesitant but graciously conceded that a tie wouldn't be necessary that night. As we turned into the car park, there was only one other car there.

'That must be the chef,' smiled Helen.

She was right. It *was* the chef's car. In a restaurant which seated somewhere between sixty and a hundred people, we were the sole guests.

After the initial embarrassment the waitress and the chef, under stern American interrogation, finally broke down and confessed that they were not only the joint owners of the establishment but they were recently married. In the end, in return for a feature in the magazine, they cooked four different dishes which we passed round as if we were in a Chinese restaurant. They were all delicious although in the heightened state of my existence I might have said the same about a tin of baked beans.

'I think I'm too full to make love,' said Helen when we got back to the hotel.

'I hope that is a deliberately provocative remark.'

'Good heavens, Mr Warren,' she said, batting her eyelashes at me furiously, 'do I understand that you have designs on my virtue?'

'Your virtue went out the window when you were seventeen years old, you shameless hussy,' I growled. 'Now come over here before I come over there.'

'But I'm only sixteen—'

I stopped her mouth with a kiss that would only come to a halt when one of us was forced to suck in air. She blinked — a small triumph for the superior male lung capacity.

I woke with a start at quarter to eight the following morning, suddenly conscious that I hadn't thought about Danny for about fifteen hours. It was the longest stretch of time I had experienced since the day he was born. There was something nagging at the back of my mind, something I had forgotten to do for Danny or with Danny but my brain was still dozy and I couldn't remember what.

Besides, I thought gratefully as I sank back into the warmth emanating from Helen's curled-up naked body, if there was an emergency he has my mobile number. He or Elaine would surely have called. But they hadn't. So I might as well just lie back and think of California.

A hand snaked out from the ostensibly sleeping California Girl next to me and sought evidence of my attention span. There was no point trying to pretend anything other than that I was in love with this woman. My body was giving both of us the clearest possible sign.

She turned over to face me. She smiled. 'Oh, you must love me a lot.'

'As it so happens I love you even more than that.'

'How much?'

'This much.' I grinned, waving myself at her and attempting to separate her thighs.

'Now, Ralph, I know you love me. It is possible to express your love for me in a non-sexual way.'

'You're absolutely right, Helen, it's appallingly phallo-centric of me. You'll have to forgive my innate male chauvinist piggery.'

'I'm not sure I can. I'd be letting down the sister-hood.'

'You have a problem with that?'

'Of course I do. I'm unmarried and nearly thirty.'

'Well, I have a bigger problem.'

'What's that?'

'I have a raging hard-on and unless you help me do something about it, the top of my head will explode and shoot off into space, orbiting the earth every sixty-three minutes.'

She laughed, lay back and like the best patient in the world opened wide and said, 'Aaah.'

CHAPTER NINETEEN

Danny

HE MISSED IT. THAT SODDING woman comes along and he's not there. It was all her fault. He'd never missed a game the whole term. Now she comes along and suddenly he's too busy with her, he's got no time for me. Well, no, I know that's not entirely fair but it's the way I was feeling. Especially afterwards.

I left for school that morning with my football things because it was games that afternoon and those of us who weren't in the school Under-13 team had to play house matches between ourselves. I had been bitterly disappointed since the start of term that I hadn't been picked for the school team this year. Last year I was top scorer but this year some new kids had joined and though I didn't think they were any better than I was I could see that they were bigger. And when you're twelve and you've got the strength of a fourteen-year-old the teacher in charge always seems to favour you. So I was dropped.

I asked Dad to make me bigger but he didn't want to.

I said I should do some weight training but he thought I was too young. Then I said perhaps I should have lots of steak because I'd heard that helps to develop the body but Dad doesn't like us to eat red meat since the BSE thing came out a few years ago and in any case he pointed out that the fashion in sports teams today is for pasta and things like that which don't increase your body weight but allow you to run harder for longer. I didn't fancy eating nothing but spaghetti seven nights a week so I knocked that one on the head too and I remained out of the school team.

The night before a game I would always pray to God to give Mark Leonard or Ollie Church, our two strikers, some terrible disease but nothing ever happened. Until that day. I got to school and we had registration and Ollie Church wasn't there. My heart leaped. I hoped desperately that he had got some horrible ailment, mumps or chickenpox or something, that would keep him off games for the rest of the term. I tried to catch Mr Banks's eye during assembly and went out of my way during break to saunter casually past him but he totally blanked me.

I supposed he had rung up Ollie's mum and found out that Ollie was coming in after lunch. He didn't have a dentist's appointment or anything like that because I had already checked with his mates. None of them knew why he wasn't in school. By lunchtime I had given up and resigned myself to playing in the house match and scoring half a dozen meaningless goals against some fatso speccy four-eyed goalie. It wasn't till we were back in our form rooms for afternoon registration that our form master made the stunning announcement. I was to report to the main changing room at three o'clock because I was playing for the school that afternoon. Yes!!!

It was the most important thing anyone had said to me for years and years and yet the master just thought it was meaningless because two seconds later it was 'Get your Latin text books out and turn to page sixty-two' — third declension nouns or some other pointless drivel. But I was in! I was back in the team for the big one, the big local derby match against our hated rivals, St Bede's School.

I had no time to tell Dad, nor any need to really, because when I left home that day he had promised to come and watch and he always kept his promises. But as we ran onto the pitch he wasn't among the group of parents on the halfway line. I kept looking beyond the pitch onto the main road during the warm-up, searching for a man in a car, on a bike, in a taxi, racing towards us, but there was nothing. I was gutted. It wasn't the same if Dad wasn't there to share it with me. Still, he'd come in the end. I knew Dad.

We kicked off and I was soon struggling. It was so different from the crappy standard I had become used to playing in regular house matches. The defenders I was up against were big strong lads and I was getting kicked on the back of my legs before I even received the ball. I kept looking at our sports teacher Mr Banks, who was the referee, but he didn't see anything wrong, he never gave me a single free kick. After twenty minutes I was tired and couldn't run until I had a bit of a breather. The big lads marking me reckoned they had kicked me out of the game and spent all their time on Mark Leonard who had nearly scored once or twice.

Then it happened. From a corner on the right Mark jumped for the ball. The two big lads went with him and the ball cannoned off one of them against the post and before the goalkeeper could drop on it I managed to get there first and stab it into the net. I felt like Michael Owen, like Pelé, like the greatest player in the history of the world. I ran all over the field (I suddenly got my second wind I suppose) until my team-mates caught up with me and jumped on me in celebration. I picked myself up, grinning like an idiot and looked round for Dad again but all I could see was Elaine Kirk, Jamie's mum, jumping up and down and smiling at me. I ran over to her.

'Where's Dad?'

'He can't come. You're coming home with me.'

I was stunned. He can't come? I stood there, rooted to the spot till Mr Banks came running over to me.

'Come on, Warren. Get on with the game.'

I drifted back to the centre circle. Much of the joy had gone out of me. I was just gutted Dad wasn't there. What the hell could ever have made him miss it? He never missed a match. Then I knew. He was with that woman.

Just before half time they equalised. It was a blatant push on our goalie but Mr Banks, leaning over backwards to be fair to the opposition, I suppose, awarded the goal, not a free kick to us. At half time he seemed to single me out for blame, telling me to work harder and pull their defenders out of position and to track back and help the defence when the opposition controlled the ball. I nodded. I was too knackered to protest.

The second half kicked off and still I couldn't get Dad out of my mind. Well, it was obvious now that I was less important to him than that bloody woman. I hated her. And I hated that horrible defender. After ten minutes of the second half when I'd got bruises all up the back of both legs and I'd been pushed and shoved every time the ball came anywhere near me, I lost it.

One of our centre backs got the ball and because we'd been told to try and play good football by passing it around, he just whacked it over the top of their defence for the umpteenth time for me to run on to. This hulking brute of a defender was pulling my shirt and tapping my ankles as we raced for the bouncing ball. He also called me 'a fucking Mummy's boy' which I thought was a bit rich in the circumstances. The red mist came down and I just let him have it. Only it was dead pathetic. I wanted to get free from him, so I tried to elbow him off. I made the slightest contact with his body, somewhere around his shoulder I think, but suddenly he went down like he'd been shot by a bullet.

The referee, Mr Banks, was back in the centre circle and we were running towards the corner flag so he couldn't see anything apart from the bully rolling over and over, holding his face though I never touched him anywhere near his face. Mr Banks came tearing over to me looking like I'd just killed Nelson Mandela.

'I saw that, Warren. There was no provocation. Off you go. Foul play.'

'You're sending me off?' I couldn't believe my ears.

'Of course I am, boy.'

'I never touched him.'

'Then what's he doing down there?'

'He's play-acting. Just like on *Match of the Day*!'

'We don't play schools who cheat.'

The opposing team's sports teacher was helping the bully to his feet. Amazingly the bully found he was able to continue.

'I am very disappointed in you, Warren. Get changed and go home. I want to see you before assembly tomorrow.'

The walk back to the changing room was the longest, most miserable walk in history. I knew now what David Beckham must have felt like when he got sent off playing for England in the World Cup. I was ashamed and embarrassed obviously but also I was angry because I didn't deserve it, not the way I looked at it. And then my dad wasn't there and I had to go home with Jamie's mum and Jamie would spend the whole night teasing me. I wish I really had elbowed that bully in the face and broken his nose. But the person I really felt like killing was Helen. If she hadn't made Dad walk out on me I wouldn't have lost my temper like that. It was because he wasn't there that I just gave up and elbowed that boy. It was all Helen's fault, the bitch.

I knew I wouldn't play for the school team again. Ollie would be back next week probably but even if he wasn't,

Mr Banks wouldn't pick me again, not this term anyway, maybe not ever. That would be my punishment. Jamie seemed to delight in spelling it all out for me because neither of us could get to sleep that night.

I hadn't told Dad but I hadn't been getting on with Jamie Kirk for quite a few months now. In fact I really hadn't told Dad much of anything since we got back from that holiday in the Lakes. I was in my second year now at secondary school and I thought the work would all be getting easier but it wasn't.

Jamie came with me from Grantchester Street Primary but even though we'd been really close friends there, by the time we got to the new school the friendship didn't mean as much as it did before. I hated staying the night with him because he wanted to talk about stupid things — about bums and girls' things and stuff like that after lights out and it made me feel uncomfortable.

Dad thought he was doing me this big, big favour letting me stay the night with Jamie but I thought if I told him the truth he wouldn't understand or he'd get upset or worried so I just said I'd like to stay in the house by myself instead. I couldn't see why not. I would be thirteen on my next birthday and Dad had always trusted me to do things round the house like putting the dishes away and leaving out the note for the milkman. I could stay by myself for the occasional night. I'd just lock the door and not answer if the bell rang. I could put the telephone answering machine on all the time and just pick it up if it was someone I knew. What could be safer?

To me it all sounded dead logical but Dad insisted that I had to stay with Jamie. So I started to blame Helen for things even before that disastrous school game because I knew that's why he wasn't paying attention to me any more. He never said anything and I didn't either but I knew.

At first I was sorry in a way that I was starting to feel like this about Helen because a) Dad liked her and I think she made him happy and b) she was always OK with me.

I wasn't too sure about Helen till she struggled her way up Bowfell, taking off her earrings and her watch which I just suggested as a joke. Plus I liked the way she moved and the way she spoke. It was dead American. She talked fast and with a funny upward twist of her voice at the end, a bit like Monica in *Friends*. She never talked down to me and she didn't do what lots of grown-ups do — be dead nice while you're alone with them in the room then when Dad comes in just blank you, sometimes in the middle of a sentence. I always thought Helen enjoyed talking to me. And in a way it was exciting when she was there. Her mobile was always ringing. People rang the house to ask to speak to her. She could talk a lot on her phone, very fast and serious and sort of threatening a bit sometimes, then she'd switch it off and we'd pick up the conversation exactly where she'd left it.

I didn't think she was drop dead gorgeous or anything like Rachel or Phoebe but I could see why Dad liked her. She was slim with dark curly hair and she had a nice shape. I looked at the girls our age and I thought they'd never grow into women like Helen. Maybe it was because she was American. She was so quick and light on her feet, like a cat. And she was real, too, not like Claudia Schiffer or Kate Moss. Sometimes she kissed me good night and then I could smell her perfume, the way I thought I remembered Mum's, but instead of being warm and comforted as I was by the memory of Mum I was confused and sort of excited by Helen in a way that made me feel very mixed up.

Once she bent over me to kiss me good night when a couple of buttons on her shirt were undone and I saw all the way down to the start of her titties. When she left the room I couldn't get to sleep for ages so I turned on the light and read for hours till I got sleepy. I didn't forget that night for a long time, especially the smell of her and the sight of those things. I wanted to touch them to see what they felt like but I knew I shouldn't and I could hardly ask permission.

So when Jamie started talking about girls and women and their bodies in a rude way I was disgusted. I thought of Helen and that wasn't the way I wanted to think of her. You could talk about some of the slags we saw on the bus or in the shopping centre in that rude way but we didn't know them so it made it easier. Except Jamie is just rude and nothing else, so that's the main reason why I didn't like staying overnight with him.

I was having problems adjusting to Helen's presence but I couldn't talk to Dad about it. That was an odd feeling, too, because we had always talked about everything till then. Dad tried to start the conversation once by explaining how he felt about Helen and how she wasn't supposed to be a mum to me and wouldn't want to be but he liked her a lot and did I mind? Well, what could I say? The moment he started I knew what he was going to say and it made me squirm with embarrassment. What I wanted to say was, 'OK, Dad, but could you ask her if I could see her naked as well?'

If I told Dad about that night ... well, I couldn't, there was no chance, no way was I going to do that. If I said that everything was OK then he'd take that as meaning he had my approval to do anything he wanted with her. I couldn't talk to Helen about these feelings because although I supposed I fancied her I didn't really feel I knew her and who knows how long she'd stay around anyway and besides she belonged to Dad. But I wanted to. I thought she might be sympathetic and tell me things that Dad couldn't – because she was a woman and because she wasn't my mum. But I didn't have the courage, though I did dream about it sometimes. They were nice dreams.

It was so difficult, so confusing, I just didn't know how to behave to Helen or to Dad so I sort of resented them both, particularly Helen who had come into our lives and messed them up. I was angry that she had stirred up something inside me but I couldn't tell anybody about it and all these feelings about her and her body and other girls and the whisperings and jokes of the older boys which I pretended to understand but didn't really, it all just left me frustrated.

That was how it was when they both buggered off and left me to face the worst crisis of my life alone. I stopped having those lustful thoughts about Helen then all right.

She was just as much to blame as I was for me being sent off and banned from the team. So I decided I was going to make her suffer just like I was suffering.

CHAPTER TWENTY

Helen

OH GOD, OH GOD, OH GOD! It was just what I didn't mean
to happen. Here I was doing something fun with the guy
I had fallen in love with and the net result was complete
disaster. Damn it!

It had been the best time. The BMW, the look on
Ralph's face, the warmth coursing through my body, the
hotel, the bed, the cute restaurant, waking up next day
and still wanting him. It all convinced me that here was
the man I had been waiting for all my life. I looked back
at myself at college in New York and as a rising executive
at Waverley Bros. Inc. and in the throes of a passionate
affair with one of the great moguls of the American press
and I thought it was utterly bizarre that I should find true
happiness with an anonymous British journalist, a single
parent with a twelve-year-old kid.

Yet I don't think I had ever been happier. I hadn't lost
my ambition, I didn't suddenly want to give it all up and
become a mommy and housewife. I just knew for sure
that Ralph Warren and I were destined to be together in

a way I had never felt about Charles Schmidt and me. I guess I was just acting out a part with Charles: female, smart, savvy, sexy exec. type, slim, thirty, into Mozart, Bacharach, books, movies and *Seinfeld*, wants to meet male, fiftyish, greying, distinguished, powerful, wealthy, sexually attractive and experienced — already married not a problem if marriage is already in trouble. I posted the personal ad. Charles was the first to reply.

But now I had everything. Ralph's love made me complete in a way that the key to the executive washroom could never do. I didn't even mind taking on Danny because he was twelve, nearly a teenager. He had his own friends, he seemed well adjusted, at least he didn't look like he'd be the classic problem adolescent. I took great comfort in the fact that he had such a good relationship with his dad. In fact they had such a great domestic routine it didn't need me to do anything except stay out of the way.

That's what I thought I was doing when I drove up to Cambridge in that softly purring BMW. It was a school day so if Danny was looked after overnight as I knew he was when Ralph stayed with me occasionally, we could have our dirty 'weekend', get back the following afternoon and nothing would have happened to shake their precious routine. The first half went without a hitch and we drove back from the south coast replete as any two lovers could be who had made love four times in twenty-four hours with a level of pleasure that never diminished from the all-time high where it started.

I dropped Ralph off at King's Cross at lunchtime,

parked the car at the office so the BMW could be picked up by the showroom and then sped across town in a black cab to an Italian restaurant in Chelsea for a meeting with some of the finance guys. I had no idea anything might have been wrong at Cambridge and when I got back to the office around four I didn't bother to call Ralph because I knew that he'd be busy picking up Danny after school and doing stuff with him for the next few hours.

Then the phone calls from the East Coast started so I didn't get the chance to make contact with Ralph till around eleven o'clock at night. It was hardly unusual and I was looking forward to one of our bedtime chats. Ralph spends a lot of time at home in front of his computer, probably more than is strictly healthy, so I find that he has a highly but pleasantly developed sexual imagination. I hope there's no one at the phone company recording our late-night communications. Ralph threatened to tape one and see if he couldn't sell it to one of those telephone sex chat lines.

When he picked up the phone I was hoping he'd be in the same still highly charged state of euphoria that I was, but his first 'hello' was enough to warn me that something had happened. Apparently Danny was almost monosyllabic after school and wouldn't talk to him about the game, so he rang the woman who usually picks Danny up after school when Ralph can't be there and got the full story. I guess he was expelled from the game for something, Ralph wasn't exactly clear, and though I know a fair amount about soccer, especially seeing as how it's taking off in the US and Bill Clinton won his re-election thanks to America's soccer moms, the ins and outs of the game are still a little unclear.

What I soon gathered was that something had gone disastrously wrong for the kid and he was mad at Ralph for not being there and Ralph was beating up on himself because he wasn't there. I was torn. On the one hand I was sympathetic. This was the man I was in love with and he was suffering, and his kid was really important to him, so of course I wanted them both to be happy again immediately. Yet I couldn't help thinking at the same time that I didn't see why Ralph should apologise to Danny or himself for going away for the night. Danny was twelve years old, not two. Ralph had sacrificed himself for eleven years for the kid; wasn't he entitled to a little happiness too? Stand your ground, Ralph, I wanted to say but I couldn't.

I couldn't because I quickly figured that at the root of it all was me. I was the reason that Danny was mad at Ralph and I sure didn't intend getting in the middle. Much as I wanted to knock Danny's head against the wall and tell him not to be so goddamn selfish, I knew that wasn't possible. We were moving into new territory here, all of us. If Ralph and I were going to make a go of it, something was going to have to give, we'd all have to adapt, all three of us. I knew that wasn't what Ralph wanted to hear that night. He wanted sympathy and love and no questioning and no judgement calls. That's what I gave him and I felt he put the phone down happier than when he had picked it up. Unlike me.

I couldn't sleep that night. My body temperature

fluctuated from the very cold to the scalding hot. I kicked the bedcovers off, then hauled them back again. At one point I thought I might be menopausal twenty years early since I seemed to be exhibiting so many of the symptoms. I flipped on the light, read a while but I couldn't concentrate. The memory of Ralph and what he had done to my body less than twenty-four hours previously kept me tingling. I turned on the TV and found the World Series but it was a pitcher's duel so nobody batted in a run, nobody even got on base. The ball was being fouled off and the count was run full and then the batter hit a feeble ground ball and we were into the next set of commercials.

Besides, the baseball reminded me of *US Sport Today* and that reminded me of Ralph so I got out of bed, grabbed my robe and sat at the desk in the living room trying to work on some financial projections. It was hopeless. Was this what true love did to you? Even when I was at the height of passion with Charles I never had any problems concentrating on work. If anything it made me work harder because I was always so anxious to impress Charles with the high standard of my professional work. If I'd turned into a lovey-dovey cutie pie, I'd have been out on my ass. But now the figures just swam before my eyes. I couldn't get Ralph out of my head.

Next day, driving to work, I thought I saw him in the street. I thought, he's come racing up to London by the first train just to be with me and he hasn't told me because he wants to surprise me just like I surprised him with the car and the hotel booking. But he was walking the other way and I had to make a huge U-turn to the sound of angry car horns to which I responded with a well-used middle finger in the upright position.

'Swivel on that, buddy!' I yelled in true New York tradition. But by the time I had raced back down the road, Ralph had disappeared. I turned left and right, hoping for a glimpse of him again but it had either been a mirage or my Ralph had turned into someone else's house. Sadly, I resumed my journey to work.

I called him at ten o'clock. I decided that I wouldn't be helping him if I mirrored his feelings of panic and despair. I had to remain calm and add a sense of perspective. This was easier said than done because when I did call I found him very down, almost despairing of the possibility of reconciling his love for Danny with his love for me. This made me mad.

Charles wouldn't have been like this, I couldn't help thinking. This was a side of Ralph I hadn't really seen before and I wasn't too crazy about it. I don't mind sensitive men but I don't much care for weak men and what Ralph was demonstrating right now was a weakness I couldn't stand. It really got my dander up.

'Ralph, you can't give in to Danny every time he sulks.'

'He's not a great sulker.'

'Well, he's sulking now.'

'He's hurting now.'

'You want us to break up? You think that's the solution?'

'Of course not.'

'You want us to have a break then?'

'How do you mean?'

'See other people for a while.'

'How can you say that? You know how much I love you.'

'Then tell him you have a life too.'

'It's not that easy.'

'It sure is. You just say that, in those exact words. If he runs upstairs and slams the bedroom door, he's going through what the experts call "adolescence". If there's a real problem he can talk it out with you.'

There was a deathly pause. I knew I had pushed him between a rock and a hard place. I was making him choose between his son and his new lover. Well, this was crunch time. If he ran away from me now I'd try my hardest to walk out of his life and castigate him for being too weak to fight for me. A split second later I realised that I loved him and I did not want Ralph Warren out of my life. Please say the right thing, Ralph, please!

'You know what?'

'What?' The world stopped spinning on its axis. Only my head was spinning. I wondered if this was how OJ felt when the verdict was being read out. The suspense kills everyone from the moment the jury files back into the courtroom. I remembered how the woman who read out the verdict couldn't say the name 'Orenthal', OJ's first name.

All this flashed through my mind before Ralph took the two seconds he needed to say, 'You're absolutely right.'

Not guilty! I thought. Now I *did* know how OJ felt.

CHAPTER TWENTY-ONE

Ralph

I HANDLED IT BADLY, NO QUESTION. It was a mistake not ringing Danny that night. It wouldn't have taken long though it might have spoiled the mood in the bedroom but then I shouldn't have spilled everything out to Helen. It wasn't her fault. She had behaved really well with Danny, she was always friendly without being overbearing, and I knew Danny liked her.

I was trying my best to have it all, I suppose — the love of this new woman and the love of my son. They were both important to me. I needed my son to love me as he always had and I needed Helen to love me as she had shown she could. Other men in my position must surely have achieved something similar. Why was it so bloody difficult for me?

It was Helen who brought me to my senses. I was entitled to my own life. I was being too soft on Danny who probably was behaving like a spoiled self-centred teenager. My only defence is that he wasn't technically a teenager yet and he had never done anything like this before. The reason we had such a special relationship was that though we were father and son, we were also best friends. There was nothing he couldn't talk to me about but in the last few months, since I'd met Helen, I suppose, he had stopped confiding in me.

Well, three or four years ago he'd also stopped wanting me to give him his bath, which was fine. It meant he was growing up. Maybe this manifestation of teenage behaviour was just another indication that he was maturing. It was Helen who pointed it out to me but when I confronted Danny as she had suggested, he didn't exactly apologise for his behaviour though he did start to calm down.

It was an awkward forty-eight hours, that was for sure. I tried to reassure him about the sending off. I told him I'd be happy to go and see Mr Banks and plead for leniency. After all, it was entirely out of character for Danny to go around elbowing defenders; I can hardly remember him ever conceding a foul before. It would certainly be unfair if he were banned from competing for a place in the school team but I accepted Danny's plea for me to stay out of it. He was nearly thirteen, he said, he had to look after himself now. It wouldn't help the perception of him at school if his daddy were seen to be protecting him quite so proactively. I took that as the evidence I needed that he was maturing so I backed off.

Helen was wonderful. She counselled me through this difficult period and I appreciated her ability to look at the position objectively. Thank God, too, she didn't shy away from a fraught family situation. I couldn't have blamed her had she decided to stay in London but she didn't and I took that as evidence that we had a future together. It wasn't just sex, though that was wonderful and totally fulfilling. It was love and for that recognition I thanked God as well as her. I hadn't realised how much I had withdrawn into myself since Angela's death, how unwilling I had been to expose any part of me to further hurt. I just wanted to love her and to have her love me.

The next weekend the three of us all went to watch Tottenham Hotspur together. Helen and I had decided that it was best if we carried on as we meant to continue. If Danny's bad temper, which by now was all I thought it was, was going to improve, it had to do so when he was confronted by the two of us behaving as a couple. All right, he had got himself sent off which was both unfair and humiliating, and all right, I hadn't told him I was going away, but I was in love with Helen and she was going to be a feature of our lives for a long time to come so he had better get used to it. As a reward I took both of them to the Spurs v. Arsenal derby match.

There were two important debutants at White Hart Lane that day. It was Helen's first visit to my spiritual home and it was George Graham's first match as the new Spurs manager, in a re-match against his old team. I was supposed to observe the game from the press box but I decided to buy tickets and watch with the other two from seats high up in the main stand but over the corner flag.

There were problems from the start.

The first was the quality of the football, or rather the

lack of it. It was a typically attritional encounter between bitter local rivals, albeit each team was leavened by exotic Frenchmen, Dutchmen and assorted Scandinavians whose acquaintance with the history and inflated importance of these matches was nonexistent. Fouls stifled the flow and despite a lot of frenetic activity, neither side created a worthwhile chance.

Before the kick-off, Helen had donated her American enthusiasm to the cause.

'OK, guys, which is our team?'

'The ones in white.'

She leaped to her feet with everyone else as the two teams emerged from the tunnel together, shouting as raucously as she could. Danny and I smiled at each other. This was going to be fun, we thought, but I had, not for the first time, misjudged the American desire for everything to be clear cut. There were no goals and no real chances. Although Danny and I revelled in the tension of the closely fought encounter, it soon became obvious that Helen was bored. And cold.

I sat between her and Danny, wretchedly torn between empathising with Helen's discomfort and being totally wrapped up in the importance of securing a win by fair means or foul over the hated enemy from the far end of the Seven Sisters Road. Every time I stood up to shout the traditional abuse at the Arsenal players and fans, I became conscious that I was widening the gap between Helen and myself. She stood up with us a few times but American sport doesn't really operate on the same hate-filled lines that powers British football and

I could see she was disenchanted by the genuine hatred and loathing for Arsenal that the crowd around us was demonstrating.

She couldn't wait for the half-time whistle and I ushered her quickly into the queue for the hot drinks. Not quickly enough, though. By the time we had manoeuvred our way out of our seats, up the aisle and into the refreshment area at the rear of the stand, there must have been fifty people in front of us. Their demands were being met by two pimply adolescents. By the time a distinctive roar greeted the teams as they reappeared for the second half, there were still twenty or thirty people between us and the sanctuary offered by a plastic cup of hot chocolate.

Helen sent us back to our seats. She was quite happy to continue waiting out of range of that vicious easterly wind and the negative football.

'She's not enjoying it, is she?' Danny was clearly taking some pleasure in her discomfort. I wanted to hit him.

'Well, unless you're an Arsenal or Spurs fan, nobody would.'

'I don't know why she came.'

I wanted to tell him that she came because she was a grown-up who was doing something nice to make him feel part of a family but at that very moment Armstrong burst free with the Arsenal goal at his mercy but pulled his shot tamely wide. After that sharp burst of adrenaline I couldn't find the anger to get into a row with Danny about Helen's presence even though I could sense he was pushing me that way.

Well, I wasn't going to give him the satisfaction. All right, I had brought Helen along in an attempt to fuse some solidarity into a special occasion for the two of us but if it hadn't worked, so be it. It was their loss.

It was nearly twenty minutes into the second half before Helen reappeared with the drinks.

'Hi! I'm sorry it took so long.'

'I was beginning to get worried about you.'

'I went for a walk.'

'Where?'

'As far as I could until I got to a locked gate.'

'Good idea. You've missed nothing here.'

'What about Armstrong's shot?' demanded Danny.

'That's what I mean. She's missed nothing. Like Armstrong and Iversen have missed everything.'

There was an awkward silence.

'What time does the game finish?'

'About ten to five,' I replied.

'Plus injury time,' added Danny sadistically.

'Do people ever leave early because they're freezing to death?'

'Only part-time supporters.'

'Shut up, Danny. Look, if you want to go, they will let you out. There's an exit down those stairs over there.'

'No, that's OK. I'll wait with you.'

'It's just that I have to file my report.'

'Offside!'

Put through by Petit, Bergkamp had left Campbell for dead and was bearing down on the Spurs goal when the referee's whistle shrilled and he stopped abruptly.

'What's offside?' asked Helen innocently.

Danny grinned. He knew how difficult the offside laws were to explain so he volunteered to do it. I let him because it seemed the easiest alternative. Of course he then gabbled them out in such a deliberately obtuse way that even I didn't understand them. He was trying to make Helen feel like a mental incompetent.

I felt frustrated. What I saw as my unselfish efforts were being undermined by Danny who knew how to wind me up. I decided I'd give him some of his own medicine and see how he liked it so, as we finally left the ground after a stultifying 0-0 draw, I insisted that Helen come and stay with us in Cambridge the following weekend and I didn't care what Danny said or thought. She accepted in the same spirit of belligerence.

There are no hills round Cambridge. It's in the middle of the flattest part of the country, the Fenlands, so we weren't going to be able to recreate the happiness we had all found fell-walking in the Lake District. However, it does have the river flowing through it and the walk along the towpath watching the college crews racing their boats is always a pretty sight.

I took Helen there on the Saturday afternoon. Offered the chance to join us, Danny looked as if he would prefer to throw himself into the river rather than walk passively with us along it. There was always the chance that one of his friends might see him and, besides, he was in some deep way still annoyed with Helen for existing and causing me to miss that school game. Instead he scuttled off into town to join his mates at the video game store. Helen and

I smiled at each other conspiratorially. What a shame! We would just have to go on our own.

We had intended to walk along the river bank only as far as Magdalene Bridge but it was such a beautiful bright autumnal afternoon that we decided we would walk a little further. In the end we walked about three or four miles all the way into Grantchester.

'Is this the honey place?'

'Pooh Bear?' I asked, not sure what kind of literary allusion this might be. Silly me. She always knew what she was talking about.

'No, stupid. "Is there honey still for tea?" Rupert Brooke and all that romantic poetry crap.'

'Oh, sorry, sure, this is the place. There's the church clock.'

'It says twenty after four.'

'That's because it's four twenty.'

'Isn't it supposed to be ten of three? "Stands the church clock at ten of three and is there honey still for tea?"'

'Ten *to* three, actually.'

'Pedant!'

'Harlot!' Her hand was unzipping me in the expectation of discovering my true interest in romantic poetry.

'Stop that immediately,' I murmured into her ear with my tongue. 'I'll have you know that no less a literary figure than Lord Jeffrey Archer of Crappola lives in that very house and if he sticks his head out of the window right now we are going to be the inspiration for another novel.'

'Well, this one might be good for a change,' she said,

withdrawing her tongue from the roof of my mouth for a moment.

'I for one am not prepared to take the risk,' I said, guiding her by the left bottom cheek into a coppice which offered partial obscurity from other Saturday afternoon walkers.

'Well?' she demanded afterwards. '*Is* there honey still for tea?'

'I think they're only open in the summer.'

We ambled down the road to the open-air tea garden, set in a now forlorn-looking apple orchard, which serves plastic teas for American tourists at inflated prices, but the owners had apparently retreated to Barbados for the winter with their tea bags and their synthetic creams, their store-bought scones and their plastic packeted honey and strawberry jam.

The village pub, however, to our delight was open and we managed a very satisfactory pint of Special for me and a cup of hot chocolate for her from a bemused landlord while we sat and watched the classified football results on a TV screen above the bar. Tottenham had managed a most unexpected 2–0 win against Manchester United at Old Trafford. That which God had brought together not even Alex Ferguson could rent asunder.

It was dark when we emerged so we took a taxi back into town. It was only when we were trying unsuccessfully to avoid feeling each other up on the back seat that I realised with a start I had walked all the way to Grantchester along the river and not once had I thought of Angela. So many times I had taken that walk in the past twelve years in the company of some woman or other and all that flashed through my mind constantly was, 'This was where Angela and I came, this was where we made love, this was where she told me she was pregnant with Danny, this was where I knelt in a cowpat (by mistake) when I begged her to marry me.' But now I was with Helen and I was so crazy for her she had succeeded in blotting out those fifteen-year-old memories. She just made me happy.

To formalise our rapture I asked the taxi to drop us off at the fish and chip shop where I impetuously bought three haddock and chips with pickled onions and mushy peas. It was a gastronomic sensation which evoked in me nothing but roars of laughter when I got home and found that Danny had raided the housekeeping jar (where I always keep two ten pound notes for him to use in an emergency) in order to buy three cod and chips with three pickled onions but no mushy peas.

'Isn't there a book called *The Cambridge Diet* or something?' I asked as I sprinkled liberal amounts of salt and vinegar over Helen's mound of chips.

'Yeah. Big seller in the States a few years back.'

'This is it,' I said, forking a huge piece of white fish into her mouth.

'I think that was Cambridge, Massachusetts, not Cambridge, England, and it involved eating only one sprout for ten days rather than two enormous portions of fish and chips every night.'

'You're quite wrong. Fish and chips contain most of

the protein and carbohydrates a body needs for healthy living.'

'Not in this quantity, surely?'

'This is the minimum quantity,' I said, swallowing heavily.

'And don't call him Shirley,' said Danny, attempting to join in the banter.

'Oh, I just love those *Naked Gun* movies,' said Helen, acquiring instant street cred.

'It's from *Airplane*,' said Danny, ever the pedant I had unwittingly raised him to be.

I basked in the warmth of my new family. We were getting on together so well. Danny had obviously had a good afternoon with his mates and I knew how exhilarated he would have been by the Spurs victory in Manchester. Helen belonged here now, she belonged with me, and Danny had thankfully, even if temporarily, abandoned his scorched earth campaign against her. Helen had been right all along. I just hadn't stood up to him properly, although I should say that I had always done so previously whenever I had needed to. I know she felt the same way. I could feel the warmth emanating from her like heat waves from an open-hearth fire. That's when she came up with the idea that we should all go away for Christmas.

CHAPTER TWENTY-TWO

Danny

WHEN HELEN ASKED IF WE wanted to go away for Christmas I thought she meant only one place.

'America?' I said immediately, because that's always been my dream to go there.

'Danny!' said Dad, annoyed, I don't know why. Helen looked a bit let down. So there it was. As usual, I'd only said one word and everyone was cross with me.

'I figured the Lake District. I really loved my time up there with you guys and I'd like to take you back there for two or three days over the holidays. My treat.'

I love the Lakes. So does Dad but neither of us said anything for a moment. So I said in a sort of small voice, 'For Christmas?'

'Sure.'

'But we always spend Christmas here. We've never stayed in a hotel before.'

'Doesn't mean you can't do it this year.'

'It would be great,' said Dad. 'Can you imagine climbing Skiddaw when it's covered in snow?'

'Is that another of those fells of yours?'

I smiled. 'It's over three thousand feet. Higher than Bowfell.' I waited for the response, the startled girly squawk, but it never came.

'Yeah. But is it tougher?'

Dad was looking at me so I had to tell the truth.

'No. It's not. It looks difficult from below but it's actually quite easy. I did it when I was seven.'

'I think I carried you the last five hundred feet.'

'Thanks, Dad.'

'Sounds cool. So what do you say, guys?'

'Are you sure, Helen? This is very generous.'

'But what about Christmas here, Dad? The Boxing Day matches and the Christmas pudding and everything.'

'Well, we can go and see Carlisle United if they're playing at home and I'm sure the hotel will serve turkey and Christmas pudding and all the things you like.'

'It won't be the same, though.'

'Might be better.'

'Doesn't Helen have to visit her mother at Christmas?'

'Well, usually I do but this year I'm spending New Year's with my mom and I thought it'd be kinda cool to have a real English Christmas with fog and carols and snow.'

'Don't you get that in America?'

'Not in California. We have Santas who wear a Santa costume coat and a pair of shorts. We don't get much in the way of snow on the West Coast.'

'But I've seen pictures on TV of New York in the winter and there's always a blizzard blowing.'

'In the East it's different. You can get buried in the stuff back East but in LA we have to buy the snow from special Christmas stores and, let me tell you, it's real expensive.'

'So what do we say to Helen, Danny?'

'Great.' There was a marked lack of enthusiasm in my voice but I don't think anyone noticed or if they did, they didn't care. I was beginning to get the feeling that Dad was insisting on sticking this woman down my throat whether I cared or not.

We left the day before Christmas Eve after we had loaded all our Christmas presents into the car but that was the last good thing that happened. We left a day early to avoid the rush but the traffic was still terrible and then the engine overheated. The needle on the water gauge shot up into the warning red bit at the top of the dial and we had to stop and call the AA and they took over two hours to come and then we had to wait some more before he could find a bottom hose to the radiator which had broken.

While we were waiting for the AA man to come back again with the replacement hose I discovered that I'd left my favourite Oasis tape at home but Dad wouldn't go back to get it even though we hadn't even got to Northampton and the M1 yet so that put me in a bad mood for a start. We usually take the M1 to Leeds and travel through the Yorkshire Dales to get to the Lake District, which is a really nice way in the summer when you can see the sheep in the fields and we can sit and have lunch in a pub garden.

This time we were late and we had to stay on the motorway the whole way there to make up time. So we had to have lunch in one of those horrible motorway service stations which are always so crowded and dirty and noisy, and you could tell Helen didn't like it and that made Dad unhappy too. So we decided just to buy sandwiches and drinks and eat them in the car which would have been OK but I put my can of Coke down for a second on the seat to change tapes in my Walkman and I accidentally knocked it over. I didn't notice immediately and it went everywhere, into the gear box and onto Helen's seat so she was sitting in it. Dad, who had been frazzled since we had to stop for the AA man, shouted at me for being careless as if I had meant to do it in the first place.

Even when we turned off the motorway and drove into the Lake District south of Windermere, it didn't get any better. The journey from Windermere to Keswick is my favourite journey in the whole world because it passes lots of different lakes on the way and the scenery is both spectacular and dead familiar so I feel like I'm coming home. As you get closer to Keswick the landscape changes again so that you can see the outline of Blencathra and I know we're nearly there. Dad and I get really excited just talking about what we can see and what's round the next bend.

But now it was about four thirty in the afternoon and it was two days after the shortest day of the year so it was dark and I couldn't see anything. Actually, I think the cloud was low and thick so if it had been light we probably couldn't have seen anything anyway but driving to Keswick with the car headlights on felt really strange and very disappointing.

It picked up a bit when we got to the hotel because there was a big Christmas tree in the lobby and the entrance was covered in lights. I knew we'd booked too late to get our usual room, the one with the alcove for Dad to read in while I watched TV after dinner, but it was on the top floor and I knew it would have a good view of Cat Bells and Maiden Moor in the morning.

Helen was booked into a single room next to our twin-bedded one which I thought was somehow significant. Four months previously she had been on the far side of the hotel looking out of the back onto Latrigg and Skiddaw. Now she was with us. I didn't mind but it was like something had happened between Helen and Dad but nobody had told me about it. Like they were engaged or something but they hadn't bothered telling me because I was only a kid.

It wasn't snowing when we woke up and for a moment I thought it was just a bit overcast. Then I saw the rain. It wasn't rain rain, if you see what I mean, nor rain like it bounces off the pavement or splatters against the windowpane so you know it's raining. It was more like a fine wet mist than a drizzle which is why it was almost invisible against the slate-grey sky and the bare trees which are usually in full bloom when we're here in the summer.

We went down for breakfast believing that it might stop and the clouds would roll away. In the summer when we had a bad day, that frequently happened and sometimes even if it was raining in the morning it could all change at lunchtime and you'd have blue skies and bright sunshine for a climb in the afternoon, with the added bonus that the wind had blown the haze away too so the views all around were as sharp as a pin.

After breakfast we walked into Keswick and bought the sandwiches and drinks as usual, which we packed in Dad's rucksack. He complained that with three people's lunches it was really heavy and he suggested I took it up the mountain and he took it down. I was quite keen to show I could do it but he said he was only joking. Since it wasn't funny I don't know why he bothered but then I thought I'll bet he was just showing off to Helen how strong he was and then I thought that if girls were really impressed by that she'd be a lot more impressed if I did it so I asked again and he said I couldn't, then I got cross and jealous all at the same time. I didn't want Dad to turn into a sort of rival but he was making it like that.

The misty rain had eased off when we were walking into town but by the time we got in the car to drive to Honister Pass, the rain had started again and this time it was much worse. The windscreen wipers were on all the time instead of just intermittently to clear the spray so we knew the rain was getting heavier.

We parked the car near the old slate mine at the foot of Green Gable. This was a much easier way to the top of Great Gable than walking from Seathwaite Farm up Sty Head Pass but Dad thought it was only fair to Helen and I didn't mind because I knew that it would be getting dark by four o'clock and I could see it was sensible for us not to get caught on a difficult descent by going up the long way.

When we got out of the car it was horrible. The wind whipped up into a gale and drove the rain into our faces. We could none of us talk because we were individually concentrating on putting one foot in front of the other. I knew it was hopeless. There was no way we were going to go up Gable like this and no point in it either because you couldn't see anything and the walk would be slippery and dangerous.

Dad was the first one to say it.

'This is pointless. I think we should go back.'

I said nothing. I wasn't going to be the one to wimp out. Let Dad do it. Let's see what Helen made of that.

'I'm up for it,' said Helen brightly, 'if you guys are.'

'Me too,' I said as the wind-driven rain lashed into our faces.

'Who would prefer a cup of hot chocolate and a Danish pastry?' said Dad.

'I think I vote for coffee and Danish but it's up to Danny.'

Oh yeah, like it's really going to make any difference what I say. I decided to be long-suffering and noble.

'I don't care.' It was supposed to be long-suffering and noble but I think it probably came out just petulant.

'OK. Danny's vote wins it.'

'And the great state of Wyoming casts all its votes for the next President of the United States — any guy who can provide a log fire and bowl of hot soup.'

I didn't understand what Helen was talking about but we turned round and there was an instant improvement because the wind drove the rain into our backs. So much for Christmas Eve.

I like Christmas Eve at home because there are always lots of good films on the telly and Dad and I would spend hours unpacking a big cardboard box stuffed full of special Christmas things which we decorated the house with — tumbling reindeers and jolly snowmen and things like that which we'd had all my life. There was even a video in the box of a *Pink Panther* Christmas special which I had loved when I was three and which I told Dad he could never record over, so he kept it in the box and I played it on Christmas Eve to get me into the Christmas mood. We didn't bring it because we didn't have a VCR in the hotel. I know it sounds silly but I really missed it.

After dinner I went off to my bedroom. There was nothing else to do really. There was going to be a quiz in the bar that Dad wanted to go to with Helen so he suggested if I didn't want to join them I should go off to the games room with 'the other kids'. Well, the other kids were like eight and nine years old. There was no one of my age, which was odd because usually there is when we come in the summer. I didn't want to play with them so I went back to find Dad. I like quizzes. Dad and me, we play quiz games all the time. I keep telling Dad he should go on *Countdown* or *Fifteen to One* and win a fortune, but when I got to the bar the quiz hadn't started yet and Dad and Helen weren't there. Instead I went back to our bedroom and watched *Escape to Victory* on telly.

When it got to the game itself, when Michael Caine and Stallone and the other prisoners of war have to play against a crack Nazi team who are supposed to be like the German World Cup side, I went downstairs to get Dad. He loves to see this film with Ossie Ardiles playing for the PoWs and he always makes jokes about what kind of a concentration camp would have Pelé and Ardiles and Bobby Moore and Mike Summerbee all in the same barracks and how Spurs should sign the lot of them up because even if they're all over fifty they're better than anyone George Graham can sign. Except Bobby Moore. He's dead now but Dad said he was the greatest even though he was only two years old himself when Moore won the World Cup with England.

I went down about half past nine but they still weren't in the bar even though the quiz was now going on. I just wanted Dad to come to the room and watch it with me and I wouldn't have minded Helen being with us because we could have explained to her why it was such a bad movie and teased her again about how Americans don't know anything about football; they don't even call it football, they call it 'soccer'. I would have started explaining the offside laws again and if she laughed that would be OK, that would make her a bit human, but if she didn't it wouldn't have mattered because it was all about me and Dad sharing the same outlook on the world, or at least on important things like films and football.

My stomach gave a lurch when I saw they weren't there because I knew now where they were instantly. They were in Helen's room and I knew what they were doing too. I didn't mind it so much at home though that might seem odd. I felt secure in my home but the hotel seemed strange to me at Christmas and Dad going into Helen's room and having sex with her as I knew he must be doing made me mad. I mean really mad. Hot tears welled up in my eyes though I didn't understand quite why I felt so strongly.

It shouldn't have been as bad as it had been when he missed the game against St Bede's School but it felt even worse. It was like when you scrape the skin off your knee and it bleeds, then it starts to heal and form a scab but if you fall off your bike and the scab gets torn off again before it's properly healed then it hurts worse than it did the first time. That's how it felt that Christmas Eve. One betrayal was bad enough but two betrayals and I wanted to lash out. Why does sex have to get in the way of everything?

If Helen was there on a Sunday morning at home I knew they must have had sex the previous night but it was over with and we could do things together on Sunday. Now they were at it in her bedroom, next door to me, and my mind was filled with horrible images of the two of them rolling over and over on top of each other. Crude, horrid images that made me want to puke. I went back to the bedroom and when Dad came in later I pretended to be asleep even though I wasn't. He kissed me on the cheek and I turned over in the bed to wipe the kiss off onto the pillow. He didn't see, though I wouldn't have cared if he had.

CHAPTER TWENTY-THREE

Helen

GOD, THAT WAS SUCH A dumb thing to do. Take them both to the Lake District, I mean. But I meant so well and they both said yes. I suppose I should have guessed, England being the 1970s backwater it is, that if it rains in that part of the country, there's nothing you can do about it. If only I'd gone back to see my mom over Christmas, which had been my first thought.

I suppose I should have learned from my mistake when I went to that freezing-cold soccer game with them both. No matter how hard Ralph tried to include me in their ritual, it was only too easy for Danny to remind me that I was an outsider. Still, I remembered what a great time we'd all had in the summer, how I felt my relationship with Ralph had deepened another notch because I'd been privileged to be initiated into one of the family's most hallowed traditions – like a sorority house haze. Maybe the Lake District magic would work again.

I'd squared things with my mom, told her the truth really about Ralph being a widower and Danny being a sweet kid who had grown up without a mother. I figured my mom wouldn't want to do anything to interrupt a possible shot at marriage and with Danny she had the attractive possibility of a ready-made grandchild. She was happy enough if I came for New Year's.

So that was the plan. I hadn't thought about the weather other than to imagine it might be like hiking up near Big Bear above Lake Arrowhead, which can be spectacular over Christmas. Charles rented a cabin for us there one year though we saw more of the cabin than we did of the Christmas-card countryside. The British are great at some things; don't push me too hard, nothing comes to mind right now except all the obvious baloney like the theatre and the TV, but they've a lot to learn about consumer welfare.

In the US if you went to a hotel over Christmas there'd be constant hoopla — costume parties, buffets, dances, that kind of stuff. In Keswick we got a pub quiz and an inedible Christmas lunch with massacred vegetables, turkey cooked to remove all the juice and a traditional fruit cake dessert smothered in brandy that I could feel shoot straight to my hips.

That wasn't why I felt so bad about the holiday though. It was the day after Christmas when it all turned really sour though Danny was kinda weird on Christmas Day itself. He just got out of bed the wrong side, his dad said when I asked him why he looked so miserable when he had a half-dozen presents to open.

A fleeting anxiety passed through me. I knew Ralph had been reluctant to go to bed with me on Christmas Eve in my room even though there was no way Danny could come in. There was much more chance of something like that happening in Cambridge but I guess sometimes the urge to express our love for each other was too strong to resist. It was certainly my idea to go up to my room. Ralph wanted to take part in the pub quiz – well, not so much take part in it as to win it, thereby demonstrating he had a brilliant mind and I should be flattered that he was showing such a strong interest in me.

'You don't need to do this any more.'

'Do what?'

'The primary courtship ritual. Beating your chest.'

'I don't want to beat my chest. I want to win the quiz.'

'You think if you know the capital of Peru this is going to make you more sexually attractive to me?'

'Is it?'

I smiled and shook my head. 'Let's just go upstairs.'

In the elevator he was unnaturally quiet.

'Should we steal one of the board games from the playroom? Then we could play strip Trivial Pursuit. Every time you get the right answer to one of the sport questions I could take one article of clothing off. What do you think?'

He didn't respond. 'I'm sorry. I was just thinking about Danny.'

'Could he wait five minutes?'

'Five minutes? I was thinking I could go on for nine or ten minutes this time.'

'I told you before, you don't need to beat your chest.'

'If you don't get that door open in the next two seconds it won't be my chest that I'll be beating.'

Afterwards we lay in each other's arms for the longest time, not saying anything. I find these moments as wonderfully satisfying as the frenetic activity which precedes them. Again I was curled up in the crook of his arm with my face nestling on his chest, inhaling the warmth and security of his smell. It was like the first time on the couch in his house in Cambridge. Every time I smelled it I wanted to smile. It was like some magic olfactory ingredient which no other man possessed. Maybe it was just love. This was what love, real love, smelled like.

That, however, was the high point and almost the last moment of innocent satisfaction we were destined to know. If it started going off the rails on Christmas Eve, 26 December, or Boxing Day as they engagingly call it in Britain for reasons no one has explained to my satisfaction, was the day it plunged over the bridge and down into the ravine.

I heard the sound of doom before I threw back the curtains, hoping against hope for a miracle – well, it was the right time of year. So baby Jesus was reborn in the hearts of millions of Christians all over the world but the rain was pelting against the window and I couldn't see more than a hundred feet in the direction of the big mountain out there whose name I kept forgetting but which sounded like 'skidding'.

Over breakfast we tried to make plans for the day though we all knew it was going to be hopeless. We turned on the TV for the weather forecast and saw nothing but little black clouds all over the country. Ralph felt it was important to take Danny out of the hotel, though if it had been me I'd have been just as happy watching TV or reading a book. But I guess when you're twelve years old you want to do things so Ralph decided to drive round the area looking for historic houses to visit.

I could have told him before we left that nothing would be open on 26 December but Ralph was convinced that because it was a holiday and lots of people like us had arrived in the area determined to enjoy themselves, all the tourist attractions would be open. I ventured the opinion that this was Britain and logic didn't have a great deal to do with it but Ralph wouldn't listen.

I was starting to become uncomfortably aware that Ralph, for all his many virtues, was a poor listener. Maybe it was all those years when his entire world was bound by Danny's needs and his own. I wondered if he was that way with Angela. So I put on my warmest coat and my thickest gloves and hoped for the best while fearing the worst.

We tried all sorts of places — ruined castles and abbeys, Wordsworth's house in Cockermouth, half a dozen historic manor houses with interesting histories and paintings and furniture — but all were closed for the holidays. The performance was always the same, a desperate examination of the tourist book, a frantic hopeful drive, a sinking feeling when there were only two cars in the car park, the frenzied scramble out of the car to put up the umbrella and shrug on our coats, the inevitable locked door and the sign saying 'Closed'.

Just before lunch we actually managed to find something that was open. It was some kind of a museum of local history. I was surprised to discover that I found it real interesting and on another day I'd have been fascinated by its re-creation of local houses with their bedrooms and living rooms and kitchens down the centuries, all furnished with local handmade items. Today, however, was not a good day for any of us.

Danny was restless, unhappy, scuffing his shoes a lot, dragging behind Ralph and me. He had wanted to have lunch as soon as we had arrived in the little coffee shop which was attached to the museum shop but Ralph told him we'd only just had breakfast and he'd have to wait till we'd finished in the museum. Danny's response was to ask for the car keys and when he came back he had his Walkman with him. He obviously planned to visit the museum plugged into his music. It wasn't a smart move. Ralph was trying, as ever, to keep both Danny and me happy. I was doing OK myself but because I was acutely sensitive to things going wrong with Danny I knew I had to stay clear of it.

We raced through the museum which was quite crowded as other families, too, had discovered this was the only open attraction in the whole of the Lake District. Ralph was constantly whispering loudly to Danny to turn the wretched Walkman off which Danny eventually did with obvious signs of long-suffering irritation. Ralph would ask Danny questions about the museum's exhibits in an attempt to get him to think and learn about what he was looking at, an intelligent way of stimulating a kid's interest, but Danny never took the bait even though I'd seen him do it willingly on many other similar occasions.

Thankfully we eventually reached the coffee shop where I ordered a cup of coffee and Danny asked for the chocolate cake that was on the menu. Unfortunately it was Boxing Day, the woman behind the till told him, and as they always baked fresh they hadn't got it today. He had to settle for a wrapped chocolate bar but you could tell that he was seething with this latest insult.

Danny rarely acted up in public and I was as surprised as Ralph as his performance continued to deteriorate. It burst into open warfare in the car on the way back to the hotel. At least we'd been out of the place for a few hours, thereby earning ourselves the reward of watching the James Bond movie on TV in the bedroom when we got back. Maybe Ralph wasn't so dumb after all. The day had been passed and we were more than ready for the comforts of the hotel. We were leaving the next day so maybe it would be a nice way to finish.

As the rain hammered into the windshield, Ralph began to talk to Danny in a voice of dangerous calm. I could hear him fighting for control.

'Danny, I'd like you to apologise for your behaviour in there.'

There was no reply. Danny was in thrall to Blur.

'Danny!' Ralph's voice rose sharply as he glanced in the rear-view mirror to see Danny's head lolling against the back seat.

Danny reluctantly removed the headphones again. 'What?'

'I said I want you to apologise.'

'For what?' Danny was outraged.

'For the way you behaved this morning.'

'What's wrong with the way I behaved this morning?'

'You were rude and discourteous.'

'Who to?'

'To Helen.'

Oh shit, don't get me involved in all of this.

'No I wasn't.'

'And to me.'

'How?'

'By wearing that stupid thing on your head when I was talking to you, by your attitude when that lady said there was no chocolate cake—'

'Well, it shouldn't have been on the menu.'

'You've been a pain in the neck for two days. Helen's given you this lovely treat—'

'Not me!'

'What?'

'She wants to be with you. She doesn't want to be with me.'

Oh Christ! Here it comes.

Ralph slammed on the brakes and the car screeched to a halt.

'Excuse us for a moment,' he said to me shortly, got out of the car, opened the back door and dragged Danny out. I watched them disappear into the mist and rain (without coats on) and prayed to be able to close my eyes and wake up in my mom's living room.

I could imagine the nature of the conversation so when they came back a few minutes later, wet and bedraggled the pair of them, I was not surprised to hear Danny's first words.

'I'm sorry if I was rude to you, Helen.'

It was spoken with all the conviction of President Clinton's first public apology for his 'improper' relationship with Monica Lewinsky.

'That's OK, Danny. It's just this miserable rain that's making everyone upset. How about we stop at one of your famous English pubs and we have a nice hot toddy?'

'The pubs are all shut, I'm afraid, like everything else,' said Ralph. 'At least till tonight, and even if they were open, hot toddies are found more easily in the pages of Dickens than in the pubs of Grasmere.'

We drove back to the hotel in silence. Danny, suitably chastened, fiddled with the Walkman for a long time before immersing himself in it, waiting for his dad to tell him he couldn't listen to it. But reprimand came there none and he retreated with gratitude into the comforting isolation offered by the headphones and the audio cassette.

By one of those strokes of irony with which the meteorological world is governed, we left the hotel the following morning in dazzling sunshine. You wouldn't call the temperature warm because the air was still bracing but the light was astonishing. You don't notice the quality of light so much in the cities but out there the mountains, sorry fells, seem to change colour as the sun's rays play on them, shifting their contours from soft to sharp. In other words it was exactly the weather we had all been hoping for when we left Cambridge.

The blue skies didn't do much to lift the depression that had settled over the three of us. If anything, the contemplation of what might have been made it all worse. As we drove out of the area we could see holidaymakers passing us coming the other way, clearly revelling in the prospect of a happy New Year. I wanted to let Ralph and Danny know that I did understand why this place meant so much to them even though the last three days had been so awful.

I cared about both of them. I knew they were upset, that something fundamental now seemed to divide them, and I knew it was in a way my fault but I was darned if I could see what I had done wrong. I wanted to apologise to them, to do anything to get the relationship between them back the way it had been before but I didn't know how to do it, other than by leaving. As the sun disappeared behind the grey clouds which loomed over us again, I was thinking more and more seriously that this was the only solution. Leave now, before I was sucked in irretrievably and all three lives went down the pan.

I had left my car outside their house in Cambridge and though Ralph wanted me to stay the night and Danny certainly raised no objections I figured it would be a mistake. They needed the time and space to talk to each other and my presence would only prolong their differences. Danny was on the phone to his friends two minutes after we walked in the door. I would think he was doing it for himself rather than us but obviously it gave Ralph and me the chance to be alone in the bedroom.

We sat on the bed, finding words difficult, whereas previously in this situation they had mostly been irrelevant.

'Do you think,' I ventured after a while, 'that he's got a crush on me?'

'What?' Ralph was genuinely surprised. I was slightly offended.

'It's possible.'

'He's twelve.'

'Exactly. He's twelve, he's not got a girlfriend of his own, has he?'

'Of course not.'

'So I'm here, I'm available, supposedly, he's got all these thoughts going through his head.'

'But you belong to me.'

'Oh thanks.'

'I'm sorry. That came out wrong. I mean we're not in competition for you.'

'Wouldn't that explain some of his behaviour?'

'He's mad because he thinks I'm spending more time with you than I am with him. I think you were right before. He's behaving badly and I've got to discipline him. It worked last time. It'll work again.'

'Sure?'

'Absolutely.'

'Ralph, I think I ought to go home now.'

'Back to London?'

'I'll feel easier. He'll feel easier.'

'But I'll feel harder . . .' He grabbed my hand but I withdrew it, though with a smile.

'I'll call you tonight. Late tonight.' I got off the bed and headed for the door.

'Wait.'

I stopped obediently. He turned me round, his hands on my shoulders as if I needed restraining.

'I think you're wonderful. I don't have the words to tell you how wonderful.'

'You got a thesaurus?'

'No. I got a . . .' And he dragged my hand towards his groin again.

'No!' I recovered my composure quickly. I just wasn't in the mood for being mauled. Ralph looked immediately contrite, like a naughty boy with his hand caught in the cookie jar.

'I'm so sorry, darling. I didn't mean . . .'

'I know.' This wasn't the time to rub his nose in it. 'I love you, Ralph. I just think a few days away from each other will give Danny and you time to work things out.'

'You *are* coming back?'

I blushed. Did he know what I had been thinking or was it just coincidence? He looked so anxious. My heart was bursting for love of him.

'You know I am.'

'I love you so much, Helen. I'd die if I lost you.'

'Ralph, you won't lose me. I'll always love you even if . . .' I couldn't finish the sentence because I couldn't, or rather didn't, want to express the anxieties that had been troubling me.

'If what? What do you mean if? Where's the if come from?' Now he looked frightened.

'If anything happened.'

'I've had a car crash destroy my life once. I couldn't deal with it again.'

'Not a car crash.'

'What then?'

Should I leave it alone or tell him? I did love him, he must know that, so maybe I owed it to our love to be honest with him.

'Ralph, I love you . . .'

'Why does that suddenly sound like a bad thing?'

'It isn't a bad thing. Our love is a wonderful thing, the best thing that has ever happened to me.'

'So why do I have this sinking feeling in the pit of my stomach?'

'Because you haven't eaten since lunch and it's nearly eight thirty and I have to go.'

'Helen!'

'What?'

'There's something bothering you.'

'It's nothing. Nothing that I haven't already said.'

'Please don't leave me. Stay here tonight. You can get up at six in the morning and drive back.'

He was getting needy. I always hated that in a man because I had trained myself so hard not to need anyone else. And then I thought that it was just another manifestation of love. He didn't need me for sex, great as our sex life was. He needed me because he loved me and I felt protected and cherished by it. I kissed him lightly but with as much feeling as I could impart. I pulled back and noticed his eyes filling with tears. This man meant so much to me but I wasn't going to be the one to come between him and Danny. I had to be strong for both of us.

'I'll call you later. I love you.'

Two days later Ralph insisted on coming to London to drive me the twenty-five miles to Heathrow Airport where I was catching a flight to Boston. I told him it was stupid, I could easily call a cab, it made no sense for him to drive two hours out of his way to take me on a half-hour journey. But I knew why he wanted to do it so badly. He needed to see me again, be with me, extract from me that promise of never-ending love which I wasn't sure I could give him.

Still, I insisted that he drop me off outside Terminal 3 and not leave the car in the short-stay multi-storey car park and come in with me. It was partly because I didn't trust myself to say the right thing in the departure terminal, nor did I want him following me like a lapdog all the way through check-in and up to passport control outside the departure lounge.

But if the truth were known I didn't want him to see me change my ticket from round trip to one way. I wasn't coming back. Not for a while. My mind was in a turmoil and had been since we'd left the Lake District. One minute I was sure we could work it out together, the next I was terrified I was going to end up ruining all our lives. Waverley was pleased with the way I'd handled the problems in the UK, so I knew they'd offer me something in California or New York. The night before I flew out I made the decision to separate — and then changed it twice more before morning.

Maybe it wasn't them, I kept thinking. Maybe it was me. I'd spent so long scrambling for my place in the sun it was hard for me to understand that love also means pain and sacrifice. I'd seen what happened to my mother. I grew up knowing I must never allow myself to be reliant on anyone except myself. Maybe I had to sacrifice the possibility of happiness with Ralph for the certainty that his relationship with Danny was always going to come first. He loved Danny and Danny loved him. Who was I to come between them? By the time we reached the freeway exit for Heathrow I felt sure it was the right decision simply because it hurt so much.

But what could I say to Ralph? How could I ever make him understand that I still loved him even though I was leaving him? Every time I said those words to myself they sounded more and more ridiculous. I was running away to save the possibility of a future relationship, but I doubted that Ralph would see it like that. He would be devastated. I knew how sensitive he was, how Angela's death had numbed his feelings for years. Now he had fallen in love all over again and I was going to break his heart a second time. It was what we call in negotiating 'a lose-lose situation'. It was just too crazy. I made the coward's decision. The drop-off zone outside Terminal 3 was not the place to start explaining my turmoil. For Christ's sake, I knew I was going to break his heart. Surely I could allow him a few more days of hope.

Was that so selfish of me? Was that really the coward's way out? Maybe things would be different once I'd left the country. Why burn bridges now when in a week's time I might see the way clear for all of us? I knew I loved him but maybe, sometimes, love isn't enough. We'd like to think it is because it seems to have an irresistible logic behind it. Ralph was a widower waiting to find love again. I was a single woman who had magically found love where I least expected it. We made each other happy. Surely that was enough to make the relationship work. But I knew in my heart it wasn't. It hurt me desperately to kiss Ralph goodbye and tell him blithely that I would see him in a week or so.

It was the first lie I had ever told him but I did love him, in fact I loved him so much I was even prepared to give him up. How could I possibly explain this convoluted piece of reasoning to him? I couldn't even try. My head was telling me I was making the sensible grown-up decision for both of us but as the wheels of the Boeing 767 left the tarmac I knew in my heart that even though I loved Ralph more than ever, Danny would always come first, so for all practical purposes it was over. When the seat belt sign was turned off and the airplane headed for the Atlantic Ocean, I burst into tears.

CHAPTER TWENTY-FOUR

Ralph

WHEN IT CAME IT WAS a bolt out of the blue. I suppose I should have seen it coming because there was all that trouble over Christmas but that was just Danny behaving like a twelve-year-old and I'd experienced his bad temper on many occasions. I didn't take it too seriously because that's what kids are like. Of course I was irritated with him, particularly since Helen had gone out of her way to be so generous and friendly. Then there was the funny mood Helen was in a few days before she left. But she kissed me as I loaded her case onto the trolley and told me she loved me. I remember her exact words. So when the call came I was shocked and then devastated.

It was almost exactly a week since she'd left and I was somewhat hurt that she hadn't bothered faxing or phoning but then I reckoned she was with her mother and maybe her mother wouldn't approve of the transatlantic phone call – it wasn't difficult to find reasons to rationalise the silence.

Sometimes when you pick up the phone, especially I

suppose when it's someone you love or someone you know really well, you can tell merely by the way they say hello or your name that there's trouble brewing. Such was my immediate sensation when I lifted the receiver that Thursday night to hear Helen's faltering voice. I never thought for a millisecond that maybe her mother was ill or that some other facet of her life unconnected to me was at the root of her distress. I knew that I was at the root of her distress.

I had never heard her so hesitant, so indecisive. One of the things that had always appealed to me about her was her clarity of thinking which allowed her to make fast decisions and stick to them. The voice which was preparing to give me the order of the boot was completely unlike her normal self. It didn't take me long to find out why. She claimed she was getting between Danny and myself and making everyone miserable. In vain I argued that she wasn't, that if there was a problem between Danny and me (which there wasn't) it was none of her making, but she didn't want to listen to a counter-argument.

I tried to calm her down, telling her there was no need for her to get upset, that when she came back at the weekend we could go out to dinner and talk it through.

'I'm not coming back.'

'Till when?' My heart sank. I knew exactly what she meant.

'Till like for ever.'

'What do you mean?'

'Just that. I'm staying here in the States. I'm moving back to Santa Barbara.'

I was too stunned to speak for a moment.

'Ralph? Are you still there?'

'Yes. I'm here. I don't understand. I mean why?'

'I told you. I'm making things worse between Danny and you.'

'No, you're not.'

'I am too.'

'But I love you.'

'And I love you.'

'So what the hell's going on?'

'Ralph, it will never work out. If I go now you'll be able to repair the damage quickly, get you and Danny back to the life you had before.'

'I don't want the life I had before. You're the best thing that's happened to my life in twelve years.'

'I'm not the one to replace Angela.'

'I don't want you to. I want you to be yourself.'

'Ralph, it's better this way.'

'Better for who?'

'For all of us.'

'Not for me.'

'Well then for Danny.'

'Danny likes you.'

'But he doesn't like me when I'm with you.'

'That's nonsense.'

'Ask him. Have you asked him?'

'I love you, Helen. I want to spend the rest of my life with you.'

'Ralph, please don't make it any harder for me.'

'This thing with Danny, he's twelve years old. We just have to give him time to adjust.'

'I saw how it was going to be when we went off to that honeymoon hotel and then again over Christmas. He wants you to be the dad he's grown up with. Go back and make him happy, Ralph. It'll make you happy as well. I can't.'

'But what about us?'

There was a pause while she searched for the right phrase. It came from *Casablanca*.

'We'll always have Bowfell.'

So that was it. She'd resigned the European job and was going back to work in Waverley's Los Angeles office. It meant she could commute from her house in Santa Barbara, which she'd scarcely seen for a year. She explained, too calmly I felt at the time, that it had all worked out perfectly for her because the lease had run out on 31 December and the agent hadn't yet rented it out for this year. Not perfect for me, that was for sure. And was it really perfect for her?

I put the phone down, numb with shock. I thought everything was going to be wonderful. She was exactly what I had always liked in a woman – bright, sharp, funny, independent, sexy. If we'd married, which I'd started to allow myself to think was the obvious culmination to the affair, I thought she would be the one woman I had ever met who would know how to deal with the Danny and the Angela situations. I could see a wonderful family life opening up for all of us, maybe one day with a new baby, a little sister or brother for Danny to look after. He'd be fourteen or fifteen years older so there wouldn't be any sibling rivalry. I know Danny, he's such a lovely kid, he'd be so pleased to be a big brother. I knew I'd deprived him of the chance so I was looking forward to nurturing that side of his character. And now it was all gone, with a single phone call.

I didn't say anything to Danny because there was no point. In one respect Helen was certainly right. The best thing I could do to repair the damage was to carry on as normal, which I did. He did ask when she was coming back so I told him the truth but not the reason why. I honestly didn't think it was Danny's fault, not really, and I didn't want him to blame himself.

Besides, I wasn't sure I agreed with Helen's diagnosis. Maybe she was the one frightened of commitment. Maybe I didn't earn enough for her, wasn't high flying enough for her, maybe she thought marrying me might set back her career. She had never said any of this obviously, never even implied it, but I was tortured with the reasons for her shocking decision and I wasn't prepared to accept the one she gave me so I searched desperately for others.

Over the next few days and weeks I tormented myself with such thoughts. On the face of it I was doing exactly the same things – telephoning, interviewing, writing and filing in my professional life, shopping, running the house, looking after Danny in my private life. I had done these things for almost as long as I could remember but whereas before Christmas I did them with a light heart, counting the hours till the next phone call or the next meeting, now I did them with a heavy heart, out of duty and necessity.

The only time I came alive during those days was when I played squash with Ian Walling who was a Fellow of St John's College. I had known Ian a long time and in the normal course of male relationships we never talked about anything that could be mistaken for emotional honesty. Our conversation ranged across the full spectrum of male obsessions – careers, sport, money, our children's progress at school, school fees, politics, college life – but though I counted him one of my closest friends, I knew no more of the reality of his marriage than he knew of the state of my affairs.

One Wednesday afternoon we were sipping some ghastly tasteless high-protein glucose drink after a hectic game of squash (which I lost 3-9, 9-6, 5-9, 3-9 to my great frustration) when Ian startled me by asking the sort of direct question we had assiduously avoided over the years.

'Is it over with Helen?'

'Why do you say that?'

'Because for the last four months you've never missed a chance to drone on about her.'

'Really?'

'You hadn't noticed?'

'No.'

'Trust me.'

'I don't know. She says it is.'

'How do you feel?'

'Like shit.'

'Well, that's the way you played today. I thought there was a reason. Other than spectacular incompetence on your part.'

I smiled. I hadn't done much of that for a couple of weeks. 'She says she can't make a go of it because of Danny.'

'What's wrong with Danny? He's great.'

'He's been a bit weird when Helen and I have been together.'

'Jealous?'

'Of what?'

'Of her.'

'I don't know.'

Ian looked surprised.

'No. Honestly. I don't know.'

'You must know. Danny tells you everything. He's the only kid I know who does tell his father everything.'

'We haven't talked. Not properly.'

'Since when?'

'Since the summer, I guess.'

'Since Helen moved into your life.'

'I thought that was coincidence.'

'Jesus, Ralph, I know you're a sports writer but you're quite a bright one. Surely even you—'

'All right, yes. I know what you're saying. I've just been unwilling to confront it. Besides, he is going through puberty, kids change. Their emotions are all screwed up.'

'Tell me about it.' Ian drained his drink with a grimace though whether it was due to the taste or the recollection of his own domestic problems was hard to tell. 'Do you love her?'

'Yes!'

'You sound amazingly sure for a man who has dithered in this area for twelve years.'

'But I love Danny too. Why the hell can't I reconcile these two great emotions?'

In professorial mode Ian sat back in his chair and thought for a long while. I felt sure he was going to come up with some pithy piece of advice. At length he stood up.

'How should I know? I can't even figure out how the video recorder works. Same time next week?'

I nodded. I was no nearer a solution.

Not only did I not talk to Danny about Helen but I tried hard to make sure he never noticed my depression. I thought I succeeded quite easily but then he was a twelve-year-old kid and the complexity and delicacy of adult inter-personal relationships were not something he was likely to spend much time thinking about. In fact, while he was around was the easiest time for me — the panics in the morning despite all the careful preparation for school which had taken place the previous night, and the homework, dinner, television scenario which followed after school tended to occupy me fully. It was only when he was at school or in bed and I was faced with a blank computer screen that I found the time dragged and my mind was filled with images of Helen.

One thing I did notice, though it didn't seem at the time to be significant. Although Helen had not yet driven the memory of Angela out of my head, she had certainly caused a certain amount of displacement. I suppose if I'm being honest now the obsession with Angela had been unhealthy, but I never saw that until after Helen had arrived in my life and I'd have denied it vehemently if I'd been asked about it before then. Helen had been totally phlegmatic about Angela, quite unfazed by the possible challenge the ubiquitous framed photographs posed to her. I felt with Helen that I could hold on to Angela in my heart without betraying her memory. Losing Helen so unexpectedly caused me to reassess what Angela now meant to me.

I had believed in an Elizabeth Barrett Browning sort of way that there was only one woman for me and that I had met her, married her and lost her to a homicidal driver outside Carmel, California. What stretched out in front of me like an empty dirt track reaching to the horizon was a life of full-time fatherhood interspersed with work which was periodically rewarding but frequently frustrating and the occasional appearance of a woman who would satisfy my carnal needs when they threatened to get out of control.

If you reversed the sexes, such a pattern of life would apply to millions of single parents who were women and it wouldn't cause the slightest comment. Obviously as single mothers the welfare of their children came first and to support their children they must find some sort of remunerative work or they would be forced into the state welfare poverty trap. From time to time a man would come along but for one reason or another it wouldn't work out. I felt somewhat freakish as a man but that was presumably because entrenched sexist attitudes weren't changing as fast as television commentators and newspaper columnists suggested they were. I couldn't help recalling the fact that I was the only father who picked up his kid outside school at three thirty on a regular basis when Danny was at primary school.

I never saw Helen as another Angela and I certainly never saw her as Danny's mother. If and when we married she would continue to have her own career; I couldn't conceive of her as a conventional mother like my own. In fact our lives wouldn't be so different from what they had been before Christmas except we would have the added security stemming from the fact that we knew we were committed to each other as a family. Helen was so utterly different from Angela, I didn't have any difficulty reconciling the previous Elizabeth Barrett Browning position with the recognition of the fact that I had fallen in love with another woman.

When I got over the shock of that initial telephone call I started to think that maybe it wasn't a shock. Maybe I knew that somehow I was unlovable and Helen's leaving had merely confirmed it. For years and years I had believed that the reason I hadn't found the right woman was that there was something wrong with the women I met. But there was nothing wrong with Helen and she had still run away. So maybe it wasn't those other women who were at fault. And it wasn't Danny either. It was me. I knew I hadn't been unlovable twelve years ago but maybe Angela's death, or rather my reaction to it, had made me so.

When I woke up now in the mornings, a heavy weight lay across my heart. It was a moment or two before I realised what had placed it there. Then it began. All those years of recovery since the death in Carmel melted away and I felt as wretched as the day the doctor looked at me with such sadness in his eyes as he drew the sheet over Angela's placid, oddly unmarked face. It was happening again. For the second time in my wretched ill-starred life a bleak and empty future stretched out in front of me.

CHAPTER TWENTY-FIVE

Danny

THE MOMENT DAD TOLD ME Helen wasn't coming back I felt really, really bad. It was so like something that happened at school a few weeks before. In the last week of term, just before we broke up for Christmas, games were cancelled because the football pitch was waterlogged and we had to do a cross-country run instead. I hate cross-country runs because I always get a stitch in my side which is really painful so I can't run and I always come in near the end with all the fatties and the saddoes and the losers. That means I get some terrible stick from the others who can't play football as well as I do but who are better runners.

Maybe I was just fed up with the teasing or maybe it was because it was the day before we broke up but I allowed myself to be persuaded by Darren Foxton and Will Stevens that we should hide in the bushes on the left of the path after it passes the outbuildings and then leap out when they all came back along the same track. That way we would only have to run half a mile instead of three and a half miles. Darren and Will wanted to do it because they wanted to smoke (not dope or anything) and I agreed though a little voice at the back of my brain said I shouldn't.

Unfortunately Piggy Harris, the master in charge, must have had inside information because when we stood up he was waiting for us ten yards away from the bushes. I always knew I shouldn't have agreed, and now here I was with my whole school career going down the drain. We knew we were going to get punished but what was worse was the sick feeling of not knowing how we'd be punished. We were just told it would be announced at general assembly the following morning when our scam would be revealed to the whole school.

I didn't want to tell Dad. He's got this ridiculously high opinion of me; he thinks I never get into trouble, which is true because I usually don't. So I couldn't tell him and I was desperately hoping he'd never find out. When I woke up in the morning I was almost sick to my stomach with anxiety. I could hardly complain, though, because we'd been caught bang to rights, as they say on *The Bill*. Going home that night one of the sixth-formers told me that he'd had the cane for doing what we did when he was in our class and how we were dead lucky that the school had abolished corporal punishment. I didn't feel dead lucky. Not then I didn't.

In the end we had two hours' detention after school had broken up, when we had to write a long essay on the theme of crime and punishment. It was dead boring but a bit of a relief because the horrible bit, the arrest and the waiting and the public humiliation were all gone. By the time next term started, no one would remember. Or so I hoped.

That sicky feeling in the pit of my stomach was how I felt again when Dad told me about Helen. It was my fault, I knew it was. I didn't say anything because I didn't know what to say. Dad didn't reproach me, he wasn't like Piggy Harris standing there with a clipboard, but my reaction was just the same only this time I couldn't see how I could make things right.

I wanted to tell Dad about the time I knew they were in Helen's room when I'd looked for them in the hotel bar but it didn't seem relevant any more. She was gone and though I felt wretched, I thought Dad would be able to cope. There had been women before who had come and gone, so I told myself that Helen was only the latest in the line but I knew deep down inside this wasn't so. Helen was special to Dad.

Life went back to what it had been before but every time I looked at Dad's face when he didn't know I was looking at him, I could see that he was miserable. The way he sat down in the armchair with a sort of whoosh, as if he had lost control of his body, or just the way he walked, which was sort of heavy, it was like he had suddenly put on ten kilos or something. But what made the whole thing clear to me was what happened after a famous football game about a month later.

At the end of January Spurs were drawn away at Ipswich in the fourth round of the FA Cup. Ipswich were a useful First Division side and we were in the Premiership but hardly setting the world alight so all the experts said it was going to be an awkward game for us. Ipswich probably fancied their chances against us. Although one of my first memories is of us winning the Cup final against Nottingham Forest in 1991, I haven't really got any other memories of famous Spurs triumphs to go with it. Still, the great thing about the new season in any sport is that we can all dream again, so after we had convincingly beaten the mighty Macclesfield Town at home 2–0 in the third round, we could see another Wembley appearance on the horizon.

Dad got the commission to cover the game for one of the Sunday papers so he would have to stay at the ground after the game was over to file his report. I didn't mind that because I usually got to eat all the leftover sandwiches in the press room and if I was lucky I could poke about a bit in the dressing rooms, maybe get an autograph or speak to one of the players.

This time I wasn't so lucky because the Spurs team was out of the players' entrance and onto their bus before I could persuade the commissionaire to let me down the stairs to the dressing rooms. I didn't care so much this time because we had won with a goal scored from a controversial penalty kick five minutes from the end of the game. Dad says we never get given decisions that favour us like that away from home so it was really wicked. Yes!!!

At the end of the game the players came over to where we were sitting and applauded us because we were applauding them. Usually people throw apple cores, coins and stuff at them because they've played like a bunch of soppy girls' blouses but this time everyone was happy so it was cool. In the car on the way home we listened to the radio to catch the final reports which always cheer us up even more and then, also as usual, Dad snapped off the radio when the man he calls 'that clown' who used to be a bad politician came on with the phone-in.

But all the way home he didn't speak. This is so unlike Dad, it really worried me. He's a fan at heart, like he brought me up to be, so it was weird him not speaking after we'd won this really difficult away match at Ipswich, and we'd be able to see it all over again on TV that night which usually doubles the pleasure. I made the odd comment about the players and the penalty and so on but he just grunted. He didn't say a word. About ten miles from Cambridge it hit me.

It had been a month since Helen had left, three weeks since the day I got that horrid feeling in my tummy. When I realised what was wrong I got the same feeling back again. It wasn't that I thought he was over it. The way he looked and walked in those unguarded moments told me he wasn't over her. But I didn't, till that moment, realise how bad it was for him. If he wasn't dead chuffed like me that Spurs had won this really difficult and important game, there was something very wrong with him. I didn't ask what because I knew and besides he wouldn't have told me anyway.

I grew up by about five years in those five minutes. As long as I can remember I wanted to be grown-up, wanted to be a sixth-former, not some little kid my dad always had to look after. Especially now because he was hurting so badly. It made me scream inside because it was my fault. I loved my dad so much, I had to do something about it. Since Mum died he had looked after me, loved me, taken care of me and helped me. Now it was time for me to do something for him.

I knew what it was I had to do to make things come out right but I couldn't think of how I could do it. It made my head spin. I was twelve years old and I was developing OK, I mean physically. I could probably pass myself off as fifteen under a baseball cap and wearing a baggy sweater and torn jeans but no way would anyone think I was older than that. I lay awake at night thinking desperately; by day I stared out of the window during lessons, willing myself to find a solution.

Then one school night we didn't get any French homework so after tea I watched TV and started flicking through the channels. On one of them was a film with Tom Hanks and that pretty blonde actress whose name I forget but who looks a bit like Mum looked just before she was killed. The film was called *Sleepless in Seattle*. By the time the film was over I knew how I could do it.

CHAPTER TWENTY-SIX

Ralph

I KNEW SOMETHING WAS WRONG almost as soon as he went back to school after the Christmas holidays. He was never a loud or particularly boisterous kid though he always made his presence felt at home. During January, however, his demeanour changed, not drastically but subtly. He no longer wanted me to test him on his homework which was unusual, but then I was so wrapped up in my own misery that I never bothered to inquire further. I kept seeing Helen wherever I went. I thought of her last thing at night and I woke up with a heavy heart when my conscious mind reminded me that I wouldn't be seeing her today – or any day soon. I had no spare strength for Danny. I needed to be alone with my misery.

One Monday lunchtime I got a call from Mrs Hargreaves, his form mistress, one of the few female teachers in the school. She was somewhat guarded on the phone, merely hinting that Danny's work was giving cause for concern and could I go into school to have a chat about it. I put on a jacket and tie and went in on the Wednesday.

I listened to her expressions of concern over Danny's recent waywardness but I wasn't exactly overwhelmed. For a start he was still only twelve years old and significant exams were three and a half years away, but the real reason I didn't react adversely to the news was that it only came as a confirmation of Danny's domestic behaviour. She tried to press me on what might be wrong at home but I wasn't keen to pursue the conversation down this track and besides, in teacher speak, there wasn't anything 'wrong' at home. My problems were my concern and I couldn't see how a discussion of the vacuum in my love life was going to help Danny's schoolwork.

I promised to talk to Danny and find out what the problem might be. I volunteered the fact that Danny had always struggled with his French irregular verbs but that still didn't explain his dip in recent weeks, which appeared also to have manifested itself in his maths and English lessons. I did mention that Danny had been growing that year, as boys rushing headlong into puberty are wont to do. We decided to shake hands and part on the understanding that it was hormonal and nothing else. I don't think she believed it either but it was a face-saving compromise.

I didn't even mention the meeting to Danny. I didn't want to start alarm bells ringing and I was anyway just too depressed by the loss of Helen. For the first time since Danny had been born, certainly the first time since Angela had been killed, I didn't put him first. His adolescent moods were making me cross and I just wanted to be back in Helen's arms, to feel her naked body against mine, to stroke her hair, to kiss her eyelids, to run my hands up and down the slim, soft, sensitive insides of her thighs. I didn't want a row about French verbs or algebraic equations. So I provoked one about a can of Coca-Cola instead.

The image of Helen was so strong in my head that it interfered with my concentration. I frequently found myself in the middle of a telephone call with someone, aware that he had been speaking for five minutes and that I hadn't heard a word he had said because I was remembering some murmured pleasantry which Helen had planted deep in my subconscious. One night I walked into the kitchen in just such a mood, trying to recall the touch of her hand on my chest, the feel of her breath on my cheek, when I stepped straight into a puddle of spilled Coke.

Danny had hurled the can across the kitchen towards the recycling bag, missed and just left it on the floor, unaware, presumably, that the can wasn't empty and that a little puddle of brown liquid was forming on the kitchen linoleum. I was certainly unaware until the moment my sock was completely soaked by the sticky stuff. I yelled for Danny.

'What?'

I took his slowness to appear as evidence of his guilt. 'Look at that!'

'Look at what?'

'You left a trail of Coke all over the bloody floor.'

'No. I didn't.'

I was infuriated. 'Yes you did. That's your bloody can. Pick it up.'

Sisyphus couldn't have exhibited a greater reluctance.

'Right, now clean it up.'

'Clean what?'

I really, really wanted to hit him. 'The bloody floor. I've got sticky goo all over my socks.'

'Well, hadn't you better clean it?'

'Danny!' I was really yelling now. Life was so unfair. First Helen breaks my heart, now Danny spills Coke on the floor.

I think he got the message that I was angry by this time and decided that co-operation of a limited kind was the better part of valour. He picked up the sponge from the sink which was still full of water and made a pathetic attempt to wipe up the Coke but succeeded only in spreading the puddle wider.

'Danny!'

'What?'

God I hate the way adolescent kids whine at you. That 'What?' sent me into orbit. 'Put the fucking chairs on the table, sweep the floor and then use the mop and the detergent and wash it properly.'

I rarely swore so the shock value worked. He did what I asked but very slowly and with evident loathing for me and the operation. I didn't care. It was that sort of attitude that had sent my darling back to America.

I left the room because I couldn't stand to watch him. When I returned ten minutes later the whole kitchen floor was almost under water and he was grinning. I wasn't going to let him get away with this. I tried hard to compose myself and spoke as slowly as I could, given my raging temper.

'Right, that's it. Go to bed.'

'Don't you want me to finish the job?'

'Not like that. I'm stopping your pocket money for a month and you won't be allowed to watch television at all except at weekends.'

'Why?' Now he was losing his cool.

'You know why.'

'That's fucking unfair.'

'And don't you swear at me.'

'Why not? You swore at me!'

I grabbed the mop off him, almost tearing it out of his hands. 'Go to bed now!' I yelled. 'Just go!'

He did. The little martyr. We didn't speak to each other again that night.

I had to leave for London early the following morning so I was out of the house before his alarm went off. I thought of waking him up and instigating an apology and a reconciliation but I thought Helen had been right when she'd encouraged me to discipline Danny a little more and I felt he could sweat out my displeasure for another day.

I got back around two thirty in the afternoon. I didn't see it at first. It was propped up on the mantelpiece in the living room, a white envelope with the word 'Dad' written on it. I thought, before I opened it, that this was strange. He'd never done this before.

I tore it open, hoping that it was an apology or a note explaining that he was going to another boy's house after school, to punish me.

Dear Dad,

I love you and I'm going to fix it. It was my fault to begin with. I'm sorry if I upset you. Don't worry. I've got money and everything so I'll be fine.

Love
         Danny

My first reaction was puzzlement. What the hell was he talking about? Then anxiety. Certainly not panic. Not at that point. I looked at my watch. I had just enough time to get to school when they came out. I grabbed my coat and raced out.

I got there before any of the kids seemed to have come out of school. Danny tended to be one of the first to sprint out of the gates so after ten minutes my anxiety started to grow. It was possible I had missed him, of course, but I couldn't be sure. Then I saw Jamie Kirk coming towards me.

'Where's Danny, Jamie?' I asked, affecting a casualness I did not feel.

'He didn't come to school today.'

The anxiety was turning into fear. I asked a couple of the boys I recognised from the school football team. They, too, confirmed his absence. A cold hand clutched at my heart. All thoughts of Helen left me as I ran into school, looking desperately for the staff room. I hammered on the door and Mrs Hargreaves, Danny's form mistress with whom I had passed a desultory half-hour two weeks before, came to open it. I'm afraid I wasn't at my most charming.

'Have you seen Danny?' I demanded.

She was slightly flustered by what I knew must be my manic appearance and all she could do was to echo the name stupidly.

'Danny?'

'My son, Daniel Warren. You're his form mistress.'

'Isn't he at home?' she asked evenly.

'No. If he was at home I wouldn't be here, would I?'

'No. Of course not.'

What the hell was the matter with her? I gabbled on, my head full of images of death and destruction. 'He didn't come out of school. Is he in detention or on a cross-country run or something? Nobody seems to know where he is.'

'He didn't come to school today. I thought he might have the flu.'

'He was fine last night.'

'Do you think he's playing truant?'

'He left me this letter.'

She took it and read it slowly, absorbing every word as if she was translating it in her head into another language.

'I don't understand. What does this mean?'

'I was hoping you might know.'

She shook her head.

I groaned in despair. 'Oh God, it's all my fault!'

'There's probably a perfectly logical explanation.'

'There is. We had this terrible row last night.'

'Oh.'

She invited me into the staff room to call the police

while she made me a cup of tea. After I'd made the call I slumped into one of the coffee-stained armchairs all staff rooms seem to specialise in. Thankfully she didn't press me for more information. She waited for me to speak.

'I've been ... a bit moody recently. When you mentioned to me that Danny's work had got worse—'

'Not that much worse.'

'I knew it was my fault. It's been a bit awkward at home recently, one or two domestic upheavals but nothing major.' I paused.

'I see,' she said, though she didn't really, not if she was thinking about the usual adolescent problems – a girl, drugs, petty crime.

'It's too complicated to explain. The point is, I suppose, that Danny and I have not been getting along in the last few weeks. I've had some problems – at work – and I thought I was hiding them from him but obviously I wasn't.' I stopped again. How much of this was relevant, I wondered. 'I made him clean the kitchen floor.'

She said nothing. Nobody runs away from home because they have to clean the floor, do they? I thought I'd better elaborate.

'He'd spilt some Coke and I pointed it out and he said he couldn't see it, then he said it wasn't him which it was and he knew it was and I'm afraid I just lost my temper.'

'Did you hit him?'

'Good God, no!' I came bloody close but there was no need for her to know that. 'I made him clean it up so he ran a sponge under the tap and just left a pool of water on the floor. I got even angrier and made him do the whole room properly, you know, put the chairs on top of the table, sweep up the crumbs, then get the mop and the detergent and do the whole thing properly.'

'Well, good for you.'

'So now he's run away from home.'

'Mr Warren, believe me, whatever that letter means, if Danny has run away it won't be because he had to clean the kitchen floor. You mustn't blame yourself.'

'Then it got worse. There was a bigger row and I stopped his pocket money for a month and banned him from watching television at all except at weekends.'

'Life imprisonment without the possibility of parole.'

'You can joke but we never, absolutely never, have rows like that.'

'I'm sorry, I had no intention of trivialising what's happened. I was just trying to make you see it wasn't your fault.'

'How can you possibly know?'

'You're right. Of course I can't.'

'It really is my fault. Even if it's nothing to do with cleaning the floor, it's still my fault.'

'Well, let's just concentrate on what the note means and where he might be now.'

As the minutes passed while we waited for the police, all likely locations were explored and dismissed. My concern grew rapidly. At this moment I would have happily settled for finding him in hospital with a broken leg and the prospect of six weeks on crutches with his leg in plaster. Anything rather than this void of uncertainty.

The newspapers carry articles about missing children all the time and television news stories seem to cover the subject every week. I had no cause to be anything but desperate. We all know the routine by now: the police issue a statement of facts asking for help in their inquiries and indicate their own alarm; then the hysterical parents go on television to appeal to the public and abase themselves in a show of ritual public despair; a few days or a few weeks later a body is discovered. Before the post-mortem identification is officially confirmed, we all know who it is. Was I really facing this end of the second millennium Calvary?

Mrs Hargreaves knew quite a few of Danny's friends, more than I did, it transpired, so before the police arrived she took the official list from the school office and telephoned them at their homes. I think they were shocked to hear their teacher invading the privacy of their homes as if the secret police were following them home to make sure they did their homework. Once they had recovered from the initial horror, they could only say they hadn't the faintest idea where Danny might have gone. He never said anything significant to them and they didn't even realise he'd acted any differently since the beginning of term. Really, adolescent boys can be quite breathtakingly unobservant. I'm sure girls of the same age would have been much more sensitive to the mood swings of their friends. With each dead end my spirits slipped further.

Mrs Hargreaves went with me to the police station where I signed my statement and then back to the house where she cooked me dinner. I didn't want much so she opened a tin of soup, made some toast from the granary bread and brewed a pot of tea. I was almost paralysed with anxiety. I was so grateful to her.

She insisted gently that we should look around the house, particularly Danny's bedroom, to see if there was something that might give us a clue as to where he had gone. Instead of seizing eagerly on this as a reason to get up and do something, I seemed to expend all my energy on getting to my feet.

In Danny's bedroom I was desperately praying that we wouldn't uncover something embarrassing but as we continued to open drawers and rummage through his wardrobe, there seemed little chance of that. After a while I straightened up.

'All I can see is his cricket bag's not here.'

'He's gone to play cricket?'

'I don't think so. His bat and his pads are still in the wardrobe.'

'Has his toothbrush gone or his toilet bag?'

'No.'

'I still think the disappearance of the cricket bag is a very good sign.'

'Why?'

'Because it looks like he's made a conscious decision to go somewhere. He's taken his biggest bag and left out the things that take up the most room.'

For a moment I felt really quite hopeful. I could see the logic in what she said. Then I shook my head. 'That note could mean anything. Anything. I don't even know what money he's talking about. How much? How much does he need to get to wherever he's going?'

'You had that argument last night. He's probably too embarrassed to explain more.'

'I don't know why I shouted at him. He's such a good kid.' My eyes began to well with tears.

She put her hand on my arm to steady me. 'We'll find him, Mr Warren. We will.' Then the doorbell rang.

I went to the door and opened it. I could see the outline of the peaked cap through the frosted glass under the porch light so I knew what to expect. Except it wasn't a policeman, it was a policewoman. My heart missed a beat. In the second it took me to open the front door and register who the caller was, I became convinced it was bad news. They always send women to deliver the bad news, I thought.

'Mr Warren?'

I nodded, wondering if the next five seconds would destroy my life.

'There's no news, Mr Warren, I'm sorry.'

For a moment I couldn't absorb the implication. Was this good or bad? If he hadn't been knocked down, if he wasn't in hospital or in a police station somewhere, was this a good thing? Or did it just increase the likelihood of his poor, beaten, mangled body lying at the bottom of the river? As if to confirm this terrible image, the policewoman told me they would send a frogman into the River Cam at dawn. Meanwhile her superior, Detective Chief Inspector Chamberlain, had sent a message to the Child Protection Services at Scotland Yard who would in turn inform all ports and airports. Nobody would be able to take Danny out of the country without being stopped. If he was still in the country, they would find him, she assured me.

'And if he's already left the country?'

The policewoman thought for a moment. 'Well, obviously it would take longer to find him but if an airport immigration authority had a record of him entering their country today or tomorrow, say, then at least we'd know where to start looking.'

Silence fell. Nobody dared to voice what we were all feeling. That she was assuming that Danny was still alive.

CHAPTER TWENTY-SEVEN

Danny

IT WAS SO EASY. I couldn't believe how easy it was. I'd always kept my own passport in the box where I keep all my special things and Dad had had this travel agent for ages and the last couple of times he had needed to fly to Barcelona or Milan or New York or wherever for an interview, he had let me do the booking on the phone. It was his way of teaching me to be independent.

Of course he was standing beside me when I did it but the travel agent didn't know that. When I was watching *Sleepless in Seattle* and I saw Tom Hanks's kid get a ticket to fly from Seattle to New York, I knew that I could do it too. In fact I don't know why the skies aren't filled with kids flying all over the world on their parents' credit cards. There must be a reason. Maybe they need a really important excuse like mine to give them the bottle.

It wasn't the regular man who did Dad's travel arrange-ments who answered the telephone but I gave him the account number Dad always uses and they had the credit card number attached to it on the computer. After we had sorted out which airline and flight number I was going to take, he asked, as I knew he would from my previous times when I was booking for Dad, if I wanted to use Dad's credit card even though it was my name on the airline ticket. I said of course I did. I mean is he stupid or what? Where was I going to get £384 including airport tax from? He never even asked me why I was travelling by myself to the US though I had my story all worked out if he had. It was so cool, I wondered why I hadn't done it before. I heard later that airlines don't accept credit card bookings over the phone but travel agencies who held a specially personalised account wouldn't need to show the same caution.

I felt very nervous and excited about what I was planning to do. A part of me wanted to tell Dad because I didn't want him to worry but the other bit of me said I shouldn't. He wouldn't let me go and I'd be in terrible trouble for using his credit card without permission. The night before I left, though, I got into this big row with Dad. He was totally out of order making me sweep and wash the kitchen floor just because there was a bit of sticky stuff on it. He said it came from my Coke can but in fact it could have come from anything. He was so unreasonable about it I had to do it but I was seething inside. I went to bed without saying good night to him, which was unusual, but in fact it meant that when I left for school in the morning I didn't feel quite so guilty about leaving home.

I planned it very carefully. I put my spare clothes in my big cricket bag and once out of the house I simply took the bus to the station, changed into my Saturday clothes in the toilet, bought a bus ticket to London and I was away. At Victoria I got the tube to Heathrow Airport. I was a bit worried about checking in but I told the woman I was on half term and I was being met by my mother in Los Angeles. I don't think she cared much. She didn't smile at me, she just asked me if I had a valid US immigration visa.

My heart stopped. I never thought about an immigration visa. All that trouble and I wouldn't get past the check-in counter at Heathrow. All that money of Dad's that I'd spent with the travel agency and I still couldn't get him and Helen back together.

My eyes began to fill with tears. I felt like such a fool. Why hadn't they asked me at the travel agency? That was their job, surely. I told the horrible check-in woman that I hadn't got one and waited for the sentence of death. But all she did was reach under the counter and give me a US visa waiver form to fill in. I could have kissed her. Obviously it was no big deal, this visa.

I filled it in and gave it back to her, by which time she had printed out my boarding card and then she seemed to rip my ticket up. I asked her to tell me if the return ticket was still there. She said it was and looked at me as if I was an idiot. And I'd waited like about an hour in the queue for all this as well.

I was a bit worried when I saw my cricket bag disappearing along the luggage conveyor belt. It looked so odd among all those suitcases. I was frightened someone would lift it off and say that it was a cricket bag and who did it belong to and I'd be discovered, but it just disappeared from sight and I went over to look at the television screen which said my flight was going to leave on time.

I knew Dad would worry so I'd left a note for him. Only I didn't want to give too much away in case he came chasing after me and hauled me back and told me not to be so stupid, that it was all over between him and Helen, and anyway it was nothing to do with me. But I knew it wasn't over and that the only way I could make Dad happy again was to go to Santa Barbara and find Helen and tell her it was all my fault that Dad and she had broken up and that if she came back to Dad, I wouldn't be this really annoying creep any more. Then Dad would be happy and she would be happy and I would be happy because the two of them would be happy.

I thought the letter I wrote was just right. I told him not to worry but I left out the reason I was going to see Helen because that was all to do with my feelings and those are very difficult things to write about. Mostly, though, I didn't want to give him the chance to ruin my cunning plan.

Yes, I know I could have telephoned Helen and said the same thing that I would say when I got there but it wouldn't have been the same thing. Telephoning Helen would have been the same as telling Dad exactly what I was doing. She wouldn't have believed me, she wouldn't take me seriously or, I suppose even worse, she'd think Dad had put me up to it and then she'd really have hated Dad. Besides, when I got to the airport I found that I didn't have Helen's phone number with me, only her address. But that was cool because I didn't see why I needed the phone number. After all, I was going straight to her house from the airport.

I reckoned that if I went to her, went to California, made everything right then rang up Dad and told him to come over or flew back with her to England, then I would be the hero. Then I would have made everything come out right. I was really looking forward to being a hero. Maybe I'd be on telly, perhaps on the evening news or *The Big Breakfast* or even *TFI Friday* with Chris Evans. They like kids who tell stories like that.

I first started thinking seriously about it when I found two hundred dollars in an envelope in Dad's desk drawer. Sometimes he leaves an opened packet of Liquorice Allsorts there and that's what I was looking for the day after the Spurs match at Ipswich. I then figured if I could get the airline ticket on Dad's credit card, I could get a bus to Santa Barbara. Even if Helen was away for a day or two I'd have enough money to stay in a cheap hotel or motel like you always see on TV and I know you can get hamburgers for ninety-nine cents at McDonald's. It was a perfect plan.

It was only after the plane had taken off that I got a bit worried. The stewardess was very nice, asking if someone was meeting me at the other end. She was American and I guessed she was used to seeing kids of divorced parents flying between London and Los Angeles. She seemed so sympathetic and had such a nice warm smile that I did think about telling her everything and then maybe she had a car in Los Angeles and she could drive me to Helen's house but I was too scared. I thought she might stop the plane or tell the pilot to return to Heathrow and that would just have been humiliating so I said nothing.

She was really pretty, that stewardess, and she was wearing lots of perfume that made me breathe heavily. I liked it though. I like women even though I grew up with only my dad in the house. What I don't understand is why I like women like that air stewardess but I don't like the girls of my own age. How do they magically get changed from those irritating things in baggy sweaters or skimpy tops with glasses and greasy hair into those really nice attractive women in smart skirts with nice hair and a big wide smile?

I fell asleep thinking about that because it was warm and now that I was past the dangerous bit I sort of relaxed. I was hoping I could sleep all the way to Los Angeles and we'd be there when I woke up but when I did wake up I looked at my watch and I discovered after doing a lot of really difficult maths in which you had to add eight hours to account for the time difference that we wouldn't be landing for another six and a half hours.

What was even worse was that I was woken up by the trolleys which they use for collecting the meal trays. I had slept through dinner or lunch or whatever it was they had just served and now they were tossing the used trays into a big bin. I wanted to shout that I hadn't eaten and I was really hungry though I didn't know whether it was for breakfast, lunch or dinner because I'd lost all track of time.

The man in the window seat pushed past me on the

way to the toilet where a long queue was now starting to form. The man in the aisle seat next to me started to read his paper and whenever he opened it to turn the page the paper almost went into my face. When he had got to the right page and folded it to a readable size, he turned to me and said that he hadn't woken me for dinner because I looked like I was really enjoying my sleep. I smiled and said thank you although what I wanted to say was, 'You stupid idiot, why didn't you wake me up? Don't you know children are always hungry?'

I wanted to go and ask that nice stewardess if she kept my dinner on one side for me but I didn't dare. I wanted something to eat really badly but now I was worried that because I'd missed the proper dinner, if I asked for something special they'd make me pay a lot of money for it. I only had that two hundred dollars and I didn't think I should spend it on the plane, otherwise I wouldn't have enough to get to Helen's.

I was too embarrassed to ask if there was going to be another meal coming soon or even if there was one coming at all before we landed. I got through another hour or so by wondering whether the next meal, when it came (as come it better had or I would die of starvation and that would be terrible publicity for the airline), would be chicken and potatoes and a nice piece of cake for dessert, or perhaps we'd already flown through the night so the next meal would be orange juice (because we were flying to California) and a huge pile of waffles with maple syrup (yes!) or maybe a big plate of corned beef hash which you always see on TV shows when they sit down to eat breakfast in a diner.

Eventually I saw the trolley coming my way and I almost cried with relief. Chicken and rice or egg and bacon, I didn't care what was on it. Then I saw people reaching into their bags for money and soon I saw why, which made me go 'Oh no!' to myself. This wasn't the free dinner trolley, this was the really expensive duty free trolley.

I couldn't buy any booze or ciggies and I didn't want any perfume or cosmetics so I didn't bother to answer when the nice stewardess smiled at the three of us and asked what we wanted. I wanted to tell her 'Food! Food! Any kind of food!' but I just said nothing. Well, my dad would be proud of me, I thought grimly. I was being the perfect guest and he was paying about four hundred pounds for it. That started to bother me a bit too. I told myself I'd pay it back out of my pocket money but at that rate it would take me four years, and that's if I continued to get any pocket money at all, and obviously that wasn't realistic. Then I thought maybe I could sell my story to a tabloid newspaper for four hundred pounds. Dad would know who to get in touch with. I felt a bit better.

I watched the movie for a while but I couldn't see the screen very well because I was so far back and the man in front of me had a gi-normous head which towered over the top of the seat and mostly obscured the screen and the man in the aisle seat kept his light on and read throughout it. Occasionally some of the passengers would burst into laughter for what seemed to be no good reason but then I realised it must be a joke in the film. By this time I'd given up trying to get into it and turned onto the comedy channel on the headphones. Some of the acts I'd never heard of and they didn't seem very funny to me. I was both hungry and tired and we still had another five hours in the air.

I dozed off for a few minutes at a time but eventually the pilot told us that if we looked out of the window we could see Las Vegas. The man in the window seat never let me see anything but after a lot of twisting and turning with my seat belt still on I eventually saw a lot of desert and some mountains which didn't look much like the fells of the Lake District. No wonder Helen was confused when she was going up Bowfell. I wished I was back there, climbing up to the top from Esk Hause with views of Coniston and Windermere in the distance.

Then they brought the landing cards and the customs forms round and I knew we must be getting close to Los Angeles. Now my heart started beating faster again. I got out Helen's address which I'd taken off Dad's computer and carefully wrote it down on the immigration card. The pilot came on the loudspeaker and said that we would be landing in half an hour. What was lying ahead of me?

I wanted to think about Helen's beautiful house near Santa Barbara. I screwed my eyes shut tight and thought so hard about her opening the door and shrieking with delight and hugging me then getting on the phone to Dad and making everything all right. Then I would have a swim in her pool and she would feed me lots of American food and a cold drink and then I would go to sleep in a really comfortable guest bedroom in between sweet-smelling soft cotton sheets which had just come out of the dryer. If wishing could make it happen, then it would happen.

But all the time I was thinking these nice thoughts a black vision of something else seemed to want to lie across it. In this vision I would be stopped at immigration and arrested. Then they would snap the cuffs on (they always do, I knew that, even if you're not going to resist arrest) and I would be forced into a police car and driven away at high speed with the lights flashing and the sirens sounding.

When my dad came out to get me I'd be wearing one of those orange (or is it red? or is that for women?) uniforms they always put prisoners in. It was such a powerful vision, I thought I was going to have an asthma attack which I hadn't had for years — and I didn't have my puffer with me. Then the wheels hit the ground and some people clapped and the pilot said nobody could move until the plane had come to a complete stop. Was that to allow the cops to come on board to arrest me?

CHAPTER TWENTY-EIGHT

Ralph

AT TWENTY TO TWO in the morning I woke up covered in sweat but with the same euphoria of discovery as has been attributed to Archimedes in the bath. He, according to legend, shouted 'Eureka!' which is Greek for 'I have found it'. I shouted 'Shit!' which is a pretty accurate modern English idiomatic equivalent. Of course! He'd gone to see Helen!

The practical difficulties were so enormous I had never considered it a serious option but when I fell into my troubled sleep that night the second person's face I saw was Helen's. She was standing on the edge of a cliff, I guess it must have been in Santa Barbara where she lives, and she had her arms wide open and Danny was running towards them. For a moment I thought Danny was going to miss her arms and plunge over the edge but she caught him and smiled at me. I was sitting unconcernedly to one side watching them. But when I woke up I soon realised that I wasn't unconcerned; I was helpless.

My eyes blinked in the harsh glare of the light bulb

over my bed as I raced downstairs stark naked to look for Helen's telephone number in California. My fingers had all the dexterity of my toes as I sought desperately to punch out the numbers. It took me three attempts to hit the right buttons only to be greeted by the worst sound of all — the busy signal. This was not good news. I knew from personal experience how long this might last. Why didn't she have call waiting, for God's sake?

I made myself a cup of tea, spilling the milk across the counter in my anxiety and inability to grasp the cold glass bottle. As the milk hit the floor, I remembered in all its painful details the argument with Danny about his spilled Coke. What wouldn't I give now to take back those words? I returned to the study and jabbed at the redial button. The same infuriatingly even response awaited me. I slammed the phone down, turned on the computer and e-mailed Helen, sitting there in an incongruous state of total nudity like the mad organist in *Monty Python's Flying Circus*.

I went back upstairs and got into bed again because the house was freezing in the middle of the night and every exposed part of me was icing up like a car windscreen. I picked up the bedside phone before I realised that I couldn't hit the redial button because I'd made the call from downstairs so I had to go back into the icy study, collect the Filofax and race back upstairs. He was there, I knew he was there. But then why hadn't Helen called me?

I dialled very slowly and deliberately and heard to my inexpressible joy the sound of an American telephone ringing. She picked it up on the second ring.

'Hello?'

'Hi. It's me. Is he there?'

'Ralph?'

'Hi. Is Danny there?'

'Danny?'

My heart slumped again. She's not a dense woman so I had to assume that she knew nothing about Danny but then it was only about six o'clock in the evening out there and maybe he hadn't got there yet. I told her, as best I could, given my somewhat turbulent, emotional state, the events as they had unfolded in the past twelve hours. Although she said nothing apart from the odd sympathetic 'Oh no!' I sensed she was with me. This was a great help. We were a team.

'How did he get a ticket?' she asked.

'I don't know yet. He must have done it through my travel agent. He's seen me do it.'

'How did he pay for it?'

'I guess he used my credit card.'

'The little rascal. How d'you know he's not gone to Hawaii on vacation?'

'This is Danny we're talking about, Helen.'

'Right. Sorry. You want me to call the cops out here?'

'If you wouldn't mind.'

'Don't be so goddamn British.'

'Hey!'

'What?'

'I've just remembered. I can ring the credit card company, say I think I've lost the card and find out the last transaction.'

'Call me back.'

The credit card company was quite happy to do business at two thirty in the morning. If only they were this approachable at two thirty in the afternoon, I thought grimly. They confirmed that a charge of £384 in favour of my travel agency had been made the previous Saturday. They couldn't tell me the details, only the figure, but that seemed to me the right sort of amount a return ticket to Los Angeles would cost. I pulled open the desk drawer. The envelope with the two hundred dollars was gone. I instantly realised the significance of this theft/loan and I started to cry with happiness. He was alive! He was alive!! Jesus Christ! Just wait till I get my hands on that kid again. I'll kill him!

I called Helen back and told her. She was so happy. I wanted to reach out for her and touch her. Did she think she had made a mistake breaking up with me or was she genuinely just moved by Danny's plight? I knew it was up to me to break the ice but in the circumstances she must surely be feeling something for me, for us.

'I'm coming out. I'm getting the first plane.'

'Hadn't you better wait till we know he's here for sure?'

'I suppose so.'

'I've told the cops out here but frankly a missing British kid isn't the kind of emergency they're going to take too seriously.'

I was outraged. 'Why the hell not?'

'Well, for a start, he's British, not American—'

'Xenophobes!'

'Don't say that to their face, they'll blow your head off. Some of them never finished high school.'

'So what does a twelve-year-old kid wandering alone through the streets of Los Angeles need before the cops take him seriously?'

'A gun.'

'What?'

'Oh sure. If he'd taken your semi-automatic out of your desk drawer we'd get their attention pretty darn quick.'

'I only keep Liquorice Allsorts in my desk drawer, you know that.'

'Well, more fool you, you Limey wimp! You never read the Second Amendment to the Constitution?'

'I don't want a political debate, Helen. I just want my son back safe and sound.'

'OK, listen. You tell the cops your end when they wake up in the morning what's going on. I'll keep a lookout for him here . . . Does he have my address?'

'I guess so. He must do.'

'OK. Let me know if you get a confirmation from Immigration Control. I'll chase it up here but really you're the parent and they might think me a bit suspicious if I'm chasing after a twelve-year-old boy I'm not related to.'

'I'll be out on the first plane.'

'What if he tries to call you?'

'Why would he? He's coming to see you. If he was going to phone me he'd already have done it.'

'Ralph . . .'

'Yes?'

'What's he want with me anyway?'

'No idea. Maybe he's stopped off at a gun store in LA and he's going to blow you away. Think the cops would be interested now?'

'I dunno. But you sure got my attention.'

'I think,' I said slowly, 'he's rumbled me.'

'What?'

'I think he knows how much I love you. He's coming out to make it all better.'

'How's he going to do that?'

'Who knows? He's a kid.'

'Some kid.'

'Helen, I'm sorry to involve you like this.'

'What the hell are you apologising for now?'

'You know there hasn't been a single minute of a single day when I haven't stopped thinking about you, loving you.'

There was another of those desperate pauses.

'Yes there was.'

'When?'

'When Tottenham defeated Norwich.'

My spirits soared. I knew the significance of this. 'Ipswich not Norwich.'

'Whatever.'

'How did—'

'I've been following the Spurs soccer team scores in the *LA Times*.'

'Really?' I was affecting a dangerous cool, one I was certainly not feeling. It paid off.

'How's Danny been these past few weeks. I've missed him.'

'Just him?'

'No. And you.'

'Just missed me?' I was really pushing it now.

'Not just missed you. I'm still in love with you, Ralph.'

Her words made my heart pound. She loved me. She still loved me. I always knew she did. We'd find Danny and everything would be OK. For ten seconds I was on cloud nine. I told her about Danny's behaviour since she'd left but not so much about mine, apart from the awful row the night before he left. I didn't want to lay a guilt trip on her and anyway I wanted to see her eyes when I told her how devastated I'd been when she called me and said she wasn't coming back. Damn that kid for the agony he's put me through these past few hours but he's given me the chance to see Helen again. When I put the phone down half an hour later my head was still swimming with all the thoughts and emotions that were in there.

I tried in a desultory fashion to get back to sleep but I managed nothing more than the occasional twenty-minute doze until the alarm went off at seven o'clock and the Radio 5 Live News and Sport came on. At one minute past nine o'clock in the morning I found the idiot at the travel agency who authorised Danny's ticket. The manager got on the line and was very apologetic but pointed out that the transaction was not made illegally and that there was nothing he could do about it. I finished letting him grovel and scrape then told him I wanted a ticket for Los Angeles for myself, leaving that day. He had ten minutes to get it sorted because the call waiting noise was bleeping in my ear.

It was Mr Plod, otherwise known as Detective Chief Inspector Chamberlain, telling me that they had just received an official fax from Immigration Control in Los Angeles. A boy answering Danny's description had passed through there yesterday afternoon. He gave his address as Helen's house in Santa Barbara. I could have kissed the Los Angeles Immigration Control even while I was wondering at their gullibility.

CHAPTER TWENTY-NINE

Danny

I STOOD BEHIND THE YELLOW line in the Tom Bradley International Terminal at Los Angeles Airport waiting to be interrogated by the secret immigration police. I kept turning round and pretending to talk to the man behind me as if he was my father or at least I was with him so the man who was going to interrogate me would know that I was just a kid coming to LA with his family. Then I panicked because my story was that I was coming to see my mum who lived in Santa Barbara and my 'dad' would have a different US address, so I turned my back on him smartly and hoped nobody had taken any notice of my clever plan.

Eventually I was summoned over the yellow line. I gave the man my passport and all the forms they handed out on the plane which I had filled in. He solemnly returned my US customs declaration which made me feel a fool. This guy was immigration not customs. I should have known that. Damn!

He flicked slowly through my newish passport. The

photograph was quite like me. He stared at me as if he had seen my face before which he hadn't and then he started tapping away at his computer. Sweat broke out on my neck and rolled in little drops down my back before coming to rest on the elasticated back of my underpants. This was it. This was the moment they came and snapped the cuffs on and threw me in the slammer with the sliding door and the orange (or red) uniform and the toilet with no seat on it.

The man stared at the screen. What was on there? My Christmas report card? 'Daniel would be much more successful in Mathematics tests if he spent more time checking his answers.' Surely not. 'Daniel needs to pay more attention in class if he is going to overcome a deficiency in his vocabulary.' The tension was unbearable. Finally, the Gestapo spoke to me.

'Vacation?'

'I'm sorry?' What did he mean? I was all ready here with my story about my mother living in Santa Barbara. What the hell was he talking about a vacation for?

'You here on vacation?'

I wanted to tell him all about my dad and Helen and so on. I was doing nothing wrong. I hadn't broken the law, had I? A little voice inside me made me say the magic word.

'Yes.'

The secret police had another flick through the passport, found a blank page and stamped it like it was a library book, stapled the appropriate bit of the landing form into it, handed it back to me and called 'Next' to my ex-dad standing behind me. I clutched the passport and my heart leaped. I was through. No more problems except to tell them I wasn't bringing any citrus fruit or meat into the country. I wondered who would bring half a dozen oranges or half a pound of meat riddled with BSE from a British supermarket into California which Dad always said had the best food in the world.

The thought of food reminded me that I hadn't eaten for twelve hours. The tension had made me forget it for the last hour or so, or maybe my stomach had shrunk like one of those terrible African famine victims you see on the news.

I was so pleased to see my cricket bag on the conveyor belt, it reminded me of home and Dad throwing my cricket clothes onto the bed before I got ready for a cricket game. A lot of people were jostling at the conveyor belt so I had to run after it for a few metres till I could find a space so I could haul it off, put it on the cart and wheel it through customs.

I had this dream, a dream I really liked, that I would be coming through customs into the part where the relatives and friends are waiting and Helen would be there and she'd be so pleased to see me and she'd drive me to her home in a posh American sports car. I knew it couldn't really happen because Helen didn't know I was coming but at the back of my mind, especially when I saw people throwing themselves into other people's arms, I hoped against hope that she would be there, maybe at the back of the queue, jumping up and down for a better look and waving with a big smile on her face. But she wasn't there.

And I know it sounds ridiculous because how could she be, but I still felt really disappointed.

Instead, I saw a brightly lit shop selling T-shirts and magazines and chocolate. I looked for something I really wanted but they all had weird names like Hershey and Juicy Fruits and Good'n'Plenty. Finally I saw a huge, I mean a gi-normous, bar of Toblerone. I love Toblerone. It said $9.95 on the label so I handed over ten dollars at the till. The cash register rang up $10.75. I said in a small voice that I thought it was $9.95. The girl at the register was chewing gum. 'Tax,' she said briefly, holding out her hand. I gave her another of my precious ten dollar bills and got a pile of one dollar banknotes back.

I wheeled the trolley over to where I could sit down on a ledge and ate nearly the whole thing. It was so nice because I love Toblerone anyway and I was really hungry. I must have eaten at least two-thirds of it before I put the remaining bit into my cricket bag. I felt ready to take on the world, though a bit sick to my stomach. Maybe I'd eaten a bit too much chocolate.

I headed outside and decided I wouldn't get a bus because it was all so confusing. Hundreds of vehicles were trying to manoeuvre their way round in about six different lanes, all of them jammed. None of the buses said Santa Barbara on the front. I counted my money again. I had $189.25, which sounded quite a lot. I wasn't too sure where Santa Barbara was so I thought the safest thing to do was to show the taxi driver the address and ask him how much it would be to drive me there.

Dad said always to look for a black cab if you need a

taxi because they were honest but obviously that wasn't going to help much in Los Angeles where they were all yellow. I stood under a sign that said 'Taxi' and when I got to be the first in the queue I asked the man how much it was to Santa Barbara. He thought for a while.

'Where you wanna go, boy?'

I showed him Helen's address – 2535 Santa Maria Street, Montecito, near Santa Barbara, California.

'How much you got?'

'One hundred and eighty-nine dollars and twenty-five cents.'

He smiled. He had big white teeth. 'OK. I take you there.'

'Thanks.'

'You show me the money, OK?'

I showed it to him. He must have been impressed because he got out of the cab and opened the boot where he slung my cricket bag. I was a bit worried because the boot was really dirty with old cans of oil and a filthy tow rope and Dad had given me that cricket bag brand new for my birthday last July. Then he opened the door for me to get in the back. It was just like he was my chauffeur. I liked that even though the seat was peculiar because it was so low – and really slippery leather. He drove too fast and screeched round corners and I kept sliding everywhere. There were no seat belts.

Still, I was sure I had done the right thing. It didn't matter that I was giving this guy all the money I had because he was taking me straight to Helen's house. As soon as she saw me, everything would be all right, like the end of *Oliver Twist* which we read in class last term, when Oliver is reunited with his grandfather and everything ends happily. There was going to be a happy ending. I could feel it in my bones. It had all been worth it.

I enjoyed the ride, looking at the tall buildings and the cars and the petrol stations and the fast food places. It was just like being in a movie or a TV series and I was glad I was in a taxi all safe and secure and not having to worry about getting on the right bus and having the right change and how to get to Helen's house from the bus station. The driver was nice because he kept looking in the rear-view mirror at me and smiling.

I tried to keep myself awake but after about twenty minutes it was like a great tidal wave of tiredness washed over me and I just lay down on the big wide back seat and fell asleep. I was so zonked I could have slept for ever.

Instead I was being shaken awake by the taxi driver who was pulling me out of the car by the shoulder. He almost dumped me on the kerb because I tripped over my cricket bag which he'd already taken out of the boot.

'Money,' he said and he wasn't half as nice as he had been before. I got my wallet out (I'd been sleeping on it like Dad always said to do) and gave him all the money except for the quarter which was still in my trouser pocket. He almost leaped into the driver's seat and roared away. I looked around at where I was standing and suddenly I got frightened. I knew Helen lived in a nice part of town and I thought I'd be on a nice tree-lined street full of detached houses like Millington Road in Cambridge where the Kirks live but I was standing on a little road with small rundown houses.

The sun was setting and there was a chill in the air now. I asked a man if this was Santa Maria Street and he said no. Now I really was frightened. The taxi driver had taken me to the wrong place and he'd driven off with all my money. The man walked away. I ran after him. 'Is this Santa Barbara?' I asked. The man shook his head. 'Montecito?' I asked desperately.

'You're in Hollywood, boy,' he said. 'You wanna be a star? I can make you a star!' He stared at me and though what he said was OK it was said in a kind of threatening tone of voice.

'I'm meeting my dad,' I said, and picked up my bag and started to run. I felt very alone and very frightened. I wished I'd never left Cambridge.

I followed the main road to a junction with another main road. I looked up at the street name and it said Hollywood Boulevard. A police car came cruising down the road towards me. My first instinct was to run away and hide but then I thought they couldn't possibly know who I was. So when the car stopped because the traffic light was on red I went over to them and asked very politely if they knew where Santa Barbara was.

'You're in Hollywood, pal,' the one who wasn't driving said in a bored voice. He was wearing sunglasses even though the sun was setting behind them.

'Could you tell me how far Santa Barbara is, please?'

'A hundred miles north,' he said as the lights changed to green and the car roared away.

A hundred miles! I had twenty-five cents in my pocket. I would have to ring her. I didn't have the number but I was sure I could get it from directory inquiries.

But I couldn't. Santa Barbara was long distance information which cost money and in any case Helen turned out to have an unlisted number which is what we call ex-directory and they wouldn't give it to me even though I said it was an emergency and I was desperate. In fact the woman was really rude and unhelpful. I wished I'd brought the number with me. I didn't think I'd need anything besides her address. But I was a hundred miles away, it was getting to be night-time, I didn't know anyone and I had no money.

CHAPTER THIRTY

Helen

I'M A REAL ACTIVE TYPE of person. My philosophy has always been that the phone won't ring of its own free will. You have to do something that prompts the return call. But after informing the authorities that Danny was missing, there was nothing I could do but look at the stupid thing and will it to ring. I knew now that I had made a mistake walking out on Ralph. I loved him and I should have stayed and fought for him. Instead I ran away and now look what's happened. This was all my fault. I just prayed to God it wouldn't turn into one of those tragedies you read about in the papers.

At first I was grateful enough to return to my old office in the Waverley Building on Wilshire Boulevard even if it was only part time at first. I didn't even mind the commute from Santa Barbara on the days they wanted me in as I tried to bathe my mind in the music from the CD player. But as soon as Ralph called me to tell me about Danny that all changed.

The phone rang often enough with work stuff but that

wasn't what I wanted to hear and I couldn't disguise the note of disappointment or impatience in my voice when the call turned out to be from an editor or an executive at work. I don't suppose I won too many friends at work that day but I didn't care. For reasons I now fully understood, I was totally wrapped up in the Danny saga. Until he was found I wouldn't know an untroubled moment.

I was driving on the 101 past Oxnard, on my way to pick up Ralph at LAX when I realised I could put a name to the nature of the condition I now found myself in. I had diverted my phone at home onto the cell phone in case the police called me at home to say they'd found him. I had been out to the store to buy some of the food he always told me he longed to eat when he came to the US and made up the guest bed for him. In fact, I realised with a sort of shock, I was behaving like a mom.

He wasn't my kid, Ralph wasn't my husband but in the last six weeks, ironically since that ill-fated expedition to the Lake District, I had turned into a wife and mother. I didn't leave Ralph because I wanted to run away. I left Ralph so he would run after me. I genuinely had no idea that this was the agenda of my subconscious but by the time I had passed the turnoff for Topanga Canyon on the way to the airport, I knew it was true. I loved Ralph and I loved Danny and what we were going through now was a family trauma. If there was anything to be gained from such a nightmare, it was the realisation that we were going through it together as a unit and not as individuals.

I never felt this way about Charles or, obviously, his

family. I never felt this way about any man, because my dad had been such a sonofabitch, I guess.

When a tuckered out Ralph pushed his battered old suitcase through the exit from the customs hall, I felt such a raging torrent of emotion that, most unlike me, I threw my arms round his neck. He was so exhausted after the flight and the anxiety that he barely had the strength to return my kiss but we stood for a long moment with our arms round each other trying to draw strength from the other body.

In the car on the way back to Santa Barbara he perked up, keeping one hand clenched in my free hand as I set the cruise control at 64mph, which avoided the need to keep looking for the California Highway Patrol cars in the mirror. I would have done anything to have taken away his pain but his mind, like mine, was tormented with black thoughts. The cell phone shrilled.

'Hello?'

It was the cops asking where I was. My heart raced. 'I'm on the 101 between Thousand Oaks and Ventura.' I kept my eyes on the road and the hand that wasn't holding the phone on the steering wheel. I could sense Ralph's desperation to listen in with me. I leaned over towards him but he couldn't hear a thing, not that there was much to hear.

'Thanks. We'll be there in fifty minutes.'

I snapped off the phone and turned to him. 'No news. That's good.'

He was quiet for a moment but I knew what he was thinking.

316 HIGH ON A CLIFF

'You know he's a smart kid. He's going to be OK.'

'He's a smart kid in Cambridge. In Los Angeles he's a helpless English kid. With no gun.'

'He's got that cash. Two hundred dollars goes a long way when you're a kid.'

'If he's still got it. If he's not penniless and wandering through South Central LA. If he's still alive.'

'Ralph, don't. Don't torture yourself.'

'What else can I do?'

I didn't have an answer.

We turned into the driveway and I thought, sadly, how often I had wanted to come here with Ralph and show off my beautiful home with such pride and anticipation. Now I was doing it but in circumstances I could never have imagined. I touched the garage opener which was attached to the sunshade. The door groaned and started to creak its way upwards. I was expecting Ralph to offer an observation about the consumer society but of course he was out of it. I said I'd fix him something light to eat, fruit or salad, get the airline food out of his system, if he wanted to take a shower first.

I busied myself in the kitchen, breaking off to stare at the irritatingly silent phone, checking the cell phone as it lay on the kitchen table in case a silent text message had flashed up. I called up to Ralph to tell him that dinner was fixed but I got no answer. I walked up to the bathroom but I couldn't hear the shower. I knocked on the door in case he was in the tub. No response. I turned the handle and went in. No sign of Ralph.

He was on my bed, fast asleep. He had made an attempt

to get undressed but hadn't managed it. His shoes and pants were off but his socks and boxer shorts were still on. Feeling like a nurse rather than a lover I disrobed him completely, pulled back the sheets and rolled him into my bed.

I don't remember doing this for any previous boyfriend. I don't remember feeling like this about any previous boyfriend. All the lyrics of all the love songs in the world suddenly seemed to make sense. Strangely enough, I had never previously associated love with tossing dirty socks and shorts into the laundry. But then if that's not love, what is?

CHAPTER THIRTY-ONE

Danny

THAT FIRST NIGHT IN LOS ANGELES was the worst night I had
spent since I was born — far, far worse than when Spurs
were hammered 6–1 in the Coca-Cola Cup by Bolton
Wanderers who were a division below us at the time.
I sat on a bench which had an advert for a mortuary
on the back. I knew mortuary was the American word
for cemetery, because I remembered a Latin vocab test
we'd done a week before we broke up for Christmas
which went 'mors, mortis, feminine, death'. I wondered
why the Romans thought of death as feminine. Then I
thought about Mum and then about Dad. The tears were
starting to prick at my eyes because though I was twelve,
which sounded old to me, I mean I'd left primary school
nearly two years ago, it didn't feel very old on the streets
of Hollywood.

Hollywood was a disappointing dump. I wondered
where the studios were. I'd heard a lot about Universal
Studios but I couldn't take the tour with only twenty-five
cents in my pocket. I wandered through Mann's

Chinese which I thought I'd heard of. I assumed it was a Chinese restaurant but then I saw lots of people behind a velvet rope, as if they were in a museum, looking at some footprints in cement. They belonged to some old movie stars so I didn't find them very interesting. I hoped Disneyland was going to be a whole lot better than Hollywood but then I felt teary again because I had always planned to visit Disneyland with Dad and maybe Helen and just thinking about the two of them made my eyes fill up again.

It was getting dark so I started to worry about where I could spend the night. It wasn't too cold, even though it was February, but I took my extra pullover out of my cricket bag and put it on. I walked westwards towards where the sun had set because the houses started getting grander so I thought that would make it a safer neighbourhood. I eventually settled down on another of those wooden benches. I was tired but my mind was racing so I couldn't fall asleep but I guess I managed to doze off because I didn't hear him come up to me.

I think I smelled him before I felt it. A horrible overpowering stink of BO that was so strong my eyes flew open. Then I felt my shoes loosening. I struggled to sit up to find a dirty, filthy, evil old tramp with a nasty stubbly beard trying to undo my trainers. I lashed out at him and he grunted. I staggered to my feet and kicked him as hard as I could. I was frightened the shoe would come off but it stayed on my foot as I connected with something soft, his stomach or his balls or something. He roared with pain like a wounded animal. I grabbed my cricket bag and didn't stop running for half an hour (except for tying up my trainers really tight) when I came to a tall sign that said 'Beverly Hills'.

I felt strangely comforted by the sign because I'd watched *Beverly Hills 90210* so it was familiar in a funny sort of way. It still didn't solve the problem of where I was going to sleep. I had no money and I knew the British police weren't very nice unless I was with Dad so the American cops were going to be worse. I didn't want to spend any time in prison, even waiting for Dad to pick me up, because Darren Foxton told me once that you can get lost in the system and you can be in prison for twenty years because nobody knows you're there.

I walked past the shops and restaurants and offices on Sunset Boulevard and turned right onto a street which seemed to have some nice houses on it. By now I was really tired. There was nobody around so I just had to find a place out of sight of everyone. On my right I saw a long wall as if it was guarding a big estate. I turned up a hill to see where the entrance was and found it was a park, Greystone Park. It had tall iron gates but there were lots of footholds and handholds and it didn't seem to be alarmed like the gates to people's houses round there. If they didn't have gates, these houses had a notice that said 'Armed response' stuck in the front garden. I didn't understand exactly what it meant except I knew it wasn't very friendly.

I tossed the cricket bag over the gate – it took me three goes to do it. Slowly I started to pull myself up. I slipped when I got to the very top and nearly impaled myself on a spike like Edward II although I think that was with a red-hot poker which sounds a lot worse. I sort of fell down the other side but I was inside and safe for the night. Or so I hoped.

I picked up my cricket bag and walked slowly into the park, navigating by the moon and the stars like Sir Francis Drake and the British sea dogs of the Elizabethan Age did. There was a big car park at the top of the hill (there is always a big car park in LA I was finding out) and from the edge of it I could see right across the city with its millions of lights winking back at me. It was a bit like getting to the top of the fells in the Lake District but the sudden view wasn't beautiful and restful like from a mountain summit.

I walked down some steps and saw a pool shimmering in the moonlight. All around it was a rectangle of grass. I threw myself on it and stretched out. I looked in my bag and put on some more shirts under my extra pullover. In fact I wore almost everything I'd brought with me. I didn't want to die in the night of that disease that old people die of in the winter when they can't afford to put the electric fire on. I had my midnight feast which comprised the last few triangles of the giant Toblerone bar and fell asleep under the stars. I told myself I was on a camping trip.

I woke in the morning a bit stiff from the position I had been sleeping in but pleased to feel the warmth of the sun on my face. I had to keep reminding myself it was February and that all my friends had been off school last week with the flu. Last week! It seemed like five years ago

— English homework, a physics test, after-school football practice, getting into a 15-rated film at the multiplex. It all belonged to another me.

I heard the sound of a car arriving in the car park so I assumed that meant the gates were open. I felt on top of the world. I had done it all myself. I had made it from Cambridge to this park in Beverly Hills. Santa Barbara was still a hundred miles away but somehow I'd make it there too. I felt really good about myself. I was going to get to Helen's today and solve everyone's problems.

I found I had passed the night in a beautiful ornamental garden like something out of a European stately home. I'd liked to have explored some more but I knew I needed to find a way to get to Helen's. I was already delayed by a day which meant Dad was probably starting to worry, even though I'd left that note telling him not to. I'd better do something about that. I passed a public phone in the car park. I hit the '0' button which said Operator on it and she answered. I asked if I could make a call to England and my dad would pay for it.

'You wanna call collect?'

'I want my dad to pay on our phone bill.'

'Station to station or person to person?'

Why was this so complicated? 'I don't know.'

'You wanna talk to your dad or anyone who answers the telephone?'

'My dad.'

'That's person to person.'

'But only my dad lives there.'

'Station to station.'

'I don't care!'

'Don't yell at me, kid!' The line went dead. I dialled again.

I was getting frustrated. Why did everything have to be so difficult? I gave our number again and eventually I heard the lovely sound of our home phone ringing, a very gentle tuneful sound, unlike the harsh American 'I won't take no for an answer' kind of ring. But Dad wasn't there. I didn't want another conversation with my operator friend so I put the phone down. I'd ring again later, maybe from Helen's house as I had always planned.

I might have been full of confidence but I was also starving. I searched through my bag but all I found was the screwed up silver foil from the big Toblerone bar I had demolished the previous night. I needed to get a bus to Santa Barbara which probably went from the town centre and I needed something to eat. I walked back to Sunset Boulevard and looked at the front of the bus to see where it was going to. It didn't say bus station or railway station or something useful like that. It just said 6th and Figueroa.

I watched as people got on and off. They got on at the front next to where the driver sat but they got off in the middle of the bus where the doors opened with a whoosh. I had no money apart from that twenty-five cents so I couldn't pay but I knew what I had to do. As soon as the next bus arrived and the doors opened I crawled onto it through the legs of the people who were getting off. I counted on the fact that nobody likes drawing attention to themselves on public transport and if the driver was busy taking fares up front he wouldn't be able to see me crawling into the back of the bus.

It worked perfectly. I soon discovered that everyone who went on the bus in Los Angeles wore the same dazed expression. It wasn't like an English bus with lots of schoolkids and women going to town to do the shopping. The kids got on separate yellow school buses (I knew that from watching *The Simpsons*) and most people in America seemed to have a car so the buses were occupied only by poor people and they obviously couldn't be arsed to turn me over to the cops. They probably hated the cops themselves.

Fortunately, too, it was rush hour and the bus soon filled up. I got out when we got to what looked like the centre of town and looked around for a newsagent's where I could spend my last twenty-five cents on something and ask for directions to the bus station. I was really annoyed to discover that America doesn't have newsagents. The newspapers are all in a plastic-fronted bin that lifts up if you put the right coins into a slot on the side.

I walked slowly down the street until I saw a 7-11. I felt a little stab of recognition. We've got 7-11 shops in England. I wandered in and was quickly appalled at the prices which I worked out by dividing by two and then adding a bit back on to get the English price. It was a dollar for a can of Coke which I can get for thirty-seven pence in Cambridge. I thought things were going to be cheaper in America. Twenty-five cents was going to get me nowhere.

I was going to have to continue my life of crime. The bus ride wasn't my first adventure into the underworld. One day after school in Cambridge I had been walking home with Jamie when he dared me to nick a Mars Bar from old Mr Patel in the newsagent's. It was like taking sweets from – well, from an old Ugandan Asian actually.

Next time the stakes were higher. Jamie and I planned a double pincer movement. My job was to act as decoy to distract the old man's attention while Jamie made off with that month's copy of *Asian Babes*. It worked like a dream. I kept calling Mr Patel's attention over to the large jar of liquorice which didn't have a price on it while Jamie climbed onto the bottom shelf so he could reach the porn mag on the top shelf, grab it and run away. Poor old guy never noticed. Seemed a shame to steal from him really. The magazine was a disappointment too. I wished Jamie had blagged a footie mag instead.

In the 7-11 store it was all different. For a start nobody spoke English. All the notices were in Mexican or something because I couldn't read them. I asked for directions to the bus station and got a torrent of Mexican back at me. It might have been the directions to the bus station but somehow it didn't sound like it. I wandered to the back of the store and took a Pepsi Max out of the cold fridge thing and a cake called a Tootsie Roll which I slipped into my pocket when I was pretty sure the horrible man at the front couldn't see me.

I made certain I left the shop with a couple of other people so I wouldn't even be visible. I was so pleased with myself because I was really starving. I decided to walk on for a bit before I unwrapped the cake and drank the Pepsi Max but I hadn't gone more than twenty yards when I heard a shout behind me. For a second I thought it had nothing to do with me then I looked back and saw the guy from the 7-11 shop racing towards me.

I turned and ran across the road and down an alleyway but this young Mexican wasn't like old Mr Patel from the Mulberry Street newsagent's. I might have dodged him for a bit longer but I was weighed down by my cricket bag. The man flung himself on me and I fell to the ground banging my head. I heard the most horrible sound in the world and I felt cold steel pressed hard into my cheek. This maniac had taken the safety catch off his gun and he was going to kill me. For a Tootsie Roll and a Pepsi Max!

My right arm was forced up my back which was really painful. I cried out in fear and alarm. I was so afraid I thought I was going to wet myself. The man took the drink and the cake out of my jacket and smacked me half a dozen times around the face really hard. Then he started kicking me. I pleaded with him to stop but he didn't till I was fainting. Then he picked up the gun and left me in the gutter.

The odd thing was I didn't cry. I was so in shock it seemed to freeze all the tears inside me. It took me nearly an hour sitting there on the ground, cradling the cricket bag to me, before I felt I could get to my feet. I hobbled away still looking for the bus station, but I had lost all that confidence I had when I hopped onto the bus in Beverly Hills first thing in the morning.

When I got to the bus station, I sat slumped on a seat watching people getting on the buses. It wasn't like the morning. They had all bought tickets at the ticket office and the side doors didn't open at all. The bus driver tore the ticket as passengers got on the bus. There was no way of getting onto the bus without a ticket. And I had no money. I wasn't going to get to Santa Barbara. Maybe it was time I abandoned this crazy idea of sorting everything out myself and just gave up.

I picked up the phone and asked for a collect call home. I knew the routine by now. The phone rang and rang. It was the middle of the night in England. I got very frightened again. Dad's always in the house at night. Where was he? I was seized by panic. Something must have happened to Dad. In trying to find me, something had happened. My head was filled with sudden flashing thoughts of how wonderful Dad was and how the last night I was home we'd had that terrible row about me spilling the Coke on the floor. Was that the last time I was ever going to see him? All I wanted to do in the whole world was to go home and be with Dad again.

CHAPTER THIRTY-TWO

Ralph

I COULDN'T BELIEVE HOW UNINTERESTED the Santa Barbara police were in Danny's disappearance. The last sighting of him was in Los Angeles, therefore it was no use complaining to them. As far as they were concerned, it was a case of 'Sorry, guv'nor, not my patch.'

Helen kept shooting me warning glances across the kitchen table but it was difficult for me to restrain my impatience which was threatening to boil over. It was ironic. She was the one given to periodic intemperate outbursts and I was usually the calm, pragmatic one. Not today. Not with my son's safety at stake.

It was Helen who persuaded them to post Danny's description on the NCIS computer which (supposedly) transmitted it automatically to every law enforcement agency in the land. The fact that he was twelve years old was the only thing that motivated them. There is growing concern in California, as there is in most places in the civilised world, that paedophiles were an increasing threat to children. So what were they going to do about it?

'We'll check all the hospitals, mental hospitals and morgues.'

'That's it?'

'That's all we're permitted to do, sir.'

'What about us? Can't we do something?'

'You can contact the FBI.'

'Aren't they in Washington DC?'

'There are field offices in most major cities.'

'And how long is all this supposed to take?'

'That's impossible to tell. If he went missing in LA it's not good news. Kids disappear all the time. It's an awful big city.'

'Well, next time I'll tell him to disappear round the back of your police station. Or would that be an inconvenience too?'

All right, I said the wrong thing but I was miserable, out of my mind with fear, and to make it worse I had slept badly. I woke up in the middle of the night, which was about ten o'clock in the morning in England, and thrashed around in the bed for a while. I couldn't stop worrying about Danny. He'd got a day's start on me, so this was his second night on American soil and no one had any idea where he was. I decided to have breakfast and let my body find its own way of adjusting to the time difference.

I couldn't find my clothes so I crept downstairs, anxious not to wake Helen. I opened the fridge and took out a plastic bottle of non-fat milk, which wasn't milk at all but some sort of chemical imitation of it, and a packet of granola, and poured them into a soup bowl which was all I could find.

'Jesus Christ, a burglar with a big schlong and a bowl of granola! You could get yourself on the front page of *The National Enquirer*.' Helen was standing there in a pair of tennis shorts, a grey sweatshirt and levelling a gun at me. I felt utterly ridiculous.

I decided to behave with all the sang-froid of a Noël Coward character so I continued to eat my granola with fastidious concentration despite my nudity, of which I was suddenly and irrationally self-conscious.

'Can I help you with something?'

'I heard a noise. I thought it might be Danny.'

'Then why the gun?' I slurped.

'Because it could have been a burglar.'

'The fact that it was more likely to be the man you knew was staying in the next room never occurred to you?'

'I'm a little on edge.'

'And I'm feeling better now I've got something inside me.'

'I'd feel better if I had something inside me too.'

'Perhaps you could put the gun down first. I don't respond well to that sort of performance pressure.'

She laughed and laid the gun on the table. I stood up and kissed her, feeling a swirl of confusing emotions – fear for Danny's plight, lust for Helen, jet lag from the plane trip, nausea from the non-fat milk. The taste of her and the feel of her body against mine was like opening the front door after a holiday. It was warm and comfortable and familiar and I belonged there. She took my hand and led me back to her bedroom, explaining why she had chosen to sleep in the guest bedroom herself. It was, as I suspected, simply her desire to let me continue to sleep, for which I could hardly blame her.

As she pulled me down onto the bed with her I suddenly realised that I hadn't showered since I had arrived. Helen seemed remarkably unaffected by the revelation but I was convinced that she was suffering nobly what must be a distinctly unhygienic experience. I pulled away from her and almost ran into the bathroom.

I let the jet of hot water wash away my tiredness and tried hard to gather my optimism for the ordeal of looking for Danny. Eventually, I stepped out of the shower, feeling at least a whole lot better prepared for whatever was now to ensue in her bedroom. The one thing I should have expected but didn't when I finally made my appearance, shaved, talced and perfumed for a battle of essences, was that my intended paramour should herself be *hors de combat*.

My initial response was of a disappointed bride on her wedding night but before we progressed too far down this sitcom road I realised that it was quarter past three in the morning and for Helen that wasn't quarter past eleven in the morning as it palpably was to my body clock. I snuggled under the sheets and felt her wonderful naked body sliding over to wrap itself, unconsciously or otherwise, around mine.

Her hand closed round me but elicited no response. I was surprised. I knew this had never happened to me before but I could hardly come out with that line of dialogue. Helen's breathing continued to be discernibly regular but her grip on my inoffensive private parts didn't lessen. I willed her to continue to sleep and retreated to my standard alternative to counting sheep by reciting in my head a list of recent Olympic Games starting with 1932 – Los Angeles, 1936 Berlin, 1948 London, 1952 Helsinki and so on up to 1996 Atlanta, 2000 Sydney. So far so good. Maybe it would all be different when I woke up. It usually was because the subconscious mind didn't worry about performance. I started afresh with my list of post-war FA Cup winners – 1946 Derby County, 1947 Charlton Athletic, 1948 Manchester United . . .

When I awoke in the morning the bed was empty and I was still no threat to the female population. I was convinced it was a physiological reaction to the fear that had gripped me but I was frustrated that now my body was betraying me. It did nothing to help me deal calmly with the negative input we received from the Santa Barbara Police. They said they would tell their officers about Danny and make sure the California Highway Patrol was kept informed in case he was wandering in their direction along the Ventura Freeway. Then they replaced their sunglasses, called Helen 'ma'am' and drove off in the glare of the California sunshine.

'Thanks for nothing,' I said as Helen closed her front door on them.

'You didn't help yourself or Danny just now.'

'Well, they were so bloody unhelpful.'

'So were you.'

'They're a bunch of arseholes.'

'Sure they're assholes. They're cops, for Christ's sake.'

'So what was I supposed to have said?'

She paused. Whatever I said wouldn't have changed their recitation of the facts about jurisdictional boundaries.

'I did tell you. If he had a gun ...'

'I'm sorry, I failed as a father. He hasn't got his own Kalashnikov.'

'Too bad. What were you waiting for?'

'His thirteenth birthday.' I must have looked thoroughly miserable.

'Would you like some tea?'

I smiled.

She bristled, defensively. 'I did learn some things in Britain, you know. Plus it wards off heart attacks, strokes and cancer.'

'I'd love a cup of tea. Thank you.'

I watched in awe as she filled two mugs with cold water from a bottle which she kept in the fridge, then dropped a Lipton's tea bag into each of the mugs. She opened the microwave door, slid the two mugs inside, slammed the door shut and set the controls for three minutes on full power.

'What are you doing?' I asked carefully.

'Making your tea.'

'In the microwave?'

'I haven't got one of those tea kettle things.'

'A teapot.'

'Whatever. Listen I've got a plan.'

'Does it involve the microwave?'

'Huh?'

'Or tea bags?'

'No.'

'Great. What is it?'

'Look, if you're not interested—'

'I'm sorry. Please, go on.'

She told me that whatever the cops did, LAPD or FBI, would take for ever unless we were incredibly lucky. By for ever she meant months, depending on what sort of a hole Danny had got himself into. We could shorten the process, but only if we got lucky in our turn. She had an idea.

Helen told me that one of the news magazines the parent company owned was a new American version of the old British photo magazine *Picture Post*. A year or so ago one of the best journalists she knew, Conor O'Neil, did an award-winning feature on the lost kids of Los Angeles. It was harrowing stuff and even though it was unlikely Danny was caught up in that underworld it was worth checking out.

It sounded like a lead of sorts, and at least we'd be doing something practical which was a whole lot better than sitting at home and waiting for the cops not to ring. At that exact moment the microwave bell sounded.

'Tea?'

'Thank you, Vicar,' I said, fishing the tea bag out of the cup with my fingers. 'Milk?'

'Only that non-fat stuff you hate.'

'Sugar?'

'Are you kidding?'

'Artificial sweetener then?'

'I got some Sweet and Low somewhere.'

I emptied the tea surreptitiously into one of the two sinks on offer. She came back into the room waving a packet of sweetener, probably lifted from Denny's or McDonald's.

'I was so thirsty,' I explained, rinsing the cup quickly and placing it firmly in the dishwasher.

'OK. You ready?'

'As I'll ever be.'

CHAPTER THIRTY-THREE

Helen

WE MADE CONTACT WITH THE Los Angeles Police Department and with the field office of the FBI but though they took notes, promised to do everything they could, they couldn't offer much in the way of hope, let alone a guarantee. They told us that only New York is a worse city for a kid to disappear in. I could see that Ralph had refused to consider the possibility that Danny might be dead so he was shaken by the options that were placed in front of him – drug runner, rent boy, Triad slave. They were too horrible to contemplate. Waiting for the cops was no choice at all. Doing something ourselves had to be the best way for us as well as Danny.

Con was an inspired idea, though I say it myself. She was a journalist whose stuff I had noticed for a couple of years before we signed her. She had arrived from Ireland as a baby with a large family, an amazing mother and no father so I felt an immediate affinity with her.

She came into the corporate building in the Miracle Mile district of LA on Wilshire and caused Ralph's next major surprise. For some reason he had assumed that Con was a man, so when she turned out to be a woman and not just a woman of conventional build but a woman nearly six feet tall with wild red hair, like Maureen O'Hara after a course of steroids, he found it difficult to articulate his thoughts for a few minutes.

Fortunately he didn't need to because Con and I did most of the talking. I had shown Ralph the brilliant series of articles she had written about the seamy underside of Los Angeles and its disappearing kids, which was complemented by some of the most poignant, searing photographs you are ever likely to see in a publication on general sale.

Conor thinks it's getting to be like Rio de Janeiro in Los Angeles but the authorities won't do anything about it because the kids are invariably from poor ethnic minorities. There are no votes in it and there's no political capital to be made out of it so the problem is allowed to get worse.

'You think Danny might be mixed up in this?'

Conor shook her head. 'White middle class kid? Dangerous. Bound to be someone looking for him.'

'So where do you think he is?'

'Sleeping rough, begging . . . could be a lot of places.'

'He had two hundred dollars with him.'

'Not now.'

'How do you know?'

'If he's not gotten in touch with you guys, he's not got the two hundred bucks.'

She was right. It made total sense. I had work to

do so I waited in the office while Conor and Ralph drove downtown and into South Central. Two was company but three was a crowd of nosy white folks. I worked as best I could until late in the evening when Ralph returned alone looking very depressed. They had spent six hours fruitlessly searching the streets, going into grocery stores and liquor stores, asking kids in the street, following Conor's route round the homeless shelters of Los Angeles. Nobody had seen Danny, nobody knew anything or cared at all.

I tried to explain to Ralph that it was hardly unusual. He couldn't expect to succeed so quickly; that would have been quite unrealistic. He was in need of some tender loving care. He had arranged to meet Conor again to continue looking at six thirty in the morning so we had to stay in town overnight. I drove him up to the front door of the Beverly Wilshire which was the nearest luxury hotel, but as the valet parking guy came out to open my door, Ralph suddenly grabbed my arm.

'No. Not here!'

'What? Why not? It's a great hotel.'

'I can't.'

'Why not, for God's sake?'

'I stayed here with Angela.'

I'd forgotten. I think maybe he'd told me months ago when we first started getting intimate. I understood instantly and jammed my foot down on the gas pedal, screaming away from the place like an armed robber. The valet parking guy leaped into the air in surprise. If Ralph still had demons about Angela, this sure as hell was not the time to confront them.

We checked into a room at a small hotel in West Hollywood near the Beverly Center between Santa Monica and Melrose. It was intimate and friendly and about as far away from the anonymity of the big Beverly Hills hotels as you could get. It was the right choice. Ralph came out of the shower to find the bed turned down and a steak and salad waiting on the table, courtesy of room service.

'Thank you.'

'You haven't tasted it. It might be crap.'

'Thank you for loving me.'

We hadn't discussed love for a while. I turned my face towards him and he kissed me. He held me and I could feel the pain of Danny's disappearance almost coursing through his body. He looked at the meal in front of him and stood there indecisively.

'What do you want? A written invitation?'

'I know it sounds crazy but I can't eat. I can't eat when Danny might be in a gutter somewhere starving.'

'This is like the conversation you have with kids when they won't finish what's on their plate and you tell them there are millions of kids starving in Africa. So they say, "Send it to them, I don't want it."'

'OK. I'll eat if you eat.'

'Sure I'll eat. I'm starving.'

He sat down opposite me in the white towelling robe the hotel provides — and bills you for if you don't watch out. Maybe it was all due to the artificially charged nature of the situation we found ourselves in but I couldn't take my eyes off him as he tentatively dragged the steak knife across the grain of the filet mignon.

'Ralph, I'm sorry I ran out on you like that. I know that's what started this whole mess.'

'It's not your fault. Why are you blaming yourself?'

'If I'd stayed, tried to make a go of it, Danny wouldn't be out here now.'

'It's nobody's fault, certainly not yours.'

'I don't think I realised how much I loved you till the plane left the ground.'

He laid the knife and fork down. 'I couldn't believe I could love someone again. I just thought you didn't love me back.'

I pushed back the chair and sat on his lap, kissing him as passionately as I knew how. He picked me up and carried me over to the bed.

'This is all very macho. What did you put on that salad?'

'I just want to introduce you to an old friend.'

'I think we reacquainted when I sat on your lap.'

He shrugged off the towelling robe. 'I love American beds. They seem bigger than English beds.'

'Everything's bigger in America,' I said, batting my eyelashes as suggestively as I could.

We fell asleep in each other's arms as the filet mignon coagulated on the plate. When I woke just before 7 a.m. he was gone. On the pillow next to me was a note scribbled

on the hotel's telephone pad. It was like a teenage kid's graffito carved into a tree in more innocent times:
'R ♥ H = D + ?'

I am greatly embarrassed to say I kissed it as I smiled.

CHAPTER THIRTY-FOUR

Danny

WHEN I PUT THE PHONE down in the bus station I just didn't know what to do next. I looked back to where I'd been sitting near the Santa Barbara bus and I saw my place had been taken by another kid, a bit younger than me maybe, about nine or ten. He looked like he hadn't stopped crying for hours. I went and sat next to him. He was making a big effort to swallow his sobs but he couldn't do it. I tried to cheer him up the way they always start on those American talk shows.

'Hi! I'm Danny Warren from England.'

He just stared into the distance as if I hadn't said anything at all.

'Where are you from?'

He took a dirty scrunched-up note out of his pocket and handed it to me. I can't remember the exact words but it was a letter 'to whom it may concern' which Dad writes to someone in authority when he doesn't know the name.

It was horrible. It was written by his wicked stepmother

who said she couldn't cope with him any longer because the boy's real father was dying of AIDS. They lived out in Montana but now they were heading to Mexico so he could die by the seaside. They couldn't look after themselves, let alone the boy who had never been to school. His real mother had died soon after he was born and the family had lived all the time in shelters and abandoned homes and eaten in soup kitchens. Stuck to the back of the note was a crumpled up official certificate which I smoothed out so I could read it. It was his birth certificate. His name was Paul. He had been born on Christmas Day.

I handed it back to him. I didn't know what to say so I said the first thing that came into my head.

'Have you really never been to school?' I couldn't imagine what it would be like to never go to school. I've known boys who were ill or broke their leg or something and they missed a whole term but I couldn't understand how a boy could just never go to school. I mean, I know there's lots of kids who live on those sink estates and everyone's unemployed and they spend their days bunking in arcades or mooching about town but even they've been to school.

Paul was still staring dead ahead but he was speaking. 'We can make ten dollars if we sell our blood.'

'Sell our blood? Who to?'

'A hospital.'

I wasn't mad for it. 'Is it safe?'

Paul didn't say anything. He still hadn't looked at me. 'You eat today?'

I shook my head.

Now he turned and looked at me. 'I found a place last night.'

He got up and walked over to where some people were boarding a bus for Bakersfield. Somebody had left a paper cup on a seat. He ran to it and snatched it as if someone was going to beat him to it, then stuffed it in his bag. He came back but walked past me. I supposed he meant me to follow him so I picked up my cricket bag and did.

I walked behind him a few paces like a wife does in Japan or China or somewhere like that. It was my choice. I wasn't sure where we were going so I wanted to be free to run away but I was so knackered and hungry I didn't have the strength to run anywhere. We walked for about half an hour into an area where there were no white faces apart from ours. I guess this is what it must feel like to be black in Cambridge but I'd never really thought about it till now. They weren't just black, they were mostly Mexican or Orientals. I was starting to feel that someone could jump on me any moment. It was a horrible feeling.

I was so relieved when we turned into a church. We went round the back, down some stairs and into the church basement where there was a trestle table and a big tureen and a large black woman was ladling out some kind of soup into paper cups. The cups were small but Paul, who still hadn't exchanged a dozen words with me, took the cup he had grabbed at the bus station and held it out. It was much bigger than the one I was given but the lady filled his up the same as mine.

Nobody was talking in the room. It was like a library. There must have been thirty or forty people there. I think some of them must have slept there because it was smelly the way a bedroom is when you get up in the morning. In the toilets off to one side I could see a mother giving her little girl a wash in the sink with a paper towel but instead of throwing the towel away, she folded it up and put it into a plastic bag.

We took our soup outside. It was a kind of lukewarm minestrone but it was mostly clear. Dad said the good bits always settle at the bottom with minestrone. It was horrible but I drank every drop. I could feel it settling in my tummy. Two other kids about ten years old came outside too. One of them had disgusting brown-looking teeth. Neither of them spoke either. They looked around warily. It was as if they were expecting some kind of attack. Everyone looked tired, worn down by life. I suppose I must have looked like everyone else.

A young black man came up to us. He must have been about eighteen or nineteen. His hair was in dreadlocks. He was holding out a bottle of something.

'You guys want some toncho?'

Paul grabbed the bottle and swallowed like a cowboy in a saloon in the Wild West. He passed it to me. I wiped the top with my sleeve and did the same. My throat nearly burned off. I couldn't get my breath. A smell a bit like petrol fumes went up my nose and I began to choke and pant for air. The black guy snatched back his bottle.

'You wanna make some money?'

'We're going to the hospital.'

'You gonna sell blood? You gonna die. You HIV?'

This conversation was starting to scare me but whatever it was that I'd drunk, which tasted like paraffin, at least it made me not feel hungry any more.

'You wanna go to the movies?' The black guy looked at both of us. I looked at my 'friend'.

'Sure,' I said. 'What's on?'

The black guy laughed. 'Say, that's good. Where you from? Australia? I know some guys from Australia talk like you.'

'I'm from England.'

'England, huh? Jolly good, old chap.' He spoke in a kind of a voice I'd never heard before but which I guessed was his idea of an English accent. 'You come to the movies?'

'I haven't got any money.'

'You get money at the movies.'

I stood up. This seemed like the best offer I'd had for quite a while. Paul had resumed his blank look, just staring off into space. I assumed this was the end of our 'friendship'.

'Just call me Batman. Everyone does.'

'I'm Danny.'

'Hey, Danny, my man, you want something to eat first?'

'I'd love something to eat. All I've had for ages is that soup and a bar of Toblerone.'

Further down the street was a small cafe. You couldn't sit down. There was a counter where you ordered and a ledge thing where you stood up and ate it. I wanted a hamburger but Batman said, 'Two hot dogs.' I noticed the hot dogs were cheaper than the hamburgers.

It was a horrid greasy place but I loved the smell of frying meat. It was the best smell I could remember. The man picked out a hot dog from a boiling vat of them and stuck it into a pre-sliced bun and handed it over. I helped myself to ketchup and mustard and onions. I nearly choked I was so hungry. I wanted to ask for a Coke or a Fanta but I didn't have the courage even though I wanted one badly.

Batman was being really nice to me and I remembered how Dad always said that Americans were so hospitable. This just proved it. I wondered why Paul hadn't wanted to come to the movies but maybe it was a 15 and he was too young to get into anything but a PG-rated film.

'What film are we going to?'

'We're gonna see porno,' said Batman as we resumed walking the streets of Los Angeles. My heart fluttered. This was cool, this was something to tell the guys about when I got back. I knew I shouldn't. I would never be able to tell Dad but my street cred would climb about a thousand per cent. This was going to be a whole lot better than that *Asian Babes* magazine we'd blagged off old Mr Patel on Mulberry Road.

It wasn't a multiplex like I expected, with a big stand for popcorn and M&Ms. It was a sleazy little place with a poster of two men with moustaches and wearing nothing but a thong. I knew instantly what was going on now. This was all-male stuff. I wasn't interested in this.

'Batman, I don't . . .'

And that was as far as I got. Batman put down fifteen dollars and pushed us through a turnstile like you do at White Hart Lane. I really, *really* wished I was back in England watching football now. I'd just have to keep my eyes shut and my cricket bag on my lap.

Batman pushed me up against a wall. 'Listen, kid, you go in there and you sit down. Someone will come and sit next to you. You just do whatever he asks and he'll give you money. Ask for twenty bucks first, OK? *Before* he does anything. You come out here after an hour and I'll be waiting for you. You give me all the money and I'll give you twenty-five bucks. OK?' He snatched my bag. 'I'll be here when you come out.'

I felt like I was drowning, the water closing over my head and I couldn't breathe. I was going to die. Batman pushed me through the swing door and I went into the cinema. It wasn't a cinema. It was just a large room with a small screen and a fuzzy picture. I couldn't make out what was up there on the screen for a good five seconds. I looked around but I could hardly see anything because my eyes hadn't got used to the darkness. I groped my way to the first empty seat and almost fell into it. On the screen I finally realised what one man was doing to another. I felt sick again. I closed my eyes and tried to think about things that made me happy, Spurs beating Arsenal, scoring runs for the school cricket team, eating pizza and watching TV with Dad at home . . .

A fat man sat down in the seat next to me. I kept my eyes screwed tightly shut. He was breathing heavily. His breath was smelly. In my mind I was trying to remember who Spurs were playing this Saturday. I had a vague memory that they were away to Middlesbrough. I felt the man's hand slide onto my thigh. I grabbed it and pushed it away. He silently put a piece of paper in between my fingers. It felt like money. He tried to unzip my fly.

'Don't!'

'C'mere, kid!' He grabbed my hand and tried to force it down into his lap. It brushed against something firm and warm. I didn't want to think what that might be.

My hand was tiny inside his and as we were both sweating I managed to slip it out of his grasp. I stumbled blindly towards the exit. The man made to come after me but then he must have found the money which I'd left on the seat and didn't bother.

I ran into the lobby and looked around for Batman and my bag but he wasn't there. I was now penniless and homeless and I'd lost my last link with my real life. I went out into the open air which felt pure and refreshing after the stinking atmosphere inside the porno house. To my relief I saw Batman standing by the traffic lights about fifty yards away. My bag was at his feet and he was talking on a mobile phone.

I raced towards him. 'Batman!'

Batman looked up. He didn't seem pleased to see me. He finished his phone conversation and snapped it back into his pocket.

'Where you come from?'

'The cinema.'

'What you doing here, man? You only just got in there.'

'There was this man and he tried to do things to me—'

'Where's my fuckin' money? Huh? Huh? Where's the money?' He had me by the collar and he was nearly strangling me.

'I haven't got any.'

At that moment a police car came roaring up the street with its siren blasting and its lights flashing. Batman let go of my collar and grabbed me by the arm, pushing me along the pavement. The police car sped past. Batman was really cross with me. He took a small manila envelope out of his pocket and gave it to me.

'Listen, kid, this is your last chance.'

Last chance for what? I wondered but I listened.

'You take this and you go two blocks down there and you take this to the guy at 1963, Apartment 5. He's gonna give you fifty bucks. You come back here with the cash and I give you five dollars. OK? Last chance, OK? You fuck up this time, I'm gonna slice you.'

'Can I take my bag with me?'

Batman thought for a moment. 'I kinda like this bag. What is it? A hockey bag?'

'Cricket bag. It was a birthday present from my dad.'

'You come back here with the fifty, I give you the bag.'

I looked at my bag like I was saying goodbye to it. I knew what was in that envelope and I didn't want anything to do with it. It wasn't like I hadn't seen stuff being dealt in town on weekends or sometimes just outside school. It was mostly dope. There were some kids who knew how to score the hard stuff — crack cocaine and heroin and all that — but I was never interested. Dad told me that if I wanted to be a professional sportsman I couldn't touch stuff like that though he spent a lot of time writing about pro players who had managed to be drug fiends at the same time.

As soon as I was out of sight of Batman I opened the envelope. Just as I thought, it was white powder. I wasn't walking round the streets of LA with this stuff. I could really go to prison now. I looked for a grid but I couldn't see one. All they have in LA is huge holes at the side of the pavement which I think must be so the rain can go down them when there's a storm but I didn't think it ever rained in California. I thought the sun always shone.

As soon as I got rid of whatever it was, I started running as hard as I could. I had to leave my cricket bag behind and I was pretty angry about that. Why should that horrible Batman get to keep my cricket bag? I thought of ringing the police anonymously and getting him arrested then taking my cricket bag off him but I didn't dare. I'd be implicated. I'd seen enough police programmes on television to know that.

I felt weird. Glad to be out of Batman's clutches, thankful that I was out of that horrible porn cinema, but I still had no money, nowhere to stay, no way of finding Dad, no way of getting to Helen's, and I was starting to get hungry again. I realised what I was now. I'd become a street kid, like the ones you see on the news who live in doorways and under bridges in cardboard boxes. I remembered with a growing sense of panic a story that Dad read out to me from a newspaper about these kids who lived wild on the streets of somewhere in Brazil. They didn't grow up to be Ronaldo. They didn't grow up at all.

CHAPTER THIRTY-FIVE

Ralph

AT THE END OF THE second day of searching, the third day since Danny went missing, a black cloud of despair descended on me. Despite Conor's help and Helen's hope, I felt utterly weary, ground down in spirit as much as energy. I remembered being told by a policeman once that if your car was stolen there were only two scenarios: if you didn't get it back in the first twenty- four hours it would either be stripped of its parts or resprayed, the licence plate changed and sold on; if it was joyriders you'd get it back with a dent in the nearside wing.

Danny hadn't made it to Helen's — that is, if that's where he was heading and already I was starting to doubt my own reasoning. I thought of all the times I'd had with him since the day he was born when I parked the car in Hampstead and sauntered into the Royal Free Hospital to see his little head sticking out. I thought of his solemn little face when I lifted him out of his cot in his grandma's house and told him with tears running down my face that his mummy wasn't coming home and from that moment on it was just him and me against the world.

I remembered rolling up my shirt sleeve and testing the temperature of his bath water with my elbow, seeing his face crack open into a wide smile as I flicked droplets of water onto him, lifting him up and wrapping him up in the bath towel like a big parcel. I could savour the talcum powder and the soft sweet odour of the top of his head, the feel of his silky thin hair. I could see him sitting up in bed at the end of his favourite stories – the hungry caterpillar and the owl who was afraid of the dark, the family who lived in the lighthouse and 'High on a Cliff' – throwing out his arms wide for a goodnight hug and kiss.

They were safe, these memories. They couldn't hurt me in the past. But reality intruded all the time. I asked Conor for details and she gave them to me starkly. She wasn't going to bullshit me. Street kids were twice as likely to be murdered, three times as likely to commit suicide. I couldn't get my head round this. Danny was only really allowed out in the daytime at weekends or during the school holidays. Otherwise I pretty much knew where he was every second of the day. He was of the generation that was ferried most places by car, though Cambridge certainly encouraged use of the bike outside the city centre. The idea that a child might be murdered obviously at some point touches every parent but my perception was that this sort of thing happened to other people's kids. This was Danny we were talking about.

Those first two or three days Conor must have driven me under every bridge and freeway overpass in Greater

Los Angeles. Under most of them there was a village of homeless people, some with kids, some without. One place under the Harbor Freeway seemed as if it was only for kids. They were all visibly malnourished. I couldn't bear to think of Danny in that condition. I got out of the car and went over to talk to them. They had the strangest names – Racoon, Little Chop Suey, the Russkie, Big Frankenstein, names that you would normally see at a dog track. It was soon obvious what was happening.

It was around six o'clock, it was dark and it was time for the people with respectable jobs to go home to their respectable families. Under the Harbor Freeway the occasional BMW or Porsche would pull off the road and flash its headlights. Two or three kids would rush over, the driver's window would glide down electronically and one of the kids would scramble into the car with the driver. A few minutes later the kid would get out again and the others would crowd around to see how much money he'd made. Was this what Danny had been reduced to? A rent boy in some equally dangerous part of the city? Every time we stopped and didn't find him I was torn by two conflicting emotions – relief that he wasn't one of these poor exploited kid prostitutes and deep depression that he might be one somewhere else – if indeed he was still alive.

I asked Conor about the kids as she drove up to yet another homeless shelter. The acrid stench of filthy bodies was overpowering. I felt like a French aristocrat in the eighteenth century holding a perfumed handkerchief to his nose as he rode in his carriage through the stinking streets of Paris. Conor answered all my questions with predictable honesty but frankly I only had to spend a couple of hours with these people to feel the hopelessness and the sense of despair.

'How much do they make, these kids?'

'Twenty bucks for a hand job, anything up to forty for oral.'

'Just sex? That's all they can do?'

'Sex or running drugs. Every one of them over the age of six can make a few bucks as a crack cocaine runner.'

'Shit!'

'It's actually quite safe. The cops want the dealers not the runners.'

'What do they spend the money on?'

'High top basketball shoes.'

'You're kidding!'

'The ones with families go home and give it to their mothers.'

'Their mothers know?'

She didn't answer. She didn't need to.

'If they haven't got families?'

'Burger King. Toncho.'

'Toncho? What's that?'

'A kind of high-octane booster. Rot gut. Worse than moonshine booze. Like a combination of nail varnish and gasoline.'

'Jesus!'

'It staves off hunger and gets them good and crazy.'

'Anything else?'

'The usual.'

'Drugs?'

She nodded. 'Many of them are HIV positive at birth. If their parents ever were together, the chances are the father's inside and the mother's on heroin or crack cocaine.'

'Do they ever go to school?'

'Some. But they get moved on so they're never in the same school for more than a couple of weeks.'

'They don't have a chance.'

'When I was researching the articles, I found a dozen kids under the age of ten with gunshot wounds.'

We walked downstairs into a church basement which served as a soup kitchen. It was strangely quiet but you could feel the tension in the air, like soldiers in the trenches waiting for the next artillery bombardment. You knew it was coming. It was only a matter of time. The faces were worn, tired, blank, reflecting the turmoil they must have been feeling inside.

The sole of my shoe picked up something from the sticky floor. Somebody had spilled something there. My mind flashed back to the last time I'd seen Danny and we'd had that stupid row about cleaning up the Coke he'd spilled. I'd have given anything in the world to have taken back those words.

There were kids here as young as three or four. Their mothers had just about given up but one kid, he was maybe five or six, he'd been given a pair of battered old Barney the Dinosaur slippers. His mother lay in a stupor on the floor. The boy was proudly putting on the slippers which had presumably come out of some charity sack. He looked down at them a long time then went over to his mother and said, 'Mom, are these new?'

It was ridiculous. They were scarcely wearable but to the little boy who had probably never had anything new in his whole life, it was very important. His mother didn't answer so he looked down again at his feet and said out loud to himself. 'They are. These are new. They're new Barney slippers!'

I was desperately hoping some other kid wouldn't come and break the illusion. I couldn't bear it. I strolled towards him.

'Hey! Neat slippers. Are they new?'

The look the kid gave me nearly broke my heart. I hurried back to Conor. 'I want to do something.'

She shrugged her shoulders. What was I going to do? Solve the whole homeless kids issue with a twenty dollar bill? I saw what she meant. If I gave the kid twenty bucks then I'd have to do something for everyone else.

I got back in the car and drove to the nearest Winchell's Donuts and spent fifty dollars on five big boxes of donuts, drove back, took out six and gave them to the Barney boy, then left the rest on the trestle table next to the soup tureen. Maybe Danny would wander in there in an hour and there'd be one or two left for him.

CHAPTER THIRTY-SIX

Danny

AFTER I'D RUN ABOUT A MILE I thought I was safe from Batman. I was utterly knackered but I didn't want to stop until I was out of his district. I saw a little park, a playground really, across the road and ran into it. The sight of the swings and the kids playing basketball made me feel more secure. I threw myself down on the ground and tried to think as calmly as my racing heart would let me.

I had to find some sort of job to earn the money that I needed for the bus ticket to Santa Barbara. I needed it quickly but not quick enough to risk my life running drugs or going with strange men in porn cinemas. I thought of all the Saturday jobs kids did in England — not my friends because we were too young but a lot of them had older brothers and sisters who did jobs on Saturdays in shops.

I couldn't do a girlie sort of a job like being an assistant in a clothes shop but I could work in a restaurant — well, not a posh restuarant where you had to know

French unless they just wanted a baguette de jambon or a baguette de fromage which was all I knew, or was it du jambon? Anyway, that put it into my head that I could work for maybe two days in a cafe sort of a place near the bus station, get tips and a wage and that way I could earn the fifty-five dollars I needed to get the Santa Barbara bus.

The place where I'd had that hot dog with Batman, that was self-service because it didn't have tables to sit down at. If there was a bigger sort of cafe that had tables and waiters, a cafe that served things like bacon, egg and chips, that would be say four or five dollars a meal so I might get a tip of fifty cents. So if I carried a hundred plates in a day I could earn nearly the full amount in tips and then there would be the day's wage and I didn't think I'd have to pay tax or anything because I was still a schoolkid and none of the kids who had Saturday jobs had to pay income tax.

I found the cafe. It didn't serve egg, bacon, sausage and chips but horrible hamburgers, I mean really horrible smelly things. I like hamburgers a lot and even I couldn't eat this stuff. The whole place smelled. They served hash browns and pancakes but they were all cooked on the same hot plate so everything was cooked in the same grease with everything else and it stank.

So did the man who owned it. He had a Chinese kind of a name and I didn't understand what he said half the time but he threw a really filthy greasy apron at me and told me to put it on. I had to clear the plates away and take them into the kitchen where it was a hundred degrees. The tips weren't fifty cents or a dollar but a quarter and often nothing at all. I didn't understand. How could they just get up and not leave anything for me?

When they did leave a tip I scooped up the quarter or the dimes and stuck them down my sock. It made walking hard but I thought it would be safe. At the end of the day I'd only made about twelve dollars and the man wouldn't give me my wages till the end of the week. I couldn't stay a whole week there. I'd die first. The man shouted all the time, mostly at me because I was new and I didn't know how to do things — well, how could I? And he also hit people.

It wasn't a clip round the back of the head like you sometimes get from the bigger kids at school. It was a punch in the shoulder as you were carrying a hot plate or a smack across the side of the face. I wasn't going to give him the satisfaction of watching me cry but I wasn't staying there a minute longer than I had to. At least he allowed me to eat there and I wolfed down a hamburger which smelled bad but tasted good. Frankly I wasn't far away from those kids I'd seen who rummaged through the rubbish looking for half-eaten food.

I didn't want to go onto the streets in case I ran into Batman so I had to spend the night somewhere near the cafe. I managed to find some old cardboard boxes at the end of the alleyway which ran behind the cafe. When the man went home and locked up, I started to construct a little tent out of them. I thought about going back to the park in Beverly Hills but I didn't want to spend my precious money on a bus and I was near to the station.

I fell asleep almost as soon as I lay down on a bed which I made out of some flattened cardboard boxes. I stole some towels from the cafe which I used as a blanket but I was so completely exhausted I could have slept standing up.

It was the middle of the night when I heard the sound of a police siren getting nearer. I thought it would pass down the main road but it didn't. I heard shouting and running feet, then the car headlights shone on me and I got up in a blind panic. It seemed like the police were chasing somebody. My first thought was that Batman had turned me in for carrying drugs and I was terrified. I knew that the cops were no friends of the homeless. This wasn't Cambridge. I couldn't ask them to look after me. I was one of the homeless now.

I scuttled over to where the alleyway was still in darkness and jammed myself against the wall. When the cops went screaming past me I started walking quickly the other way. I hung around the streets for an hour or so until I thought it might be safe to go back. When I got to the alleyway again my tent had been demolished and it was starting to rain. I couldn't stay out in the open. This wasn't Lake District fine drizzle. This was real rain and it was coming down hard.

I tramped the streets again looking for a doorway to shelter in. Eventually I found one and slumped to the ground, relieved but dripping wet. I stretched out on the cold tiles and was in a world that wasn't quite asleep and wasn't quite awake when I felt a violent pain in my side. It took me two or three seconds to realise I was being given a good kicking by an old tramp.

'This is mine, you fucking thief!' he kept shouting as he continued to boot me in the side and the legs and chest. I staggered to my feet and ran off. I didn't care which doorway I slept in. I just wanted to sleep.

I was woken at eight in the morning when the shopkeeper came to open up. He was another Oriental and he wasn't exactly pleased to see me. I wasn't going to hang around to get beaten up again so I scooted off. It took me another half an hour to find the cafe. I had been kicked from pillar to post and I'd totally lost my sense of direction.

The owner shouted at me that I was late, that I should have been there at eight when the cafe opened. I tried to say it was illegal to work kids so hard for so many hours but as soon as he heard the word illegal he clouted me across the face so I stopped. I could have walked out but I was so near to the money I needed I thought it was better to stick with the devil I knew. And he was a devil. This man was pure evil, like in all the *Nightmare on Elm Street* movies.

By the second day I was almost getting used to it — the constant screaming, the thumping and the slapping. I thought of the worst sort of day I'd had at school — getting my lunch money stolen by one of the bigger boys, waiting for the Piggy Harris punishment, getting sent off in the school match. None of them came even close to what I was going through now. It all seemed so petty compared with trying to find something to eat, somewhere to sleep. Just staying alive took all my concentration. Who could learn Latin vocabulary if his whole mind was taken up by just surviving?

Just before we closed at the end of my third day there, I'd collected $27.30 in tips. Then the man saw me scoop three dollars from the table and fold them into my pocket. It had been a party of four and they'd ordered a lot because it was their dinner and they were going home. The man screamed at me that I was stealing from him and that the money was his. I shouted back and said it wasn't, it was mine, but he wouldn't listen and he hit me again and dragged me and the three dollars over to the cash register. I went mental. If he stole my tips from me I'd never get to Santa Barbara and make everything all right again with Helen and Dad. I'd be a prisoner here for the rest of my life.

As he snatched the three dollars from my left hand, I thrust my right hand into the open cash drawer and grabbed whatever I could and fled. He bellowed at me but he wasn't as young or as nimble as I was. I thought of one of my favourite nursery rhymes, 'Jack be nimble, Jack be quick, Jack jumped over the candlestick' – pretty stupid at a time like this, I know. Dad used to read it to me from a beautiful cream-coloured book with bright, colourful illustrations. When I was much younger of course. And now here I was being as nimble as I'd ever been in my life.

I outran the man easily and went all round the block with him racing after me screaming in Mexican or

Japanese or whatever it was he spoke. Nobody helped him, thank God. I guess they saw this sort of sight every day on those streets. It was a great feeling and I had all that money in my pocket. I counted it. Eighty-seven dollars. It was enough to get me onto the Santa Barbara bus!

CHAPTER THIRTY-SEVEN

Helen

ALTHOUGH RALPH AND I STARTED off by becoming real intimate, just the way I wanted it, as time slipped by and we got no closer to discovering anything about Danny, I began to feel the mounting tension. Danny was destroying us by his absence as surely as he had with his presence. I was coming to the sickening realisation that I would not be able to get Ralph through this tragedy, if that's what it turned out to be.

I had read all those articles about families who are destroyed by a murder, not necessarily at the time but months later. It's not only murder; serious illness can also do this. Parents who are loving and supportive, who watch their child die of cancer, are likely to be found in the divorce courts the following year. I had no intention of abandoning Ralph but the Danny trauma was starting to weigh down our relationship. He couldn't give himself to me, he didn't want anything from me, he was just totally and understandably obsessed by what had happened to Danny.

I didn't blame him. I fully supported him. I loved him. How could I not? But as the days went by I was dreading the call that I knew must surely come. A body had been discovered. Could Ralph come down to the morgue and identify it?

On the third day it happened, just the way I had been predicting. I called Conor in the car. Ralph was buying lunch in a McDonald's. Conor said she'd break it to Ralph and they'd meet me down at the city morgue.

I squeezed Ralph's hand tightly as they pulled the drawer out and zipped open the body bag. Ralph pulled away and stepped forward. His expression seemed not to change. He stared for the longest time as if he couldn't recognise his own son any longer. I moved forward too. It wasn't Danny. It wasn't anything like Danny. We said no politely and went back outside.

There was no sun. It was a bleak LA February afternoon. There would be showers before long and I shivered. Ralph put his arm round my shoulder and pressed his face to mine.

'What were you thinking of back there?' I asked him.

'I was thinking of his parents. How long had they been looking for him?'

'You know, Ralph, this could go on for quite a while.'

'I don't care how long it takes. I'm going to find him.'

Our lives were full of such conversations. I felt so helpless, I guess because he felt so helpless.

The following afternoon the phone on my desk rang.

I'd been working in a desultory sort of way so when I heard a strange excited voice down the phone I wasn't at all sure who it was. Eventually it became clear the excited jabbering belonged to Ralph and what he was yelling was 'We've found him!'

'You have! Oh my God, that's amazing! I mean, like how— ?'

'Well, we haven't got him with us exactly.'

'What have you got exactly?'

'You know that picture of the two of us you took at the top of Bowfell?'

'How could I forget?'

'We've been showing it around these horrible dives and we got lucky. Some Chinese bloke – sorry, Conor says he was Korean. Anyway, he went ballistic when he saw it. He said Danny robbed him.'

'Thank God! Thank God! No wonder you sound pleased.'

'He's alive, for Christ's sake.'

'I know, I know, it's just great. And pretty amazing considering the way you trained that kid to be so polite in other people's houses . . .'

'Yeah, well, I don't think I was anticipating him having to survive on the streets of South Central Los Angeles.'

'How much did he take?'

'Eighty-seven dollars.'

'Eighty-seven bucks? What kind of hardened criminal are you raising, Ralph Warren?'

'Helen, can't you see, he's alive, I'm so happy!'

'And I'm just so happy for you. For both of us. Now what do you want to do?'

'I want to hang around here for a bit. Keep showing the photograph. Find out where he's gone with the cash. Conor wants to talk to you.'

He handed the cell phone back to Con who said it was best if they waited now till night because a whole new bunch of weirdos come out when the neon lights come on. She would take Ralph back to crash out at her place. We agreed I should go back to Santa Barbara and see if Danny showed up there. In any case, my brother Michael was coming to stay the night before taking a flight to Nairobi the next day. They both knew how to contact me.

Meanwhile, of course, there had been no word from the uniformed upholders of the law, which I decided to take into my own hands. Now that Danny was more of a reality and less of a supposition, I summoned every available resource. Every radio and TV station was told and every researcher and runner however minimally connected to Waverley Bros. Inc. on the West Coast was conscripted to aid in the search. Apart from my own private interest, this was going to be a hell of a story. This way, at least, I squared my appropriation of other people's resources with the greater good of Waverley Bros. Inc.

I drove back to Santa Barbara with the commute hour traffic. Why they still call it commute hour God knows. The journey back north on the 405 and west on the 101 starts backing up from around three thirty in the afternoon and rarely clears much before eight. I wouldn't normally travel too much in commute hour traffic during the week. I used to make use of the company service apartment in West LA so that I only needed to travel home for the weekend but I hadn't been regularly based in LA for over a year and I had forgotten how horrible it was to be trapped in six lanes of stationary traffic. Thank God for my four-speaker stereo and CD player.

The message light was flashing on the machine when I got home. I tried to suppress my hopes but I played back the six calls with an increasing sense of disappointment because none of them was the one I wanted. I wondered whether Danny had copied down my address and phone number or just the address, because he could always have placed a collect call. He must know that I'd always go and find him wherever he was. Unfortunately my number was unlisted so calling Information wasn't going to help him out.

The pasta was boiling away on the stove when the phone did ring. I grabbed it, my heart pounding, only to hear the familiar voice of my brother, Michael. I drove over to the airport in Goleta to pick him up.

I was delighted that he was here. We don't get to see each other too often these days and we had much to catch up on. Michael works for the United Nations and is always on a plane or just getting off a plane or just boarding a plane. He finds boarding cards in his pyjama pockets, air miles in his breakfast cereal. If he ever lost this job he would hardly miss it if he got another one tearing tickets at a gate, handing over duty free and anxiously scanning the departure screens; the environment would be just the same.

We have always been close, could always rely on each other for support since we left home. Growing up he was a royal pain in the ass, hogging the TV, taking Mom's car to football practice when I wanted it to go to the movies, but after we left home I discovered that he was really a great guy. He's separated from his wife but married to his job, being capable of giving of himself to the underprivileged peoples of East Africa but not to Jane, his wife.

Michael polished off two helpings of pasta and arrabiata sauce while I poured a glass of white wine and told him all about Ralph and Danny. He regarded the Ralph saga with amused tolerance. I don't think it is biologically possible for brothers and sisters to take their siblings' love affairs too seriously. There is always the feeling that this is the current month's toy and by Christmas there'll be an overwhelming need for a new one.

On the other hand his face went all grave when I told him Danny was missing. Funnily enough, when I described my own feelings for Danny and the mess we were now all in, his attitude to Ralph changed as well. Ralph as a boyfriend was an object of gentle fun between a brother and a sister, neither of whom seemed capable of settling down into the traditional nuclear family unit. Ralph as the father of a twelve-year-old, middle-class British kid missing on the streets of Los Angeles was another guy completely.

By the time I had poured out my heart to Michael, I knew that the emotion I had been feeling about Danny was true and honest. I had become that little boy's mom. I didn't ask to be. I flew six thousand miles back home to avoid it but somehow what had happened this week only confirmed that I was being drawn ever deeper into a situation in which I appeared to have lost my own free will. Michael was moved by my confession, got out of the deep armchair in which he had sunk and came and sat next to me on the couch, putting his arms round me and holding me, not saying anything.

It was an extraordinary and touching gesture because we weren't a particularly tactile family. I think he really appreciated that I was going through a life-changing experience and he wanted me to know that he was right there for me. The phone rang and I raced for it, imagining it to be Danny with only seconds to go before some horrible guy who was chasing him caught up with him and dragged him back into his den of iniquity.

It wasn't Danny, of course, it was Ralph, a bit depressed. After the wonderful, miraculous discovery that Danny was alive and thieving, the trail had gone completely cold. I praised him as much as I could, trying hard to lift his spirits, reassured him that at least Danny now had money to look after himself with and reminded him that Conor was a supremely gifted investigative journalist. Better than any shamus she'd sniff out where the trail went if anyone could. We kissed each other goodnight down the phone but neither of us exactly felt in the mood for phone sex. Michael had retreated to the guest bathroom.

He knocked on my door and came into my room to wish me good night. He was catching an early connecting flight to LA so he had called the local cab company for a taxi to pick him up in the morning.

'That's crazy. I'll drive you.'

'I can afford the six dollars.'

'I like taking you to the airport.'

'That could be misinterpreted.'

'You know what I mean.'

'Look . . . this is awkward.'

'God, is this going to be some kind of revelation? Are you coming out?'

'You want a slap in the mouth?'

'OK. Stay in the closet. See if I care.'

'You're not making this easier.'

'I'm sorry.'

'I haven't been a great husband. I know that 'cause my wife keeps telling me. I'd like to be a better brother. If I can do anything . . .'

That was as far as he was going to get. I hugged him. This was a record number of physical encounters for us over the course of a single day. For a guy who rarely expressed his emotions to his own wife, what I heard spoke volumes. It was a warm, deeply appreciated verbal fumbling. Words and Emotions were my side of the family; he was responsible for Deeds and Moral Strength.

Michael was a solidly built man and when he put his arms round me I felt his strength, hoping it might somehow pass into me by osmosis and fortify me for the terrifying things which I suspected were still lying ahead. Ralph was built entirely differently, more slender, strong but in a wiry sort of a way. Ralph had a strength that came from jogging or playing sports, Michael got his from working out in a gym. They were both attractive in their own way. Right now I really appreciated my brother's support.

I'm a pretty light sleeper at the best of times but, weighed down by the current anxieties, there was no way I was going to sleep through Michael's attempts to get out of the house without waking me. For a start he failed to get to the front door before the chimes rang.

I glanced out of the window and saw the cab driver sauntering back to the taxi, smoking a cigarette. I was shocked. I hadn't seen a cigarette in California since the late 1980s.

I flew out of the house, gathering my robe around me. The driver slammed the trunk lid down and smiled as he saw this slightly demented female in a state of undress hurling herself on a man who was being driven to the airport. I knew he had gotten hold of the wrong end of the stick but I had no desire to set him straight. I hugged and kissed Michael, suddenly unwilling to let him go.

Michael searched for the right note of sincerity. 'I'll stay if you'd like.'

'OK.'

'No, I mean it.'

'I know. That's why I said OK.'

'Well, you'll have to let go of me so I can call the government of Kenya and tell them to put the famine on hold for a while.'

'Go on. Get outta here.'

'I'm sorry.'

'I was just playing my sisterly role to perfection.'

'That's what I thought.'

'Then why are you sweating like a stuck hog?'

'Am I?'

I laughed. I didn't want him to say anything else. His fumbling attempts at expressing himself and the knowledge that he truly cared for me were all that I really needed from him.

CHAPTER THIRTY-EIGHT

Danny

WHEN I SAW HELEN KISSING that man, my whole world collapsed. Everything I had gone through had been a waste of time. All that planning and dodging and being robbed by the taxi man and starving and doing those horrible things in that porn cinema and the drug-running and the horrible cafe owner and sleeping in the alley and stealing that money ... I only kept going because I was so sure, *so sure*, that Helen loved Dad and I'd been the one to louse it up.

And now I felt like a total spas. She didn't love Dad. She'd never loved Dad. She loved this man, this guy getting into a taxi. Why else would she be kissing him wearing a nightie and nothing else? Why would she kiss someone in public unless she loved him? Maybe he was her husband. Maybe he was her husband when she was in England. Did Dad know all this and not tell me? Is that what all the whispered conferences were about when I was in bed?

I thought and thought so hard, my head started to

hurt. What had I done? I hated it when Dad interfered in my life, when he went to see my teacher when I was in primary school and complained about Luke Josephs bullying me. He got it all wrong. I told him about it because he was my dad. I didn't expect him to go and solve anything. He just made things worse. The teacher made Luke write out Psalm 121 about 121 times and he hated me for ever — it made everything so much worse. He'd lie in wait for me after school (if Dad wasn't there to walk me home) to try and beat me up. Fortunately I could run faster than he could. I swore to myself I'd never do anything like that to my children. So I did it to Dad instead.

Maybe Dad talked to me about Helen because he had no one else to talk to. Then I thought back to just after Christmas, when Helen left, and I remembered that in fact Dad hadn't talked to me at all about Helen. Why did I think he had? Did I make everything up? I felt so confused.

I never wanted Helen to be my mum, not even when I was trying to get her back together with Dad. My mum was my mum, Angela, nobody could ever replace her and I didn't want Helen to try. But the reason I think I sort of liked her was that she didn't try. And now that I wanted her to, she was off with some other guy. I know I didn't behave too well before when I thought she might have been moving in on Dad and me, and then after she went I knew Dad wanted her, but the weird thing is, over the past week or so when I had become so totally uptight about getting to Helen's house, I was looking forward to her coming to live with us and making us into a real family.

Helen wouldn't be a mum like Darren Foxton's mum. She's got an important job and she'd be travelling a lot which would be cool because she'd bring back lots of presents and then when she wasn't at home it would just be me and Dad as usual. So that's why I was telling myself, all the way over on the plane and then in Los Angeles and then on the bus to Santa Barbara, that if Helen and Dad got back together again, it would be so worth all the aggro. And I did think maybe she could explain to me why I felt so strange when she kissed me good night that time. She could be like a grown-up sister to me but someone Dad could love who would make him happy.

But now Helen stood there in her nightie in front of her house and watched the taxi drive away. She was smiling and blowing a kiss. I felt like she had stabbed me in the gut with a kitchen knife and then twisted it about. I was fifty metres or so away down the hill and behind a parked car. I ducked down as the taxi came past where I was. I knew at once that I didn't want her to see me. I didn't know if she'd pretend that there wasn't a man but I did know she wouldn't be happy if she knew I'd seen her with that guy. And I knew she'd never come back to Dad now.

I sat on the pavement and cried. There was no one about. There's never anyone on the street in the nice parts of California, only in the horrible bits where I had been. I cried more than I've cried for — well, I suppose I've been crying a lot these last few days which is strange because I never cried much, not even when I was a little boy. I had a friend at primary school called Hugh who cried all the time and everyone made fun of him though I tried not to join in because I hated to see him being teased like that. But I was glad it wasn't me.

Now I felt I was just like Hugh because I knew. I knew exactly what was going on. I'd seen it now with my own eyes. Dad had broken up with Helen after Christmas, that's why he was sad, and now she had come back here to live with her husband or her boyfriend or whoever the man was. There was no point in staying around. I had suffered too much in the past few days to go and see Helen now. All my dreams were like the end of those books, like *Oliver Twist*, where the door opens and the long-lost parents or grandparents run outside and sweep the child up in their arms. I wanted that to happen to me too, but I'd got it all wrong as usual.

I started to wander back down the hill. I was used to walking long distances now. At home I used to hate walking to school on cold mornings in the winter or back home after school when it was raining and Dad wasn't there to collect me. I would never have believed how far I had walked these last few days. It must have been miles and miles. I'd be dead fit for the rest of the football season. And then I started to think about playing football with my friends and diving about on the grass in Jamie's back garden and the tears started to prick at my eyes. I was just crying all the time.

I had two banknotes worth twenty dollars each, three one dollar notes and a handful of change left from the money I took because I had got a child's fare bus ticket from Los Angeles to Santa Barbara. I didn't steal it. It was mine. The man lied to me, robbed me, hit me, cheated me, so I had no guilty feelings about taking the money. Besides, it was in a good cause – the best possible cause. If he hadn't been so horrible I'd have asked Dad to pay him back.

Dad! Where was he? Where was my dad now? Going off his nut with worry, I guessed as I walked back towards the bus stop where I'd got off. When I reached the main road I found a payphone. I dialled the operator – I knew the routine so well by now – and rang home but there was no reply. I wanted to see him so badly, just to hug him and say, 'Oh Daddy, I'm so sorry. I'll never do anything like this again as long as I live.'

I caught the bus from Montecito to Santa Barbara which cost me one dollar and twenty-five cents. I kept trying to think about what I could do next but I was now really, really tired. I hadn't slept properly for days and days. I couldn't think straight. I couldn't go back to the airport because Dad might have already arrived and be looking for me somewhere. But where, where? Where would he go that he knew I would go too?

I got off the bus at the station and sat on a bench. It wasn't as bad as Los Angeles. Santa Barbara seemed safe and clean in comparison and the sky was blue and the sun was warm. I thought this was what it must have been like for Dad and Mum when they were on their holiday in California. I thought about the pictures of Mummy in our house back home, especially the one I liked so much, lying on the sun lounger. She'd have liked today's weather.

The tears were coming again. I couldn't stop them. I had never cried like this before. I felt so alone and I wanted my dad and my mum around me. My mum would know where Dad was because they loved each other so much and she would help me too because though she was dead I knew her spirit watched over me, like Dad always said. I didn't have a hankie or anything so I just wiped my nose on the back of my hand and rubbed my eyes furiously to block the flow of tears.

I got up and walked towards the exit where there was a travel agency or ticket office or something. It had lots of posters in the window. I recognised the Golden Gate Bridge because underneath was a sign saying 'San Francisco – Special Weekend fare $59.95'. There was a picture of a lake which said Lake Tahoe and a bus fare next to it and a big Disneyland-type castle which was called Hearst's Castle San Simeon. I wasn't thinking much about these places because my mind was filled up with thoughts of my mother. Then I saw it.

It was a picture of a lighthouse standing on a rocky island while the waves smashed all around it. And then it all came together in my mind like the missing piece of a gigantic jigsaw.

I stared at the lighthouse for the longest time. There was only one place in California that I knew about and that must be the place where Dad would go too. How ⸻en had I heard about it? Almost from the time I was old ⸻ remember anything I knew about this place.

There had to be a reason why that story about scattering Mummy's ashes in front of the lighthouse high on a cliff was so special. Apart from the obvious one, that is. And now I knew. That's where I'd go. If my dad wasn't there, my mum was and she'd know where he was. She'd know what to do. Somehow she'd find a way of telling me where he was. High on a cliff Mummy's soul watches over us both.

CHAPTER THIRTY-NINE

Ralph

I ARRIVED BACK AT HELEN'S house exhausted and frantic at the same time. I was on the verge of hysteria. I needed to watch some sport just to calm me down but there was no football on TV because the Superbowl had taken place three weeks before and spring training for baseball was a week away, so I was left with college basketball and ice hockey, neither of which really grabbed me. I needed to watch Spurs playing Arsenal or the England cricket team battling away in Australia. In fact I got something far better than either of those. I got a totally focused Helen.

She knew that I hadn't found him because I'd been on the mobile to her all day. I wanted to stay in LA overnight again but she wouldn't hear of it. I was out on my feet and, besides, she'd been organising. She was still excited about our having found the cafe where Danny stole some money. I wasn't because I'd been so disappointed at how quickly the trail had gone cold.

Galvanised into action by my earlier phone call Helen

seemed to have tipped off every journalist in southern California. She had a private army down in South Central combing the streets that Conor and I had exhausted ourselves on. I wondered who was paying these guys but she just smiled, pointing out that when we found Danny it would be one of the great journalistic stories of all time. I couldn't even raise the obvious question of what would happen if . . .

She ran a bath for me with a handful of bath salts. I enjoyed the touch of her hands on my belt buckle as she snapped open my jeans. It was the first time I had undressed in front of her, or rather been undressed by her when sex hadn't been the object of the exercise. We were in a different mode tonight.

She wouldn't hear any kind of defeatist talk. I was to stay with her that night and the following morning we could leave at five thirty before the freeways clogged and we'd be in LA soon after seven. She placed or rather caused to be placed a number of telephone calls to the Los Angeles Police Department.

The LAPD changed their tune when they realised the scale and the nature of the search Helen had organised. Like any major law enforcement organisation, they couldn't afford the bad publicity that would come their way if the journalists found Danny and they didn't. They were in bad odour anyway with a couple of investigations for internal corruption constantly on the local TV news so finding Danny would be a major coup for them.

Helen was just wonderful – so calm, so organised, so supportive. I kept having to remind myself that I shouldn't expect too much. After all, Danny wasn't her son. But I wanted so much for her to be a part of our lives and I felt that she would spend the rest of her life with us — unless tragedy struck, and I kept trying to suppress that fear. I also kept reminding myself I wasn't betraying Angela; that Angela, if she could see us now, would be cheering us on. She would want me to find Danny, she would want Danny to have Helen as a friend and a supporter. This could be the most magical time in our lives if . . .

The 'if' wouldn't go away. I fell asleep with Helen's beautiful body wrapped around me and dreamed of Danny. I dreamed of the time I flew back home without Angela and of driving to her mother's house and seeing his little face, questioning but unable to articulate the words. I felt a failure then, having returned without his mother, and I felt a failure now. Somehow this whole tragic ordeal was my fault. It had to be. I had failed my little boy. I didn't communicate with him. I'd lost his trust and in trying to win it back himself, he had given his life.

Afterwards I rationalised that the dream was a result of those heartbreaking days with the street kids, and in particular of that traumatic moment at the morgue when I thought I was going to have to formally identify Danny's wretched broken body. I'm one of those people who rarely dream, or if I do I never remember the substance of it in the morning. This was different. This was a nightmare the like of which I have never experienced.

When I saw him, it was as if he was asleep. He was thin,

with dirty clothes and tousled hair, and he bore the marks not of violence but neglect. There was nobody around him. It was just chance I found him as I walked along the street. There was a kid under a filthy blanket. I rolled him face upwards and saw that it was the dead body of my child. I screamed and screamed but nobody came. Nobody cared. A policeman told me to move the kid away, he was causing an obstruction. I yelled at him that it was Danny, my son, but the cop just said something to the effect that the world couldn't stop just because my son was dead.

When I lifted him up he felt like a bundle of feathers. It wasn't just that he'd lost weight, it was like picking up a toddler. And that was the thought that overwhelmed me. He was just a boy, a baby, and I, his father and only parent, the one person in the world who should have looked out for him, had neglected him. I hadn't meant to. I loved him so much, always had from the moment of his birth, but when it came to it I hadn't been there for him. 'Oh God!' I cried to a deity who seemed very real. 'Give me back my son and I'll do anything! Anything!'

What kind of a deal could you do with God? What did the monks and nuns do, those wholly holy people who spend their lives on their knees praying to God, to understand His Will? I will become a better person? I will stop eating cakes and chocolate? Surely the pursuit of deep spiritual commitment can't be like going to Weight Watchers? I will give one hundred pounds to charity? One thousand? What price do you put on the life of your own flesh and blood?

I awoke in a cold sweat. It was still dark outside. Helen

was with me but where I was in my head she couldn't follow. I needed my son. I needed Danny back or I wouldn't be able to live any longer. To lose Angela when I was twenty-three was a nightmare. To lose my little boy as well would be insupportable. I went back to sleep as dawn broke over the islands off the coast of Santa Barbara.

Helen had to shake me awake in the morning. I was so out of it she almost had to push me into the shower which she turned on cold at full blast. I woke up pretty damn quick then. She was waiting for me as I stepped out, holding the towel. I started to dry myself, looking for the right words.

'Helen . . .'

'Shhh!' She put her index finger to my lips and kept it there. I took it off and kissed it.

'I'm sorry if I haven't been much of anything . . .'

'Ralph, don't. Don't say anything.'

'I just want to tell you how much I love you.'

'You've done that. Now let me tell you something.' We sat together on the edge of the bath. She took my hand and kissed the palm tenderly. 'Ralph, when I met you, I thought I was still in love with Charles. I know now I was living a shallow, silly life really, full of the wrong people and the wrong values. Now I want to tell you what you've done for me. You and Danny. You've made me feel like a whole person. I can't say I care about Danny like you do but as far as I'm capable, I love him just as much in my own way because I love you so much. We're going on and we're going to find him. OK?'

My eyes filled with tears as she spoke. The words were so kind. All I could do was nod. She leaned forward and kissed me.

She made some coffee, the tea-making fiasco having been abandoned permanently, and we hit the freeway. I wasn't too talkative because I rarely am in the morning and my mind was still dashing maniacally from one possible scenario to the next. South of Oxnard, Helen, obviously concerned again by my returning sombre mood, began to apologise for California's appearance in my life as nothing more than a background for my personal tragedies. I demurred.

'It's not like that. I love California.'

'I don't see how you can, seeing as how we've done nothing but screw your life up.'

'I love you. And you're in California.'

'You should never come back here. You should stay home and look at *Baywatch*. Keep the whole thing a fantasy.'

'I disagree. I should come here all the time. If Danny knew his way round the state . . .' My voice trailed away.

'You've never been back? In twelve years?'

'I come to golf tournaments and so on but mostly on the East Coast so I don't feel so far away from Danny then.'

'But you talk to Danny about California. He told me.'

'Sure. I talk to him about Angela, about what happened. I've always tried to make her death into a story.'

'Like a fairy story?'

'When he was little I used to tell him a bedtime story

about how I scattered his mother's ashes high on a hill overlooking the ocean.'

'Sounds creepy.'

'It wasn't. Honest. Danny loved it. It was his favourite bedtime story as a kid.'

'Is that how you finished it? With her cremation and scattering her ashes?'

'Yes, but there was always a moral.'

'Don't drink and drive?'

'No. For us, the two of us. I used to say "High on a cliff, Mummy's spirit watches over us both."'

'That's cute.'

'I wanted him to feel that Angela still had a presence in his life. If I wasn't there he could somehow turn to . . . Shiiiiiit!' I flung my arm out across Helen's chest.

She screamed in panic. 'Ralph!' She jammed on the brakes. Vehicles behind hooted and flashed their lights but she managed to keep control of the car and bring it to a stop on the hard shoulder.

The cars continued to zoom past with the sound of their horns trailing behind them as I turned and looked at Helen. Gathering as much composure as I could manage, I stammered out the words like a stroke victim.

'I'm sorry! I'm sorry, I didn't mean to scare you.'

'Well, you sure as hell did!'

'I just remembered. That's where he is, Helen! I'm sure of it. He's gone to High on a Cliff!'

CHAPTER FORTY

Helen

HE TOLD ME THE WHOLE spiel as we headed north. About the bedtime stories he used to read, the one about an owl, the one about a hungry caterpillar, the family that lived in a lighthouse and always ending with Angela and the special place high on a cliff. As he did so, his whole attitude changed. It was like he'd had some deep religious experience or he'd watched his beloved Tottenham Hotspur soccer team defeat some other team. His face shone with certainty.

'How can you be sure Danny knows?'

'He's always known.'

'How old was he when you told him these stories?'

'I told them almost every night for about five or six years from the age of two onwards. I can't tell you what a powerful effect they had on him.'

'And you think he's going to find his way in a strange country to the exact spot? Ralph, honey, be realistic.'

'I am, darling, I am. Oh, Helen, please believe me. I used to say if he was ever in trouble and I wasn't there to help him he must always ask his mummy what to do. Her soul was with both of us always, watching over us.'

While I was delighted that Ralph now had a strength and an assurance that I had not seen since he had arrived at LAX, I couldn't help feeling concerned at the possible consequences. The chances of Danny having found his way to the exact spot were on the far side of remote. How was Ralph going to feel then? Were we going to have to sit in some goddamn state park for a week waiting for the impossible?

I let Ralph take over the driving because I wanted to stay in touch by cell phone with the continuing search for Danny in South Central LA where I was sure they'd eventually find him. It was a struggle to get Ralph to keep to the speed limit.

'There are Highway Patrol cars all over the place.'

'Who?'

'Cops.'

'I thought they were all out looking for Danny.'

'LAPD jurisdiction ends two hundred miles south of here.'

'You know just about everything.'

'I don't know where this place is you're taking me to.'

'I do.'

He certainly drove like he did.

'What's it called, this place?'

'I dunno. But I'll recognise it when I see it again.'

I groaned inwardly. The roadworks on Route 1 just beyond the turnoff for Hearst's Castle at San Simeon caused the first crease to furrow his brow. He started to slow down.

'This is it?'

He looked round, puzzled. 'Looks familiar.'

'This is the John Little State Reserve.'

'Looks sort of familiar but I'm not ...'

'Why don't we stop?'

We were in Mill Creek, at the southern tip of the California Sea Otter State Game Refuge and it was a truly beautiful sight. The rain which had swept across the state during January had blown away and we were experiencing a glorious fresh February morning with the sun shining brightly out of a cloudless California sky. Ralph stopped the car in the official car park and almost ran towards the sound of the ocean. There were already picnickers at the wooden tables and little kids holding their parents' hands were venturing further out to find the sea otters.

'Is this the place?'

Ralph's face betrayed his anxiety. 'I sort of recognise the mountains behind us but I just can't be sure ...'

It was hopeless. We must have spent nearly an hour combing the place. Every time he thought he recognised something, a patch of ground, a clump of trees, he sprinted forward and then came to a stop, shaking his head in frustration. I tried to be positive. It just came out negative.

'You'd know it if this was the place.'

What neither of us said was that Danny wasn't here. I wanted to get Ralph back to LA as soon as possible. This was just so crazy, a wild goose chase. There was no way Danny had made his way this far upstate.

Eventually Ralph turned back towards the car. 'Let's drive on. It's been twelve years.'

We got back in the car and headed north again. I tried not to stare at Ralph but I couldn't help it. I could read him like a book just by looking at his eyes. Something was stirring. I could see his face change. There was an intensity about him now that I hadn't seen before, like a dog sniffing some old familiar smell.

'What?'

A smile crept across his face. 'I can feel it. Sense it.'

'This is it?'

'I know it is. I know it.'

I looked at the map. 'We're coming up to Vista Point.'

'Makes sense, doesn't it? High on a Cliff? Vista Point.'

'Yes, but there's a hundred vista points on Route One.'

'This is it!'

We skidded to a halt. He leaped out of the car, leaving the engine running. I leaned over and turned it off, locked the car and tried to catch up with him. Ralph was running around like a chicken with its head cut off. He was screaming, 'This is it!'

He plunged on through the woods and out onto the open grassland. In the distance I could hear the roar of the ocean as it pounded the rocks.

Ralph was waving his arms about. 'This is the place. This is high on a cliff. That's where we made love and over there is where I stood. Come on!'

He grabbed my hand and pulled me towards the edge of the cliff.

'Whoah, Ralph. Hey, hold it right now!'

'I stood here, Helen, right here. I opened the urn . . .'

He threw out his arm like a man scattering ashes. He turned to me. His eyes were burning bright. 'You do believe me, don't you?'

'Yes, Ralph, I do believe you. But look, Danny isn't here.'

It took a minute for it to sink in.

'He's not here,' whispered Ralph. 'Danny! Danny!' He was now yelling and racing around as if he believed that Danny would magically appear from the forest of trees and come racing towards us. Eventually the manic behaviour stopped and he slumped to the ground. I sat down next to him, cradling his head in my lap.

'I was so sure.'

'I know, darling.'

'High on a cliff. It's here.'

I stroked his hair and kissed his face, chapped by the winds that blew off the ocean.

'Shall we go back?'

'No!' Ralph scrambled to his feet. 'He's here. He's at high on a cliff.'

'But you just said— '

'Well, maybe *I'm* wrong. Maybe I'm wrong and this isn't high on a cliff but Danny's just up the road.'

We drove on northwards through Big Sur because that's what he wanted but the atmosphere in the car had changed. What had, at first, seemed such an overwhelming certainty became an increasingly forlorn hope. We stopped the car at every conceivable possibility – the Ventana Campground, Cooper Point, Riverside Park, the Andrew Molera State Park.

At each juncture the routine was the same. Ralph was certain this was the place, a clump of trees, the sound of the waves, the view of the Los Padres National Forest behind us, and then nothing. No Danny, no recognition of the famous spot. We would trudge back to the car feeling that we were trampling on Ralph's dreams. This place had achieved mythic status in his mind and now it had gone.

Eventually the beauty of the day began to fade for us and the sun shone out of the blue sky to mock our efforts, not to celebrate them. Each time we got back in the car to drive ever northwards, Ralph drove slower and slower, as if reluctant to encounter the next disappointment. By now I was paralysed with fear. This was worse than the fearful dragging of the scummy streets of LA. I didn't know what to say to cheer him up.

We left the Los Padres National Forest behind and headed on towards Carmel and Monterey. Ralph had always been sure that he had driven south from Carmel with the ashes so the chances of our finding the place now were almost nonexistent. Besides, from my point of view I believed him when we stopped at Vista Point. That was high on a cliff all right but Danny hadn't found it because he was still living on the streets of LA.

With every disappointment and negative response,

Ralph got crazier with anxiety. I was beginning to be seriously concerned for his mental health.

'Ralph, let's stop somewhere and talk this thing through.'

'I've got to find Danny. If I don't, it'll happen all over again.'

'What? What'll happen all over again?'

'Like after Angela died. My life will disintegrate.'

'You'll still have me. I'll be there for you. I'm not going to run away again.'

'But I will.'

'What?'

'I know myself too well, Helen. If I lose Danny, there'll be nothing left. I won't want to be with anyone and you won't want to be with me. Believe me.'

My cell phone rang. It was Conor. There had been a serious incident at one of the homeless shelters. A fight had broken out and some guy had been ejected by the authorities. Half an hour later he returned with a can of gasoline and a box of matches and torched the place. Ten people had died, at least half a dozen of them kids. Many more were in the hospital with horrific burns.

I told Ralph as calmly as I could. 'We've got to go back. He might be in this hospital.'

'No! He's here!'

'Ralph! Listen to me! Danny might be hurt. He might be in the hospital, in pain because of these burns. We've got to go and find him.'

Ralph swung the car off the highway and along a forested track. He seemed to have calmed down. His eyes were fixed on something in the distance. I tried again.

'Ralph, I'll drive, if you like.'

'Look, Helen, can you see that?'

'What?'

'That lighthouse.'

'It's the Point Sur lighthouse. What about it?'

'Such a coincidence. Right next to high on a cliff, there's a lighthouse.'

'It's hardly right next to it. It's been thirty miles since Vista Point.'

'I wonder. I wonder.'

Ralph got out of the car, his eyes almost magnetically attracted to the lighthouse. I could hear the sound of the crashing surf but I couldn't see it because the grassland ran to the top of the cliff and the ocean was a hundred feet below.

'Ralph, let's go back to LA. That's where we'll find him.'

'He's here, Helen.'

'What? You're crazy.' I looked around. The place was deserted. 'Is this high on a cliff then?'

'No. We found high on a cliff. But Danny's here. Can't you feel it?'

'I can feel the cold. Let's get back in the car.'

'Somewhere. Danny's here somewhere.'

But he wasn't. There was no Danny. There wasn't a soul. Just something that looked like a bunch of old clothes on the far side of the grassy headland. I wondered why the Park Rangers hadn't tidied it up. They're usually real good about keeping these state reserves in great shape. Ralph was staring at it.

'He's not here, Ralph.'

Ralph wasn't listening. He started to walk towards the pile of garbage. Then he broke into a run, then a sprint. Suddenly he was yelling.

'Danny! Danny!'

The pile of garbage sat up, startled, animated. It stood up. 'Dad! Daddy!'

'Oh my God! It's him! It's Danny!'

It was. It was Danny. I ran after them both, screaming my head off, but they both ran faster. I thought for a moment they would knock each other out, such was the force of their impact. It wasn't a pile of old clothes. It was Danny. And he was there, I really believe, because of what Ralph had always said. Angela's spirit was watching over the two of them. It was she who found them and made them whole.

Ralph just held Danny in his arms for the longest time. Both of them were crying and I stood there like a third wheel, watching. I was so pleased, so happy for both of them, so relieved that it hadn't all ended in tragedy. I wanted to join in but I knew my place so I hung back.

'I knew you'd be here, Dad. I knew it. This is the place, isn't it? This is High on a Cliff, isn't it?'

'What? No ... I mean yes, darling. It is. This is the place.'

'I knew it was here somewhere. I just had to find the lighthouse. I knew you'd find me if I could get to the lighthouse. Oh Daddy, I thought I'd never see you again.'

'Shhh, it's all right now. I'm here. I'm never going to leave you again.'

'I'm sorry about spilling the Coke and I'm sorry I didn't clean the floor properly.'

'Oh Danny, don't. I love you so much.'

'Mummy's soul is watching over us. Just like you always said.'

'That's right, I did, didn't I?'

I couldn't help the tears either. They were just tears of relief. I didn't have their history but I felt it almost as deeply as they did. They turned towards me. I didn't know what to do. I don't think Ralph did either. But Danny did. He broke away from his father and came over to me. He looked at me, the tears still streaming down his face.

'Helen, I'm sorry, I went to your house. I saw you with that man. I didn't know what to do. I thought it must be your husband. I'm sorry. I've just messed everything up.'

A cold stab of realisation pierced me. Michael! He saw me with Michael! He'd gotten so close . . .

'Oh Danny! That was my brother you saw. My brother Michael. He works for the United Nations.' What his job had to do with it I don't know apart from somehow legitimising the embrace which had so nearly ended in tragedy.

'The man who drove off in the taxi? He's your brother?'

'Just my brother. I haven't got a husband.' I dropped to my knees and held and kissed him, feeling at that moment as passionately about him as Ralph. I kissed his dirty tangled hair. He looked up at me.

'I'm sorry I was horrible to you, Helen. I didn't mean it. Will you come and live with us?'

I couldn't speak. I could only nod.

'I tried to come to your house to tell you that Dad loved you but I got robbed and I had to . . .'

I hugged him again, rocking back and forth, kissing and kissing him on his precious head. 'It's all right, Danny, it's OK. I do love your dad. And I love you and we're all going to be together now. For ever and ever. We've got the rest of our lives to spend together now. OK?'

Ralph came over and kissed me and the three of us stood in a group clinging on to each other for dear life. After all this, what could possibly break us apart now?

And so we stood, the three of us, high on a cliff overlooking the Pacific Ocean while the pounding waves which somehow symbolised the forces that had tried to destroy us dashed themselves unavailingly against the rocks below.

Our Kid

Billy Hopkins

It was on a Sunday night in 1928 that Billy Hopkins made his first appearance. Billy's tenement home on the outskirts of Manchester would be considered a slum today, but he lived there happily with his large Catholic family, hatching money-making schemes with his many friends.

When war came, and the Luftwaffe dominated the night sky, Billy was evacuated to Blackpool. There he lived on a starvation diet while his own rations went to feed his landlady's children – 'I might as well be in Strangeways!' But even the cruel blows that were to be dealt to the family on his return to Manchester would not destroy Billy's fighting spirit – or his sense of humour.

Nostalgic, sad and funny, OUR KID recalls an up-bringing and an environment now vanished.

OUR KID, originally published under the author name Tim Lally, was warmly acclaimed:

'How wonderful to have a book like this. A book . . . that pulls readers back to that different world . . . A glimpse of a lost reality' *Manchester Evening News*

0 7472 6153 9

HEADLINE

Suddenly Single

Sheila O'Flanagan

What do you do when you find yourself suddenly single?

Go suddenly suicidal?

Suddenly sex-crazed?

Or simply collapse in self-pity?

Alix Callaghan, who thought she was in control of her work-packed life, feels like doing all three when her long-term boyfriend insists on settling down to a sensible existence – complete with children, proper meals and early nights – but without her.

Though motherhood is the last thing on her mind, losing Paul hurts more than Alix will ever admit – especially to herself.

Now, with the men at the office eyeing up her job, not to mention the discovery of her first grey hair, she's beginning to wonder if being single again is all it's cracked up to be . . .

'Sparkling and inspiring . . . a must for the contemporary woman' *Ireland on Sunday*

'Fabulous . . . thoroughly enjoyable' *RTÉ*

'A rattling good read' *U Magazine*

0 7472 6236 5

HEADLINE

If you enjoyed this book here is a selection of other bestselling titles from Headline